SPECI...

THE U...
(register...
was estab...
research, di...
Exam...
the...

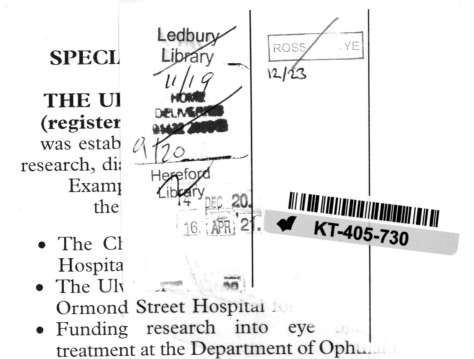

- The C...
  Hospita...
- The Ul... ...
  Ormond Street Hospital ...
- Funding research into eye ...
  treatment at the Department of Oph...
  University of Leicester
- The Ulverscroft Vision Research Group,
  Institute of Child Health
- Twin operating theatres at the Western
  Ophthalmic Hospital, London
- The Chair of Ophthalmology at the Royal
  Australian College of Ophthalmologists

You can help further the work of the Foundation
by making a donation or leaving a legacy.
Every contribution is gratefully received. If you
would like to help support the Foundation or
require further information, please contact:

THE ULVERSCROFT FOUNDATION
The Green, Bradgate Road, Anstey
Leicester LE7 7FU, England
Tel: (0116) 236 4325

website: www.foundation.ulverscroft.com

740009839635

AMBER

When Kitty Farrell is offered a trinket by a
street urchin, her impulsive response will
change both of their lives forever, and place
an unexpected strain on Kitty's marriage. For
the past four years, she has sailed the high
seas on the trading vessel *Katipo* with Rian,
her wild Irish husband; but when they return
to the Bay of Islands in 1845, they find
themselves in the midst of a bloody affray.
Their loyalties and their love are sorely
tested, and Kitty's past comes back to haunt
her when she encounters the bewitching child
she names Amber. As the action swirls
around them, Kitty and Rian must battle to
be reunited as they fight for their lives and
watch friends and enemies alike succumb to
the madness of war and the fatal seduction of
hatred.

Books by Deborah Challinor
Published by Ulverscroft:

TAMAR
WHITE FEATHERS
BLUE SMOKE
UNION BELLE
KITTY

DEBORAH CHALLINOR

AMBER

Book Two of the
Smuggler's Wife Series

Complete and Unabridged

AURORA
Leicester

First published in Great Britain in 2018
by HarperCollins*Publishers*

First published in New Zealand in 2007
by HarperCollins*Publishers* (New Zealand)

First Aurora Edition
published 2019
by arrangement with
HarperCollins*Publishers* (Australia)

A catalogue record for this book is available
from the British Library.

ISBN 978–1–78782–197–2

Published by
F. A. Thorpe (Publishing)
Anstey, Leicestershire

Set by Words & Graphics Ltd.
Anstey, Leicestershire
Printed and bound in Great Britain by
T. J. International Ltd., Padstow, Cornwall

This book is printed on acid-free paper

Dedication

This one is for my brave mother,
Pat Challinor, who was very
like Kitty in that she always did
everything she could to keep
the people she loved safe.

Acknowledgements

The characters in this story are all fictional, except for the ones already in the history books.

As always, loads of thanks go to the team at HarperCollins Publishers for being encouraging, supportive and enthusiastic. Likewise to Anna Rogers, who once again has managed to turn a sow's ear into a silk purse.

Now, a note about the Irish ballad referred to most commonly these days as 'Whiskey in the Jar' and beloved by Thin Lizzy and Metallica fans the world over. In my search for the original lyrics, I had to look fairly hard as there are dozens of versions. The one that appears in this story was published as a broadside (or broadsheet) in 1850, and could be purchased for a penny from the Poet's Box, 6 St Andrew's Lane, Glasgow. The address possibly explains why the title appeared as 'There's Whisky in the Jar', with no 'e' in the whisky. But I'm sure there must be even earlier versions of these lyrics somewhere.

Interlude

Norfolk, England, 1841

Dereham, April 1841

Mrs Carlisle! Post!'
Emily Carlisle carefully set aside the mazarine blue satin bodice she was embroidering. She didn't receive mail very often, so it was an excellent excuse to take a break from the painstaking and fiddly work, even if she did have to have it finished by Friday. Her client was a valued one, but, really, trust her to demand the world's tiniest seed pearls for her daughter's wedding gown. And peacock-hued ones at that. They must have cost a fortune!

Emily listened to the heavy tread of her housegirl-cum-sewing assistant approaching along the hallway. She was a lumpy girl, Nellie, but with surprisingly nimble fingers and a good eye for the way cloth draped, and Emily was pleased to have her. She was even more pleased that she could once again afford help in the house, now that her dressmaking business was doing so well.

Nellie hesitated at the parlour door and knocked timidly, having learned some time ago not to creep up on her employer while she was concentrating on her work.

Emily beckoned her in. 'What do you have for me? Anything interesting?'

Nellie separated the two envelopes in her pudgy hand. 'Well, there's a letter from Mrs

3

Feather . . . um, Featherstone . . . haugh? Is that how you say it?' Nellie was literate, but not terribly, especially when it came to ridiculously difficult-to-say upper-class names.

'It's pronounced 'Fanshawe', Nellie. Put that one aside — I haven't even started on her gown yet. What else?'

'Aaaand,' Nellie announced, stretching out the moment because she knew Mrs Carlisle would be delighted, 'one from a Miss Kitty Carlisle!'

'Kitty?' Emily repeated, her face lighting up. She darted across the room and snatched the envelope from Nellie's hand, her heart quickening at the sight of the familiar, elegant handwriting. 'Why don't you go and put the kettle on, Nellie? It must be morning-tea time.'

Nellie also knew when her presence wasn't required, but she smiled as she left the parlour. Mrs Carlisle didn't get many letters from her wayward, twenty-year-old daughter, so she didn't begrudge her wanting a few minutes alone to savour the latest news. And news there would be, Nellie was sure; Kitty sounded like a right tearaway, running off from New Zealand like that, then popping up in Sydney, Australia, and now sending letters from the four corners of the world. Nellie had never met Kitty, but nevertheless she lived in awe of her. Or of her reputation, at least.

Emily waited until Nellie had gone, then tore open the envelope. The address at the top was stated only as *The High Seas*, which made Emily's brow crease with both exasperation and worry. The date, however, was February 1841, so

4

her heart leapt again. Did that mean that Kitty was actually somewhere quite close to England?

Emily had been worrying herself sick since the previous May, when a letter had arrived from her sister-in-law Sarah Kelleher in New Zealand, bearing the shocking news that Kitty had run away from the mission station at the Bay of Islands, and also that Emily's brother George, Sarah's husband, had disappeared in 'mysterious circumstances'. A dreadful tragedy, Sarah had written — but, frustratingly, she had not elaborated any further in subsequent correspondence.

Sarah's supposition in her initial letter that Kitty had sailed off aboard a schooner, possibly bound for Sydney, had been borne out by a letter Emily had received some weeks later from Kitty herself. She had written that something awful had happened in New Zealand and she was now in Sydney, but safe and sound, and among friends. That had assuaged Emily's fears slightly, but not enough to allow her to sleep more than fitfully until the next letter. In that, Kitty had written that she had found work, that she was being chaperoned by a nice Irish woman who lived next door to the house Kitty was renting, that she would not be returning to New Zealand in the foreseeable future, and that Emily should not be concerned. There had been no return address.

Not concerned? Emily had been *beside* herself, anger growing in tandem with fear as more short letters had arrived from her daughter, but with very little additional information. She had written back to Sarah, asking for more details of the 'tragedy', but her sister-in-law had been equally evasive. Emily wondered what on earth could have happened. And where was George? She had asked Sarah repeatedly for news of his whereabouts, but Sarah would reply only that he had not been found, but that the Lord worked in mysterious ways and perhaps George had received the reward he so richly deserved.

Emily sat down on the sofa, unfolded the letter, and began to read.

> My Dearest Mama,
>   I hope this letter finds you well. I am very well myself, and I have some Wonderful News. I am to be Married, to a Sea Captain! I know you will be very happy for me, as I realise how anxious you were for me to find a Husband, and I can almost see your face as you sit reading this letter!

Her hand to her mouth, Emily thought it very fortunate that Kitty couldn't see her face, as she knew her expression to be nothing short of appalled horror. A sea captain!

> But do not worry, Mama, I will never be a 'Seaman's Widow', as they say, as I will be sailing constantly with my Husband and sharing his Adventures on the High Seas every day for the rest of our wonderful, married lives!

Emily almost swooned.

You will like him, Mama, I know you will. His name is Rian Farrell, he is twenty-nine years old, and he is Master of his own Schooner and Trading Enterprise. We wish to be married as quickly as possible —

Swallowing nervously, Emily wondered why.

— so I will be bringing him Home soon, to meet you and so you can be present at our Wedding. I would like to be married at Home in Dereham, in the garden, and I would very much like to wear your Wedding gown, if you do not mind. I know Papa cannot be with us, but, as you and he had such a Happy Marriage, I believe it will bode well for mine if I wore the gown you wore for him.

We only wish for a small Wedding. I expect that Tongues are still wagging over what happened before I went away, so there may not be many people you care to invite anyway. Rian's crew would like to attend. They are a colourful lot, I think you will find, but all wonderful people. Can you please organise publication of the Banns, the Vicar to officiate, and something that will pass for a wedding breakfast? Rian has asked me to inform you that he will Reimburse you for all costs when we arrive.

We have just sailed from San Francisco, and we have Business in Rio de Janeiro which may take several weeks, so I expect we will be Home some time towards the end

7

of May. Rian says we will put in to King's Lynn, as there are good shipyards there and the Katipo (that is his Schooner) needs some work.

So, in anticipation of seeing you soon, my dearest Mama, I will say Goodbye and all my love for now.

Your Loving Daughter,
Kitty

Emily allowed the letter to flutter onto her lap. She didn't know whether to weep, faint or stamp her foot. In the end, she simply went to the parlour door and called out to Nellie regarding the progress of the tea.

Then she reread the letter, wondering how well she might actually still know her daughter when Kitty finally did come home. Even Kitty's manner of expressing herself had altered: her words were different, and — more disturbingly — so, obviously, were her assumptions and attitudes. There was a lightness, an informality — she sounded almost . . . colonial.

Emily sighed raggedly. A sea captain. Oh dear. In the past, Kitty's judgement concerning men had proved rather alarming, and Emily had no reason to suspect that it had changed. There had been the extremely unfortunate business with that terrible rake Hugh Alexander nearly three years previously, which was why she had had to send Kitty out to New Zealand in the first place, and she couldn't imagine what might have occurred in the interim to encourage her daughter to make a less misguided choice.

And that was the trouble, wasn't it? Owing to the apparent unwillingness of either her daughter or her sister-in-law to offer any detailed information, Emily had only her imagination to fall back on, and of course it had run riot, conjuring all manner of appalling scenarios. And this latest news only fuelled her fears. Had Kitty actually been sailing around the world in the company of a gang of adventurers and buccaneers? Unchaperoned, and with the man she intended to marry? Such a thing was unheard of! And Emily would have to ensure that it stayed that way, at least so far as the inhabitants of Dereham were concerned. People were still talking about Kitty and Hugh Alexander, she knew they were, and this new development would only be an additional source of delight to the village's gossipmongers.

Nellie came in and set the tea tray down on the occasional table at the end of the sofa.

'There's only the shortbread left, Mrs Carlisle, but it's still fresh. I tested a piece.' Nellie took a closer look. 'Mrs Carlisle? Are you feeling poorly?'

Snatched from her unpleasant reverie, Emily started. 'What?'

'You look as like you've seen a ghost.'

'Oh, no, it's just some . . . unexpected news.'

'Not bad, I hope?' Nellie asked with genuine concern as she poured the tea.

'Well, that depends on how you look at it, really.' Emily took the cup and saucer handed to her and waited for Nellie to sit down. They

9

shared all their meals and refreshments, an arrangement that many women wouldn't allow, Emily knew, but she and Nellie also worked together so the boundaries were somewhat blurred, and anyway, she suffered badly from loneliness. She reached for a piece of shortbread. 'My daughter is to be married.'

'Well, then, that's wonderful news, isn't it?' Nellie replied enthusiastically.

'To a sea captain. She will be arriving here with him in May.'

Nellie dunked her shortbread. Normally Emily told her off for doing this, but that day she didn't seem to have noticed.

'So will he collect her?' Nellie asked. 'Where from? That's nice of him, isn't it, escorting her like that?'

'Not really,' Emily replied flatly. 'It seems that they are already, er, together.'

Nellie's round eyes grew even rounder over the rim of her teacup. She coughed slightly and put down the cup. 'Together? On his ship?'

'I can only assume so, yes.'

'Do you mean, *together* together?' Nellie looked aghast.

'Oh, stop it, Nellie,' Emily snapped. 'You sound just like a parrot. And not a very clever one at that.'

Nellie's estimation of Kitty Carlisle shot up several more degrees. The thrill of it, sailing around the world with a sea captain you weren't even married to! He must be so exciting. He must be at least six feet tall and with flashing eyes and gorgeous dark hair that flopped over a

10

wide, clear brow permanently sheened with sweat from making daring and momentous decisions every hour of the day!

'He's a tugboat captain,' Emily said.

Nellie's face fell. 'Oh, is he?'

'No, but I wanted to wipe that silly look off your face. This isn't a Jane Austen novel, Nellie, this is my daughter we're talking about!'

Chastened, Nellie stuck another piece of shortbread in her mouth.

'She has asked to be married here, in this house,' Emily said. She didn't add that it had always been her dream to see Kitty walk down the aisle of one of the larger churches in Norwich, perhaps even one of the cathedrals, although in all honesty there would never be the money to pay for an event of that magnitude.

'But that will be nice, won't it?' Nellie insisted. 'The vicar does a lovely service and the spring flowers will all be out by then.'

'Yes, but I wanted . . . ' Emily trailed off. One of the things she had been most looking forward to was the proud expression on her husband's face as he escorted Kitty down the aisle, but Lewis had been in his grave for over three years now. She sighed again. 'Yes, the vicar does do a lovely service. I'll have to go over and see him tomorrow.'

Later that day, Emily went upstairs to the attic and opened the trunk in which was stored her wedding gown. She carried it — still wrapped in tissue and undyed calico to stop it from spoiling — down to her bedroom and laid it across the bed she had once shared with Lewis. Carefully, she opened the layers until the dress was revealed.

It was of figured muslin in a deep ivory, with copper-coloured silk trim and cording around the low scoop neck and at the cuffs of the short puffed sleeves. A matching silk sash ran across the high waistline and tied at the back, and copper-coloured glass beads embroidered around the hem formed a subtle but very pretty design. In the afternoon light filtering through the gauze curtains at the bedroom windows, the copper silk gleamed dully. There was also a pair of matching satin slippers, which Emily already knew would not fit Kitty because Kitty had rather long feet for such a slender girl. On her own wedding day, Emily had worn her hair up, with her mother's pale pearls wound through the strands, pearls that were now carefully stored in her jewellery case.

Unconsciously twisting her onyx mourning ring, Emily gazed down at the dress spread across the white counterpane, tears threatening as she remembered how happy she had been the day she and Lewis had wed, and how that happiness had carried on unabated until he had died so unexpectedly. They had married in June of 1815, just after Napoleon's defeat at Waterloo. Napoleon had been exiled to St Helena after that, and these days Emily felt as though she had been exiled as well, to a life without Lewis and therefore without love. All she had left was Kitty, and it seemed that despite her best intentions, and possibly even because of them, she was losing her now, too.

As a mother, it was her duty to forbid Kitty to marry someone whom she, Emily, had not even met, and especially a man so amoral that he had evidently consented to allow, if he had not indeed encouraged, Kitty to sail with him unchaperoned and in the company of what must be an all-male crew. But Emily knew her daughter well enough to realise that the decision would not have been this mysterious Rian Farrell's alone; Kitty would not have done anything against her will.

No, if she tried to stop this marriage, Kitty would simply leave, and Emily would possibly never see her again. Her only choice was to see to the arrangements Kitty had requested, and wait and see. And trust that her daughter knew what she was doing.

★　★　★

On the very last day of May, as spring slid gently into summer, Emily was in the back garden tidying the last of the peonies and staking hollyhocks when the sound of wheels turning in the gravel at the front of the house made her pause. She slowly straightened and held her breath. There was a nerve-wracking hiatus of a minute or more, and then it finally came — the voice she had been waiting for so long to hear again.

'Mama?'

Emily turned, and there she was, framed by the honeysuckle that grew around the back door. She tugged off her gardening gloves and ran.

'Kitty! *Kitty*, my *darling!*'

Kitty stepped out to meet her, her lovely face wet with tears.

'Mama! Oh, Mama, it's so wonderful to see you. I've missed you so *much!*'

They embraced fiercely, both crying now.

'Sweetheart,' Emily sobbed, 'I thought I might never see you again! Sarah said there had been a terrible tragedy. I've been so worried!' And so angry, she added silently.

'I know, Mama,' Kitty murmured. 'It must have been awful for you. Let's sit down, shall we, and I'll tell you all about it.'

'That sounds like a very good idea.'

Emily blew her nose daintily, then took a good, long look at her daughter. Kitty still looked more or less as she had when she'd left Dereham in November of 1838. She was still slender — though Emily noticed with an anxious twinge that her daughter's bosom had grown a little fuller, and her hips perhaps just a hint more rounded — and still very beautiful, her black hair gleaming in the sunlight and her cheeks rosy with good health. Her skin had acquired a slightly darker tinge, no doubt from being exposed to the southern sun, and her hands were not quite as soft and manicured as they had once been, but otherwise she looked the same.

Kitty said, 'But first, Mama, I would like you to meet Rian.'

It was only then that Emily noticed a shadowy figure standing in the dimness of the hallway beyond her daughter. The figure stepped into the light, revealing himself to be a well-built man of

14

a little over average height with blond hair tied back in a queue, a slightly weathered face and thoughtful grey eyes. He looked honest, open and really quite ordinary.

'Mrs Carlisle,' he said, coming forward and taking her hand. 'I'm extremely pleased to meet you. Kitty has told me so much about you.'

His voice was low and very pleasant, and Emily was shocked to discover that it appealed to her in a manner she hadn't experienced since Lewis had died. She withdrew her hand.

'Good morning, Captain Farrell,' she replied, then stopped because what *did* one say to a man who had in all probability been having very intimate relations with one's unmarried daughter?

Kitty sensed her hesitation. 'We met Nellie, your housegirl. She's getting us something to eat. How long has she been working here?'

Emily shifted her gaze to her daughter. 'About a year. She's my assistant as well as my housegirl. I took her on when my dressmaking business started to become too much for me to manage by myself.'

'Well, that's good news.' Kitty sounded pleased.

'Yes. And it's news you would already know if you'd ever put a return address on your letters, Kitty.'

Kitty said brightly to Rian, 'I think Mama and I would like a few moments alone. Would you like to wait in the parlour? I'm sure Nellie will bring you something to drink.'

A look of understanding passed between

15

them, which Emily absorbed with a sharp pang of grief because it was the sort of intimate communication she had so often shared with Lewis.

Rian smiled at Kitty and murmured, 'Mo ghrá, of course,' then turned and went back inside.

After a moment, Emily said, 'He's not what I expected. And he's Irish.'

Kitty sat down on the wooden bench set against the whitewashed wall of the house, untied the ribbons of her bonnet and took it off.

'Sit down, Mama. We have a lot to talk about.'

'We most certainly do,' Emily said. 'I've been so very worried, Kitty. What on earth did you think you were doing? What do you think you are doing?'

'It's a long story,' Kitty replied.

Emily sat. 'Oh, I knew it would be that, my dear. I'm delighted to see you, I really am, but you have a lot of explaining to do.'

'I know, Mama, and I'm not sure where to start.'

'Try at the beginning.'

So Kitty did. She told her mother about her first year at the mission station at Paihia with her Uncle George and Aunt Sarah, and her growing friendship with a man called Haunui and his niece Wai, one of Sarah's Maori housegirls — things that Emily already knew from Kitty's earlier letters. And then she hesitated.

'The next bit isn't very nice, Mama. You'll be shocked and I think quite upset.'

'Nothing could shock and upset me more than

16

hearing that you'd run off from Paihia and having no idea why, Kitty, so just tell me, please.'

Puzzled, Kitty asked, 'Did Aunt Sarah not tell you anything at all?'

'No, she has been as close-mouthed as you have, much to my intense annoyance and confusion.'

Kitty frowned slightly, then made a resigned face. 'Well, I'm very sorry, Mama, and there's no easy way for me to say this, but what happened was that Uncle George . . . well, Uncle George formed an attachment with Wai, and she became pregnant. When Aunt Sarah found out, she threw both of us out of the house, me and Wai.'

Emily looked as though she had swallowed the bumblebee that had been buzzing lazily around them a minute ago.

'Mama?' Kitty prompted.

'George made a girl *pregnant?*'

'Yes. Wai, my friend.'

'How . . . how old was she?'

'Fifteen.'

Emily stared at Kitty, horrified.

'Unfortunately,' Kitty went on, 'Wai's father was the chief of the area . . . well, we *thought* he was her father, and it was vital that he didn't find out what Uncle George had done because it was the eve of the signing of the treaty — '

'What treaty?'

'The one in which the Maoris ceded sovereignty over New Zealand to the Crown. Was it not in the newspapers here?'

Emily thought for a moment. 'Yes, I do remember something. But what did that have to

17

do with George?' Suddenly, she covered her face with her hands. 'I simply cannot believe that about him, Kitty. He can't have been in his right mind. Are you sure that it was George, that this girl didn't just make it up?'

'Yes, Mama,' Kitty replied in a very frosty voice. 'It was Uncle George. Wai never told lies, and I'll thank you never to suggest again that she did. You have absolutely no idea.'

Startled and somewhat chastened by Kitty's tone, Emily realised that her daughter had changed far more than she had first assumed.

Kitty went on. 'We were terrified that if Wai's father found out that his daughter had been made pregnant by a Pakeha, particularly a man of the cloth, he wouldn't sign the treaty. But he did find out, and because of that we had to leave immediately.' She decided not to add that she and Wai had literally had to run for their lives. 'Rian took us on his schooner, and thank God he did, or I might not be here today to tell you this. And no, Mama, Uncle George wasn't in his right mind. He'd lost it steadily over the year we were at Paihia, and at the end he was almost a raving lunatic, and I'm sure he was beating Aunt Sarah.'

'Oh, poor Sarah,' Emily said.

'Poor Sarah, my backside,' Kitty retorted.

'Kitty!'

'Mama, she didn't even stop to ask whether Wai had wanted to . . . to lie with Uncle George! No, straight away she called her a trollop and then she threw us bodily out of the house.'

Stunned, Emily stammered, 'She never said

18

anything about that in her letters.'

'Well, would you?'

'No, I suppose not. But why did she throw you out as well?'

'I don't know,' Kitty said. 'Because I was Wai's friend, I expect. Perhaps she thought I'd known about what was going on.'

'And had you?'

'No, I had no idea,' Kitty said, feeling a shadow of the old guilt pass over her.

'So when did George go missing?'

Kitty shrugged. 'I'm not sure, but it must have been after Wai and I had gone because I'd seen him earlier that day. You've not had any news at all about him?'

'No, Sarah has only ever written that he'd disappeared.' And then Emily recalled Sarah's cryptic comments, which made a little more sense now, and said, 'Oh dear, poor George.'

'Mad George,' Kitty corrected.

'I can't say I'm particularly surprised,' Emily confessed suddenly. 'About George losing his mind, I mean. He was always a bit . . . unstable. Your father often said it was likely. It was one of the reasons there was never much love lost between George and myself. I am horrified by what he did, though. I would never have thought he had that sort of behaviour in him.'

'Well, he did. And it ruined Wai's life.'

'What happened to the child?' Emily asked with a startled glance at Kitty. 'I suppose it would be my niece or nephew, wouldn't it? And your cousin!'

' 'It' is a little boy named Huatahi, and he'll be

19

almost a year old now. Wai gave birth to him in Sydney, but quite soon afterwards he was taken back to Paihia.'

'By his mother?'

'No,' Kitty said. 'By Wai's real father, Haunui. It turned out that Tupehu wasn't her father at all, although her mother had been Tupehu's wife. That's another long story.' She bit her lip and was silent for several seconds. 'Wai died giving birth.'

'Oh, Kitty, I am sorry,' Emily said. She touched her daughter's hand gently. 'I really am. I know she meant a lot to you.'

'She did, Mama, she really did. Which is why, one day, we're going back to Sydney to collect her bones and take them home to New Zealand.'

⋆　⋆　⋆

Rian sat in the parlour, alternately wading his way through the plate of cake and biscuits Nellie had brought him, and twiddling his thumbs. Kitty had been outside with her mother for almost two hours. He realised they had a lot to talk about, but he wished they'd hurry up; he'd had three cups of tea and was dying to relieve himself, and, assuming that the privy was out the back somewhere, he would have to pass them on his way and he didn't fancy his progress being monitored by Mrs Emily Carlisle, whose huge dark eyes were so much like Kitty's and whom he suspected wasn't overly enamoured with him. Perhaps he could nip out the front and do it in

20

the garden somewhere. But it would be just his luck to be standing there pissing on a lavender bush when someone went past, then it would be all over Dereham village that Kitty Carlisle was marrying a man who didn't even have the grace to use a privy when he needed one. But he was saved when Kitty and her mother appeared at the parlour door.

Kitty smiled, and Rian noticed that the little worry lines that had been forming between her brows over the past couple of weeks had disappeared. 'Don't worry, we haven't forgotten you, my love,' she said.

Emily Carlisle walked over to him, and he was struck afresh by the uncanny resemblance between mother and daughter, even though he knew that one was more than twenty years older than the other. He was almost tempted to say to Mrs Carlisle that he understood now where her daughter's fine looks had come from. But not quite tempted enough. It was true, but it was also trite, and he had no wish to appear shallow and ingratiating in the eyes of his prospective mother-in-law.

'Please, let me start again, Captain,' Emily said, offering him her hand. 'I'm delighted to meet you and I would like to formally welcome you to this family.'

Rian lurched to his feet, crumbs tumbling off his jacket onto the rug, and grasped her hand. 'Thank you very much indeed, Mrs Carlisle. I'm honoured.'

Emily smiled. 'And so am I.'

She was stunning when she smiled, Rian

thought, just like her daughter. And she seemed noticeably more pleased to see him now than she had earlier.

He had no idea, of course, that Kitty had been busy telling Emily that Rian Farrell was all she'd ever wanted in a man and that she intended to marry him no matter what, that he had saved her life on at least one occasion, that he was kind and decent and loved her deeply, and no, she wasn't in a delicate condition. Also that he wasn't your run-of-the mill sort of man and that Emily should never expect them to settle down and live what most people would consider to be a 'normal' life. The past eighteen months had made Kitty realise that happiness was something to be grasped whenever it presented itself, because it could vanish just as quickly — Emily of all people should know that — and she intended to grasp hold of a life with Rian Farrell, and all that that entailed, as firmly as she could. And if Emily didn't like it, well, she was sorry but she and Rian would get back into the gig they had hired and return to King's Lynn and, when the *Katipo* was ready, simply sail away again.

Emily had known that Kitty meant what she said, and it had taken her only a few seconds to decide that a daughter married to a slightly scruffy sea captain and gallivanting around the world was better than no daughter at all.

'You must tell me all about yourself, Captain,' Emily continued. 'But first I'll talk to Nellie about some more tea. I'm quite parched — that sun really is rather draining.'

At the mention of more tea, Rian tried not to pull a face.

When Emily had gone, Kitty came over and kissed his nose. 'Well, that went better than I thought it would.' She gave him an odd look. 'What's the matter? You look as though you're in pain.'

'I bloody well am. Is the privy out the back?'

Kitty grinned. 'Oh, poor darling, I didn't even think to tell you. Yes, it's just beyond the vegetable garden.'

When he'd hurried off, walking slightly stiffly, Kitty sat down on the sofa and looked around. The parlour hadn't changed much since she'd been away. Her mother's dressmaking business did indeed seem to be prospering, though, because there was a good-quality rug she hadn't seen before on the floor and a new pair of leather armchairs flanking the fireplace. She was pleased to see, however, that her father's favourite tatty old chair was still in its usual place near a table lamp, where he had liked to read at night. She wondered if his clothes and books and other personal bits and pieces were still upstairs. Probably, knowing her mother. There was a study lined with bookshelves on the upper floor, and three bedrooms, the largest of which had always been her parents'. She would sleep in her own room for the next few nights, although she wasn't at all looking forward to it; she and Rian hadn't spent a night apart since that day in July of the previous year when Haunui and baby Tahi had disembarked from the *Katipo* at Paihia and she had decided to stay on board with Rian. It

23

was Monday today, and she hoped they would be married by the end of the week, but even that seemed too long to wait to sleep next to him again, to feel his warm, hard body against hers and listen to him breathe at night while she lay awake marvelling at how lucky she was.

Nellie appeared with more tea, followed by Emily, then Rian, looking markedly more at ease.

'Captain Farrell's just been telling me about his schooner,' Emily said gaily. 'He says it's been logged as one of the fastest for its size. Isn't that right, Captain?'

'It is,' Rian replied. 'Although Kitty already knows that, of course, having sailed on her for . . . a while.' He shut his mouth before he could put his foot into it any further.

'Yes, quite,' Emily said as she sat down in a rustle of skirts. Signalling for the tea to be poured, she stared hard at Nellie, who was in turn staring at Rian.

Nellie thought Captain Rian Farrell was one of the most dashing, romantic men she'd ever laid eyes on. It was true that he wasn't six feet tall and his hair wasn't dark, but strands of it did flop and his eyes certainly flashed quite a bit, especially when he smiled.

'Nellie, pour the tea, please, will you?' Emily prompted briskly.

'Oh, yes,' Nellie said, and did just that, all over the tray.

'Oh dear,' Emily said, and tutted. 'Go and get a cloth.' When Nellie, mortified, had rushed from the parlour, Emily added, 'She's not normally quite that clumsy. I don't know what's come over her.' She suspected she did, however, and hoped that Captain Farrell's crew weren't as mesmerising as Nellie clearly found the captain himself to be. 'So, Captain, tell me a little about yourself. You're Irish, I gather?'

'I am,' Rian replied. 'Dublin born and bred. Well, Kingstown, to be precise. My family have some land there. And, please, call me Rian.'

'Rian, then,' Emily agreed. She hesitated, then asked bluntly, 'How much land? Roughly?'

Kitty rolled her eyes towards the ceiling.

'Enough to generate an income that will keep Kitty in comfort for the rest of her life should anything ever happen to me,' Rian answered, 'if that's what you mean.'

'Oh, no, I wasn't ... ' Noting the keen intelligence in his pale grey eyes, Emily trailed off and decided not to bother with denial. 'Well, actually, yes, that is what I mean. Forgive me, but I am only thinking of my daughter's best interests.'

'Of course,' Rian said, although he failed to offer any further information about his family. Emily didn't think it mattered; she would prise it out of Kitty later if necessary.

Nellie returned with a cloth, her round cheeks still flushed. She mopped up the spilt tea, poured three cups, then left again.

'You'll be pleased to know, Kitty,' Emily said, offering the cake plate to Rian, who declined, 'that Reverend Goodall has assured me he can perform a marriage ceremony at any time, so long as he has a couple of days' notice.'

'Did you have the banns published?' Kitty

asked, taking a piece of cake.

'Yes, I did that in April. You could go and see Reverend Goodall tomorrow to talk about what you'd like. And I've managed to find someone to make the refreshments. Nellie's mother, actually. She's the cook at the Ormsbys' house.'

'Not Bernard and Ida Ormsby?' Kitty said, appalled.

Emily nodded.

'Oh, no!' Kitty exclaimed. 'You haven't invited *them*, have you?'

'Of course not. Not after the things they said about your poor father! No, Mrs Ingram has agreed to come here for the day instead. And at quite a reasonable cost. I don't know what arrangement she has made with the Ormsbys, and, frankly, I don't care.'

'The Ormsbys own one of the local mills,' Kitty explained to Rian. 'I don't think you'd like them. They're overwhelmingly awful.'

Rian shrugged, quite happy if there were no guests at all at the wedding ceremony. Except for his crew, of course.

'Who else have you invited?' Kitty asked.

'Oh, you know, just a few,' Emily replied evasively. 'And I've only mentioned it in passing, because I wasn't sure when you'd be home.'

'You mean you weren't sure whether you could talk me out of it or not,' Kitty said artlessly.

Emily looked at her for a moment, then laughed. 'Something like that, yes. But we can send invitations out as soon as you've spoken with the vicar, if you like. Very short notice,

26

though. I've only a handful of people I'd like to attend, but you might have a few.'

'Not really, no,' Kitty said. 'All the people who are really important to me will be here anyway.'

'Are you sure?'

'Very,' Kitty confirmed.

Emily turned to Rian. 'What about your parents, Rian?'

'No, there isn't time. And anyway, my parents and I are currently, shall we say, estranged.'

Dying to know why, Emily was nevertheless far too polite to ask.

'And my sister went out to Australia,' Rian added, 'so I'm afraid it will only be my crew. They're on their way now. I expect they'll be here by Wednesday, Thursday at the latest. I noticed a tavern as we came through the village. The White Hart? We'll stay there, I think.'

Kitty set her teacup down in its saucer with a rather sharp clink.

'Good, that's settled, then,' Emily said brightly, trying but failing to keep the relief out of her voice. 'Now,' she said, turning back to Kitty, 'let's see about this wedding gown, shall we?'

★　★　★

The dress was too tight for Kitty across the bosom, and a little short, so Emily skilfully let out the bodice seams and added a length of ivory lace to the hem. By the time she had finished, it looked as though it had been made for Kitty.

'What shoes were you thinking of wearing?'

27

she asked her on Wednesday morning as she hung the finished gown in the armoire in Kitty's room.

But Kitty wasn't listening; she was leaning on the windowsill gazing down into the backyard at Rian, who had arrived early for breakfast and was now making himself useful by chopping wood. Emily was very quickly growing to like her soon-to-be son-in-law, and had to admit she was beginning to appreciate what her daughter saw in him. He was obviously intelligent and had a sharp wit that Emily appreciated. In some ways he reminded her of her beloved Lewis. He also had an air about him, and she couldn't decide whether it was one of quiet but supreme confidence, or an undercurrent of danger. Either way, it was very attractive. And the way he looked at Kitty, especially when he thought he wasn't being observed, left Emily in no doubt that he both adored her and lusted after her. 'Kitty?' she said more loudly. 'I asked you a question.'

Kitty dragged herself away from the window. 'Sorry, Mama?'

'I said: What shoes will you wear?'

'Well, I have my black boots.'

'Oh, Kitty, you can't wear black boots on your wedding day!'

'I know that,' Kitty replied impatiently. And on the *Katipo*, she usually wore them with a pair of men's trousers, but she didn't think this was the right time to tell her mother *that*. 'And I have these, but they won't go with your gown.' She lifted the hem of her dress to reveal a pair of rather tatty brown button boots.

Emily made a disparaging face. 'No, those won't do either.' Then she added, 'And it's *your* gown now, love.'

Kitty gave her mother a little, sad smile. 'I'm very grateful for that, Mama. It means a lot to me.'

'It means a lot to me, too,' Emily said, her eyes suddenly bright with tears. 'Oh, sweetheart, when I first read your letter I was horrified, I really was. But now that I've met Rian and come to know him a little, I think . . . well, I'm beginning to think that it might be all right.'

'It will be, Mama. I know it will.'

Emily regarded her daughter's lovely, calm face and said, 'Yes, I think you do.'

Kitty started to say something, but was rudely interrupted by a piercing shriek from downstairs.

They stared at each other, eyes wide.

'My God, that's Nellie!' Emily exclaimed, and hurried out of the bedroom, Kitty close behind her, their feet clattering on the wooden stairs.

Nellie was standing in the middle of the kitchen, cut flowers strewn around her on the floor, and her hand clapped over her eyes.

'Nellie, what on earth's the matter?' Emily demanded.

'Outside, Mrs Carlisle, there's a giant!' Nellie babbled hysterically. 'I've never seen the like! Black as the ace of spades, he is!'

Kitty peered through the kitchen window into the garden. Then she grinned, and waved vigorously. 'The crew,' she said delightedly, 'they're here! Come and meet them!'

Followed by Emily and a hesitant but wildly curious Nellie, Kitty stepped through the back door and out into the bright sunlight. The crew, clustered around Rian, who had his shirtsleeves rolled up and the axe resting over his shoulder, looked every inch the pack of gunrunners and smugglers Kitty knew they were.

Emily, who was becoming near-sighted but was too vain to wear spectacles, didn't gasp until she was quite close to them.

They stood in a half-circle. On Emily's left was a ruddy-faced man with a long, black plait, wearing a shirt and trousers made from some sort of pale, soft fabric. A leather belt with silver embellishments sat on his hips, and there was a sheathed knife tucked into it. He nodded to her and said, 'Good morning, ma'am.'

'Mama, this is Running Hawk, a Seneca of the Iroquois,' Kitty said excitedly. 'But we just call him Hawk.'

'Er, good morning, Mr Hawk,' Emily responded, her manners coming to the fore automatically.

Next to him stood a surly-looking article with red-brown hair, a large scar running down his face, several missing teeth and a glinting gold hoop in each ear, who inclined his head and said curtly, 'Missus.'

'John Sharkey, from Newcastle,' Kitty explained before her mother could respond, then indicated the next man: this one short and wiry with dark, oiled hair, a goatee beard and a moustache with the ends waxed, and a cheerful

30

expression on his weathered face. 'And this is Pierre.'

The little man bowed extravagantly low and said, '*Bonjour, Madame. Je suis Pierre Babineaux, et je suis enchanté pour faire votre connaissance.*'

Slightly startled, Emily struggled to resurrect her own rusty French. '*Bonjour, monsieur. Je suis heureux également de vous rencontrer. De quelle région de la France êtes-vous?*'

Pierre shook his head. '*Non, Madame, pas France. Je suis Arcadien de bayou, de Louisiane.*'

'Oh, I beg your pardon,' Emily said.

'She is a simple mistake,' Pierre replied, lifting his arms in a not-to-worry gesture and wafting the scent of lavender towards Emily. Then he smiled widely, revealing what appeared to be several solid-gold teeth.

Next to him was a brown-skinned man whose wavy black hair hung down to his shoulders. He had a slightly hooked nose and was rather good-looking in an untamed sort of way, Emily thought, though he seemed a little reserved.

'Mama,' Kitty said, 'this is Ropata, a New Zealand Maori from the Ngati Kahungungu tribe on the East Coast.'

Emily regarded him with interest: he was the first Maori she had encountered. But her attention was soon diverted by the light-skinned man standing on the Maori boy's left; a young man who no doubt had broken plenty of hearts already in his time. He had the most alluring, sparkling black eyes, a head of the loveliest black

31

curls, and beautiful white teeth revealed by a very charming smile.

He bowed slightly. 'Top of the morning to you, missus. And it's clear to me already where Kitty gets her lovely looks, so it is.'

'Thank you,' Emily replied, trying not to smile. Typical Irish blarney!

'This is Mick Doyle, Mama,' Kitty said. 'His mam looked after us when we were in Sydney.'

'In that case,' Emily said, 'please pass on my heartfelt thanks to your mother the next time you see her, Mr Doyle.'

'I will that,' Mick replied, and then, although Emily wasn't entirely sure, she thought he might have winked at her.

Finally, Kitty came to the man Emily had been trying very hard not to stare at. He was *huge*, an enormous fellow with massive arms and legs, skin as dark as blue-black ink and a completely shaved head.

He stepped forward and said, in the deepest voice she had ever heard, 'Your servant, ma'am. I'm delighted to make your acquaintance, and equally delighted to be able to attend your daughter's nuptials. Kitty is a wonderful young lady and we are all very pleased that our captain has convinced her to become his wife.'

Emily blinked.

'And this is Gideon,' Kitty said, thoroughly enjoying herself.

'Thank you very much, Mr Gideon,' Emily replied. Out of the corner of her eye she saw that Nellie had subsided onto the garden bench, her hand over her mouth now instead of her eyes.

'No, ma'am, it is just Gideon,' Gideon corrected.

Emily felt like collapsing onto the bench herself. Over the past few days she had managed to . . . accommodate the idea of Kitty marrying Rian Farrell and sailing off with him. But that 'accommodation' was receding rapidly now that she had seen the sort of men that Kitty would be living with. She'd been prepared for a fairly rugged group, but certainly not this extraordinary, motley and decidedly untrustworthy-looking collection. But the wedding wasn't until Friday; perhaps she could manage to dissuade her daughter after all.

She glanced across and saw that Kitty was gazing straight back. Then, very slowly, Kitty simply shook her head, and Emily knew in her heart that it really was too late.

★　★　★

Kitty woke up with a smile on her face, and she knew why: today was the day she was marrying Rian.

She sat up, stretched, then climbed out of bed and looked beneath it for the chamber pot. She used it, then put it aside to take downstairs later, reflecting that one of the many good things about living on a schooner was that you just threw everything over the side. She sat down for a moment on the window seat.

The day before, Thursday, had been rather draining. She and her mother had visited a shoemaker and had managed to find a pair of slippers for the wedding. That had gone well, but when they had stopped at a tea shop Emily's smile had slipped and, halfway through her ginger cake, she'd burst into tears.

Kitty knew why, of course. She felt for her mother and she loved her dearly, but she couldn't bring herself to deliberately close all the wonderful doors that had slowly opened to her over the past two years, and give up the chance of a lifetime of love and passion, challenge and excitement. And these, Kitty knew, were almost as important to her as the promise of love. To have to return to a life of silly etiquette, limited horizons and grinding predictability now would cripple her.

So instead of yet again trying to explain and justify her reasons for marrying Rian, and then probably arguing with mother anyway, she had simply asked Emily to trust her. Her mother had continued to weep, in a very lady-like manner naturally, but the tears had eventually slowed and she had nodded her agreement, then made Kitty promise to come straight home if anything ever went wrong. And Kitty *had* promised, and meant it.

She smiled again, shivering with delighted anticipation at the thought of becoming Mrs Kitty Farrell, although, unexpectedly, she was feeling nervous about the actual ceremony. But the thought of spending the rest of her life with Rian; of waking next to him every morning, of knowing he would love and respect her to the very best of his ability, and of rising each day to a new adventure, together — what heaven!

Nellie knocked and stuck her head around the bedroom door. 'Miss Kitty, your mam says are you ready for breakfast yet?'

Kitty climbed off the window seat. 'Honestly, Nellie, stop calling me 'Miss Kitty'. It makes me feel like somebody's desiccated old maiden aunt.'

'Beg pardon,' Nellie said contritely, and produced a tray containing a plate of poached eggs on toast and a pot of tea, next to which stood a tiny vase holding a single cream rose.

'Did Mama pick the rose?' Kitty asked.

'First thing,' Nellie confirmed.

Kitty's eyes pricked with tears. She sat in the white wicker chair in front of her dressing table, stared down at the lurid yellow eggs and felt her stomach lurch ominously.

Quickly, she handed the tray back. 'Oh, no, I really don't think I can eat anything this morning.'

Nellie looked uneasy. 'Your mam said you have to. She said you can't get married on an empty stomach.'

'I'll have the tea,' Kitty bargained.

'I'm not to take your plate down with anything on it,' Nellie insisted.

Even the smell was making Kitty sick now. She rose, took the plate from Nellie again and crossed to the window. Unlatching it, she tossed out the eggs and returned the plate to Nellie. 'There, there's nothing on it now,' she said.

Nellie looked astonished, then burst into a high, tinkling laugh that was most unexpected from such a staid girl.

'Nellie, will you be my bridesmaid?' Kitty asked impulsively. 'Hawk will be Rian's best man, but I haven't invited any of my old friends.'

'Me?' Nellie squeaked.

Kitty nodded.

A deep, pink glow suffused Nellie's round cheeks. 'Ooh, yes, please. I've never been a bridesmaid before.' Then her face fell. 'Oh, but I don't have anything nice to wear.'

'Don't you have a dress for church or something like that?'

'I've got my dark green calico. It has lace on it, but it's a bit old.'

'Well, wear that and pin a rose in your hair. You'll look lovely!'

Nellie grinned hugely and trotted away happily to draw Kitty a bath.

★　★　★

Kitty sat anxiously in her room. It was half past ten and she had just finished getting dressed. Her mother's gown looked beautiful on her, she had to admit, and she had twisted her shining black hair up into a loose knot and tucked three or four cream rose buds into the folds. Her hair fell past her shoulders these days; it had grown very quickly since she'd had most of it cut off fifteen months before after an almost-fatal accident on the *Katipo*. Pierre had been regularly dosing her with the most disgusting concoction, which he insisted was a secret Arcadian potion guaranteed to make hair grow. It smelt like sick and tasted worse, but it

36

certainly seemed to be working. Her mother had also given her the rope of small but very pretty family pearls to wear at her throat, where they sat now, gleaming softly against the faint tan of her skin.

She had been nervous before, but now she was close to having a very uncharacteristic attack of the vapours because, sitting in the bath, it had suddenly occurred to her that Rian might not turn up. He had not come to the house for his dinner last night, as he had done for the previous three evenings, because the crew had insisted that, as it was his last night of 'freedom', he was entitled to spend it getting drunk at the tavern. Kitty had only laughed when he'd told her, but what if he'd changed his mind? What if, sometime during the evening, he had come to the conclusion that he didn't want to be saddled with a wife after all, and had simply gone back to King's Lynn and sailed out of her life forever? The thought had been so awful that she had contemplated not even bothering to put on her wedding dress. Her mother had told her not to be so silly, that even she could see that the man was absolutely besotted with her, and to get out of the bath before she caught a chill.

So here she was, clean and fragrant and looking lovely, but feeling sick with anxiety. Her mother had invited several guests, and Kitty knew they had arrived and were downstairs. Mr Sanders, a teacher at the school at which her father had also taught, had come with his wife Maud, who was a close friend of Emily's. The neighbours, Mr and Mrs Moon, were also here, and so was old Hector Billingsworth, who tended Emily's garden once a week, and of whom Emily was extremely fond. And of course, Mrs Ingram, Nellie's mother, had been at the house since six that morning, preparing food for the wedding breakfast. And that was all. Kitty was aware that her mother had invited only people she knew would not pass judgement on Kitty's behaviour, past or present, and for that she was grateful.

'Kitty?' Emily appeared in the doorway. 'The vicar is here.'

'I don't want to go downstairs. I don't want to see him,' Kitty muttered.

'Well, you'll have to if you're expecting him to marry you, darling.'

'No, I mean I don't want to see him before Rian gets here. If he gets here,' Kitty said gloomily. 'It might be bad luck.'

Emily refrained from rolling her eyes. 'It's only bad luck if your future husband sees you in your wedding dress before the ceremony. Now, come on, don't be silly. Reverend Goodall would like to have a word with you.'

'In my bedroom?' Kitty asked, sounding shocked.

'Yes, if you won't come down.'

'But, Mama, what will people say?'

Emily had had just about enough of Kitty's surly mood this morning. 'Oh, for goodness sake, Kitty, it's a bit late to be worrying about that sort of thing, don't you think? Now stop sulking and try to look a little more like a blushing bride. I'll bring the vicar up.'

Kitty gazed after her mother as she left the room, wanting to shout out that she was scared stiff, but something — could it have been pride? — prevented her.

A minute later Reverend Goodall appeared. A short, round man, he had known Kitty since she was six years old. He was wearing a cassock, surplice and scarf, having decided to forgo his alb and chasuble because of the informality of the wedding. By nature a cheerful person, he was having a rare moment of melancholy as Emily Carlisle had just informed him that there still had not been any news of her brother George's whereabouts. The disappearance of clergymen serving in far-flung corners of the empire was not unheard of, of course, but to have known one personally was somewhat disturbing. However, he produced his jolliest smile, hoping that it didn't look as false as Kitty's. Oh dear, he thought, surely not trouble already?

'Good morning, Kitty, my dear.'

'Hello, Reverend Goodall,' Kitty replied, her tenuous smile evaporating.

'That's a long face for someone about to be married, I must say!'

Kitty didn't respond.

'It's not wedding jitters, is it?' the vicar asked. 'Because if it is, I can assure you that almost every bride I have ever married has suffered from them. It's perfectly normal when a young woman is about to embark on a new — ' He stopped. He had been going to say 'adventure', but as he knew that Kitty Carlisle had had plenty of those already, and very colourful ones by all accounts,

39

he hurriedly changed tack. 'A new life. And it's a big responsibility, taking on a husband, you know!' He chuckled heartily, but he did it by himself.

He saw then that Kitty was genuinely upset, and sat down to explain to her exactly what the ceremony would entail, thinking that it might help to settle her nerves. He'd just got to the bit where the newly married couple sign the parish register when the sound of someone arriving came through the open window.

Kitty leapt up and ran to look. When she pulled her head back in she was transformed, an enormous smile lighting up her face and her eyes shining.

'He's here!' she exclaimed to the vicar. 'Rian's here!' And she ran across the room, gave Reverend Goodall a resounding kiss on the cheek and darted out the door, leaving him sitting speechless in the wicker chair.

Kitty tore down the stairs, along the flagstoned hall and out through the front door, where she launched herself at Rian. He caught her and swung her around, then took her in his arms.

'What's all this?' he asked gently, looking down at her.

'I thought you weren't coming,' Kitty said breathlessly, feeling the warmth of a blush finally begin to creep across her face.

'Sweetheart, wild horses couldn't keep me away.'

'I thought you might have changed your mind.'

Rian kissed the tip of her nose. '*Mo ghrá*, I

have never been more certain of anything in my life.'

Kitty laughed out loud. 'Good. Let's get married then, shall we?'

And so they did.

Part One

Restless Bones

1

Sydney, December 1844

Kitty hung over the rail of the *Katipo*, watching rubbish bob past the hull as the schooner eased herself into Sydney Harbour. It was hot, even out there on the water, and Kitty's shirt was sticking to her back although it was only nine o'clock in the morning. Bodie, the ship's cat, lay curled in the centre of a rope coil at Kitty's feet, her black fur sleek and gleaming.

This was the first time they had been back to Sydney since everything that had happened four years earlier, when Wai had died in a small tenement in a narrow street on The Rocks. Now, it was time for Kitty to fulfil her promise to her dear friend, and to Wai's father Haunui: they had come to collect Wai's bones and take them back to New Zealand, where she belonged.

'I'd forgotten how hot it gets here,' Rian said as he appeared beside her.

Kitty turned to look at him. He was tired and there were dark shadows beneath his eyes. It had been a rough trip this time around the Cape of Good Hope and across the lower latitudes, very rough, and they hadn't yet recovered from the shock of losing Sharkey during a brief sojourn in Durban. As usual he'd been in a pub all night and as he left he was set upon by a group of seamen he'd had an altercation with earlier, and was stabbed in the throat. He had died almost immediately, his blood seeping into the dirt of a Durban street as the rest of the crew stood over him in helpless silence. Knowing that his first love had always been the sea, they had taken his body back to the *Katipo*, wrapped him in a weighted sail and lowered him into the ocean the following day.

So now they were a crew member short, but Rian wasn't in a hurry to take anyone else on — waiting, Kitty suspected, until the wound left by Sharkey's death was a little less raw. Even she missed him, and Sharkey had been the only one of the *Katipo*'s crew she had never really taken to.

They had been all over the world during the past three years, buying, selling, trading and doing a little bit of smuggling when the situation made the opportunity worthwhile. Rian never referred to it as smuggling, though. He liked to say that they were providing a service to those in need by furnishing at a competitive price certain items that various authorities frowned upon, such as alcohol, tobacco and firearms. It had long since ceased to bother Kitty, as Rian was always fairly circumspect regarding whom he supplied with what, and never did anything his conscience could not live with. If pioneers and settlers wanted to drink and smoke themselves into a stupor, then who was he to deny them? But if they insisted on actively forcing their rule onto the natives of the lands in which they had settled, then he felt morally obliged to supply those natives with the means to fight back. It was a matter of principle, he had said to Kitty on several occasions.

Their life together had so far been all she could have hoped for. Despite Rian's initial worries, she had never grown bored with being at sea, and spent much of her time learning the craft of sailing and helping out on deck whenever possible. And even if she had wanted to do those dull domestic things a wife was supposed to do, like cook for her husband, Pierre wouldn't let her into the *Katipo*'s tiny galley, unless he was specifically teaching her how to prepare a certain dish. And the rest of the crew, being true sailors, were very tidy and did all their own cleaning and washing, so there was nothing for her there either. She read, and sewed and embroidered occasionally, but mostly she was up on deck, learning what she could about the world's great, wide, beautiful oceans. And she loved Rian now more than ever, even though they still argued on a fairly regular basis. They fought above decks, below decks and in the mess-room, but never in bed, which was the one place where they put their differences of opinion aside and revelled in the passion, excitement and comfort of each other.

The only thing that saddened her was that there had been no babies so far. She didn't know why. Her courses had been late on four or five occasions over the past few years, but had always arrived eventually, albeit a little heavier than normal, and a little more painful. Sometimes she wondered, as she washed out her napkins in a bucket of sea water, whether she was rinsing away the beginnings of a new life, but there was no one to ask, and she wasn't sure she really wanted to know.

And she had to admit that, until a year or so ago, her desire to become a mother hadn't exactly been all-consuming. But if a baby had come along she was sure she could have managed very happily. Lately, though, something inside her seemed to have changed and she found herself thinking more and more about what it would be like to have a child of her own. And sometimes the daydream became an actual yearning, an ache she felt somewhere deep in her belly and in her heart. It was as though her body were starting to clamour for something it needed, without even bothering to consult her consciousness.

It also bothered her that Rian had been rather evasive on the rare occasions she had raised the matter, although she knew of course that his first wife and child had been lost at sea, and attributed his reticence to that. All he would do was kiss her nose, say that a working schooner was no place to raise a child, and tell her that he loved her.

Bodie stretched, climbed out of her rope nest, sharpened her claws on the back of Rian's leg and wandered off across the deck.

Rian rubbed absently at the scratches, then raised his spyglass and swept his gaze across the sparkling, deep blue harbour.

'Can you see him?' Kitty asked.

'No. I would have thought he'd be out here like a robber's dog the minute he spotted our

48

ensign.' Rian lowered the glass, gazed for a minute longer towards the red brick and white stone warehouses and sheds crowding the shoreline of Sydney Cove, squinted, raised the glass again and swore. Then he shouted for Hawk.

Hawk appeared a moment later, and Rian handed him the spyglass. 'Someone's coming out. Is it him, do you think?'

'No, that is not Kinghazel,' Hawk answered eventually. 'Too skinny.'

Rian looked again at the rowboat that had been launched from the wharf in front of the customs house and was now moving steadily towards them. 'Drop anchor!' he called to Ropata over his shoulder. Almost immediately, the anchor chain rattled furiously as it paid out.

'Perhaps he's been watching his diet,' Kitty suggested.

'I doubt it. That man is as much a glutton as he is a prick,' Rian replied. He frowned, and the three of them leaned on the rail in silence to wait as the rowboat drew closer and closer.

Kitty felt a bubble of unease form in the pit of her stomach. Walter Kinghazel was the customs and excise man who had arrested Rian in 1840 for failing to pay duty on a shipment of alcohol and tobacco. Unknown to Kitty, Rian hadn't paid it, but, believing that the receipts had simply been lost, she had risked her own freedom to obtain counterfeit receipts from a master forger incarcerated in Hyde Park Barracks, a very unpleasant piece of work named Avery Bannerman. The forged receipts had been presented in court and the charges dropped, but

Kitty knew she would not have been able to secure those documents if it hadn't been for Daniel Royce, a young soldier at the barracks who had turned a blind eye at a crucial moment.

Rian had walked free, but Walter Kinghazel had known damn well that Rian hadn't paid any duty, receipts or no, and everyone on board the *Katipo* was sure he would have another attempt at bringing Rian to justice the very next time they showed their faces in Sydney. Their cargo was completely licit this time, and they had had to return so they could take Wai home, but still they were very uneasy; Walter Kinghazel was a powerful and notoriously malicious man.

When the rowboat was no more than a furlong away, Rian raised the glass again. 'It's definitely not Kinghazel. But it's someone in the Queen's uniform.'

A minute later, whoever was in the boat set down his oars and took up a loudhailer.

'Ahoy the schooner! Customs and excise preparing to board!'

'Shite,' Rian said.

When the rowboat bumped against the *Katipo*'s hull, Rian dropped the rope ladder over the side and waited until an unfamiliar face appeared at the rail. The man stepped onto the deck and adjusted his hat, which had come adrift during his ascent.

'Good morning. Bartholomew Nixon, customs and excise. Ma'am,' he said, nodding to Kitty and offering Rian his hand.

Rian shook it. 'Captain Rian Farrell, at your service.'

50

'Captain, I need to inspect your vessel in accordance with — '

Rian waved the end of Mr Nixon's sentence away. 'Yes, we're familiar with all that. What's happened to Walter Kinghazel?'

Nixon, a tallish man with red hair and fair, freckly skin that obviously wasn't taking to the harsh antipodean sun, paused for a moment. Then he said flatly, 'Mr Kinghazel is deceased.'

Rian tried to keep the elation out of his voice. 'Deceased? That's dreadful, Mr Nixon. I'm astonished.'

Mr Nixon regarded Rian thoughtfully. 'I'm sure you are, Captain. Particularly given your past dealings with him.'

Oh dear, Kitty thought.

'Walter Kinghazel was murdered,' Nixon went on. 'His throat was cut, on his own front doorstep, no less.'

Kitty had despised Walter Kinghazel, but she was still shocked. 'That's awful, Mr Nixon. Did they catch whoever did it?'

'No, Ma'am, unfortunately they haven't. Not yet, anyway.'

'When did this happen?' Rian asked.

'In May of this year.'

'Surely the trail will be cold by now?'

Nixon shrugged. 'I'm not privy to the constabulary's criminal investigations — not to that extent, anyway. But it has been rumoured that, of late, there have been one or two strong leads. Unfortunately Mr Kinghazel was not a popular man, which has somewhat muddied the waters of the investigation, so to speak.'

Kitty was extremely relieved that they hadn't been in Sydney six months earlier, or fingers might well have been pointed directly at Rian. He wasn't popular with the authorities and his long-running battle with Walter Kinghazel had been very public knowledge.

'But back to matters at hand,' Nixon said. 'I need to inspect your vessel. I can do it now, or I can come back with an official escort.'

'Do it now. I'll take you down to the hold, if you like,' Rian offered.

'Thank you, Captain. That is most co-operative of you.' Nixon sounded as though he had been expecting something else entirely.

It took him an hour to pick through the cargo in the *Katipo*'s hold, but he found nothing to concern him and Rian paid the small amount of duty due. By the time Nixon had finished, the crew were ready to go ashore.

★ ★ ★

'Not much has changed.' Gideon stepped over a pile of horse manure as they walked up George Street and turned into Suffolk Lane. 'More buildings, perhaps.'

Gazing around, Kitty agreed: The Rocks was as crowded, dirty, noisy and vibrant as it had been when she'd arrived in March 1840. And that distinctive combination of smells — freshly baked bread mixed with the stenches of sewage and the slaughteryard further up the hill — was as strong as ever. Then, though, she had had Wai beside her, and she frowned as a pang of

52

grief stabbed at her.

'All right?' Rian, walking next to her, asked quietly.

Kitty nodded. 'Just remembering the first time we were here.'

Rian took her hand. He knew how much she still missed her friend, and he recalled very clearly himself the appalling shock of Wai's death.

They would be there for only a week or so this time — just long enough to unload their current cargo, take on another for New Zealand, and make the arrangements to finally take Wai home. When they reached the juncture of Suffolk Lane and Gloucester Street they parted ways, agreeing to meet up again later in the Bird-in-Hand public house.

Rian and Kitty continued along Suffolk Lane to visit Rian's sister, Enya Mason, who owned a dressmaking business there. Her shop was empty when they stepped through the door, so Rian vigorously rang the little silver bell on the counter. Nothing happened for a moment, then a voice called from the recesses of the shop, 'I won't be a minute!'

Eventually Enya appeared, an enormous smile lighting up her face. 'Rian! You're back!' She darted around the counter and hurried to her brother, her arms wide. They embraced, then Enya stepped back and looked him up and down. 'Still the same,' she said, laughing. 'Still scruffy!' She turned to Kitty and gave her a warm hug. 'And Kitty, it's so lovely to see you. Has my brother been looking after you?'

'Oh, yes,' Kitty said happily. 'I couldn't ask for

more. It's wonderful, being married.' She smiled warmly at her stunningly beautiful sister-in-law, of whom she had once been searingly jealous when she'd thought Enya was Rian's lover.

Enya looked wistful for a moment, remembering, Kitty guessed, her own husband who had died in 1839. 'Yes, it is wonderful, isn't it?' she said. 'I recommend it wholeheartedly.'

'No one on the horizon?' Rian asked.

Enya looked coy. 'Well, actually, now that you mention it, there might be.'

'Oh,' Rian said, clearly surprised because for so long Enya had seemed content to live her life as a widow. 'Do I know him?'

'No, and so what if you don't, big brother?' Enya replied. 'I'm a successful businesswoman and I'm perfectly capable of knowing my own mind, thank you very much.'

Rian said exasperatedly, 'I *know* you know your own mind, En. It's the successful businesswoman bit that I'm worried about. He might be after your money.'

'Unlikely. He has far more than I have.'

'Oh,' Rian said again, his sails suddenly without wind. 'But I think I should meet him.'

'Not this time. He's at sea.'

'Oh Christ, he's not a bloody merchant seaman, is he?'

'What's wrong with merchant seamen?' Kitty said.

Rian frowned at her. 'Well, they do tend to drown, don't they?'

Kitty laughed. 'What? Like traders and part-time smugglers?'

'I suppose,' Rian conceded. 'But you can't blame me, Enya, you've already been widowed once.'

'I'm perfectly aware of that, Rian. I know what I'm doing. And anyway, he isn't a merchant seaman, he's a captain in the navy.'

Rian was surprised. 'The *Royal* Navy?'

'Yes.'

'And he knows you were transported?'

Enya said, 'I've never made a secret of it, and I never will. You know that.'

'Well, if he's in the navy, how does he come to have money?' Rian ploughed on, grasping at straws. 'He must be lying — the pay's atrocious.'

Enya was about to tell her nosy, overprotective brother that it was none of his business when someone entered the shop, so she sent them both out the back, where Kitty was very pleased to be able to sit down. After any extended period at sea her feet always felt as though they were made of lead when she stepped onto dry land, and her legs felt most strange not having to adjust to the constant roll of the deck. Rian insisted it was because she was turning into a mermaid.

When the customer had gone, Enya rejoined them.

'Now,' she said, 'it's time for your wedding presents.' She crossed the room to a series of floor-to-ceiling shelves which were stacked with large, flat boxes. Reading the labels, she eventually found what she wanted, and slid out two. She handed one to Rian and one to Kitty.

Kitty opened hers eagerly and gasped as she

lifted out a dress. 'Oh, Enya, it's absolutely *beautiful!*'

It was lilac charmeuse with a chiffon overskirt, the bodice decorated with Enya's exquisite trademark beading and embroidery. The sleeves were slightly puffed at the shoulder but fitting from the elbow down, the waist very snug, and the neckline low. Kitty was overcome; she owned a handful of nice dresses these days, but nothing as gorgeous as this.

'I hope it fits,' Enya said. 'I made it after Rian wrote about the wedding, from the measurements we took when I remodelled the dress you wore to go to see Avery Bannerman at the barracks. But you don't look as though you've changed size.'

Kitty desperately hoped she hadn't; the dress was so beautiful it would be the cruellest of blows if she couldn't fit into it. 'I'm going to try it on,' she said, and immediately started unbuttoning the much more ordinary dress she had worn to come ashore.

Rian was torn between watching the ever-tantalising spectacle of his wife undressing and opening his own present. Watching Kitty won. When Enya had done up the fastenings for her, Kitty twirled around the room, the sun slanting through the small window catching the glass beads on the silk bodice and making them sparkle.

The dress fitted her perfectly.

Rian gave a long, appreciative whistle and patted his knee. 'Here, love, come and sit down for a minute. I think I might have something for you.'

Kitty laughed and flicked the hem of her skirt at him.

'Honeymoon not worn off yet, then?' Enya observed, her eyebrows raised in amusement.

Kitty hugged her again. 'Thank you so much, Enya. It's absolutely divine!'

Enya went pink with pleasure. 'You can wear a fichu if you'd rather not have quite so much décolletage on display.'

'Such as any time you wear it in the company of anyone else but me,' Rian said, only half-jokingly.

'Yes, dear,' Kitty replied dismissively. 'Go on, open yours.'

Rian carefully took the lid off his box and lifted out a beautifully cut and finished tailcoat in dark grey cheviot wool with gleaming silver buttons. He went over to his sister and kissed her on her cheek.

'Thanks, it's very nice. It's about time I had something decent to wear,' he remarked.

'Yes, but will you?' Enya asked.

'When the occasion demands it. We don't get out much, being at sea as much as we are. But thanks, En, it's very smart.'

Enya sat back. 'So, are you in Sydney for a reason, or are you on your way somewhere?'

'We're here for Wai,' Kitty said. 'It's time to take her home. Well past time, actually.'

Enya knew about what had happened, of course, and had been told about the Maori protocols that decreed that Wai be returned to New Zealand so her soul could finally rest in peace.

She asked, 'The little boy will be four by now, won't he?'

'Almost four and a half,' Kitty replied.

'And you haven't seen him since you took him home?'

'No, we haven't been back to New Zealand at all.'

'And you're sure it's all right for you to go back? No one there will still be holding a grudge?'

Kitty thought for a moment. 'I don't know. I hope not.'

'Well, be careful anyway,' Enya said incisively. 'Have you heard about the unrest there, in the Bay of Islands?'

Rian said, 'We saw something in the paper in Durban about Hone Heke having a go at the flagstaff at Kororareka.' He looked at Kitty. 'Or was that in Montevideo?'

'Durban,' Kitty replied. 'It was just after Sharkey died.'

Enya's fine eyebrows arched in surprise. 'John Sharkey, your crewman? The one with the scar and the earrings?'

Rian nodded grimly. 'He was knifed in a street brawl.'

'Oh dear, I'm very sorry to hear that. I know you thought well of him, Rian.' Enya paused, then said, 'Well, as I said, be careful. There's talk that war might be imminent.'

Startled, Kitty blurted, 'War? In New Zealand?'

'Yes, between the natives and the Crown, apparently.'

Rian frowned. 'Is it in the north, or throughout the country?'

'Just in the north, I believe. There was an incident at Wairau — is that how you say it? — in New Ulster, but they say that was over fairly quickly. But Governor FitzRoy moved troops into the Bay of Islands earlier this year.'

'Just because Heke cut down a flagstaff?'

'I'm not entirely sure. We don't get all the news from New Zealand.' Enya's eyes narrowed. 'Your cargo this time doesn't include guns, does it?'

'No,' Rian said. 'But still, they might come in handy, mightn't they?'

Enya gave her brother a long, apprehensive look, but said nothing.

★ ★ ★

Kitty watched Gideon as he carefully carried a tray loaded with jugs of ale and tumblers of spirits across the crowded public room of the Bird-in-Hand. In fact it only had a public room: its clientele wasn't particularly discerning, unlike the St Patrick's Inn a few doors along, where Kitty had once worked and which had both a public room and a private lounge.

Following Gideon at a respectful distance was a serving girl, whose wide eyes seemed to be drawn to Gideon's enormously broad back. The Rocks attracted all sorts of unusual and exotic people, particularly sailors, from every corner of the world, but Kitty had to admit that Gideon was more or less in a league of his own. He spoke extremely cultured English, though, and it always amused her to watch the expressions on people's faces when he opened his mouth.

He set down the tray on the long, scarred wooden table and squeezed himself onto the bench beside it.

Rian reached for his ale and said to the serving girl, who was now hovering nervously at his elbow, 'Do you still have that bread, cheese and pickle plate?'

She nodded.

'One of those then, thanks.' Rian glanced at Kitty. 'The same?'

Kitty said yes. Pierre replenished the ship's larder every time they called into port, and he had a very good eye and nose for interesting, good-quality foodstuffs, but she'd become partial to Australian cheese and had missed it while they'd been away.

The girl took everyone else's orders, then trotted off.

'How did you get on?' Rian said to Ropata, who had made considerable inroads into his ale already.

Ropata stifled a burp. 'We found someone who can contact him, and we passed on a message.'

Gideon added, 'He must be close by, because we will hear by tonight.'

The man they were talking about was Mundawuy Lightfoot, the Aborigine who, through his friendship with Gideon, had allowed Wai to be interred in the ancestral burial cave of his people until it was time for her to go home. They had all agreed that it would be deeply

60

disrespectful to return to the caves on the western shore of Sydney Cove and collect her without consulting Mundawuy. But there were very few Aborigines in Sydney town, and to make contact with one required a considerable amount of tapping on the right shoulders.

Rian asked, 'Does this messenger know where to find us?'

'Yes. I told her to come here,' Gideon replied.

'*Her?*'

Gideon said, 'Yes. A relative, I believe. A niece?' His eyes bright with amusement, he added 'Ropata took a fancy to her.'

'I did not!' Ropata protested.

Rian said, 'What time tonight, did she say?'

'Just evening,' Gideon replied.

'Well, I suppose we'll just have to sit here and drink until she turns up,' Rian declared, not sounding at all bothered by the prospect.

'I haven't been to see me mam yet,' Mick said, setting his empty tumbler on the table.

'I thought you were going to see her when we parted company earlier?' Kitty said.

Mick smirked. 'I was waylaid.'

'On the way past the whorehouse on Argyle Street?' Pierre asked slyly.

'Aye. 'Tis a terrible thing, human nature, so it is,' Mick said solemnly while everyone else laughed. Except for Kitty, who still wasn't completely at ease with the men referring so casually to that sort of thing.

'Anyway, *you* can talk,' Mick said to Pierre, 'considerin' where you've been all afternoon.'

Having spent the past few hours in the

61

company of the lady friend who regularly accommodated him whenever he was in Sydney, Pierre looked affronted. 'Ah, but there is *une petite difference*: I have the special friend, not just some ratty whore. And that is what makes the world go around — good food, friendship and *l'amour*.'

Mick snorted, opened his mouth to say something, then glanced at Kitty and shut it again.

'When are you going?' Rian asked Mick.

'Soon as I've had me dinner.'

'We might come with you, then.'

'Aye, that'll be grand.'

An hour later, Kitty, Rian and Mick turned off Cribb's Lane into Caraher's Lane and walked along the familiar, narrow cobbled street until they came to Mick's mother's house. Kitty slowed as she approached, feeling surprisingly and disconcertingly close to tears.

'It's very strange, being back here,' she said after a moment. 'Sort of comforting, like coming home, but sad at the same time.'

Rian slid his hand around her waist as Mick knocked on his mother's door and stood back. When Biddy Doyle opened it, she launched herself down the two front steps and threw her arms around Mick.

'My boy, my baby boy!' she cried, kissing him all over his face and squeezing him until Kitty feared that his dinner of pickle and cheese might burst out of him.

'Hello there, Mam,' Mick said slightly breathlessly. 'You're looking well.'

Mrs Doyle was barely changed from when they'd last seen her. She was perhaps a little more plump, but everything else was the same — the grey hair, the shawl folded across her bosom, the shrewd, sparkling eyes.

'And Rian. And young Kitty!' Mrs Doyle went on, delighted. She hugged them both, then stood back. 'Still together then, I see?'

Grinning, Kitty proudly held up her hand to display the wide gold filigree band she wore on her ring finger.

'Aye, and wed, too! Well, I never saw that one coming, so I didn't!' Mrs Doyle said, laughing. She turned to Mick and clipped him smartly across the ear. 'You could have written and told your old mam there'd been a wedding!'

'Sorry, Mam. I didn't think of it.'

'Well, never mind,' Mrs Doyle said. 'Lucky for you Enya gave me the news. So, how long have you been man and wife?' she asked Rian.

'Three years and five months.'

Mrs Doyle nodded knowingly and remarked, 'You must really love the lass. It's usually her that counts the months as well as the years, not the man.'

Kitty took Rian's hand and squeezed it.

Mrs Doyle noticed. 'Aye, 'tis both of you. Well, that's grand, isn't it, Mick?' she said, raising a hopeful eyebrow at her unmarried son.

'Mmm,' Mick said noncommittally.

'No babbies?' Mrs Doyle went on.

Kitty shook her head. 'Not yet. One day, perhaps.'

'Aye, there's time enough yet, I suppose. Just,'

63

Mrs Doyle added pointedly. She believed in big families. 'So what brings you back to Sydney town?'

'We've come to collect Wai and take her home,' Kitty explained.

Mrs Doyle muttered, 'And not before time, I'd say.'

Kitty started to ask her what she meant, but Rian interrupted. 'How's business?' he asked, gesturing at the tenement houses attached to Mrs Doyle's.

'Fair,' she said. 'Good in all but downstairs at number four.'

'Where we lived?' Kitty said.

'Aye. Anyway, come in and have a cup of tea. You're just in time — I've just made a lardy cake.'

Inside, when Mrs Doyle had served tea and happily watched them each eat a slab of cake, Mick asked, 'Why can't you rent out number four, Mam?'

'Well, it's not the renting that's the problem,' his mother replied, collecting cake crumbs from her plate with her finger, 'it's keeping the tenants in there.'

'But it's a lovely little house,' Kitty said.

'It is. But as you know I only rent that one to ladies, and all the ladies I've had in there over the past eighteen months or so have complained about there being a *taibhse* wandering about.'

There was a short silence, then Rian said, in a not altogether disbelieving tone, 'A ghost?'

Mrs Doyle nodded, and the hairs on Kitty's arms began to stand up.

'Aye, they all insist that they've seen a young girl with long black hair sitting on the daybed, just under the front window there, keening and wailing and asking for her babby.' Mrs Doyle paled slightly as she uttered her next words. 'Me, I think it's the wee colleen Wai.'

Kitty burst into tears.

★ ★ ★

They arrived back at the Bird-in-Hand just before eight o'clock. The rest of the crew were still there sitting at the long table, but a young woman had joined them. She had a brow heavy enough to suggest that Aboriginal blood flowed in her veins, and beautifully curved, full lips, but her skin was lighter than Ropata's and her black hair was straight, though there was masses of it. Kitty guessed she was somewhere in her early twenties, and also that she was very uncomfortable sitting in the pub, as she had her back to the wall and kept looking around, her dark eyes wary.

Hawk said, 'This is Leena, Mundawuy's niece.'

Leena inclined her head, but said nothing.

'She says Mundawuy will take us to the caves tomorrow night,' Hawk added.

Leena spoke up then. 'He say to meet him at the shore, like last time. When the moon is up. And to bring shovels.' Her eyes darted around the pub again. 'That is all. I have passed the message. I will go now,' she said, and stood up.

As she slid out from behind the table, Kitty

could see that she was tall and slender, and probably younger than she had first assumed. She also saw that Ropata was staring intently at her, watching every graceful movement of her limbs. He opened his mouth to say something but was too late, because a second later she had slipped through the door and out into the night. When he realised he had missed his chance, his handsome face assumed such an expression of childish disappointment that Kitty almost laughed.

'Will we all go?' Mick asked.

'No,' Rian said. 'Just me and Kitty. And you two?' he asked Gideon and Ropata.

They both nodded.

Pierre let out an audible sigh of relief, as did Hawk and Mick. Pierre was the most superstitious person Kitty had ever met. Not only did he abide by the full quota of traditional sailors' superstitions, he was also steeped in the codes of his personal religion, the *voudou* of his native Louisiana. Some days on board the *Katipo*, if the sun was shrouded in hazy cloud, or a particular bird had been seen wheeling in the sky two days before, or for no apparent reason the bread hadn't risen in the galley oven the day before, Pierre could barely force himself to get out of his bunk without performing a wide range of rituals designed to ward off the evils he insisted that any one of those portents might evoke. So digging up the bones of a long-dead girl was not the sort of thing he relished at all.

Hawk also was very wary and reverent of death rituals — his own as well as those of others

66

— and had made it clear that, although he would help in any other way required, he would not be visiting the Aborigines' sacred burial ground. Mick, however, wasn't particularly superstitious, just very keen on paying another visit to the whorehouse on Argyle Street.

Kitty sighed. She had a headache from crying and fully expected that by the time the following night was over, she would have shed even more tears.

2

Kitty had the strangest sense of déjà vu. But then, they were doing exactly as they had the first time they'd landed on the little beach on Sydney Cove's western shore, except that this time Gideon was rowing the boat instead of the taciturn waterman who had ferried them on their previous journey. And this night the moon was high and bright, which would help them negotiate the steep, narrow track that would lead them to the Aborigine burial caves.

Gideon guided the rowboat onto the beach, and Rian and Ropata jumped out and pulled the bow further up onto dry land. Then Kitty disembarked, holding her skirts up around her knees to avoid getting them wet, and waited while Gideon carefully lifted the box out of the boat.

It was a box, that was true, but it was also a waka taonga, as Ropata called it: a place to store treasures. It measured two feet long, one foot wide and one foot high, and had been made from a teak log Rian had had milled almost two years before in Batavia. Since then, they had each taken many hours to carve into it the symbols and scenes that held importance for them, a way of honouring Wai's memory and easing her journey back to New Zealand. Hawk had carved the spiritual motifs of the Seneca people, Pierre those of Louisianan *voudou*, Ropata the whorls and lines of Ngati Kahungungu, and Rian and Mick the designs unique to those with Celtic blood. Sharkey had carved a scene on the lid that depicted Wai rising out of the ocean on the back of a whale, and Gideon, who had been baptised as a young man, added an ornate cross. Kitty couldn't carve, no matter how hard she tried, so her contribution had been the padded, flower-embroidered silk lining inside the box.

Gideon set the box down and they settled in to wait. It was eerily quiet on the small beach, the silence broken only by the hissing of small waves scurrying across the sand. The night air was warm and heavy, barely stirred by the breeze coming off the sea. Occasionally, one of Australia's exotic and noisy birds gave voice, making Kitty jump.

Ropata spoke for them all when he said eventually, 'It is scaring me, this place. When is he coming?'

'Should be soon,' Rian replied, squinting up at the full moon.

'Too right,' a voice said, then Mundawuy Lightfoot himself stepped into the moonlight. Like Biddy Doyle, he looked exactly as he had when they'd first met him; long-legged, lean, bearded and cocoa-skinned.

'G'day, black man,' Mundawuy said to Gideon, who had risen to his feet.

'Good evening, friend Mundawuy,' Gideon replied, warmly shaking hands with the Aborigine. 'I believe you have met everyone except Ropata, who is Ngati Kahungungu of the East Coast of New Zealand.'

Mundawuy looked Ropata up and down, and

said, 'G'day, brown man.'

Ropata stepped forward and hongied him. Mundawuy looked startled for a moment, then his face broke into a wide grin, his teeth gleaming in the moonlight. 'That's good, eh?' he said.

Ropata smiled. 'It is. From my people to yours.'

'That is good,' Mundawuy agreed, then shook hands with Rian and Kitty. 'You got shovels?'

He waited while the others gathered together the box and everything else they would need, then he turned away and padded silently off into the shadows.

This time the walk up through the great slabs of rock and in and out of clumps of hard, scratchy scrub seemed shorter, but journeys always did, Kitty knew, if you'd done them once before. It wasn't long before they started going downhill again, and she knew they would soon be at the cave.

As they walked in through the shadowed entrance, the moonlight slowly faded until they were moving in complete blackness. Rian struck a flint, sharply reminding Kitty again of the first time they had been here, and lit an oil lamp. As they walked on in silence, their boots sinking into the soft, dry sand, she saw once again the ancient drawings that Mundawuy's ancestors had scored and burned into the walls so long ago. She also heard the leathery flutter of bats' wings, and felt rather than heard their high-pitched squeaks, glad that this time she had thought to wear a bonnet.

70

As they walked further and further into the cave, she began to worry that they might not be able to find the spot where they had buried Wai, but then, up ahead, Mundawuy came to an abrupt halt and held up his hand. He squatted down, spread out his fingers and repeated the strange sniffing that had so unnerved her when they had first come with Wai.

After a minute, Mundawuy stood, moved several yards further in, squatted again, then pointed. 'She under here.'

They set down their tools and the box, and waited while Ropata said a short karakia to Hine-nui-o-te-po, the great goddess of death, asking for her permission to temporarily release Wai. Then they started digging, the sand whispering off the metal of their shovels as they worked.

It suddenly occurred to Kitty that, because the sand was so dry, there might be more left of Wai than they had been expecting. She shuddered, envisaging her friend's mummified head, the dried flesh shrunken onto her yellowed bones. She felt someone's gaze on her and looked up.

'No worry,' Mundawuy said quietly. 'This sand special. No meat left, no stink.'

Kitty stared at him, almost as alarmed by his reading of her mind as by the thought of finding Wai only partly decomposed. But she nodded and let her gaze slide back to the grave. When the digging stopped a moment later she stepped forward, feeling her heart thud rapidly in her chest.

She looked down.

In the flickering yellow light of Rian's lamp, she could see that the shroud in which they had buried Wai had been reduced to dusty shreds, the remaining wisps draped over her bones, which were indeed bare and pearly white. Surrounded by lengths of long black hair, her pale skull gleamed softly, and between her ribs, where her heart would have been, lay the greenstone earring her father had left with her. The sand had sifted down through her delicate bones but it was obvious that she hadn't been disturbed. She might have been lying here for a thousand years, Kitty thought, not for just four and a half. She moved back, her eyes filling with tears.

'Little bird girl,' Mundawuy said.

Gideon and Rian stepped carefully down into the grave while Kitty brought the box closer and opened it, resting the hinged lid on the sand. As they started to pass out Wai's bones, Ropata began to intone another prayer. Suddenly not frightened any more, filled now with only an aching sadness for her lost friend, Kitty took each bone as it was handed up to her and laid it carefully in the silk-lined box. Last to go in was the greenstone earring. Kitty gently closed the lid and looked up at Rian.

'All right?' he asked.

She nodded, although there was still a lump the size and sharpness of a peach pit in her throat; then she gave in and allowed herself to weep as Rian helped her to her feet. She leaned against him, grateful for his warmth, his strength and his understanding. Beside her Gideon was also weeping, although silently; the twin line of tears flowing down his wide, black cheeks reflected the lamplight, as though he were crying tiny threads of fire. Ropata had finished his karakia on a very wobbly note and was now intently studying the cave wall, blinking furiously.

Mundawuy started speaking then in his own tongue, and Kitty saw that he was directing his words to a spot in the air above Wai's empty grave. She looked away, not wanting to intrude: she knew enough now about native peoples to accept and respect the fact that most had their own ways of appeasing gods, thanking ancestors and soothing spirits.

Gideon bent down and hoisted the box onto his wide shoulders, although Kitty thought that even she could have managed to carry it. Wai's bones could hardly weigh much; it was her memory that lay heavily on them all.

★   ★   ★

The day before the *Katipo* set sail for New Zealand, Kitty and Enya went shopping. Kitty bought slippers to go with her new dress, some rather fine bed linen, and several pairs of men's trousers, which she would tailor to her own shape as the trews she had been wearing over the past year were almost threadbare and coming apart at the seams. She also bought a boy's cap, to keep her hair out of the way while she was working on deck. She had been using a head scarf but it tended to slide off, especially when her hair was freshly washed.

After that, she found herself being steered by Enya into a pharmacy.

'Why are we in here?' she asked, mystified.

'Because you can't keep sailing about on the high seas the way you are and expect your complexion to remain as lovely it is,' Enya replied. 'And you're not exactly a girl any more, are you?'

Kitty knew Enya's comments were meant affectionately, but she still felt somewhat put out. 'What's wrong with my complexion?' she asked, a tad grumpily.

'Nothing yet. Apart from those tiny crow's feet starting at the corners of your eyes. That's probably from squinting into the sun.'

Kitty went over to a mirror mounted on the pharmacy wall and glared into it with her eyes wide open. 'I can't see any crow's feet.'

'That's because you're pulling a face. How old are you now?'

'Twenty-five. But I only had my birthday last month.'

'Then it's time to start doing something before it's too late.' Enya took Kitty firmly by the elbow and led her over to the counter, behind which the pharmacist, a small man with neatly trimmed whiskers, stood patiently waiting.

'Good afternoon, Mr Turvey,' Enya said.

'Good afternoon, Mrs Mason,' he replied genially.

'I buy all of my beauty preparations from Mr Turvey,' Enya explained to Kitty. 'He's very skilled.'

He must be, Kitty thought grudgingly, because her sister-in-law certainly had a flawless complexion, all smooth cream and pink. She was beginning to feel like an old hag now.

'So what I think we'll start with, Mr Turvey,' Enya said, 'is some of your best cold cream, the one with the lanolin base. That's to use at night,' she explained to Kitty. 'It can be a bit greasy, so don't use too much. Then perhaps we'll try an oatmeal-and-buttermilk face mask, though you'll have to use that quickly or it will go off. It leaves the face feeling marvellously clean and firm. And some witch-hazel eyewash for that puffiness we get when we're tired.'

We? Kitty thought: she had *never* seen Enya with puffy eyes. She knew hers were puffy, though, mostly from sitting in the hot, smoky public room of the Bird-in-Hand until after midnight the night before. But it had been worth it, because they'd caught up on the latest gossip about Walter Kinghazel's murder. Apparently, so the farrier sitting at the next table had informed them — and he should know, he insisted, because he was on very friendly terms with one of the local constabulary — a new suspect had been identified, a man who had been seen in the same drinking establishment as Mr Kinghazel on the night of his murder, then a little later in the immediate vicinity of his house. Now all of Sydney was busy speculating about who the suspect might be.

Enya leaned in close to Kitty's face, studied it for a moment, then said, 'Hmm.'

Kitty steeled herself for more bad news.

'You're developing a few freckles,' Enya declared. 'We'll take a large pot of your elderflower-and-zinc-sulphate cream, too, thank you, Mr Turvey. And is that a hint of ruddiness in your cheeks? We'd better have some of the white castile, cuttlefish and orris root soap as well.'

'It's not ruddiness, I'm just hot,' Kitty insisted, but Enya ignored her.

'Show me your hands.'

Kitty reluctantly presented her hands for inspection.

'Oh dear,' Enya said. 'And a large tub of almond-oil hand-cream. Now, have you started using cosmetics yet, Kitty?'

Kitty was surprised to discover that she was faintly shocked, because everyone knew that only whores wore face paint. 'No, I haven't!'

'All the best ladies do, you know.'

'They do not!'

'Yes they do, but it's so subtly applied you'd never know.'

'So why bother, then?' Kitty retorted.

'Because, applied artfully, cosmetics will always enhance the complexion. I'm only talking about a dusting of rice powder, a dab of lip balm and just a hint of rouge on the cheekbones.'

'Well, as I've already got ruddy cheeks I won't need rouge, will I?' Kitty grumbled. 'I do have some lip balm, though. But it's a bit old. I think it's gone rancid.'

So Enya ordered some cosmetics and a small case of castile-and-chamomile soap for Kitty's hair. 'How long will all that take to make up?'

she asked the pharmacist.

Mr Turvey looked at his pocket watch. 'If you come back at four o'clock, I'll have it ready by then. Will that suit you, Mrs Mason?'

'Very well, thank you. Good day until then, Mr Turvey.'

Outside the shop, Kitty said, 'How much is all that going to cost? Because I still have some shopping to do yet.'

'Oh, don't worry, I'll pay for it,' Enya replied blithely. 'As part of your wedding gift. And for your birthday.'

Kitty felt embarrassed by her sister-in-law's largesse. 'But you've already given me a beautiful gown.'

'Yes, and a beautiful gown deserves a beautiful complexion, don't you think?'

Kitty walked on in silence for a moment, then suddenly stopped. 'Enya, am I really looking that rough?' Then another, far worse, suspicion hit her. 'Do you think Rian might lose interest in me if I start to look old and weather-beaten? Is that it?'

Enya looked aghast. 'No, not at all! You look wonderful, Kitty, you always have. And I know my brother. He loves you very much and I don't think a few wrinkles or a bit of windburn would make an ounce of difference to him, I really don't.' She frowned, and touched Kitty's hand. 'I'm sorry if I've offended you. I certainly didn't mean to. Rian always said I can be a little too blunt at times, which is quite hypocritical coming from him, don't you think?'

Kitty smiled, because Enya was right. Then

she said, 'But *do* I look awful? Why do I need all of those preparations?'

'I don't think you *need* them, Kitty, I thought you might *like* them. You spend most of your time in the company of sailors, and, let's face it, as fond of them as I am, they're not the most urbane of men, are they? I just thought you might like to pamper yourself now and then, treat yourself like the beautiful woman you are. You might like to enjoy being *feminine*, I suppose is what I'm trying to say.'

Kitty was absurdly touched. Enya was right, she did sometimes miss the things that most women of her age enjoyed — wearing pretty gowns and dressing her hair and what have you — but she simply didn't have the time, especially when they were at sea. And she could hardly go shinnying up the ratlines in a tea gown with her hair elaborately coiffed and decorated with fresh flowers. The crew would laugh themselves silly. And the fact remained that, because she had spent first a year with the missionary women of Paihia, for whom personal appearance wasn't a priority, then the next four on board the *Katipo*, she'd never really had the opportunity to learn the art of enhancing her femininity.

She gave her sister-in-law a quick kiss on the cheek. 'Thank you, Enya, I appreciate it, I really do.'

They went into David Jones's after that, and spent a very satisfying hour making more purchases: the store was quite small, but Mr Jones stocked something for everyone and hours

78

could be whiled away just looking at everything he had for sale.

In particular, Kitty wanted gifts for the people with whom she had lived in Paihia, assuming that they were still there, of course. For Marianne Williams, the wife of Reverend Henry Williams, she bought an ornately decorated case for holding spectacles; for her friend Rebecca Purcell, wife of a lay missionary, she found a lovely quilted sewing box; and for Jannah Tait, whose husband was also a lay missionary, she bought a beautiful recipe book, which she hoped wouldn't be misinterpreted. She had never particularly liked Jannah, but she had respected her. And for her widowed Aunt Sarah — who certainly *must* be calling herself a widow by now, as to Kitty's knowledge there had not been a single piece of news regarding George's whereabouts since the day he had disappeared — she purchased a gorgeous bonnet in navy silk with black grosgrain ribbons and black feathers. She still wasn't sure if she had forgiven her aunt, but she thought it better to go prepared for a reconciliation. If there wasn't one, then she would simply keep the bonnet for herself.

She also bought gifts for two men — Simon Bullock, another lay missionary serving at Waimate Mission, and Haunui. If, again, Simon was still there. It had once been assumed — even hoped by some — that Kitty would marry Simon Bullock. Neither had thought it a particularly good idea, for various reasons, but they had become firm friends and Simon had been very fond of Wai. For Haunui, Kitty purchased a very smart top hat in black silk, in the largest size she could find, as a sly reference to the straw sunhat he had once stolen from her; and for Simon she found a lovely cream linen shirt, in the hope that he might wear it instead of his usual motley garments.

It was half past three when both women decided they were desperate for a drink and went into a coffee house. Kitty wilted onto a chair at the closest table, and sat fanning her face with her hand. Her chemise beneath her corset was stuck to her torso, and she suspected there were large wet patches under her arms.

'Yes, it *is* very warm, isn't it?' Enya agreed, untying the ribbons on her bonnet and pushing strands of damp hair back from her forehead.

Kitty surreptitiously blew down the front of her dress. 'It's nearly as bad as the Dutch East Indies, but not quite.'

'I've never been there,' Enya said. 'Is it nice?'

'I'm not sure I'd call it nice, but it's certainly interesting.'

A girl approached to take their orders, and Kitty waited until she had gone before she continued.

'Enya?'

'Mmm?'

'Will you tell me about Rian's first wife?'

Enya looked at her. 'Has he never said much?'

'Not really. He told me before we were wed that he'd been married before, and that his wife had fallen overboard with their baby, and that he'd lost them both. It must have been absolutely awful for him.'

'It was. He was inconsolable. He blamed himself, of course.'

'Because she fell overboard? How could that have been Rian's fault?'

'She didn't fall.' Enya sat back. 'Meagan was pretty and sweet and I believe Rian did love her, but she was never a strong girl, Kitty, not like you. She was quite fragile, and when I met her I thought Rian had made a mistake.' She shook her head. 'No, I knew he had. He left her in Dublin while he was at sea, but she pined for him and, frankly, made such a fuss that he finally gave in and took her with him. She became pregnant and after she had the baby she developed a mania. You've heard how some women can be afflicted like that after childbirth?'

'Yes.'

'Rian had convinced her to see a physician at their next port of call, but he was too late. She threw herself and the baby overboard one night and they both drowned.'

Kitty felt sick. 'Oh, my poor love,' she whispered.

Enya said, 'Yes, it was a terrible shock. Rian believed it was his fault because he'd allowed her to sail with him, but it wasn't. No one could have foreseen that.' She paused. 'And I didn't know Meagan well enough to realise she had the type of character that might be prone to hysteria. If I had, I think I would have done everything I could to stop her sailing with him. But I'd been transported by then, anyway.'

'Losing your wife would be bad enough but,

81

oh God, to lose a child would be so much worse,' Kitty said.

Enya nodded. Then she said, 'Kitty, pardon me if I'm being too personal, but have you thought much about a family?'

'Having babies?'

'Yes. You've been married for over three years now, and some people might say it's time to start considering it.'

'Well, they can say what they like,' Kitty replied shortly, 'but I'm not altogether sure it's going to happen.' And she told Enya about her suspicions about her ability, or lack thereof, to successfully conceive.

But instead of the sympathy Kitty was expecting, Enya appeared relieved.

'Well, that is sad,' she said. 'But I really think it might be for the best.'

Kitty leaned back as the serving girl returned with their refreshments and set them on the table. When she'd gone, she asked, 'Why do you say that?'

'Because I don't think Rian could bear to sail with a child on board again, after what happened with Meagan. Have you talked to him about having children?'

Kitty stirred her coffee. 'Not really. He doesn't seem to want to discuss it.'

'But you understand why, now?'

'Well, yes, I *understand* it, but — '

'And knowing my brother as well as I do,' Enya interrupted, 'I suspect that if a child were to come along, Rian would feel he would have to leave you, and it, ashore. And that would

82

break his heart as much as losing the pair of you altogether.' She looked beseechingly at Kitty. 'So, if you want babies, please think very hard about how it might affect your marriage. I know it's none of my business, but that's my advice to you. I love my brother and I'm very fond of you, Kitty. I'd hate anything to come between you.'

Kitty thought for a moment, then something else occurred to her. 'Is what happened with Meagan the reason Rian didn't want women on board the *Katipo*?'

'Yes, he swore he would never allow it again. You must have meant a lot to him already by then, for him to have let you on board.'

Remembering the mad, terrifying dash to get away from an enraged Tupehu and out to the *Katipo* before she sailed away, Kitty said, 'He didn't have a lot of choice, really.'

'Oh, I think he did, Kitty. He could have put you down anywhere.'

'I asked him to, but he said nowhere in New Zealand would be safe.'

'See? He didn't want to be parted from you even then.'

And Kitty smiled, because she suddenly saw that it was true.

★ ★ ★

Eight days after they had arrived in Sydney, the *Katipo* had been reloaded with an assortment of goods for trade in New Zealand: crates of soap, bales of shirts, duck trousers and blankets, sheet lead, dozens of bottles of turpentine and linseed oil, nails, window glass, white lead and green paint, a range of iron gardening implements and — at Kitty's request because she could clearly recall the women of Paihia bemoaning the fact that they couldn't get nice fabric — a dozen bolts of quality assorted dress materials.

Now they were all aboard, waiting for the tide to turn so the *Katipo* could be towed out into the harbour and set sail. Everything was shipshape and Wai's box had been stowed in the hold, inside a larger trunk packed with straw. They expected the trip to take a brisk eleven or twelve days, as the tail wind was likely to favour them at this time of year.

They lounged on deck, fanning sweaty faces and feeling sorry for Pierre who was in the galley preparing supper. Finally, the tugmaster came alongside and signalled that he was ready to tow them away from the dock and out into deeper water where they would be able to pick up the sea breeze and fill their sails.

Kitty watched as the dock slowly receded, the solid buildings along the cove's shoreline shrinking to the size of a child's toys as she leaned on the rail. Then, as the sun went down behind the upper reaches of The Rocks, the sunset turned the soil and rock of Sydney even redder, and for thirty minutes or so the whole harbour looked aflame, even the sea. She wondered when they would return to Sydney again. Quite soon, possibly, given that the unfortunate Mr Kinghazel had been despatched and they no longer had to concern themselves with any ideas of revenge he might have been harbouring.

By the time the crew sat down to Pierre's supper in the mess-room, the *Katipo* was passing between Dawes Point and Bennelong Point in the mouth of the harbour, and was about to move out into the dark rising swell of the Pacific Ocean. They would sail directly across the Tasman Sea, heading for Wellington to make the most of the trade winds, then through Cook Strait and up the East Coast of the North Island until they reached the Bay of Islands. As they ate, the ocean became progressively more choppy, and Kitty decided that after supper she would go down into the hold to make sure that the trunk in which Wai's remains had been packed was well secured. It would be unthinkable if the trunk toppled over.

It was truly dark by the time she lifted the hatch to the hold and, being careful not to spill any oil from her lamp, she made her way down the steep ladder, Bodie bouncing lightly down behind her. Kitty was pleased she had changed into a pair of trousers; the ladder was difficult enough to negotiate as it was, without layers of skirts hampering her.

At the foot of the ladder she paused and waited until her eyes had become accustomed to the semi-darkness. It was odd, she reflected, how the darkness of a night sky was always crisp and sharp, while the blackness contained within walls seemed to be much more palpable, and somehow thicker.

When she could see she moved forward,

threading her way through bales and crates and barrels until she reached Wai's trunk. Setting the lamp carefully on a box, she bent down and checked that the ropes lashing the trunk to the deck were secure. She patted the lid of the trunk fondly.

'You'll soon be home,' she whispered. 'Back with your people and your father and your baby, I promise.'

She stood for a moment, thinking about everything that had happened since she had last talked to her friend, then turned to retrieve the lamp. But as she did, the *Katipo* rolled mightily and she fell against the box, knocking the lamp over. It shattered, spilling a puddle of burning oil onto the deck. Kitty squeaked and scrambled out of the way, wildly looking around for something with which to douse the small fire.

But suddenly, a large black shape rushed at her from the shadows at the far end of the hold, banging and crashing and knocking things over as it came. Bodie screeched and leapt onto a stack of crates. A second later something rough flapped across Kitty's face, a gust of air whooshed past her and the puddle of flame disappeared, followed immediately by the muffled sound of the lamp being crunched and smothered underfoot. Terrified, Kitty staggered backwards until she connected with Wai's trunk, and groped for the broom she knew was lying behind it. She snatched it up and began swinging it through the darkness, at the same time screaming out for help.

The broom hit something and a male voice

cried, 'Ow! Christ!'

Kitty swung even harder, this time connecting solidly enough to jar her forearms.

'Ow, stop that, Miss Carlisle. It's me!'

Bodie chose that moment to attack, launching herself at the intruder's head, spitting and scratching. The swearing increased.

Panting, Kitty cautiously lowered the broom. 'Who is 'me'?'

The disembodied voice squawked, 'Daniel Royce, the sergeant from Hyde Park Barracks. Ow, Jesus *Christ!*'

★   ★   ★

Rian came skittering down the ladder into the hold at neck-breaking speed, followed by Hawk with another lamp, then Gideon and Mick.

Rian's boots thudded on the deck and he dodged across the hold towards Kitty, his drawn pistol glinting. Seeing that she appeared to be safe he stopped, peered at the shadowed figure next to her still scrambling to protect his face from Bodie's claws, and demanded, 'Who the hell is this?'

'Sergeant Royce, from the barracks,' Kitty replied, her voice wobbling slightly and her heart still racing.

'Who?'

'The sergeant from Hyde Park Barracks. The one who helped me,' Kitty said. 'At least he says it is. I can't see him properly.'

'Are you all right?' Rian asked her.

Kitty nodded as Rian disconnected a still-spitting Bodie from her victim's head.

'But I broke the lamp,' Kitty said. 'There's oil on the deck.'

'See to it, Mick,' Rian ordered, then he grasped the man's arm and bundled him roughly towards the ladder.

By the time Kitty had followed them up to the mess-room, both Rian and the intruder were seated at the table. Bodie was perched on the far end, glaring malevolently. Rian's pistol rested on the table in front of him, within easy reach. It was obvious in the light of the cabin lamps that the man was indeed Daniel Royce. He had a beard of four or five days, Bodie's handiwork had left deep scratches on his left cheek, and his clothes — not his smart barracks uniform, Kitty noted — were grubby and creased, but she clearly recognised his handsome, boyish features.

'Good evening, Miss Carlisle,' Daniel said sheepishly.

'Hello, Sergeant,' Kitty replied as she sat down. 'Actually, it's Mrs Farrell now. Captain Farrell here is my husband,' she added.

Something indecipherable flitted across Daniel's face and he seemed to deflate slightly. 'Oh,' he said after a moment. Then, 'Please accept my congratulations.'

'Never mind that,' Rian barked. 'What the hell were you doing in my hold?'

'Stowing away,' Daniel replied candidly.

'Really? Why, may I ask?'

'Unfortunately, I can't tell you that,' Daniel said.

Rian's eyes narrowed, which meant he was about to lose his temper. 'In that case, unfortunately, you'll have to swim back to Sydney Cove because I'm not taking you anywhere.'

Apparently either unconcerned by, or unaware of, the veiled menace in Rian's tone, Daniel said, 'But now that you know I'm aboard, could I perhaps work my passage to, well, wherever it is you're bound?'

Astounded, Rian glanced at the rest of the crew standing near the door watching with great interest, then back at Daniel. 'Am I correct in understanding that you stole aboard my schooner, without even knowing our next port of call, hoping to conceal yourself in my hold for God knew how long, eating rats and drinking your own piss?'

'Not exactly, no,' Daniel said. 'Not the rats and the piss, anyway. But I'm more than happy to work my passage. I've been to sea before.'

Rian shook his head at the pure cheek of the man. 'I won't even consider it until you tell me why you've stowed away. If you wanted to leave Sydney, why didn't you secure a passage aboard an outgoing vessel like everyone else?'

Daniel dropped his gaze then and stared hard at the scarred table top, apparently in the throes of some sort of internal debate. Finally, he seemed to come to a decision. No longer sounding quite so confident, he replied, 'The reason I couldn't secure passage like everyone else is because I'm wanted by the Sydney armed constabulary.'

'What for?' Rian said flatly.

'Suspicion of murder.'

Rian's expression didn't alter at all. 'The murder of whom?'

'Walter Kinghazel.'

3

Ah,' Rian said, and sat back. 'And what spurred you to despatch such a fine, upstanding citizen as Mr Kinghazel? Or is murder something you're in the habit of committing?'

'Certainly not,' Daniel replied indignantly. 'I've never killed anyone in my life. Until now.'

'So why Kinghazel?'

'He was a bastard.'

'Yes, well, we all knew that,' Rian agreed. 'But surely you must have had a more specific motive?'

Daniel looked deeply uncomfortable. 'I'd rather not say.'

Rian let the silence stretch out until Daniel began to fidget.

'It concerns Miss Carlisle,' he said eventually.

'Mrs Farrell,' Hawk interjected pointedly.

'What about her?' Rian said.

'I can't say.'

Rian looked up at Kitty. 'Would you mind waiting in our quarters?'

'Yes, I would,' she shot back. 'If it concerns me, I want to know.'

Rian's eyebrows lifted barely perceptibly, and after a moment Kitty stamped off into the cabin, banging the door unnecessarily loudly behind her, then yanking it open again a second later as Bodie scratched furiously to be let in.

Rian planted his elbows on the table. 'Right,

Sergeant, out with it.'

'It's probably only 'Mister' now, as I suppose I've deserted,' Daniel said. Then he sighed. 'I killed Kinghazel because he'd been going around for the past year telling anyone who would listen that he'd . . . that he'd had relations of a sexual nature with Miss Carlisle when you were last in Sydney. And that she is a doxy.' He swallowed and looked directly at Rian. 'And I know she isn't.'

There was a very heavy silence in the mess-room, which Hawk broke by saying somewhat aggressively this time, 'It is *Mrs* Farrell. She is married now.'

Rian's face had paled and his lips barely moved as he said, 'Well, Royce, if you hadn't slit the prick's throat, I would have.'

'And me,' Mick added. The others all nodded, and Pierre had gone positively puce with outrage.

Daniel went on. 'When I met Miss — *Mrs* Farrell, at the barracks, when she was visiting Avery Bannerman, I didn't know her very well, of course, but I could see that she was a lady. And that she would never do anything of the sort, especially with a jumped-up little shit like Kinghazel.'

Rian looked at him for a long moment. 'So why do you think he was he saying it?'

'Revenge, I suppose.' Daniel made a contemptuous face. 'You had dealings with him, Captain, you know what a nasty piece of work he was. He was *incensed* when you got off that customs charge, almost mad with rage, and he never forgot it. It grew in him like a cancer. God knows what he had up his sleeve for when you showed your face in Sydney Cove again. But you never did, and I imagine he thought the worst he could do instead was to slander the lady who had been in your company.'

'Did you hear the slander with your own ears?' Hawk asked.

'Yes. Kinghazel sometimes drank in the same public house I did. The Erin-go-Bragh? I heard it coming out of his foul mouth four or five times before I finally lost my temper.'

Rian turned the pistol on the table so the barrel no longer pointed at Daniel. 'You hadn't planned it?'

'No, I just lost my temper,' Daniel said. 'I followed him home one night, just meaning to give him a good kicking to teach him a lesson, and then he said it.'

'Said what?

'He said, 'I suppose you tupped her yourself, did you, when she was flogging her wares at the barracks?' And then before I knew it my knife was in my hand and I'd slit his throat. But I've never regretted it,' Daniel added defiantly. 'Not once.'

Rian said, 'Did you expect to get away with it?'

'Not really. But I'm not prepared to swing for the little bastard either. I'm surprised it's taken so long for the rozzers to find out that I was outside his house the night he died. But Kinghazel wasn't liked and people haven't been particularly helpful.'

'So when they did put you in the picture you

decided it was time to leave Sydney?'

Daniel nodded.

'So why choose my schooner?' Rian asked.

Daniel's gaze met Rian's and they stared at each other across the mess table for almost a minute.

Then Daniel said, 'Because I thought you'd be the least likely person to turn me in, given that Kinghazel tried to have you gaoled.'

He was lying, and Rian knew it. Or he at least knew that Royce wasn't giving him a completely frank answer. But for some reason he was beginning to warm to the man, and he admired his principles, especially as they had concerned Kitty's virtue, although he was starting to wonder whether Kitty was actually Royce's reason for being on the *Katipo*. Royce hadn't said as much — he seemed far too circumspect for that — but it was written all over his face every time he looked at her.

'Well, you're right in assuming I won't turn you in,' Rian said. 'As far as I'm concerned, you've done me a favour. Several, actually. You can sail with us to New Zealand, but you *will* work your passage. And let me make something very clear at the outset, Royce. This schooner, and everything on it, is mine. That includes the gear, the cargo, and the crew. It also includes my wife. Do you understand?'

The cabin became very silent; even the creaking of the *Katipo*'s hull and the cracking of her sails overhead seemed to cease for a few, heavy, seconds.

Eventually, Daniel nodded.

Kitty was already in bed, scowling and sitting with the sheets pulled up to her chest, Bodie dozing across her lap. Rian sat down in the wooden chair at his desk and wrestled off his boots, kicking them across the rug towards the wardrobe.

'Are you unhappy with me?' he asked.

'What do you think?' Kitty replied tartly. 'You made me look a fool in there, Rian. Telling me to go to my room like a naughty little child!'

Rian sighed, reached for the brandy decanter on his desk and poured himself a sizeable tot. 'I didn't tell you to go to your room, I asked you to wait in our quarters.'

'It's the same thing, though, isn't it?' Kitty snapped. 'You didn't think it appropriate that my little shell-like ears hear whatever it was Daniel had to say, so you told me to go away.'

'You don't have shell-like ears, Kitty, and you know as well as I do that over the past four years they've already heard every inappropriateness they're ever likely to.'

'That's not the *point*, Rian! You're always doing that, making decisions on my behalf when I'm perfectly capable of making them for myself.'

'How can you make a decision about something you're not even aware of yet?'

'Oh, shut up,' Kitty said crossly. 'You know what I mean.'

Rian dared not look at her, in case he laughed.

Kitty adjusted the sheets, pulling them up even higher across her chest. Rian noticed that she was wearing the nightdress he was particularly fond of, the floaty white one he'd discovered was almost transparent whenever he asked her to hop out of bed and fetch him something from his desk.

'So what was Daniel's great secret, anyway?' she asked. 'The one not fit for my ears?'

'*He* was the one who didn't want to say it in front of you, if you'll recall,' Rian replied, not feeling like laughing any more: Kitty's familiar use of Royce's Christian name was beginning to make him feel uneasy. He took another sip of his brandy. 'Kitty?'

'What?'

'How well did you get to know Daniel Royce? At the barracks, I mean?'

She looked at him warily. 'Not particularly well. Why?'

Rian paused while he considered how best to ask his next question. 'Well, did anything . . . happen while you were there?'

'Yes. I was scared witless on each occasion and I had to lie myself blue in the face and flaunt myself in a dress any self-respecting tart would kill for. Is that what you mean?'

'No. I meant . . . with Royce.'

Something briefly flickered in Kitty's eyes, but she blinked and it was gone. 'Such as?'

But Rian had seen it. 'Such as, did he make advances towards you of any sort?'

Kitty looked so genuinely surprised by the question that Rian's unease instantly receded. He didn't for a second suspect that Kitty was keeping secrets from him and he trusted her implicitly. He always had. It was his own fear making him nervous: he could not bear even the notion of being forced to live from day to day suspecting that she did not belong wholly to him. There was a part of her spirit he could never lay claim to, and he loved that about her even if it did lead to some fairly energetic disagreements, but he knew that her heart was his alone, just as she knew that he loved her unfailingly. And he did, he loved her as much as he loved the sea herself. It had taken him some time after they had wed to allow himself to relax and accept that she was finally his, but something small and unpleasant lodged deep within him still occasionally persisted in asking whether she would be his forever.

'Advances? From Daniel Royce?' Kitty exclaimed. 'Hardly. He's one of the most courteous, honourable men I've ever met.'

'He never implied that he liked you, or anything like that?'

'Of course not! Rian, what is all this about?'

Knowing that there was no way to avoid telling her, Rian said reluctantly, 'Royce has just informed us that he murdered Kinghazel to avenge your honour.'

Hoping fervently that his lovely wife was not going to suddenly decide that she had to take responsibility for Royce's actions, Rian said gently, 'Kinghazel was evidently going about insulting your personal reputation. Your virtue. Royce had had enough of it and killed him.'

Kitty looked mystified. 'What sort of insults?'

Oh God, he had known she was going to ask

that. 'He was implying, *suggesting*, that he had received, well, sexual favours from you.'

'From *me?*' Kitty cried shrilly, causing Bodie to leap off the bed in fright. 'That little *toad!* If I'd known that, I would have killed him myself!'

'No, Kitty,' Rian said, his voice suddenly harsh. '*I* would have, make no mistake about it.'

'But why, Rian? Why would he say something like that?'

'Your Daniel believes it was for revenge.'

'He's not *my* Daniel!' Kitty shot back, and then her faced sagged with dismayed realisation. 'Oh no, Rian, are you telling me he murdered Kinghazel for *me?*'

'To avenge your honour? Yes, it appears so.'

'But I don't understand. I hardly know him.'

'Well, you appear to have made quite an impression on him.'

Kitty disentangled her feet from the sheets and hung her legs over the side of the bed. 'But surely he didn't say that? Not to you?'

'No, he didn't. But obviously he's infatuated.'

'Oh dear.' Kitty frowned. 'Is that why he stowed away with us?'

Rian took another sip of brandy. 'He said it was because he didn't think I'd turn him in for Kinghazel's murder.'

'Was he right?'

'Well, of course he was. I've agreed that we'll take him as far as New Zealand. But after that he'll have to make his own way. He did us both a favour, Kitty, but we can't be responsible for him beyond what I've agreed to.'

Kitty nodded, then looked down at her bare

feet. 'Does it matter, that he did what he did for me? And that he's sailing with us now?'

Rian stared into the bottom of his brandy glass. 'Are you asking me does it bother me that he admires you?'

'Yes,' Kitty said after a moment.

'Should it?' Rian asked.

Kitty climbed off the bed and crossed the cabin to sit on his knee. She drew his head to her until his face rested against her breasts, and began to stroke his hair. 'No, my love, it shouldn't. I love you with all my heart and there is nothing in this world that will ever come between us, I promise.'

And then she bent her head and kissed him.

★   ★   ★

But later, when Rian was asleep beside her, his breath gentle on her bare shoulder, she stared up at the planked ceiling, listening to the steady hiss of the waves as they swept past the *Katipo*'s hull.

She had lied to Rian, and it didn't sit at all well with her. She had been almost speechless with surprise when the intruder in the hold had turned out to be Daniel Royce, and even more startled when Rian had told her of the crime he'd committed on her behalf. And then she'd begun to recall what she had suspected about Daniel four and a half years before, during those visits she'd made to Hyde Park Barracks, but had ignored because even then her heart had belonged to Rian, even if she hadn't been willing to admit it. Daniel Royce had been falling in love with her. Or was at least well on the way to becoming infatuated, as Rian had suggested. He had known what she was up to, and had in fact seriously risked his position as a barracks officer by allowing her to smuggle in contraband to Avery Bannerman. She had flirted with him and taken advantage of him when she should have discouraged him, but she'd been so anxious to obtain Rian's freedom, perhaps even save his life, that she'd not thought for a second about the consequences of her actions. She should never have gone back to say goodbye to Daniel before they'd sailed from Sydney, she knew that now, and she most certainly should not have kissed him.

She sighed, but quietly so she wouldn't disturb Rian. Daniel Royce very obviously wasn't a boy any more. She had guessed at the time that he had been twenty years old, if that, which meant that he would now be twenty-four or twenty-five. He'd filled out noticeably and was really rather attractive, beneath the grime and the beard. Clearly, he also had a mind of his own and considerable determination, which, Kitty knew, Rian would find far more worrying than a pair of alluring brown eyes and a winning smile. And that was why she had not told him the truth about what had happened at the barracks.

But Rian had no need to be worried: Daniel Royce was not, and never would be, a threat. What worried Kitty, however, was the flicker of unease she had seen in her husband's eyes when he had been talking about Daniel. She turned to look at Rian, loving the way the shadows from the moonlight touched the planes of his sleeping face and made his eyelashes look at least an inch long.

'I love you, Rian Farrell, and I always will,' she whispered.

Then she rolled carefully onto her side, snuggled her bottom into Rian's lap, lifted his arm over her and pressed his hand tightly against her belly.

Behind her, Rian's lips curved in a tiny smile.

★   ★   ★

'You are making a mistake, Rian,' Hawk said the next morning.

They had almost left the Australian coast behind them, although a flat, bluish line on the horizon beyond the Katipo's stern, and the abundance of sea birds still wheeling in the sky, suggested it would be several hours yet before they had the ocean completely to themselves.

Rian tapped the contents of his pipe over the side and said nothing.

Hawk turned away from gazing down at the Katipo's churning wake and leaned his back against the rail. 'Did you hear me?'

'I heard.'

'The man is in love with Kitty,' Hawk declared. 'It is as plain as the nose on my face.'

'Maybe.'

'Maybe definitely. Why did you allow him to sail with us? It will only mean trouble.'

Rian spat, the saliva dissipating before it reached the sea's restless surface. 'Well, what was

I supposed to do, Hawk? Turn around and dump him on the dock outside the Sydney customs house? Or perhaps even the gaol?'

'Why not?'

'Because I owe him a debt.'

'But what will it cost you to repay it?' Hawk asked cryptically.

Rian said angrily, 'What do you mean? What are you implying? That Kitty will actually respond to Royce's infatuation? Is that it?'

He knew Hawk meant nothing of the sort, but he was out of sorts because he really wasn't at ease with Royce being on board, and he felt like having an argument.

But Hawk didn't rise. 'Do not be an idiot, Rian. Of course she will not respond.' He gave his friend a sidelong glance. 'Are you sure that this is not your pride speaking?'

'What?'

'Could it be that you are worried that Kitty may actually have some feelings for Royce, but you are ignoring that worry because you refuse to countenance that such a thing may be? Because your pride refuses to countenance it?'

'Don't be so bloody stupid, Hawk,' Rian snapped, annoyed at the accuracy of his friend's perceptions. 'When have I ever let *pride* interfere with my decisions?'

Hawk simply stared at him, his ruddy face impassive.

'Anyway,' Rian went on somewhat defensively, 'she told me last night that he means nothing to her. And that's all I need to know. It's all you need to know, as well.'

Hawk said, 'The men are very protective of her, Rian. There may be unrest.'

'Well, that's just unfortunate, isn't it? They'll just have to behave.' Rian sighed. 'Look, Hawk, I'm not pleased about him sailing with us either, but I don't see that I have much choice. And he doesn't seem a bad sort.'

'Except that he is a murderer and covets your wife.'

'More a rat-catcher than a murderer, Hawk.'

Hawk shrugged. 'You are the captain.'

'That's right, I am. And we're a man down, remember? He might even be useful.'

It turned out that Daniel Royce was in fact very handy on deck. But Hawk had been right — the crew did resent his presence and the threat he posed. Not that he ever made his admiration for Kitty known. He rarely spoke to her, and she spoke to him even less frequently. In her opinion, the crew were initially rather mean to Daniel, although she never said as much to Rian. Hawk allocated him the most boring and menial jobs, such as swabbing the deck and recoiling various lengths of rope — the same chores, in fact, that Rian had made Kitty perform to teach her a lesson on their first voyage together from Paihia to Sydney. But Daniel completed them all expertly and with good grace, until even Hawk had to admit he would be better doing something more relevant to the day-to-day running of the schooner. By their fifth day at sea Daniel was up the ratlines and working on the masts, demonstrating that he was an unexpectedly skilled seaman. When Rian asked him where he had attained those skills, Daniel explained that he had gone to sea with his uncle from the age of fourteen to eighteen, before he decided to settle in Sydney and join the armed constabulary.

However, Gideon, Ropata and Mick began to thaw towards Daniel only when they saw that he shared their affinity for the sea, that he was keeping as far away from Kitty as was physically possible, and after Rian had told them in no uncertain terms that they had to stop treating Daniel as though he had leprosy.

From the outset, though, Pierre couldn't bring himself to ostracise Daniel. He toyed briefly with the idea of serving him only the scraggiest cuts of meat and the dregs from the bottom of the coffee-pot, but, try as he might, he couldn't really see anything wrong with having Daniel Royce on board. What could a man say? Pierre thought it a splendidly honourable and gallant thing to do, to slit the throat of a scoundrel who had besmirched the name of your beloved, even if your beloved was married to someone else. And anyway, Kitty would never consider dallying with Daniel Royce, Pierre knew that or his name wasn't Pierre Babineaux. And if Royce did behave improperly towards Kitty, then Rian could kill him. It was as simple as that.

The tension eased as the days passed, and on the tenth night Daniel was invited to join the crew after supper on deck for a pipe. He didn't say much, but the others addressed him from time to time, and he seemed happy with that. The only crew member who continued to pillory

Daniel was Bodie. He had been allocated Sharkey's old bunk, and on the very first night she piddled on his blanket. The next evening he discovered a reeking fish-head from the galley stuffed under his pillow, and the day after that a small, fresh turd in his boot. At first he'd assumed that one of the crew was responsible, but no human could be capable of producing such compact yet eye-wateringly noxious ordure, surely? Pierre took pity on him after that and suggested that the culprit was almost certainly Bodie, told him to keep the door to his cabin shut at all times, and regaled him with various other Bodie stories. Daniel laughed politely, but privately dreaded what the cat might do next. The crew found it all very entertaining.

By the time the *Katipo* had passed through Cook Strait then turned north-east to sail up the eastern coastline of New Zealand's North Island, the calendar on the mess-room wall read 21 December. They continued on all that day and throughout the following night, aiming to reach harbour at the Bay of Islands by early morning.

Rian's timing was perfect: just as they passed through the stretch of calmer seas between Waitangi and Waihihi Bay, the sun began to bleach the eastern horizon. As a mark of respect, and to alert those on shore to the fact that they were arriving with a body on board, Rian gave the order to lower his ensigns to half-mast. He flew two — the orange, white and green flag of Ireland, and the green ensign featuring a golden harp, which had been used widely during the Irish rebellion almost fifty years before, and which Rian belligerently insisted on flying even in English ports.

The anchor clanked loudly in the muffled silence as it was lowered, and the crew waited patiently for the Paihia shoreline to be revealed as the sun climbed higher in the sky and burned off the heavy sea mist.

But, as Rian gave the order to launch the rowboat twenty minutes later, Hawk pointed towards the shore and said, 'Look.'

At first all Kitty could see were the blue-green hills above Paihia, still wreathed in shreds of mist, and the solid shapes of the mission's small buildings. There were a few more now, she noticed, and she wondered how many people the tiny settlement supported these days. But then she saw them — a large crowd of people standing motionless on the beach, at the point where the coarse sand succumbed to tough coastal grass. She squinted, but still couldn't judge how many people were there. A hundred, perhaps? Or was it even more?

The sight was so eerie and surreal that she found herself whispering as she asked Rian, 'Why are they all on the beach? What are they waiting for?'

Rian didn't reply, but stared towards the shore a moment longer, then motioned to Mick to continue lowering the rowboat. It hit the water with a faint *whump*, then the rope ladder was released over the rail.

Mick went down first, followed by Ropata, Gideon, Pierre, Hawk, then Rian one-handed and balancing Wai's waka taonga on his hip, and finally Kitty. Daniel was told to stay aboard. When Kitty was seated, Rian handed her the box, which she cradled on her knee. Gideon took up the oars, manoeuvred the boat around so that the prow was pointing away from the *Katipo*, then struck out for the shore.

No one spoke: the only sound was the rhythmic splash of oars dipping into the sea as Gideon leaned forward and pulled, leaned forward and pulled, his muscles flexing and his face set in concentration.

The hairs on Kitty's arms had risen: something out of the ordinary was about to happen. From this distance the faces of the people on the beach were still indistinct, but she thought she could make out a small knot of Europeans standing well to one side of the larger crowd, whose height and shape — and the weapons they appeared to be carrying — suggested that they were Maori. Kitty's heart sank. Was it a taua, a war party? Had the old wounds from nearly five years ago not healed after all?

As the rowboat neared the shore, Kitty began to recognise faces she had known, both Maori and Pakeha. She glanced at Rian seated next to her: he rested his hand on her knee and squeezed, and she felt a little better.

When they were still a hundred yards out, several dozen men detached themselves from the larger group and danced down to the hard sand just beyond the hissing waves. The strands of their piupiu rattled as they advanced, their bare feet making no noise at all. Some wielded taiaha adorned with feathers and dog-hair, and the long thin spears called tao, while others carried feather-tufted tewhatewha, or long-handled battle-axes. A dozen held patu of both stone and whalebone. Their eyes wide and rolling grotesquely, the whites in stark contrast to their brown faces, and their tongues snaking in and out of wide-stretched mouths, they hissed and grunted, not chanting, but not silent either. Backwards and forwards across the sand they came, stabbing with their weapons and challenging the approaching rowboat, daring the occupants to set foot on land.

Kitty's hands felt sweaty and she wiped them on her skirt, then asked Ropata nervously, 'Is it a wero? Are they angry with us?'

Without looking at her, Ropata replied, 'No. The jumping is from side to side so it is a tutu ngarahu, a haka of welcome, not war. But it is still a challenge.'

The rowboat grounded gently a minute later, and Mick and Pierre, somewhat warily, climbed out and began to nudge the prow up the beach. When they had all disembarked, they stood and faced the taua as the haka continued. Kitty, with the box in her arms, stood behind the men. From the tension in their stances, she could see that Gideon, Mick and Pierre were ill at ease. And not surprisingly: the haka party was, at the very least, alarming.

The crowd had formed into a horseshoe, and she could see Haunui now, standing in the centre, a small boy next to him. She couldn't tell if Haunui had recognised her or not: if he had, he wasn't acknowledging the fact. He stared resolutely towards the front, his eyes unwavering and his jaw clenched. Beyond the Maoris stood the missionaries. Kitty recognised Rebecca and Win Purcell, Marianne Williams, and Frederick Tait, Jannah's long-suffering husband, but there were also several unfamiliar faces.

As the haka group receded towards the horseshoe, a lone warrior came prancing through them, taking quick, light little steps that tautened the muscles of his calves and thighs, moving as gracefully as though he were gliding on ice. His hair was tied up, greased and adorned with two of the coveted huia feathers, and his moko covered his entire face, indicating that he had considerable mana. He made a downward slash with the long blade of his taiaha, cutting the air audibly, and began to manoeuvre it from hand to hand with breathtaking speed and dexterity, beginning the wero, the challenge proper. He grimaced and hissed, thrust and twirled, never once breaking eye contact with Rian. Then from the waistband of his piupiu he plucked a fern frond, dropped it on the ground at his feet and danced away backwards, the sharp tip of his taiaha pointing directly at Rian's heart.

There was a moment when there was no sound at all, when the tension became so thick that Kitty could feel it ringing in her ears, then Rian stepped forward, picked up the frond and tucked it into his own waistband.

A collective sigh came from the Maoris, and suddenly a karanga began. The horseshoe broke and an ancient woman stepped forward, her powerful but grief-laden voice soaring in a lament for the dead. Her wrinkled face was green with the blurred lines of old moko, and Kitty recognised her as Erunora, the oldest and most revered kuia of Wai's hapu. Her thin, white hair was crowned with a wreath of green leaves, and only then did Kitty notice that all the other women wore, or carried, greenery as well, and she realised that they were in mourning. For Wai.

When Erunora had finished, her voice dying away on a note thinner than the wind and sadder than anything Kitty had ever heard, Ropata stepped around Rian and began to reply. He spoke in Maori, and Kitty understood that, in accordance with tradition, he was stating who he was and where he was from, and also that he belonged to the hapu who sailed on the *Katipo*, whose chief was Rian Farrell.

He gestured to Kitty then to come forward. Gideon, Mick and Pierre stepped aside and she moved to the front, the waka taonga containing Wai's bones held out before her. The weeping and keening began in earnest then, and a great tide of grief flowed out from the Maoris and washed over them all.

Kitty began to walk, feeling her eyes fill with tears and her face grow hot with the pain of mourning her dear friend. Her heart felt swollen and her throat ached with the sobs she longed to release, but knew she couldn't, not yet.

Erunora limped down the sand to meet her, resting a gnarled hand on the box to lighten at least the spiritual load as they walked together towards Haunui, who stood in silence, tears coursing down his homely face. When Kitty was only a few feet away, he raised his arms to receive his daughter's remains. Kitty settled the box in his arms. He nodded once, a simple gesture so filled with gratitude, dignity and grief that Kitty thought her heart might break.

She had so much she wanted to say to him, but knew not to disturb the protocol of this intensely personal moment of mourning. She desperately also wanted to crouch down in front of the little boy who was now hanging onto Haunui's trouser leg, to tip up his chin and look into his face and see how much of his mother was in it, how much of her had been passed on to live another longer and happier life, but she knew that would have to wait as well.

Erunora then formally invited Rian's 'hapu' to Pukera village for the tangi, for which, she stated, preparations were already under way. Ropata thanked her, and the crowd began to break into smaller groups, awaiting word to return to the village themselves.

Haunui sat down cross-legged on the sand, gripping the box so tightly that the knuckles of his big hands were almost white, his tears splashing onto the carved lid. Four or five people stayed near to him, ready should he need their physical or emotional support. Erunora was one.

Kitty knelt on the sand before him, and touched his sleeve. 'Hello, Haunui,' she said.

He raised his swollen red eyes to her. 'Hello, my little Pakeha daughter.'

4

The women were still wailing, and Kitty wished they would stop. But she knew that this was the way they mourned. She had sometimes thought that the Maori approach to death and grieving — the public weeping and the embracing, and the long, three-day funeral — was a far more satisfactory arrangement than the English tradition of quickly burying the deceased, then grieving behind closed doors; but this way was also so very exhausting.

'How did you know we would be arriving today?' she asked Haunui. 'And how did you know we would be bringing Wai?'

Haunui blew his nose fastidiously into an enormous handkerchief, then shoved it in his pocket. 'Tahi had a dream.'

Kitty raised her eyebrows questioningly.

'He woke up one morning,' Haunui explained, 'and said he had dreamed that his mama would be coming home on this day, just as the sun was rising. So we started making the preparations. He has had visions before. He has never been wrong.'

Kitty knew better than to question the importance the Maoris attached to visions and other mysticisms. She sat back on her heels and regarded the little boy sitting close beside his grandfather, his small, brown hand resting lightly on the waka taonga containing his mother's remains. He had

112

his head bowed and Kitty could see his scalp through his parting. His black hair was fine and glossy and reached his shoulders, the heavy wave common to most Maori hair absent.

'Did you know your mama was coming today?' she asked him.

He looked up then, and Kitty almost cried out with startled delight. 'But he looks so like Wai!' she exclaimed to Haunui.

The boy had his mother's little pointed chin, her wide cheekbones, and her slanted eyes, though his were hazel, not the deep chocolate of Wai's.

Haunui smiled. 'Ae, he does. Better his mother than his father, though, eh?'

'Yes, indeed,' Kitty agreed, recalling her uncle's long, dour face and his thin lips, pinched tight with hypocritical piety. 'You're a clever little man, aren't you?' she said to Tahi.

He nodded, his hair swinging. 'Whaea Williams says so.'

Kitty opened her mouth to ask him if he realised that they were cousins, then abruptly shut it again and turned slightly away from him. 'Does he know?' she whispered to Haunui.

'Ae. I have not kept much from him. Only the . . . nature of it.'

'My papa has gone away,' Tahi announced.

'I know, sweetheart,' Kitty replied gently. 'He's in heaven, with your mama.'

Tahi shook his head vehemently. 'No. He is somewhere else.'

'Oh.' Kitty wondered if he meant hell. He was probably too young to be attending the mission

113

school, but the more florid aspects of the Church Missionary Society's version of Christianity did tend to get passed around rather indiscriminately, and she knew for a fact that Maori mothers sometimes told troublesome children that if they didn't behave they would go to hell.

'He is down there,' Tahi said, pointing at the sand.

Kitty glanced at Haunui.

He shrugged. 'It is as good a place for him as any.' Then his expression softened. 'It is very good to see you again, Kitty. I have missed you.'

Kitty felt tears threatening again. 'I've missed you too, Haunui.'

'Thank you for bringing her home. I will sleep easy now. And so will she.'

'I hope so.'

'And you are happy, being Rian's wife?' Haunui asked, gesturing at the ring on Kitty's hand.

'Oh, very. But how did you know?'

'Your mother wrote to your aunt. I am very happy for both of you. And you have not had to give him too many kicks in the pants?'

Kitty grinned. 'Not yet.'

'Ah, that is good. That is always a sign of a successful marriage.'

Just then, Erunora tapped Haunui on the shoulder and said in her thin voice, 'It is time to return to the village. We have much to do.'

Haunui nodded. 'You will all be at the tangi?' he asked Kitty.

'Of course. We would be honoured. Thank you.'

'And where will you stay? There is plenty of room at Pukera.'

'Well, I was considering staying at Aunt Sarah's. But she wasn't with Rebecca Purcell and the others. Is she avoiding me, do you think?'

Haunui gave her an amused look. 'Yes, she was with the others.'

'Well, I didn't see her.'

'She is there now.'

Kitty turned around and stared at the group of missionaries still standing on the sand a hundred or so yards away. Someone waved — Rebecca. Kitty waved back.

'I still can't see Aunt Sarah,' she said.

'Look more closely.' Haunui stood up. 'You will come to the village soon? Most of the manuhiri are here now.'

Kitty knew that if the visitors from other areas had arrived, the tangi would start shortly. 'Yes. I just want to say hello to everyone first. After that?'

'Ae,' Haunui said. Then his face broke into a grin as Rian approached, his sea boots crunching on the shelly sand. He took the hand Rian offered, and returned the greeting with a hongi. 'It is good to see you, Rian. Thank you for bringing Wai home.'

'It was an honour,' Rian said. 'It's good to see you, too. I regret that it's in such unfortunate circumstances, though.'

'Ae. But at least she is home now.'

Kitty walked across the sand towards the small group of missionaries. As she neared them,

Rebecca Purcell detached herself and came to meet her, her arms wide.

'Kitty Carlisle!' she exclaimed as she enfolded Kitty in a generous embrace. 'How wonderful to see you! Or rather, I should say Mrs Farrell, shouldn't I? Congratulations, dear. I'm so happy for you.'

'Thank you, Rebecca. That means a great deal to me,' Kitty replied, standing back to inspect her friend. 'You look very well.'

Rebecca hadn't changed much since Kitty had last seen her. A little heavier around the middle, perhaps, and there were feathers of grey streaking the red hair at her temples, but her welcoming smile and kind eyes were the same.

'That's very nice of you to say, Kitty, but I must admit I'm having to let out my stays a little more each year. Of course, having two more babies hasn't helped.' She grasped Kitty's hand. 'Are you happy? Have you been having lots of wonderful adventures sailing the Seven Seas?'

Kitty laughed. 'Yes, I am happy. Very.'

Rebecca looked rather relieved. 'Oh, I *am* pleased. When Sarah told us that you and the captain had married, well, I did wonder if that may not have been the wisest thing for you to do. Then I thought, no, that girl knows her own mind. And her own heart. She won't have made a decision like that lightly.'

'No, I didn't, and I haven't regretted it for a moment. Rebecca, where is Aunt Sarah?'

Rebecca stepped aside and pointed to a short, plump woman standing next to the much taller figure of Marianne Williams. The woman waggled her fingers in a hesitant wave, the early morning sun glinting off her spectacles.

Kitty blinked. 'Aunt Sarah?'

'Hello, Kitty.'

Kitty took several steps closer, finally recognising her. It was indeed Aunt Sarah, but not the thin, faded, harried-looking woman who had bodily thrown her and Wai out of the house one hot February afternoon in 1840. This Aunt Sarah was pleasingly plump, even stout, with pink cheeks and markedly smoother skin. But she must have been weeping, because her eyes were rimmed with red.

Kitty stepped forward to embrace her aunt, but Sarah raised her hands to stop her. 'No,' she said, and Kitty's heart plummeted with disappointment.

But then Sarah said quickly, 'Kitty, I need to say something to you.' She cleared her throat nervously. 'And that is that I am so sorry for the way I behaved towards you and Wai on the day you left Paihia. I am sorry that I doubted you and accused you both of those vile things. You were not at fault, either of you, I know that now, and I have regretted my actions every single day since.'

Kitty opened her mouth to speak, but Sarah cut her off again. 'No, please, I need to finish. I have asked God for forgiveness, and He has seen fit to grant that to me. Now I'm asking you for forgiveness also. I do not expect it, Kitty, but I would like it.'

Kitty reached out and hugged her aunt tightly. 'Oh, Aunt Sarah, of course I forgive you. And

I'm sure Wai would too, if she could. It wasn't your fault that we had to leave. Please believe that. We had to go anyway, because of Tupehu.'

Sarah burst into tears, sobbing damply on Kitty's shoulder while Rebecca and Mrs Williams looked on, dabbing at their own eyes.

Kitty awkwardly patted Sarah's back until her aunt finally stepped back, fumbling for her handkerchief. 'Oh dear, I'm so relieved,' Sarah mumbled, then blew her nose. 'I've dreaded this day.'

'Well, you shouldn't have,' Kitty admonished, feeling that a weight had finally been lifted from her own shoulders. 'How have you been faring, Aunt Sarah? Has there been any news of Uncle George?'

Her aunt's face changed, and for a second the old Sarah was back. 'No, there has not,' she said testily. 'But in his case, no news is definitely good news. And I hope there never *is* any news, come to that.'

Kitty stared, shocked by the vehemence in her aunt's voice, even though God knew she had reason for it.

Sarah's tone softened and she added, with a twinkle in her eye, 'You see, dear, I have a suitor. I believe one is supposed to wait seven years until one's missing spouse can be declared dead, and I've still got two years to go. Still, I am hopeful.'

Kitty exclaimed, 'Aunt Sarah!' and burst out laughing. 'Oh, I'm sorry, but that sounded really funny.'

Sarah said, 'I know that's a dreadful thing to

118

say about the man I once loved, and I did love George for many years, I truly did. He was a good man, and very devout, and he was so inspiring in the pulpit. But something went terribly wrong with his mind. Well, you know that, Kitty, you saw him.'

Kitty said nothing, recalling with a shudder how progressively more deluded, demanding and frightening George had become during his time as a reverend at Paihia.

Sarah's face hardened again, but in it Kitty could also see a shadow of sadness for the man her aunt had once loved. 'In the end he was evil. There is no other word to describe him. He must have been to . . . to do what he did. Not even the Lord could forgive him for that. But now he has gone, and I believe that is for the best.'

Kitty nodded, but now she was thinking about someone else, someone she very much wanted to speak to but with whom she had absolutely no intention of reconciling. 'And Amy? Is Amiria still here?'

Amy — cunning, wilful and hot-headed — had been a housegirl in the Kellehers' Paihia household at the same time as Wai, her cousin, and it had been Amy who had told Tupehu that Wai had become pregnant by the Reverend George Kelleher. Tupehu had gone insane with rage and chased Kitty and Wai, and his own brother Haunui, down the beach and hurled spears and curses at them as they escaped out to the *Katipo*.

'Amy has gone as well,' Rebecca said, her tone suggesting that this wasn't a bad thing either.

119

'When?' Kitty asked, a horrible notion taking shape in her mind.

Sarah saw it. 'No, she went about six months after George disappeared. That was the same day you and Wai left. He was last seen on his way home from Waitangi, on this side of the river. He was walking around Ti Point at Te Ti Bay, apparently.'

Kitty wondered whether Tupehu had come across him, and her uncle's bones were now lying hidden somewhere between here and the mouth of the Waitangi River. 'And nobody has seen him or heard from him since?'

Sarah shook her head. 'Not a single word.'

'We have had word of Amy, however,' Rebecca said. 'She left the village here when Haunui came back with the child, and apparently went out to Hone Heke's settlement at Pakaraka. I'm not sure if she is still there now. It's rumoured that she has been seen with the rebel Maoris.'

'What rebel Maoris?' Kitty asked.

'Heke's people. The ones who have been cutting down the flagstaff at Kororareka.'

Kitty opened her mouth to ask more, but suddenly noticed that the last of the Maoris were leaving the beach and heading back to the village. Her questions would have to wait.

★   ★   ★

Wai's tangi began that afternoon and went on for two days and two nights. The population of Pukera had increased considerably for the occasion, swelled with visitors come to pay their respects to Wai and her family. But there was plenty of food — pork and kai moana and kumara and potatoes — and the weather so balmy that most people slept outside.

On the first night were the formalities. As the wharenui was too small to hold everyone, Wai's waka taonga was laid in the porch and the people gathered on the paepae before it to hear the speakers and take part in the grieving. First came the speakers from Pukera, including Te Rangi, Haunui's half-brother who had ascended to chief when Tupehu died, then at least half a dozen orators representing the manuhiri. Then Reverend Augustus Dow, the Church Missionary Society minister standing in for Reverend Henry Williams, who was away, said a prayer and read some passages from the Bible, followed by Pukera's tohunga, who also led prayers, although they were definitely not Christian. Wai had been baptised, and was therefore entitled to an Anglican service, but Haunui had evidently insisted she also have a traditional Maori farewell.

Kitty's old friend Simon Bullock arrived at eight in the evening — she recognised him immediately, hovering with his hat in hand and waving discreetly at her across the paepae.

'Look, there's Simon,' she whispered excitedly to Rian. 'I'm going to say hello.'

Rian lifted his hand in greeting and Simon replied with a salute.

Kitty waited until the current speaker paused to contemplate his next words, then wove her way to the back of the sitting crowd towards Simon.

Grinning broadly, he took her hands and kissed her cheek. 'Kitty! It's marvellous to see you! I heard this morning that you'd arrived. How are you?'

'I'm well, Simon, thank you. It's lovely to see you, too.' Noting that he looked as sartorially uninspired as he always had, she was pleased she had bought him the new shirt.

'I see you brought her home,' Simon said, inclining his head towards the wharenui. 'I knew you would, when you could. You always were a good person, Kitty.'

Kitty's eyes grew hot with unexpected tears. 'I'm so pleased you're still here, Simon.'

Simon sighed. 'Yes, I'm still out at Waimate growing oats and barley and trying to indoctrinate small defenceless children with the teachings of the CMS.'

Kitty felt a twitch of disquiet; he sounded jaded and even slightly bitter, and, just for a moment, most unlike the Simon she knew. She regarded him more closely, and noticed lines fanning out from his kind eyes and his generous mouth that definitely hadn't been there five years ago.

'Oh dear,' she said. 'You're not having a crisis of faith, are you?' Such a question would be considered extremely rude if she had asked it of anyone else, but she knew Simon wouldn't mind.

'Not so much a crisis of faith, as such. More a crisis of, shall we say, denominations?'

'Oh.'

'Yes. But I'll tell you about that later, shall I? And by the way, Kitty, you're a dreadful liar.'

'What? Why?' she demanded in bewilderment.

Simon reached out and tapped the wedding ring on her finger. 'You told me you weren't the marrying kind. You turned me down, remember?' But he was smiling again. 'Well, you would have if I'd asked you.'

Kitty did remember; she'd been terrified he was going to ask for her hand, so she had spurned him before he'd had the chance. As it had turned out, he'd had no intention of asking her to marry him, so it was all a bit embarrassing. But amusing, eventually.

'Well, clearly I was mistaken, wasn't I?'

'He's a good man, the captain,' Simon said, and for some reason his approval pleased Kitty inordinately. 'No children yet?'

'No.'

'That's a shame. I've always thought you'd make a wonderful mother.' Simon looked around. 'Are the Paihia people not here? That's a bit rude, I must say.'

Assuming he meant the missionaries, Kitty said, 'Yes, they were for a while, but they left when the tohunga got up to speak.'

Simon's *moue* of disapproval suggested that he still thought the missionaries' decision to leave was discourteous.

'Come and sit down with us,' Kitty suggested. 'Come and say hello to Rian. And the rest of the crew are here somewhere as well. Except for Sharkey, of course.' And she told Simon what had happened in Durban, and also that they had a temporary crewman on board, although not the story of how he came to be sailing with

123

them; she wasn't sure if Simon would approve of Rian's decision to harbour a self-confessed murderer. 'But Rian told him to stay on the *Katipo* because he's not had anything to do with Maoris and we didn't think this was a suitable time to introduce him.'

Simon resolved to stay the night at the village — perhaps, Kitty thought, to make amends for the other missionaries — although at eleven o'clock she and Rian made their way by the light of an oil lamp back to Paihia. They spent the night with Sarah and returned to the village the next morning to find that even more people had arrived for the tangi.

For the rest of that day, between eating from the huge hangi that was opened three times a day and meeting up with people neither of them had seen for a long time, Kitty and Rian sat sweating in the merciless sun, listening to the speakers on the paepae. Sarah had lent Kitty a parasol, but she didn't want to use it in case she blocked the view of those behind her, which would surely be the height of bad manners.

They also heard the news about the disturbance Hone Heke and his followers had been causing over the past six months, prompting Rian to mutter darkly, 'I knew he'd regret signing that bloody treaty.'

Or rather, they heard several different versions of it from a range of people. Kitty wished they could talk to Haunui, but he was keeping vigil in the porch with Wai and she didn't wish to disturb him.

It was Simon, however, who gave them the

most sensible account of what had been going on. He started by relating to them developments since the treaty had been signed. Evidently, the first major rumble of Maori discontent had come after Governor Hobson's decision to move the capital of New Zealand from Kororareka to Auckland, which deprived the Bay of Islands Nga Puhi Maoris of many economic benefits. The government had then introduced customs duties, which forced up prices, and had claimed the revenue from shipping duties that had previously gone to the Maoris. The whalers subsequently moved to other less-policed ports, the felling of kauri was also banned for a time, and land sales slowed when the government took over their management. Hard times followed, and Heke began to complain that his authority, and that of the Maoris in general, was being undermined by British power.

Then Maketu, son of Nga Puhi chief Ruhe, had been hung for the murder of four European settlers and a high-ranking Maori woman. When Heke had discovered that some of his own Nga Puhi relatives had given permission for Maketu to be tried under British law, he, according to Simon, went mad, his party performing a vicious haka and firing loaded muskets into the air. Since then Heke had been gathering around him a group of very loyal and influential warriors and doing everything he could, and not always pleasantly, to ensure his people's loyalty when the time came. Which it did, in July of 1844, when he sent his men to cut down the flagstaff flying the British flag at Kororareka.

'He sent a letter to Governor FitzRoy in Auckland, insisting he wouldn't do it again,' Simon said. 'You know FitzRoy took over after Hobson died in 1842?' Kitty and Rian both nodded. 'Well, actually, Willoughby Shortland did, but he was a fool. Fortunately, FitzRoy replaced him at the beginning of this year. But I'll wager he *will* do it again. Heke, I mean. Things are very tense here at the moment. There's a lot of talk flying about.'

'Who's doing the talking?' Rian asked.

'Mostly Heke and his lot. And the government, I suppose. We've heard rumours that a blockhouse could soon be built across at Kororareka.' Simon swept his arm in a wide arc, encompassing the large crowd. 'And everyone here now is talking, too. In a way it's a little unfortunate that you brought Wai back when you did. I'm very glad you did, and so is Haunui, but it's given everyone an excellent excuse to get together.'

Slightly alarmed, Kitty asked, 'Hone Heke won't be coming here, will he?'

'I don't know. Probably not. The last we heard he was down in Auckland.'

Kitty leaned back on her hands, relieved. Her feet were roasting in her black leather boots, her petticoats were sticking to her legs and sweat was trickling down her sides, but at least she wouldn't have to worry about encountering Hone Heke as well. She had seen him only once, the day before the treaty was signed at Waitangi. He had frightened her then, and the stories she was hearing of his trouble-making

126

and rabble-rousing made her fear him even more now. She knew, though, that Rian would not see it like that. She could tell by the thoughtful look on his face that he was thinking about what they'd heard, possibly even about what he could do to help the Maoris in their fight against the Crown.

★ ★ ★

That night was the time set aside for storytelling: stories about Wai, stories about the ancestors, and about the great and wondrous deeds of Nga Puhi in general. Kitty found the tales fascinating, and laughed as heartily as everyone else when people remembered Wai as a little girl and how she had vexed her father, Tupehu. Or, at least, the man everyone had believed was her father. Kitty wondered if the people of Pukera now knew of Haunui's long-standing love for his brother's dead wife. Poor Haunui, losing her as well as their precious daughter. But at least he had his grandson, Tahi, now.

On the morning of the third day, Haunui carried his daughter's remains from the village to the urupa a short distance away, Tahi walking beside him, his head up but his dark eyes struggling to blink back tears. What a brave little boy, Kitty thought, and knew in her heart that his mother would have been so very proud of him.

At the graveside, Reverend Dow spoke first as Wai was lowered into her grave, next to that of her mother, Hareta, his words urging Wai's soul to enter the Anglican kingdom of heaven. The tohunga who followed him, however, spoke of how Wai's spirit would now finally be free to travel to the ancient pohutukawa at Cape Reinga at the northernmost tip of the North Island, climb down the long, twisted roots, and from there journey on to Hawaiki, spiritual home of the ancestors.

'I suppose we should bring Royce ashore,' Rian said as they walked back through the bush to Paihia. 'He's been out on the schooner by himself for three days, and it *is* Christmas Day tomorrow.'

'Mmm, but he's had Bodie for company,' Kitty replied.

They looked at each other.

'Yes, perhaps we'd better bring him in,' Rian muttered.

So Gideon and Mick were sent out to the *Katipo* to collect Daniel and Bodie, and everyone's luggage, as Rian had declared that they would stay at Paihia for at least a week while he investigated the possibility of taking a load of kauri spars back to Sydney — if there was any kauri to be had.

When Kitty reached Aunt Sarah's house there were ginger gems waiting, baked by one of Sarah's housegirls, named Ngahuia. She was small, as Wai had been, and seeing her in the kitchen gave Kitty a poignant stab of grief. However, Ngahuia was darker-skinned than Wai and had a club-foot. Sarah had sent to Auckland for a special pair of boots to help her to walk more comfortably, but so far they hadn't arrived.

128

Kitty greeted Ngahuia and told her that Sarah would be home shortly. Then she flopped down on the chaise in the parlour and unbuttoned her boots and kicked them off, relishing the touch of the slight breeze from the open windows on her toes. The parlour was quite different now. There was more furniture, some pretty watercolours on the walls that Sarah had said she'd painted herself, and several vases of bright summer flowers. The pieces of furniture, Sarah had explained, were gifts from her 'suitor', Caleb Jenkins, a lay missionary out at Waimate and a skilled cabinetmaker.

To date, he had made for Sarah a large sideboard from solid mottled kauri with rewarewa drawers and door panels, two beautifully turned and upholstered kauri armchairs to replace the old pair in the parlour, and a chiffonier cabinet, which Sarah had displayed in the hall under the mirror Amy had spent so much time looking into. The chiffonier was a particularly fine piece. Smaller than the sideboard, it had ornate rimu, kauri, totora and miro intarsia in the two door panels and knobs of imported rosewood and mother-of-pearl. Kitty doubted that you would find much finer furniture in the home of a well-to-do gentleman in England. But as beautiful as Mr Jenkins's cabinetry was, she didn't think any of it demonstrated quite as much flair as the armoire Haunui had once made for her and which she had been pleased to note was still upstairs in her old bedroom.

Sarah appeared at the parlour door, her face

pink from the energetic walk back from Pukera and her fingers plucking at the ribbons of her bonnet.

'Well, that went quite nicely, didn't it?' she remarked as she laid her bonnet on the sofa. 'Well, as nice as a funeral can ever be.' She sat down, fanning herself with her handkerchief. 'And I'm so pleased I could be present when she was finally laid to rest. I still feel terribly . . . well, I'm still not entirely at peace with myself about how I treated the poor little thing.'

'She forgave you, you know,' Kitty said. 'She knew you were very upset. And really, Aunt Sarah, who wouldn't have been?'

'But I am a servant of God, Kitty. I should have been able to find it in my heart to see past my own distress and extend to her the hand of Christian charity.'

'I'm not sure many women could have done that,' Kitty said wryly, 'no matter what their vocation.'

'Yes, well, at least I was able to pray for her today.'

Kitty lightly flapped her skirts to create a bit of a breeze and wished she was in her cabin on the *Katipo*, where she quite often wore only her shift when the weather was particularly hot.

'Aunt Sarah?'

'Mmm?'

'Why didn't you go home after Uncle George disappeared? Back to England, I mean.'

Sarah didn't answer immediately. Eventually she said, 'At first all I could think about was George's disappearance. I was so distraught. I thought he must somehow have heard about Wai's accusations and run off in fear of his life. We searched everywhere for him, Kitty, we really did, but to absolutely no avail. Then I thought Tupehu must have killed him and disposed of his earthly remains somewhere. But the more I thought about it, the more I began to wonder whether Wai's claims weren't true. I started to recall ... well, the way that George was, especially in those last six months. And then I did a terrible thing — and I truly pray that God has forgiven me for it.'

'What was that?' Kitty leaned forward, poised for a revelation.

'I read George's private diaries.'

'Oh.' Vaguely disappointed, Kitty relaxed into the chaise again.

'And it was all in there, all in dreadful, shocking detail. How God had told him to ... ' a red flush appeared on Sarah's plump neck and spread across her face ' ... to seduce Wai to save her from depravity and sin. But do you know what the worst of it was? It was that in my heart I knew that Wai, and you, Kitty, had been telling the truth. Right from the day you told me. And I had refused to acknowledge it.' Sarah was silent again for a long moment. 'And once I had admitted that, well, I felt so ashamed of myself, and of course of George, that I couldn't go home. I couldn't even write about it to your mother, even though George was her kin.'

'Was? So you think Uncle George is dead?'

'I don't know, Kitty. Probably.' Sarah removed her spectacles and polished them on her handkerchief. 'Either dead or run away to some far-flung corner of the world. Although I very much doubt the latter. I suspect the mania that afflicted him so badly would also have prevented him from travelling any great distance.'

'And is that the only reason you've stayed? Because you were ashamed?'

Sarah brightened. 'To be honest, not entirely. I'm very much enjoying my work here. I seem to have taken on a new lease of life since George went. And there is Mr Jenkins, of course, whom you will meet tomorrow at our Christmas lunch and of whom I have become very fond over the past two years. And to return home I would have to endure that appalling sea voyage again, and I truly believe I would not survive it a second time.'

Kitty gave her a sympathetic look, recalling the awful time Sarah had had on the journey out from England.

Then Sarah suddenly said, 'Oh, that's right, I've got something for you', and hurried out of the parlour, her tread heavy on the hall stairs.

A minute later she was back. 'I believe this is yours?' she said, smiling, and handed Kitty a small velvet drawstring bag.

Kitty opened it and withdrew the milky blue coral bangle carved with flowers that Rian had given her one sunny afternoon in Sarah's garden. Delighted, she exclaimed, 'Oh, Aunt Sarah, I'm so glad you kept it!' and slid the bangle over her wrist and admired the colour of it against her lightly tanned skin. 'It's the first gift . . . '

'Rian ever gave you. I thought so,' Sarah

132

finished for her, her eyes moist. 'It was in your work basket. I almost threw it away after . . . well, after that terrible business. But something made me put it aside, and I'm very glad that I did.'

Ngahuia came in then with a pitcher of lemonade, a pot of tea and half a dozen generously buttered ginger gems; Kitty eyed them speculatively as Ngahuia set them down on the small table between the sofa and the chaise, but decided it was far too hot to eat anything.

'Oh good, I thought I could smell something nice,' Rian said from the doorway.

He looked even scruffier than usual: the heat of the day had prompted him to forgo his coat and undo the top three buttons of his shirt.

'Ah, Captain, please join us,' Sarah invited. 'We were just about to take tea.'

Despite the fact that Rian was obviously still as forthright, intolerant and disregarding of social conventions as he had been five years before — qualities that hadn't always endeared him to the Paihia missionaries — Sarah seemed to have taken quite a shine to him. Perhaps, Kitty thought, it was because George wasn't around to disapprove of him. Or maybe she had simply capitulated now that he was family by marriage.

'Thank you,' Rian replied, sitting down on the chaise so close to Kitty that he was on her skirts.

Sarah stood and offered him the plate of ginger gems.

He took three and bit into one immediately. 'Very nice. I've been talking to Win Purcell,' he

133

said, crumbs flying out of his mouth. 'He's worried that this business about Hone Heke and the flagstaff is going to flare up again. He says he wouldn't be surprised if Heke had another go at it.'

Kitty picked crumbs from the front of Rian's shirt. 'Simon said that, too, didn't he?'

'Did he really?' Sarah said, pouring the tea. 'Mr Bullock's not normally one for gossip. It's high time that young man found himself a good woman.'

Rian and Kitty exchanged a clandestine glance: a wife would be the last thing to interest Simon.

'It seems to be the general consensus,' Rian remarked. 'That Heke will take the flagstaff again, I mean.'

Sarah said, 'Well, so long as it isn't tomorrow during our Christmas dinner.'

Kitty frowned at her aunt. 'Doesn't it bother you? What if he attacks the mission here?'

'Oh, he won't do that, dear,' Sarah replied serenely. 'Hone Heke has an abiding respect for us and what we are achieving here with our work.' Her brow creased briefly. 'Although I must say he didn't get on very well with Bishop Selwyn. And the bishop seemed to have no regard for his mana whatsoever. But then none of us got on with the bishop particularly well, I'm sad to say. It was quite a relief when he went back to Auckland and left us to get on with it.'

Rian swallowed his last mouthful of ginger gem. 'Those were very good, Mrs Kelleher. Did you bake them?'

'No, Ngahuia did. She has quite a talent in the kitchen. Would you like the recipe?'

'Pierre might,' Kitty said. 'Have you invited anyone from the village to Christmas dinner?'

'Yes, we have actually. Haunui and his grandson, and Te Rangi and his wife. I hope they enjoy the repast — we really have gone to a lot of trouble this year.'

Clearly bored by talk of Christmas dinners, Rian looked at his watch. 'I think I'll go and have a talk to Frederick Tait, see what he thinks about what's been going on.' He looked meaningfully at Kitty. 'And then I believe I might just have an early night.'

'Do you now?' Kitty said, her eyebrows arching playfully.

'Yes, I do. I'm very . . . tired.' He extended his hand to caress her thigh, but stopped himself just in time.

5

Rian and Kitty did have an early night, but Rian fell asleep the minute his head touched the pillow. Some time over the past five years Sarah had replaced the single bed in Kitty's room with a double bed, so Kitty was able to snuggle behind Rian as he slept, listening to him snoring softly.

She awoke feeling much better for her sleep, but hot and sticky from the humid night air. She hoped it wouldn't rain that day, as the Christmas feast was to be held outdoors in the Purcells' garden.

She rolled carefully onto her back so she wouldn't wake Rian, and pulled the hem of her cotton nightgown up to her hips so the morning air could cool her damp skin.

'That's a grand view,' Rian said, sitting up and gazing down at her long, pale legs and the dark triangle of hair.

Kitty smiled. 'I thought you were asleep.'

Rian lifted the sheet covering his lower half and peered beneath it. 'No, definitely not asleep.'

He bent down to kiss her, but she wriggled away from him. 'Let's go for a swim, shall we?'

'In the sea?'

'No. Have you ever been to the swimming hole here? In the river?'

'Yes, and I'm sure it will be full of shrieking, splashing children already.'

'No, not that one. There's a smaller one where the river branches.' She climbed out of bed. 'Come on, let's go before everyone else wakes up.'

Ten minutes later, quickly dressed and each with a ginger gem pinched from the kitchen, they were walking along the beach towards the track that would take them into the bush. At the formation of rocks at the end of the beach, where Simon Bullock had once not asked Kitty to marry him, they turned left and followed the well-worn path into the base of the hills. There were indeed children in the main pool already, laughing and screaming and making almighty splashes leaping off the bank into the cool, slow water. Kitty and Rian waved and carried on, further into the bush. Soon the sounds of children playing were almost behind them and the songs of birds and cicadas had taken over again.

As Kitty had predicted, the smaller pool was empty, its surface rippling smoothly as the waters from the stream eddied into it. They sat down together on a log bleached silver by the sun, and watched as a large leaf was propelled from the stream into the pool, where it spun slowly around before drifting beyond the current to float almost motionless near the bank. Kitty removed her boots and set them aside, relishing the feel of the early morning sun on her bare feet and ankles.

'Are there koura in here?' Rian asked.

'Yes, little ones.'

They sat for a moment longer, then Rian stood and pulled Kitty to her feet. He drew her into his arms and kissed her deeply, his hands unravelling her plait so that her silky black hair fell past her shoulders.

'Mmm,' he murmured against her ear. 'This is nice. I fell asleep last night.'

'I know.'

'I won't now, though.'

Kitty agreed, thinking it very unlikely judging by the hardness of him against her belly.

'Take your clothes off,' he whispered.

She turned around and held her hair out of the way as he began to unbutton her dress. When he reached her waist he slid the sleeves off her shoulders and kissed the skin at the base of her neck. She gasped and closed her eyes in anticipatory pleasure.

Goosebumps ran down her spine as he slowly undid the rest of the buttons and she stepped out of her dress, leaving it lying on the ground, then allowed him to turn her around and pull gently on the ribbon that gathered her sleeveless chemise across her breasts. It opened and he ran a finger down her cleavage and caressed an upturned breast.

'Mmm,' he murmured, moving her chemise aside and bending his head to gently suck on her nipple.

Kitty clasped the back of his head, and moaned as his hands roamed across her bottom. She felt him smile against her skin and he straightened and pulled her to him again, pressing his hips against her stomach.

'No drawers, Mrs Farrell? I'm shocked.'

'It's too hot. And I was in a hurry.'

He grunted and cupped her buttocks. 'So am I, *mo ghrá*, a terrible hurry.'

He pulled her chemise all the way open and pushed it down so that it pooled around her bare feet, and moved back and stared at her, openly admiring her nakedness. Then he lifted her in his arms and carried her across to the log, kicking her boots out of the way as he sat down with her on his knee. She wriggled against him, enjoying the sensation of her naked skin against the coarseness of his trousers and the worn chambray of his shirt.

'Cold?' he murmured.

'No, not at all,' she replied against his neck. He tasted salty and he was sweating slightly, and she knew it was because of her and she loved it. She wriggled some more.

'Christ almighty, woman,' Rian gasped, and clamped his hands on her hips to stop her.

Kitty giggled. 'A little sensitive this morning, are we?'

'I'll give you sensitive, you cheeky wench,' Rian growled and kissed her hard, his hand creeping between her legs where he began to massage lightly but insistently.

Kitty almost swooned. Her knees parted and she moved again, unable to stop herself this time.

She moaned and Rian whispered into her ear, 'That will teach you.'

'I doubt it,' she whispered back, then removed

his hand so she could concentrate on unbuttoning his shirt.

He shrugged it off and tossed it aside, then stood up, taking Kitty with him, her arms wrapped around his neck. He looked around for a suitable spot, then put her down in a sunny nest of long grass while he hastily tugged off his boots and unbuckled his belt, sliding his trousers down and stepping out of them. The hair on his muscled chest, belly and legs gleamed gold in the sunlight: Kitty reached up for him and he lay down beside her.

He began to kiss her again, running his hand over her breasts and flat stomach. She slid her hand around to the back of his neck and pulled off the ribbon holding his hair back in its customary queue.

'You need your hair cut,' she said, her lips moving against his.

'I know,' he mumbled, but she knew he wasn't really listening.

He moved to roll on top of her, but she pushed him onto his back and climbed onto him instead, straddling his hips. Setting her hands on his chest, she lowered herself slowly, gasping as he filled her with a single, slippery stroke. His hands came to rest on her waist and she began to move up and down, frowning with concentration as the tantalising itch deep inside her began to intensify. Rian tightened his grip and thrust back, watching her face as it contorted in ecstasy, delighting in her pleasure and biting his lip in an effort to control himself. When she came, she cried out. She clawed at his chest and threw back her head, her long throat exposed and the veins in her breasts blue against the flush of her skin. Then she slumped onto him, her warm belly pressed against his and her face against his neck.

He lay still, holding his breath until she caught her own, then rolled quickly over. She clung to him and he pushed into her, driving her down into the grass, thrusting with increasing urgency until, his eyes screwed shut and his teeth bared, he let himself go and exploded. Seconds later his strength deserted him and he collapsed on top of her.

'Christ,' he said faintly, and moved to push himself off her but she hung on tightly so he couldn't move.

They lay like that for some time until Rian finally said, 'Someone has stolen my knees and replaced them with jelly.'

Kitty laughed and he smiled at the sheer loveliness of the sound. Then, after a moment, he whispered, 'Kitty?'

'Mmm?'

'Never leave me, will you?'

Her arms and legs tightened even more firmly around him and she whispered back, 'No, my love, I won't.'

⋆　⋆　⋆

The Purcells had joined together five long dining tables in their front garden, and decorated them with silver candlesticks that gleamed softly in the sun, arrangements of red and white flowers from

141

the missionaries' gardens and a perfect peach from the Waimate mission orchard next to each plate. There was no decorated Christmas tree, however, although it had been reported that Queen Victoria and Prince Albert had taken to erecting one each year. The missionaries had deemed this a practice just a little too frivolous.

Kitty sat down at her place next to Rian, unfolded her linen table napkin and spread it across her lap. She had given everyone their gifts privately, taking care to explain that they weren't Christmas presents really, just tokens of her pleasure at seeing them again, because the missionaries didn't really favour the giving of Christmas gifts either — at least, not lavish ones. But the presents had been received with much gratitude, and Haunui had liked his top hat so much that he had been wearing it all morning. Kitty wished she had bought something for Tahi but, when she had gone shopping, in her mind's eye he had still been only a few months old, not the solemn little boy sitting at the table today in freshly laundered long trousers, rolled up at the bottoms and clearly cast-offs from one of the missionary children.

'Take off your hat at the table,' she whispered to Haunui sitting on her left.

'Eh?'

Kitty pointed to his hat, and he removed it and placed it reverently beneath his chair. She looked across the table and saw that Simon, talking animatedly to Pierre, was also wearing his new shirt, although he seemed to have got something on the sleeve already.

The crew of the *Katipo* had been invited at the last minute, Mrs Williams insisting that they couldn't very well be left to their own devices with no dinner on Christmas Day. Kitty knew that they would have been just as happy at Pukera where they'd been sleeping, but they had accepted the invitation with good grace and appeared in the morning in time for church, shuffling self-consciously into the back pew with their various hairstyles tidied for the occasion and in their best clothes, such as they were. Daniel was with them, wearing a pair of Mick's trousers and his shirt recently mended of cat rips.

Bodie herself was lounging under a tree, flicking her tail imperiously at a grey-striped male tabby — Bodie's own grandson, according to Rebecca — who was paying far too much attention to her nether regions. Fortunately, as Kitty had said to Rian on the way back from the pool that morning, Bodie showed no signs of being in heat, or there may well have been miniature Bodies all over the *Katipo* some time in April.

Reverend Williams was still away, but everyone else was there, including Caleb Jenkins, Sarah's beau. He was the complete opposite of George: of medium height, with a fairly wide girth, sandy hair, bushy whiskers, and a ruddy face wearing a smile that was frequently directed towards Sarah, who seemed to positively glow under his gaze.

The Purcell children were also all present. Albert had developed into a very pleasant-looking if slightly spotty young man, and the other children had all grown like weeds too. Alice was now fifteen, tall and willowy and very pretty, and little Jasmine, who had been three when Kitty had left Paihia, was now eight. The baby, Harriet, named for her brother who had died in the measles epidemic when he was only a year old, was now five and had a younger brother and sister, bringing the Purcell contribution to the mission's population to nine. Kitty wondered how Rebecca managed, but she seemed as content as ever. Jannah Tait had also had two more children, although in her case the additions seemed only to have deepened the lines on her face. But she had seemed happy to see Kitty, and had actually been rather pleased with the recipe book Kitty had given her. There was also another young couple, John and Emily Henry, who had evidently arrived from England fourteen months before, and had managed to produce a set of twins since. The twins, named Samuel and Luke, lay gurgling in wicker baskets beneath the tree next to the table that had been set for the mission's smaller children. And at which Tahi had absolutely refused to sit.

Kitty saw that the women were ready to begin serving the meal, and got up to help. The first course was ham-and-pea soup, with a side dish of pig's head brawn.

Sitting next to his wife, Charlotte, Reverend Dow stood and tugged at the hem of his black coat in which he was sweating profusely. He was a slightly younger version of Henry Williams, with the same curly hair and bushy sideburns, but Augustus Dow did not wear spectacles and

144

his chin was considerably weaker. Charlotte Dow, on the other hand, was the complete opposite of Marianne Williams, with her short, round stature, sharp face and beady mouse eyes. Staring up at her husband, waiting for him to speak, she twitched her nose, and across the table Kitty hurriedly disguised her laugh as a cough.

Reverend Dow tapped the side of his glass with a spoon. 'May we bow our heads in prayer and give thanks to God for this wonderful repast, and for our health and our spiritual salvation in general.'

The chatter died down, heads were bowed and he began:

Almighty God, Father of all mercies, we Your servants give You most humble and hearty thanks for all Your goodness and loving kindness to us and all people.

We bless You for our creation, preservation, and all the blessings of this life; but above all for Your inestimable love in the redemption of the world by our Lord Jesus Christ, for the means of grace, and for the hope of glory . . .

Kitty opened her eyes and glanced around the table. Rian was staring off into the distance, obviously thinking of anything but a means of grace, but Pierre had his eyes screwed shut in devout concentration, even though Kitty knew his religion was more closely aligned to Catholicism than Anglicanism. Mick was cleaning his

145

fingernails with the point of a knife, Simon had his eyes closed but an unreadable expression on his face, and Daniel was staring at Te Rangi and his wife.

Despite the heat, Te Rangi was wearing a magnificent dog-skin cloak, a pair of huia feathers in the oiled hair pulled tight above his tattooed face, a heavy bone earring, a waistcoat with no shirt beneath it, beige trousers and bare feet. His attractive wife, Mahuika, was only marginally less decorated, a large bone pendant around her neck, and her ears stretched by the weight of the greenstone suspended from them, her chin moko in sharp relief against skin that wasn't much darker than Tahi's, and her high-necked European gown damp under the armpits from sweat. She also had her head down and her eyes closed, but looked vaguely cross, as though she were wishing she had worn something a little more suited to the weather.

Haunui had explained that when he had come home with Tahi, it was to find that Te Rangi had stepped in as chief of the local people after Tupehu had been killed at Taupo. But unlike Tupehu, who had been arrogant, overbearing and quick-tempered, Haunui had always found his half-brother — the product of his father's union with his second wife — quite reasonable, if at times overly conservative. Te Rangi had offered to stand down as chief, but Haunui had declined, wishing only to live a quiet life and raise his mokopuna. However, as he had told Rian and Kitty, Te Rangi often turned to him for advice, particularly after Hone Heke had begun stirring up Maori sentiment against the British.

Noticing that Sarah was looking at her from beneath her lace cap, Kitty bowed her head obediently and tried to listen as the prayer droned on.

. . . show forth Your praise, not only with our lips, but in our lives; by giving up ourselves to Your service, and by walking before You in holiness and righteousness all our days; through Jesus Christ our Lord, to whom with You and the Holy Spirit be all honour and glory, world without end. Amen.

'A men,' Kitty murmured as Reverend Dow sat down and signalled that the meal could begin.

The ham-and-pea soup was very tasty, and so it should be — Kitty had prevailed upon Pierre to give her his recipe — even though it was perhaps a little more spicy than the missionaries were accustomed to. The pig's head brawn, however, had been made by Rebecca, and was also very good.

Kitty was surprised to see that alcohol was served with the meal. She knew the missionaries were as partial to a good drop as anyone else, but she thought they might have refrained, given that Haunui, Te Rangi and Mahuika were present: the CMS had always gone to great lengths to ensure that the Maoris were not given alcohol. But when Haunui was offered the claret, he placed his hand over his glass and shook his head, an expression of exaggerated piety on his face. Te Rangi and Mahuika did the same.

Kitty stared at Haunui incredulously, knowing full well from their time in Sydney that he was more than capable of matching the amount that any of the *Katipo*'s crew might drink. He smiled innocently back.

The second course consisted of stewed rump of beef, roast fowl, kumara, roast potatoes and peas, served with fresh bread baked to Mrs Williams's own recipe. Kitty knew that some settlers made bread from buttermilk and carbonate soda, or even from yeast made from shredded flax, but Mrs Williams made her yeast from flour ground from wheat grown at Waimate, sugar, porter and water, shaken in a bottle and left to ferment, and always managed to produce light, white loaves.

The third course was plum pudding with custard and cream, and gingerbread, and several bowls of sugarplums — although the plums were actually carefully pitted cherries because the plum crop had apparently failed that year — which Te Rangi and Mahuika almost polished off between them.

At the completion of the meal, port was served, and again the Maoris present declined, except for Ropata, who sipped his luxuriously while studiously ignoring the missionaries' frowns.

Rian moved his chair back from the table and surreptitiously let out his belt a notch. 'That was an excellent meal, thank you very much,' he declared.

'*Oui, absolument magnifique!*' Pierre agreed

148

expansively, even though Kitty had noticed him poking at his beef and frowning.

There were murmurs of agreement from around the table, and the mission's collective housegirls, who had had their Christmas dinner on the Purcells' verandah, swooped in and began to clear the table. Rebecca got up to clean the faces of her two youngest children, and Eliza Henry gathered up her twins and disappeared inside with them, presumably, Kitty thought with a pang of envy, to feed them. They were darling little boys, with tufts of fluffy brown hair and bright blue eyes.

Marianne Williams folded her table napkin neatly and suggested, 'Ladies, shall we adjourn to the parlour?' When they were settled inside, leaving the men in the garden to sit back, pour themselves more port and light their pipes, she said, 'That was a wonderful meal, ladies. Thank you.' She opened her workbox and withdrew a piece of embroidery. 'And it is lovely to have you back, Kitty. I trust you are adjusting to life as Mrs Rian Farrell?'

Kitty glanced at her, noting the twinkle in her eye. 'Oh, definitely, Mrs Williams. I am finding that it suits me very well.'

'You must have the most wonderful adventures, sailing about the high seas.'

'Well, sometimes we have adventures, but usually our daily lives are quite routine.'

'Just like any life, I expect,' Mrs Williams noted.

'Do you not get bored on that little schooner, Kitty?' Rebecca asked.

Kitty thought about it. 'Not really. I have my daily chores and my handiwork, and I read. And there is always something new on the horizon. And we're not at sea all the time. Sometimes we're in port.'

'In England?' Eliza Henry asked, trying to settle both babies on her lap at once. Apparently they didn't want to settle and Samuel began to grizzle.

'Occasionally,' Kitty replied, 'but more often than not somewhere else. We were in Sydney a few weeks ago, and before that Durban.'

'That's in Africa, isn't it?' Eliza gave up and set the babies on the floor, where they immediately crawled off in different directions.

'South Africa, yes,' Kitty said, scooping up Luke and sitting him on her knee.

Eliza nodded. 'The CMS almost sent us there instead of here, but I'm glad they didn't. I'm not at all sure I would have managed with those Zulus. Such ferocious people.'

Kitty eyed Eliza's small frame, tiny hands and feet, and golden hair, and decided she probably had to agree.

'We are all God's children, Eliza,' Mrs Williams remarked, squinting despite her spectacles as she threaded a needle.

Jannah Tait turned a sock inside-out and inspected the hole she was about to darn. 'Mind you, things have been somewhat hectic here, too.'

'Yes, it has been rather an anxious time,' Eliza agreed, darting over to a plant stand to stop Samuel from pulling it over on himself. 'Why aren't these babies sleepy? They nearly always sleep after they've been fed.'

'You've heard about Hone Heke's antics, Kitty, I presume?' Jannah asked.

'We've heard various versions of what's been happening, yes,' Kitty said.

Jannah selected a length of grey wool from her workbox. 'Well, I feel he is behaving in a very belligerent and disruptive manner. It shows a marked lack of gratitude on his part, if you ask me. No good will come of it, I'm sure.'

'From cutting down the flagstaff, do you mean?' Kitty asked.

'Actually, Heke himself did not actually cut down the flagstaff,' Sarah said. 'It was Te Haratua apparently, his second in command.'

'So they say. It's the same thing, though, isn't it?' Jannah insisted.

'I think so, too,' Charlotte Dow agreed, her head bent low over her embroidery. 'A very alarming man, that John Heke. And arrogant.'

Mrs Williams snipped a piece of thread with her sewing scissors. 'Perhaps we might remember that the flagstaff was given by Heke himself nine years ago, specifically to fly the ensign of the Confederation of the United Chiefs and Tribes. Also that it was moved from Waitangi to Maiki Hill across the bay without his permission. Therefore, given the economic restrictions the Crown has imposed upon the Maoris since the treaty, particularly here in Northland, one can imagine what effect the flying of the Union Jack from that very flagstaff day after day might have had on his sensibilities.' She sighed. 'But I fear that you are right, Jannah. No good will come of it.'

Rebecca added, 'And he has alienated Tamati Waka Nene, so now there's a fear that tribal warfare will resurface, on top of everything else.'

The women were silent for a long moment, concentrating on their work. Then, recalling something that Enya had mentioned while they'd been in Sydney, Kitty asked, 'What happened at Wairau?'

Jannah and Rebecca exchanged an oh-dear-wasn't-that-dreadful glance, and Rebecca said, 'It was over disputed land, near Marlborough. It was originally Te Rauparaha's land but the New Zealand Company believed they had purchased it, although in retrospect they clearly had not, and sent a party to survey it. Te Rauparaha opposed the survey, so thirty armed settlers — '

'*Fifty* armed settlers,' Jannah amended, her darning forgotten for the moment.

Charlotte also interrupted. 'And it was straight after that terrible murder at Cloudy Bay.'

Jannah frowned. 'No, it was six months after that.'

Kitty turned to Mrs Williams, who explained, 'A Maori woman, Rangihaua Kuika, and her baby were murdered by a European whaler. He was tried under British law but went free. Most unfortunate.'

'Anyway,' Rebecca went on, '*fifty* armed settlers arrived to arrest Te Rauparaha — '

'And chief Te Rangihaeata,' Charlotte said, interrupting again.

Jannah stabbed her sock with a darning needle

and said sharply, 'Charlotte, please let Rebecca finish', apparently forgetting that she had interrupted the story twice herself.

Rebecca sent her a grateful look. 'Te Rauparaha resisted arrest, fatal shots were fired, and some of the arresting party were captured. But when it was discovered that one of those killed was Te Rongo, Te Rangihaeata's wife and Te Rauparaha's daughter, the twenty captured settlers were — '

'Were *murdered*,' Charlotte blurted. 'Including Captain Wakefield himself, who was to be head of the new town!'

Jannah rolled her eyes.

'And how many Maoris were murdered?' Kitty asked quietly.

'Oh, no, no *Maoris* were murdered,' Charlotte exclaimed. 'But six were killed in battle.'

'So how is it that they were 'killed in battle', but the settlers were 'murdered'?' Kitty said.

Charlotte looked slightly confused for a moment. 'Because the settlers were prisoners when they were killed. The Maoris weren't. They were resisting arrest.'

Unable to restrain her anger any longer towards the silly, ignorant woman, who after all was supposed to be an advocate for the Maoris, and a Christian one at that, Kitty enquired icily, 'But why wouldn't they resist, if they were being arrested for trying to protect their own land?' Charlotte opened her mouth to reply but Kitty kept on. 'And hadn't Te Rongo just been killed, and six months before that Rangihaua Kuika and her child, without justice being served to their murderer? Have you not heard of utu, Mrs Dow?'

'Yes, of course, but — ' Charlotte began, but was spared from digging herself any deeper when Luke gave a resounding burp and regurgitated milk and puréed kumara all over Kitty's sleeve.

'Oh Lord!' Eliza cried, mortified, as she hurried over to Kitty and hastily mopped at the splatter on her dress. 'I'm terribly sorry.'

'Don't worry,' Kitty replied, patting Luke on the back. 'It's only sick.'

'You'll need to sponge that or it will smell,' Sarah said unhelpfully.

Eliza gathered up Luke and he gurgled cheerfully, clearly much happier.

Still dabbing half-heartedly at the stain with Eliza's cloth, and deciding it wasn't worth arguing with Charlotte Dow, Kitty asked Mrs Williams, 'So what happened after Hone Heke cut down the flagstaff?'

'Oh, there was a huge fuss in the press and Bishop Selwyn organised a meeting at Waimate of local chiefs, at which Heke agreed to erect a new flagstaff to replace the one he'd cut down. I believe he handed over a small number of arms as well. But Governor FitzRoy had already requested military aid, and one morning a contingent of two-hundred-and-fifty imperial troops appeared across the bay.'

'I hadn't realised there were that many soldiers in New Zealand,' Kitty said. There certainly hadn't been when she'd left in 1840.

'There weren't,' Rebecca explained. 'These were seamen and marines from the warship

HMS *Hazard*, and soldiers from Point Britomart in Auckland, and a hundred-and-fifty men sent over from the 96th Regiment stationed in Sydney.'

'They're not still here, are they?' Kitty asked. 'We didn't see any military vessels when we put in.'

Rebecca said, 'No, they returned to Auckland when Heke capitulated and matters seemed to be in hand.'

'And since then Hone Heke has been going around stirring up anti-British sentiment?'

'More or less,' Mrs Williams replied. 'Along with a few other rather prominent chiefs, which does not bode well, and some very hot-headed young men.'

'Do you think trouble is on the way?' Kitty said bluntly.

Mrs Williams looked at her over the top of her spectacles. 'Unfortunately, Kitty, yes, I do.'

6

It rained torrentially and almost solidly for the following two weeks, but it was a warm rain that turned clothes and bread alike mouldy overnight, prevented freshly laundered linen from drying properly, and sluiced mud and leaves across walking paths so that several people, braving the deluges, slipped and turned their ankles, and, in one case, broke a wrist. As a result, Mrs Williams was kept busy preparing poultices made from boiled flax root and the oil of pulped titoki berries, and handing out arnica pills. The rain also confined the mission's children indoors, making them irritable and fidgety, a state compounded by the discovery that many of them were suffering an outbreak of threadworm. Subsequently everyone at the mission, including visitors, had to be treated with an aperient of castor oil and sal volatile, then administered three or four grains of santonin. Although the treatment was guaranteed to clear the bowel of any remaining eggs, most of the adults also became irritable after repeated trips to the privy.

The rain prevented Rian from scouting out possible sources of kauri to ship to Sydney, but Kitty had the distinct impression that he was in no hurry to leave Paihia. He was, of course, waiting to see what might happen with Hone Heke, as she had known he would since they'd first heard of the growing tension. But Sarah seemed glad to have them, and Kitty had to admit that it was very pleasant to spend time in the company of women she knew and cared for. Well, mostly cared for — Charlotte Dow had continued to irritate her and that state of affairs showed no sign of abating.

Kitty had asked Rebecca whether Mrs Dow was normally so galling or was it perhaps just the mugginess and the never-ending rain? And Rebecca had smiled and replied that Charlotte was indeed a unique spirit, but that the teachings of the Society strongly favoured the practices of tolerance and acceptance of others. Or had Kitty forgotten that? No, Kitty said, she hadn't, but Mrs Dow appeared to have done so, and that was a particularly distressing thing to see in a missionary. Rebecca had pointed out that Charlotte's heart was in the right place, and asked if Kitty would mind checking whether baby Joshua's nappy was wet, which meant that she didn't wish to discuss Charlotte any more.

But by 8 January the sun was out again in all its stewing heat and turning the bush into a steaming wonderland. The children were instantly happy and consequently so were the adults, delighted to send little and not-so-little ones off with a picnic lunch for an adventure. They were farewelled, however, with the warning that were they to encounter any Maoris they did not recognise, or even a war party, they were to run home straight away. Heke and some of his followers had been in the area lately, and had in fact dined at Pukera the evening before last, and while the missionaries were confident that he wouldn't attack mission children, or indeed the mission itself, they believed it would be prudent to keep their children out of his way.

On the following day, the temperature was high even at seven in the morning, and when Kitty awoke, her hair plastered to her neck with sweat, it was to discover that Rian wasn't next to her. She rose, slipped into her cotton robe and padded down the wooden stairs, yawning and tying her hair back with a piece of ribbon. The parlour was empty except for Bodie, stretched out in the sun on Sarah's chaise.

'Hello, little madam,' Kitty said. 'I thought you were out at Pukera with Pierre?'

Bodie opened one eye, yawned and meowed at the same time, then rolled onto her back so that her tummy could be tickled.

Kitty obliged, but confided, 'I'm not sure Aunt Sarah really wants you depositing black hairs all over her cream upholstery. Actually, wouldn't she be your *great*-aunt? By marriage?'

'Cats don't have aunts,' Rian said from the dining room.

Kitty found him at the table in his shirtsleeves, eating a large plate of porridge swimming in milk and honey. She sat down.

'I didn't hear you get up.'

Rian ran his spoon around the edge of his plate. 'Then you shouldn't snore so loudly, sweetheart, should you?'

'I don't snore. Has Aunt Sarah risen yet?'

'She's been down, but I assume she's getting dressed now.'

Kitty reached for the teapot, tilted it over a cup and frowned when nothing came out. 'Damn, is there no more?'

'I believe Ngahuia's just refilled the kettle,' Rian mumbled through his porridge.

Kitty took the pot and went to find out: the kettle was indeed heating on the grate over the kitchen fire but Ngahuia was nowhere to be seen. Neither was Rangimarie, Sarah's other, extraordinarily timid, housegirl. But when Kitty went outside she saw them both, crouching in the kitchen garden and talking, their heads close together.

She called out to Ngahuia and both girls started and looked up, then Ngahuia rose and limped hurriedly towards the house.

'Good morning, Missus Kitty,' she said.

'Good morning, Ngahuia,' Kitty replied, wondering why the girl looked so guilty.

'Would you like me to serve you the pareti?'

'Only if you're not busy.'

Kitty followed Ngahuia into the kitchen and emptied the teapot into the bowl where Sarah saved the old leaves to dye her crochet and tatting, then opened the tea canister. Rangimarie came in a moment later with four string beans in her hand. Surely it hadn't required the pair of them to pick four beans?

'Are the beans not very good at the moment?' she asked. 'Was it the rain, do you think?'

Both girls stared.

Kitty tried again. 'Do you think the rain has spoiled the beans? Stopped the flowers from setting, I mean?' She inclined her head towards

159

Rangimarie's hand. 'You don't seem to have found many.'

Ngahuia ducked her head and mumbled, 'No, we did not find many.'

Suspecting that something was amiss, Kitty touched her arm. 'Is something the matter? Can I be of help?'

The boiling kettle hissed onto the fire and Ngahuia lifted it off and poured water into the teapot, all the while avoiding Kitty's gaze.

'Ngahuia?'

Rangimarie turned to leave the kitchen but Kitty grabbed her sleeve. 'Tell me, please.'

'It is nothing, thank you,' Rangimarie mumbled. Gently but firmly disengaging Kitty's hand, she walked out.

Ngahuia, her head still down, said, 'I will bring your pareti and the tea.'

Kitty regarded her worriedly for a moment, then went back into the dining room and sat down again.

'They're in an odd mood this morning.'

'Who?' Rian asked.

'Ngahuia and Rangimarie. Rian, I think something might be happening. Something bad.'

'It is,' Rian replied, pushing his empty plate away.

Kitty's heart lurched. 'What?'

'Pierre came by earlier this morning to say that there have been rumours out at Pukera that Hone Heke may be about to make another attack on the flagstaff.' He sighed and rubbed his hands over his unshaven face. 'Christ knows what FitzRoy will do. Send every bloody soldier

160

he can get his hands on up here, I expect.'

Ngahuia appeared and set Kitty's plate of porridge in front of her, then poured a cup of tea. She turned to go, then paused and said, 'I am sorry. I did not mean to be rude.'

'Oh Ngahuia, it doesn't matter,' Kitty replied. 'I understand.' When Ngahuia had gone, she said, 'They wouldn't tell me what was wrong, but obviously they've heard the rumour too.'

Rian crossed his arms. 'Well, we'll have to stay. At least until things settle down.'

Kitty was silent for some time, staring down at her porridge. Then she said, '*Why* do we have to stay, Rian? I sympathise with the people and what's happened to them since the treaty, you know that, but it's not our fight. And apart from that, do you really think there is anything we could do that would make a difference?'

Rian shrugged. 'I don't know yet.'

'And if we did get involved — '

'No, Kitty, you won't be getting involved, no matter what eventuates.'

Kitty didn't bite. 'All right, if *you* got involved, you would be branded as a traitor to the Crown and the punishment for that is hanging, Rian. I am *not* going through that again.'

'How can I be a traitor to the Crown?' he asked innocently.

Kitty gave him an exasperated look.

'What? I don't have any allegiance to the British. I'm Irish, remember?'

'So if you're not Maori and you're not British, why do you want to get involved?'

Rian said stubbornly, 'Because there's a

principle at stake here.'

Kitty sighed inwardly: Rian and his damned principles! 'Well, what is it, then?'

'You know very well what it is. It's *wrong* for one people to force another to submit to their rule. You can't just go around subjugating whole countries! And that's what the Crown is doing. Bloody English, I hate them!'

'Rian, *I'm* English!'

'No you're not. You're . . . you're Kitty.' Rian paused. 'And I'm not sure you really understand what all of this means.'

Kitty thought she did, actually. 'Well, what do *you* think it means?'

He took her hand. 'What it means, love, is that the Maoris will lose their way of life for ever. It means they'll be persecuted for their beliefs, even killed for them, like the Catholics are in Ireland. It means they'll be forced to live and die by a system of law weighted so heavily against them that they'll never be able to extricate themselves from it.'

Kitty frowned, recalling uncomfortably that Enya had been tried and transported to Australia by an English judge. And so had Mick's mother, Biddy Doyle, although Kitty had never found out what Mrs Doyle's crime had been.

Rian was becoming more and more passionate as he spoke. 'It also means they'll become deprived of almost all political and economic power, and that's happening already, isn't it? And it means their spirit will be crushed and, believe me, that's the hardest thing of all to recover from. Kitty, listen to me: the English have been interfering in Ireland and destroying it for nearly seven hundred years. Do you want that to happen here?'

Kitty blinked. 'Of course not, Rian. You know I don't.'

'Well, it will if this isn't stopped.'

'But *you* can't stop it, Rian. You're only one person.'

'No, I know, but I must do something.'

With a sinking heart, Kitty knew he wasn't going to be dissuaded. She dipped her spoon into her congealing porridge and stirred it listlessly. 'Will you promise me one thing?'

'If I can.'

'Don't take up arms against the British. Please. They'll kill you one way or another.'

Rian leaned across the corner of the table and kissed her cheek. 'Don't worry, *mo ghrá*, I'm not going to take up arms for or against anyone. But I will do what I can.'

Kitty pushed her plate away, her appetite gone.

⋆ ⋆ ⋆

The morning of 10 January was again fine and warm, so Rian decided to go across to Kororareka and pick up a few supplies. Pierre also wanted to inspect the stores there: he didn't know when they would be leaving the Bay of Islands, but he wanted the galley to be provisioned when they did.

However, when the crew, plus Haunui and Tahi, arrived at Paihia, it was obvious that they weren't all going to fit into the *Katipo's* rowboat, so they borrowed one of Pukera's waka. There was much hilarity as they set off, the waka changing direction with every stroke of the oars until Haunui, counting the cadence and laughing his head off, managed to synchronise Mick, Rian, Pierre, Daniel and Hawk as they rowed. Kitty — minus her bonnet, as she knew from past experience that the brisk winds of the bay would have it off her head in minutes — and Tahi sat in the prow with Ropata, who was thoroughly enjoying watching his crewmates making idiots of themselves. They stopped off at the *Katipo*, anchored in the bay among six or seven other ships, to collect Gideon, who had been keeping watch on the schooner, then set off again for the sweeping curve of Kororareka's beach.

They were all damp with sea spray and in high spirits when they arrived, Kitty looking forward to fossicking in the stores, and the others to a pint or two in one of the grog-shops. The town looked picturesque in the bright sunshine, with rows of ships' boats and waka pulled up on the shingled beach before two small palisaded pa, and the street of one- and two-storey weatherboard buildings that paralleled the shore. Behind them, the tall-windowed Anglican church squatted solidly next to its graveyard, houses and gardens sat on the lower slopes of the hills, and the American flag was flying from consul James Clendon's house. At the southern end of the beach were clustered Bishop Pompallier's chapel, houses, workshops

164

and printery. The tranquil scene belied the settlement's reputation as 'a perfect picture of depravity' — a sobriquet that was, by most accounts, nevertheless thoroughly deserved.

Behind the town lay a large swamp, and behind that a series of rugged hills, their seaward-facing slopes peppered with coarse fern and dwarf cypress. At the northern end of the bay rose Maiki Hill, topped by the now-infamous flagstaff flying the Union Jack. On closer inspection, Kitty saw that Governor FitzRoy's economic sanctions had not been kind to the town: it might have grown, but it seemed even more dilapidated than it had been during her only other visit, back in 1839. She had been with Wai, then. And Amy.

Walking up the potholed main street she eyed the shabby trading stores, private dwellings, boarding houses and grog-shops, and the sailors and other rough-looking individuals openly eyeing her, and was glad she was with a party of eight men. And one little boy, even though she wasn't entirely convinced that this was the sort of place Tahi should be visiting. But he was strolling along beside Haunui, his hands in his pockets, calmly taking in the sights. When a pair of gaudily-dressed young women sitting outside a small house and showing rather a lot of stockinged calf called out, he waved to them cheerily.

One of the women stood up and struck a pose, her hands smoothing the cheap, shiny fabric of her dress over her hips. Kitty stopped and stared, wondering if they were the same whores she, Wai

165

and Amy had encountered five years before, but after a moment decided they couldn't be.

'Good morning, gentlemen,' the woman on her feet called out invitingly. Belatedly noticing Kitty, she added unenthusiastically, 'Oh, and lady. Are yis looking for a little bit o' comfort? Because yis've come to the right place if yis are.'

Pierre looked her up and down and shook his head disdainfully. The woman made a rude gesture at him. Daniel went pink. Hawk, Ropata and Gideon ignored her, and Mick looked as though he was having a terrible time deciding between the sort of comfort the woman was offering and the sort that could be purchased over a bar.

'What about you, little man?' the woman called, pointing at Tahi, and both she and her companion burst into ribald giggles.

Mick bent down and said to Tahi, 'Now's your chance, so it is.'

Kitty gave Mick a stern look, which only made him grin.

'Pardon?' Tahi said, his big eyes turned up to Mick.

'Never mind, love,' Kitty told him. 'Mick's only being silly.'

Nevertheless, Haunui manoeuvred Tahi protectively between himself and Gideon.

'They won't bite,' Mick teased.

Haunui made a face. 'They bloody might.'

Pierre spotted a likely-looking trading store, gave a grunt of satisfaction and veered off towards it.

'Hey!' Ropata shouted, and when Pierre

turned Ropata raised his elbow in a drinking gesture. 'Are you not coming?'

'*Oui*,' Pierre replied. 'But first I buy the food, then I drink.'

Ropata shrugged and followed the others across the street to a rather seedy-looking establishment that was clearly a grogshop. Noting the envious expression on Haunui's face, Kitty took Tahi's hand and steered him towards the trading store.

'But I want to go with Koro,' Tahi complained, dragging his feet.

'Well, you can't,' Kitty said. 'Little boys don't go into places like that.'

'But Koro said I am allowed,' Tahi insisted.

'I did not!' Haunui called from the verandah of the grogshop. 'Go on, boy, go with Kitty.'

Tahi's bottom lip came out, but he reluctantly allowed himself to be led across the street.

The light inside the trading store was dim, but when Kitty's eyes adjusted she saw that the interior was entirely lined with shelves reaching from the bare, uneven floorboards to the ceiling. There were lower shelves in the middle of the floor and a solid counter ran across the back of the store, presumably blocking off access to the smaller, more expensive items on display behind it. The aproned storekeeper, leaning on the counter and concentrating on lighting his pipe, ignored them. The whole place smelled of chaff, leather, wet wood, and some strange, dusty sort of spice.

The shelves, which weren't overstocked by any means, held rolls of coarse cloth suitable for men's work clothes, and sturdy shirts and moleskin trousers, woollen undergarments and socks that looked as though they would be horribly itchy to wear, hobnail boots, broad-brimmed hats, leather belts, lengths of canvas, plain tableware, cutlery, iron griddles, hooks, cheap pots and pans, rope of all sizes, lamps and lanterns with fresh white wicks, buckets and basins, jars, sacks — in short, everything a person might need for a basic life. Behind the counter were tobacco, pipes, razors and strops, soap, sharp gleaming knives, alcohol, laudanum, and various other bits and pieces.

Pierre had headed straight for the shelves containing edible provisions. Kitty went after him, the heels of her boots clacking on the wooden floor, Tahi padding silently beside her.

'Do they have what you want?' she asked Pierre, who was peering into a bin of flour.

He took up a pinch between his fingers, looked at it closely, then sniffed it. 'Pah! There have been the weevils in this flour!'

'I beg your pardon!' the storekeeper exclaimed from behind his counter, puffing clouds of rank-smelling smoke towards the stained ceiling.

'Your flour, she is spoiled!' Pierre declared, theatrically rubbing his fingers together to clean them.

'That is perfectly good flour,' the storekeeper replied.

'It has had the weevils,' Pierre insisted.

The storekeeper looked sceptical. 'What makes you say that?'

'I smell them. I smell where the little feet have

168

been. She is inferior! I will not pay you for that.'

'Don't then,' the storekeeper said, shrugging.

Pierre moved on to a bin of dried peas, sniffed a handful and discarded those as well. 'Stale,' he announced disgustedly.

He had a little luck eventually, though, selecting three bottles of white vinegar, several packets of spices and a small cask of salt. He paid the surly shopkeeper for them, plus six pieces of butterscotch in a paper twist for Tahi, and arranged to collect the goods later. As they left the store, Kitty was sure she heard the storekeeper mutter, 'Cheeky bloody Frog.'

Outside, she asked, 'Were there really weevils in the flour?'

Pierre shook his head. 'But you can get a better price sometimes that way, eh?' Then, casually, he inclined his head towards Tahi.

Kitty followed his gaze: there was a large piece of butterscotch making a lump in the boy's cheek and he was clutching his penis through his trousers.

'Do you need a mimi?' she asked.

Tahi nodded.

Kitty looked up and down the street. 'Oh dear. I wonder if there's a privy anywhere?' she said to Pierre.

'He don't need a privy when there is a wall.'

'Well, you take him then,' Kitty urged, 'I'll wait here.'

She turned her back while Pierre took Tahi around the side of the store: she couldn't see them, but she was certainly still within earshot because, after a long silence, she heard Pierre say, 'Don't he want to come now?'

Another silence, shorter this time. Then Pierre saying, 'I have one too, then we be two men together, eh?'

A few seconds later came the sound of a stream of liquid hitting the wall, followed by Pierre's voice: 'See Monsieur Spider there? Let's drown him.'

Tahi giggled, then exclaimed, 'Haere ra, pungawerewere!'

Kitty was still grinning when, out of the corner of her eye, she noticed three men crossing the street towards her. She stopped smiling and quickly glanced over her shoulder to see where Pierre was.

One of the men doffed his hat and drawled, 'Morning, little lady. Lost, are you?'

'Not at all,' Kitty replied quickly, alarmed to see that the trio were very rough-looking. And drunk.

'Ye def'ny look lost to me,' another said. 'Come with us, we'll look after ye.'

At that all three of them guffawed. The first man stepped up and took her arm in a firm grip, his expression turning mean. 'Come on, girlie, I got a surprise for you.'

Kitty wrenched her arm out of his grasp, then saw something that allowed her to relax somewhat: Pierre had appeared from around the other side of the trading store and was standing behind the trio with his pistol drawn. Despite his lack of height, he cut an intimidating figure, with his wiry, muscled body, his scowling face, pointed beard, and long, exotic plait — and his pair of fighting knives in full view at his belt.

'Leave the lady alone,' he growled. 'She not be interested. Go! *Cassez-vous!*'

They turned around, but took a hasty step back when they saw the pistol. They stared at him for a moment, then one slowly raised his hands, palms out. 'Sorry, didn't realise she was taken.'

Pierre steadied his pistol, cocked it and aimed it at the man's chest. The man backed away, then turned and hurried off with as much dignity as he could muster, followed quickly by his companions.

Kitty blew out a great sigh of relief, her heart thudding wildly. Pierre whistled and Tahi appeared from his hiding place behind the building.

'Shall I get Koro?' he asked breathlessly, gazing up at Pierre.

Pierre shook his head. '*Non, mon fils*, they be gone now.' He holstered his pistol and spat in the dirt.

'Thank you, Pierre,' Kitty said.

Pierre bowed theatrically. 'At your service, Madame.' But when he straightened, he added so that Tahi wouldn't hear, 'It is not safe here. We will go to the others.'

'The others' were already well away in the grog-shop, which was quite crowded even at this early hour. Mick had procured a mandolin from somewhere and, accompanied by a morose-looking man on a *bodhrán*, was giving a rendition of his favourite song. Kitty also liked it, so she leaned against the doorway with Pierre,

171

ignoring the stares of the men inside, and listened as Mick sang in his rough but rather sensual voice:

I'm a bold Irish hero, who never yet was
*   daunted,*
In the courting of a pretty girl I very seldom
*   wanted,*
In the courting of a pretty girl I own it was my
*   folly,*
I'd venture my whole life for you, my very pretty
*   Molly.*

Then he winked at Kitty and launched into the chorus, the words of which he knew she thought were nothing more than made-up nonsense.

Mush a ring fal a do fal a da,
Whack fol a daddy-o,
Whack fol a daddy-o,
There's whiskey in the jar-o.

As I was walking over old Kilgary Mountain,
I met with Captain Powers, his money he was
*   counting,*
I pulled out my sword, and likewise then my
*   rapier,*
Saying, stand and deliver, for I am a bold
*   deceiver.*

It's when I got the money it was a pretty penny,
I put it in my pocket and I took it home to Molly,
She said, my dearest lover, I never will deceive
*   you,*

But the devil's in the women, they never can be easy.

But Mick didn't get to finish the song because, just as he started on the third chorus, Kitty was shoved rudely out of the doorway by a man who was breathless and red in the face from running.

'He's done it again!' he shouted as he barged in. 'The bugger's attacked the flagstaff again!'

For a moment there was no sound at all. Then Rian started to laugh.

★   ★   ★

The general consensus seemed to be that Hone Heke had lost his mind. After the flagstaff attack, he had threatened to destroy the gaol, the police and customs houses, and the post office at Kororareka, although all this, fortunately, was thwarted by two hundred Nga Puhi men led by the formidable chief Kawiti, and a contingent of armed locals. FitzRoy offered a £100 reward to anyone who apprehended the renegade chief, payable on his delivery either to Thomas Beckham, the police magistrate at Kororareka, or the magistrate at Auckland. He also declared that anyone found assisting, harbouring or concealing Heke would be charged. Heke promptly offered his own £100 reward for the capture of the governor.

As Rian had predicted, FitzRoy sent a garrison of thirty soldiers of the 96th to Kororareka and requested even more military assistance from New South Wales: two companies of the 58th

173

Regiment were despatched to New Zealand immediately. The flagstaff on Maiki Hill was replaced and its lower section heavily reinforced with iron, but Heke managed to fell it a third time on 18 January, only eight days after his second attack. Tamati Waka Nene, now openly supporting the government, had been guarding the flagstaff at the time, but such was Hone Heke's mana that no one made a move to stop him.

Rian was chopping wood for Sarah — a chore for which he seemed to be in high demand by Kitty's relatives — when Win Purcell came by to relay word of FitzRoy's latest measures.

Rian rested his axe against the chopping block and wiped the sweat out of his eyes with his shirtsleeve. 'So what do you think? Will it be war?'

'I hope not,' Win said, his red face shining even though he had done nothing more than walk a few hundred yards up the beach. 'But ordering blockhouses to be built across the bay doesn't look good, does it?'

'No, it doesn't,' Rian replied, gesturing for Win to sit on a bench in the shade of a nearby tree.

Win did so gratefully, while Rian sat on the chopping block and got out his pipe. 'And I don't like the sound of more troops coming from Sydney, either,' he added. 'The last lot that arrived are still in Auckland, aren't they?'

Win nodded, withdrawing his own smoking accoutrements from a deep pocket.

'And that makes four hundred men, plus the fifty special constables you say Beckham has just

174

sworn in at Kororareka?'

'Aye.'

Rian frowned. 'And if FitzRoy has said there'll be no protection for settlers anywhere else, that means that Paihia won't be defended, I assume?'

Win concurred gloomily. 'Nor Waimate, nor Kerikeri.'

Rian used a twig to scrape the last of the old ash out of his pipe, then tapped the bowl against the chopping block before he tamped in fresh tobacco. 'So what will you do if there *is* war?'

'Well, we're hoping of course that it won't come to that. We're not strictly pacifists, but we are servants of the Lord. We don't condone violence.'

'And you won't be taking part in any?'

Win lit his pipe. 'No, we won't.' He puffed vigorously until the tobacco caught. 'What about yourself?'

A good minute went past before Rian finally said, 'I'll tell you what I told my wife. And that is, if it comes to war, I won't fight for one side or the other.'

Win looked at him shrewdly. 'You say you won't fight, but will you assist in any other way? Say on the side of the Maoris, perchance?'

Rian returned the look. 'Did Reverend Williams send you down here? Or was it that long-winded bigot, Dow?'

'Neither. Augustus Dow may be long-winded at times, and I concede that he hasn't yet been in New Zealand long enough to appreciate the many intricacies of the Maori race, but he does have a good Christian heart.'

'Well, I'll take your word for that,' Rian said. 'And you've certainly had worse than him here, haven't you?'

Win's face darkened. 'Indeed.' He stared at his boots for a long moment. 'Look, Captain, I know we haven't always seen eye to eye, but these are trying times. There may be war, and that in my experience means loss of lives. There are children here, and women.'

'I'm fully aware of that.'

Win went on as though Rian hadn't spoken. 'I'll be blunt, Captain. I need to know if your cargo on this trip included arms.'

'No, it did not,' Rian answered immediately. 'Not this time. You saw what we unloaded after we arrived, and that was everything we shipped. The *Katipo* is sitting well above her waterline at the moment.'

'Well, that's a good thing to hear,' Win said.

He looked so pathetically relieved that Rian felt sorry for him. 'I've made no secret of my views of colonisation, whether it be by missionaries or thieving land-grabbers like the New Zealand Company. And, to be as blunt as you were, I'm sometimes hard put to see a difference between the two. But I fear it may already be too late for this country, for these people. I also believe that war is inevitable, and there's nothing I can do to change that.' Rian suddenly grinned. 'Who the hell am I, anyway? A scruffy sea trader with an even scruffier crew. Although I do have a very beautiful and charming wife.'

Win almost smiled. 'So why don't you just sail

away with her, Captain, and keep her safe? Take her beyond harm's reach?'

Rian peered into the bowl of his pipe, stirred the contents slightly with his twig, and drew on it to strengthen the embers. 'Because I have friends here, Mr Purcell, and so does she. And if it comes to war, I *will* do what I can for my friends. Surely you must understand that?'

'Yes, I believe I do.'

'And although, as you say,' Rian added, 'we haven't always seen eye to eye, I hope that there are some in this community I can also now name as friends, just as I can say the same thing about Pukera.'

Win settled his weight against the back of Sarah's garden seat and crossed his arms. He looked vaguely pleased. 'Well, if it *does* come to war, I dare say we would be glad of your presence. And that of your men. We have little fear of Heke himself, but sometimes in the heat of battle, as I'm sure a man such as yourself will know, events can occur that are deeply regretted afterwards. And there are young warriors aligned with Hone Heke who have little experience and even less discipline, and who may succumb to the bloodlust that can afflict many men in times of war. *That* is what I am frightened of, Captain.'

7

A mild panic spread throughout New Zealand, fuelled by speculation from settlements nowhere near the Bay of Islands, and by genuine fear generated in Auckland, which was considerably closer to the seat of unrest. And FitzRoy's very public preparations for war belied the official call for calm.

Nonetheless, the Paihia mission station quietly prepared for a siege, although some of the children, who were having trouble linking their brown-skinned playmates to any notion of danger, had to be persuaded that it was not all a game. Te Rangi had already declared that Pukera would remain neutral should a conflict arise, both because of the village's close relationship with the mission, and because he (or rather, Haunui) did not particularly agree with Hone Heke's heavy-handed tactics.

Extra grain and other produce was brought to Paihia from Waimate, which was also readying for war, and visits were made to smaller outlying European settlements to offer shelter at either of the missions should the need arise. The idea of visiting the smaller Maori communities in the area had also been considered, but discarded; the Maoris had been at war for decades and were quite capable of keeping themselves out of the way if necessary, and there were also fears that rebel Maoris might infiltrate European settlements under cover of 'good' Maoris.

Rian countered this argument, which held strong sway with many of the British settlers filtering through the Bay of Islands on their way down to Auckland, by pointing out that, so far as could be ascertained, Heke had no intention of alienating the settlers: that would limit his declared aim of improving relations between the races. The response to that was, inevitably: so why had Heke thrice cut down the flagstaff, the ultimate symbol of British authority? And if Rian attempted to argue further, it only made anyone listening decide that he was a supporter of Heke and subsequently regard him with deep suspicion. Heke himself had gone quiet and was rumoured to have temporarily retired to his stronghold at Kaikohe.

Then, late in February, reports came through that he had been joined by two hundred men from the Hokianga and was on his way to Waimate for further discussions with Henry Williams, and also with Tamati Waka Nene. But Heke failed to provide an assurance that he would not attack Kororareka, And then came worse news: the great chief Kawiti had also aligned himself with Heke.

'Well, I think this is probably it,' Rian said grimly to Kitty the morning they heard, before setting off for Pukera to bring the crew back to Paihia.

When he returned later that day he had with him not only the *Katipo*'s men, but also Haunui and Tahi, and a dozen of the village's children

179

aged between about two and ten.

'Te Rangi thought they might be safer here at the mission,' Haunui explained to Aunt Sarah as they all gathered on her front verandah.

'Does he think there *is* going to be trouble?' Kitty asked, handing around a platter of bread and blackberry jam to the children.

'No. Just to be sure,' Haunui replied, helping himself to a couple of slices.

'Where will we put them?' Sarah wondered aloud, looking down at the sea of little faces. She knew most of them already from the mission school, but not the children under the age of six. 'Did you carry the little ones?'

'Ae, we all did,' Haunui replied. 'The babies are still at the village with their mothers.'

'Did you not ask them to come in as well?'

'We did,' Rian said, 'but they chose to stay.'

'Why?' Sarah asked. 'Surely they would be safer here?'

Kitty eyed her aunt, wondering if Sarah was more nervous about the impending conflict than she was admitting. She'd been fairly calm and cheerful so far, but Kitty knew she'd been listening to Charlotte Dow, who'd been regaling the mission women with hair-raising stories of what had happened to missionaries in other parts of the world who had found themselves caught up in wars. Stories that involved large cooking pots, escapes that ended in fatal shipwrecks, and people who were lost forever in hostile jungles. All of it was hearsay, so far as Kitty could gather, and no doubt liberally enriched by Mrs Dow's penchant for alarmism.

The woman needed a good slap across the face, and Kitty had decided that when the time came she would be first in line.

Haunui said, 'They do not believe so. But they sent these children because they are the tutu ones. It is much easier to watch a child who cannot yet walk, than a whole lot who run away all the time and do not listen.'

Kitty laughed. 'So are we to be nannies to Pukera's most badly behaved children?'

'Ae,' Haunui said, grinning widely. 'I think so.'

But Sarah wasn't laughing. In fact she had paled visibly, as though something had just occurred to her. 'But what if we are overrun ourselves? What will we do with them all? We can't be responsible for them. What will we do if we can't protect them?'

Rian laid a hand on Sarah's forearm and said in his most panic-dispelling voice, 'I very much doubt that the mission will be overrun, Mrs Kelleher. Heke won't attack here, you've said so yourself.'

Sarah looked at him with a flicker of hope. 'Yes, I suppose I have, haven't I? But, oh, I wish Mr Jenkins were here. He would know what we should do.'

Rian's eyes narrowed slightly, although his voice remained calm. 'What we should do, Mrs Kelleher, is go surely and steadily about our business. For example, I suggest you set up bedding for these children in the schoolroom, and won't arrangements need to be made to feed them all?'

'Yes,' Sarah said after a moment. 'Yes, that's a

good idea. I'll go and talk to Mrs Williams now, in fact.' And off she bustled.

When she was out of earshot, Rian said to Kitty, 'Christ almighty, your aunt certainly knows how to make a mountain out of a molehill, doesn't she?'

'I think you can blame Charlotte Dow for that,' Kitty muttered.

Rian looked at her for a moment, then lifted her hand and brought it to his lips. 'What about you, *mo ghrá*? Are you frightened?'

Kitty leaned against him. 'Not exactly frightened, no. But I am . . . well, I am apprehensive, Rian. I'm worried that it will all get out of hand and that people will be killed. People we care about.'

Rian nodded, just once. 'So am I, love. But with luck it will all be over soon. That's if it ever starts.'

'I think it will, don't you?'

'Yes, I do.'

A discreet cough came from behind them: it was Hawk. Kitty couldn't help noticing that he was carrying all his weapons.

'Excuse me, Rian,' he said. 'The men would like a word.'

Kitty looked beyond him and saw that Haunui had joined the crew on the beach. Tahi was squatting on his haunches, poking at something under a small rock with a stick. 'Bring them in,' she suggested. 'I'll put the kettle on.' She turned then to the Pukera children who had made themselves comfortable on Sarah's verandah and asked them in Maori if they would like some

182

more bread and jam.

Smiling to herself at the enthusiastically nodding heads and chorus of 'Ae!', she went inside, for a second not realising that they were all following her, their bare feet soundless on the hall carpets. When she did notice, she stood in the doorway to the kitchen and watched them, amused, as they touched everything they could reach — the white-painted walls, the hall mirror, the fine woodwork of Mr Jenkins's chiffonier, the crocheted runner draped along it, the flowers in the porcelain vase on the occasional table at the base of the stairs. When a very small child picked up the vase and almost dropped it, Kitty decided they would all be better in the courtyard between the house and the kitchen garden.

By the time she returned, she saw that Rian and the crew had settled themselves in Sarah's parlour — except for Gideon, who was prowling around the room looking at Sarah's nice things, much as the children had done.

In the kitchen she busied herself making a large pot of tea and putting more jam on slices of buttered bread. She thought about what to give the crew to eat: there was only half of a seed cake left, which she knew wouldn't go far.

'Should I make scones?' she wondered out loud, and started violently when a voice responded, 'I could do that.'

It was Daniel, standing in the doorway watching her, a gentle smile on his handsome face.

'I almost had a fit of the vapours then,' Kitty exclaimed, her hand over her thudding heart.

'Beg your pardon,' Daniel said. 'But I could, you know. Make scones, I mean. My mother taught me.'

'Your mother taught a big strapping man like you to make scones?' Kitty echoed disbelievingly, then stopped, suddenly worried that he might interpret her comment as a flirtation. Or that someone else might.

'No,' he said, 'I was only a boy when she showed me. And to be honest I haven't made them for years. There wasn't much call for them at Hyde Park Barracks.' He moved further into the kitchen. 'Do you have plenty of flour?'

Kitty checked the bin. 'Yes.'

'What about baking soda and cream of tartar?'

Kitty already knew there were ample quantities of both of those. 'And buttermilk,' she said.

'Shall I make cheese or plain?' he asked, moving nearer to the bench and rolling up his shirtsleeves.

Kitty saw that his forearms were tanned and muscled and dusted with fine black hair.

'Whatever you like,' she said quickly. 'I'll just check on the children.'

At the back door she stood with her back pressed hard against the doorframe, wondering what on earth had come over her.

'Missus Kitty?'

She looked down at one of the older boys. 'Mmm?'

'Where's our bread?'

'Oh.' She turned and almost walked straight into Rian, coming through the door with the platter of bread and jam.

184

'You forgot this.'

'I know. Thank you,' Kitty replied, taking the platter.

'What's Royce doing in the kitchen?' he asked.

'Making scones.'

Rian frowned. 'Scones?'

'Yes.' Kitty handed the platter to the boy and watched as he was almost knocked over by the other children rushing to grab pieces of the jammy bread. 'What were *you* doing in the kitchen?'

'Nothing.'

They looked quickly at each other, then they both laughed and it was on the tip of Kitty's tongue to say 'You were checking up on me, weren't you?' but she stopped herself just in time.

'What sort of man admits to knowing how to bake scones?' Rian asked as they went back to the kitchen, where Pierre was now standing over Daniel.

'*Non, non, NON!*' he was saying. 'The *crème du tartre*, she go in *before* the *bicarbonate du soude!*' He grabbed a wooden spoon from Daniel's hand and waggled it in the bowl in front of him so that flour puffed out everywhere. 'See, the scones they will not rise now!'

'That sort of man,' Kitty said. Clearly, Pierre's acceptance of Daniel did not extend to matters of food preparation.

Daniel snatched back the spoon. 'No, the cream of tartar goes in first, and they *will* rise.'

'Who tells you that?' Pierre demanded.

'My mother,' Daniel shot back, 'and don't you dare insult her!'

Pierre looked aghast. 'I would never insult *une mère!* 'cept I only say that 'cause — '

'Shut up, the pair of you!' Rian barked, while Kitty covered her smile with a hand. 'Pierre, leave him alone. Daniel, finish the bloody scones then come into the parlour.'

They were all waiting by the time Daniel appeared, hurriedly drying his hands on a tea towel. He said nothing but squeezed onto the end of the chaise next to Gideon.

'Right,' Rian said. 'Now, what are we going to do?'

Everyone looked at him blankly.

'About?' Hawk prompted.

'About this war between Heke and the British.'

'But it hasn't even started yet,' Mick pointed out reasonably.

Hawk frowned. 'I thought you had already decided. Is that not why we are still here?'

Rian said, 'I've given my assurance . . . ' he glanced at Kitty, ' . . . that I will not be supporting Heke, and I certainly won't be supporting the bloody British. But surely it wouldn't do any harm if we, well, kept an eye on things?'

'What sort of an eye?' Kitty asked suspiciously.

'Well, what if we just watched what was going on? From a safe distance, I mean. Then if anything untoward were to happen, we could . . . warn the appropriate people, perhaps?'

Kitty felt a flush of anger suffuse her face. 'You mean if Heke looks like he's losing, you'll give him a helping hand? Rian! You promised!'

'No, I said I won't be taking sides,' Rian insisted.

Kitty stood up so quickly she felt a momentary wash of dizziness. 'Oh, so you're just going to look down on everything like God from on high and decide who needs help here and who needs help there?' She was so angry she stamped her foot like a three-year-old. 'You can't do that, Rian! This isn't even your fight! What if you're captured? What if you're *shot*?'

'But I won't be,' Rian replied in a bewildered tone.

'How do you know that?'

'Because we won't be anywhere near the battlefield.'

'Oh, sometimes you're such a *fool*, Rian Farrell!' Kitty shouted, and stormed out of the room. They heard her pounding up the stairs and, a second later, a door slammed.

For a brief few seconds Rian wondered whether he actually was a fool, then quickly pushed the thought away. He glanced at his crew: half of them were looking at their boots and the rest were gazing steadfastly out the window. Daniel, his face red, clearly didn't know where to look.

Something occurred to Rian. 'I suppose I'd better ask you all whether you're with me or not. Are you?'

With no hesitation, the crew all confirmed that they were.

To Daniel, Rian said, 'What about you? Can you shoot straight?'

Daniel nodded. 'I'm a crack shot. I'm with you.'

Hawk fixed Rian with a long and level stare.

'Why does he need to shoot straight if we are only to be observers?'

'Well, we should be prepared,' Rian replied. 'Just in case.'

Hawk's face remained impassive. 'It would be a mistake to get involved to the point of firing weapons. Kitty is right.'

Rian slammed the arm of his chair with his fist. 'Christ almighty, Hawk. I can't just sit by and watch a wholesale slaughter, can you? You know it can't possibly be an even fight!'

'I am with you, Rian,' Hawk said calmly. 'Just be sure you know what you are doing. Do you?'

Rian slumped in his chair. 'No. Not really.'

They were all silent for moment, each contemplating what might lie ahead. Then Ropata wrinkled his nose. 'What's burning?'

'Daniel's scones,' Pierre replied with a smirk.

★ ★ ★

Paihia, March 1845

During the next few weeks HMS *Hazard* arrived and anchored in Kororareka Bay, carrying one-hundred-and-forty soldiers, sailors and marines. Two blockhouses were erected to accommodate a detachment from the 96th Regiment — one next to the flagstaff on Maiki Hill, and another equipped with three cannon further down the slopes — and a barracks was built in the town itself. Defences were also manned by two hundred armed townspeople, and volunteers from the merchant ships anchored in the bay. A one-gun battery was set up at Matauwhi Pass to cover the road leading into Kororareka from the south, and the town gaol and settler Joel Polack's house, hastily stockaded against accidental bombardment from the *Hazard*, were designated places of refuge for women and children.

Settlers too frightened to stay in Kororareka had fled, and those who had decided to sit it out had moved into the town: there had been a spate of robberies, allegedly committed by Kawiti's men, at outlying properties, and three houses at Okiato south of Kororareka had been plundered and burnt to the ground. Although Henry Williams had almost worn himself out trying unsuccessfully to broker a peace deal between Heke and the Crown, there seemed no chance now that the rebel Maoris would back down.

At Paihia, the dozen Maori children returned to Pukera because the mission simply could not accommodate them for any length of time, and because they were homesick. Tahi went back with them, but Haunui elected to stay at Paihia. Privately, Kitty suspected it was so he could keep an eye on Rian, although she never said so to either of them.

Hostilities still had not officially been declared, but the tension and expectation were immense, and nerves became more frayed by the day as people did their best to go about their normal business.

The crisis came on 3 March when a large party of Kawiti's men attacked a settler's property at Uruti Bay, only two miles south of

Kororareka. The house was destroyed and two horses were stolen from a nearby paddock. Troops from the *Hazard* set off in pursuit, and shots were exchanged, but the Maoris melted into the bush.

Then came another week of nothing other than reports of sightings of numbers of Kawiti's and Heke's men beyond the township. But when Bishop Selwyn arrived on 9 March aboard the sloop *Flying Fish*, he was told immediately by a lieutenant from the *Hazard* that an attack by the rebel Maoris was imminent.

At Paihia the next day the mood was one of intense foreboding. Those Maoris who were at the mission, adults and children alike, could not seem to settle: they talked well into the night and did not sleep. Nor could the missionaries settle. Rumours had been circulating for the past thirty-six hours that Heke would be attacking Kororareka some time in the early hours of the following morning.

That evening, Haunui, whom Rian had advised to stay behind at the mission, stood on the Paihia shore and gazed across the darkened bay towards Kororareka, wondering uneasily how his friends were faring.

★   ★   ★

When Rian had informed Kitty that afternoon that he and the crew were going to row across to Kororareka and offer their services as defenders, Kitty gaped at him in outright shock. But then he'd explained that if they approached the town

190

by any other route, they risked being shot at by trigger-happy troops and nervous settlers. Once they were safely in the town, they would slip away into the hills to find a suitable vantage point. At that point Kitty's shock had turned into anger, and she had insisted on accompanying him.

'No,' Rian said flatly. 'It's out of the question.'

They were standing in Sarah's garden, Kitty clutching a bowl of freshly picked peas, which, so far, she had only just managed to refrain from throwing at him.

'Why is it out of the question?'

He looked at her in genuine bewilderment. 'Because it won't be safe. There will be guns and things,' he added unnecessarily.

'Don't take that sarky tone with me, Rian Farrell!' Kitty snapped. 'If it's safe enough for you, why wouldn't it be safe for me?'

'Sweetheart, a battleground is no place for a woman.'

'But you won't be near any battlegrounds, you said so yourself!'

'I know I did, and I meant it. But the fighting could be very intense. You could be hit by a stray bullet.'

'So could you!'

'Not if I'm on a hill above the town.'

'So if it will be that safe for *you*, why can't *I* come?'

Rian's eyes narrowed. 'Because I've said no, and that's that.'

Kitty hurled the bowl of peas onto the hard-baked ground. The bowl shattered and bright green pods flew everywhere. 'No, that is *not* that, Rian! I'm coming with you and you can't stop me.'

Stepping over the broken bowl she marched off towards the house, so angry her eyes were stinging with tears. When would he ever understand that every time he did something deliberately dangerous it almost frightened the life out of her? Her head would fill with ghastly visions of him being badly hurt or even killed, and she didn't think she could bear it if either of those things happened. And he was such a stubborn man she was powerless to stop him — although she had certainly tried every method she could think of. So all there was left to do was go with him, whether he liked it or not. Then, if anything did go wrong, at least she would be at his side.

'You will stay *here*, Kitty Farrell!' Rian shouted, then started after her. 'I'll make you stay if it's the last thing I do!'

We'll see about that, Kitty thought grimly as she slammed the back door in his face.

★   ★   ★

Kororareka Bay was smooth and tranquil in the approaching dusk, as the *Katipo*'s rowboat glided through the shallows and grounded with a slight bump on the shingle beach. The atmosphere on board, however, was tense — partly because no one knew quite what to expect, but more as a result of the iciness between Rian and Kitty, who hadn't exchanged a

192

single word on the trip across the harbour.

They had pushed off from Te Ti Bay on the other side of the promontory from Paihia, as Rian hadn't wanted to have to explain his actions to Win Purcell or anyone else. So the crew had been the only witnesses to the tremendous shouting match that ensued when Kitty had calmly proceeded to climb into the boat. In the end, Rian had climbed in himself and ignored her, wanting very much to wring her lovely neck. He was terrified that something would happen to her, and had told her so over and over, but it hadn't seemed to make a jot of difference.

She ignored him even when they were all out of the boat again and had dragged it up Kororareka beach to a spot above the high-water mark, but by then he didn't want to argue with her any more; he only wanted to take her in his arms and tell her how much he loved her.

Every man on Kororareka's dusty main street seemed to be armed, and imperial troops were very much in evidence; so much so that, before Rian had even stepped off the sand, he and his men were stopped by soldiers at bayonet point. They wore blue forage caps, grey trousers and red jackets criss-crossed with bright white shoulder belts, which Rian thought was typically idiotic and English: the points where the belts converged on the chest and back made perfect targets.

'Identify yourselves,' one of the soldiers ordered tersely.

Rian did so, explaining that they had rowed

across from Paihia to help defend Kororareka.

'You live across the harbour? All of you?' the soldier asked.

'No, we're visitors to this part of the world. That's my schooner,' Rian said, pointing out towards the *Katipo*, resting small and black on the harbour, silhouetted before the sinking sun. 'I'm a trader.'

After several more questions they were escorted through the town and up to the blockhouse on the lower slopes of Maiki Hill. The building was constructed from thick split logs, on the outside still retaining their bark. Instead of windows there was a series of small loopholes in the walls through which muskets could be aimed at approaching enemy. The furnishings were minimal — rough benches along the sides and a single table on which sat several oil lamps, enough to dispel the gloom in the dark interior.

There, they were interrogated again by a pale, nervous-looking man who introduced himself as Lieutenant Barclay. Rian suspected the nervousness was caused by Ropata, who was carrying not only a musket but a knife and a small but lethal patu. Eventually Barclay seemed satisfied that Ropata was a 'friendly' Maori and relaxed slightly.

'And who is this?' he asked, indicating Kitty.

'My wife,' Rian said. 'I didn't want to leave her alone.'

The lieutenant nodded. 'There's a place for women and children. Polack's Stockade? You'll have passed it on the way through town.' He went to the door of the blockhouse and shouted, 'Corporal Shand!'

A burly-looking soldier appeared. 'Sir!'

'Take this woman to the stockade,' Barclay ordered.

Kitty's heart sank.

Rian, although delighted that Kitty would be somewhere relatively safe, was offended by the way the lieutenant had referred to her. 'Mrs Farrell,' he corrected sharply.

The lieutenant seemed pre-occupied. 'What? Oh, yes, I do beg your pardon, ma'am. Corporal Shand will escort you to the stockade. You'll find that most of the town's womenfolk are there already. And the children.'

'How long will I have to stay there?' she asked.

Barclay looked at her blankly, as though he wasn't quite sure what she meant. 'In the stockade? Well, until it's safe to come out. After the attack and we've driven the rebels off, I expect.'

Kitty had an unwelcome vision of being stuck in there for days while Rian raced about getting into God only knew what trouble. 'But I don't want to go in the stockade.'

Lieutenant Barclay shot Rian a glance that suggested that he, too, had had experience with a wilful and headstrong wife. To Kitty's chagrin, Rian made a sympathetic face.

'I think you'll find the arrangements comfortable enough,' Barclay said placatingly. 'And there are plenty of provisions.'

Kitty saw that she could hardly insist that she remain with her husband, not while he was busy despatching rebel Maoris, so she reluctantly went with Corporal Shand.

Joel Polack's house was indeed crowded with women and children, many of them in a high state of anxiety. Some of the children, however, seemed thoroughly excited, and were dashing about or peering expectantly through the windows: perhaps a little too excited, Kitty thought, as she noticed that one little boy had wet his trousers.

The corporal left her in the care of an older woman who introduced herself as Martha Geddes, whose home was at Matauwhi Bay. Her husband had insisted they come into town the morning before.

'It's very frightening, isn't it?' she said. 'We brought as many of our possessions with us as we could, but I'm afraid we still had to leave a lot behind. It's heart-breaking, really. If our house is burnt down we'll lose so much. Not to mention the house cow. We couldn't bring her, of course. Mr Geddes said just let her wander and she'll come home when she realises we've returned. If we have a home to return to, that is.'

As she prattled on, Kitty looked around the large parlour. Every available surface had possessions piled onto it and there were bags and small trunks all over the floor. The women in the room all looked at her expectantly, as though she might have some vital news to impart, and there were babies crying, one on the lap of a white-faced girl who didn't look much older than eighteen.

Mrs Geddes pulled a child off a windowsill and drew the curtain. 'They told us we should close the curtains at nightfall. To confuse the rebels,' she explained to Kitty.

'Who told you?' Kitty asked.

'Commander Robertson, from the *Hazard*. He said if there are no lights then the Maoris won't know where to attack.' Mrs Geddes made a disparaging face. 'I'm not so sure about that myself. I've lived here for five years and I'd lay money on those Maoris knowing the town like the backs of their hands, whether it's dark or not. They've probably been shopping at Clayton's trading store for the past year.'

Kitty made a noncommittal sound, even though she agreed: Heke and his people were probably up in the hills even now waiting for the right time to strike, and they would know exactly where to go if they wanted to come into the town. Haunui — who seemed to have rather a lot of information for someone who professed to have no connections whatsoever with Heke — had been of the opinion that Heke was probably only going to attempt to cut down the flagstaff again, but Kitty and almost everyone else at Paihia thought it a reasonable assumption that, if the British troops fought back, then a battle would ensue. They clearly thought so here at Kororareka, too.

Martha Geddes said, 'I'll introduce you to the other ladies, and then I think supper should be ready. It will be a bit of a pot-luck, I'm afraid. Now, I'm sorry but where did you say you were from?'

'We're only visiting the Bay of Islands, actually.'

'Oh, what terrible bad luck!' Mrs Geddes exclaimed.

'Yes. My husband is a trader, he owns the schooner out in the harbour. The one with the black hull and the red stripe?'

'Oh yes, we were admiring that only the other day.'

'And then this trouble blew up and my husband thought we should offer our help. Well, that he and his crew should.' Kitty didn't want to tell too much of a lie; she quite liked Martha Geddes.

Mrs Geddes bent down and, with her handkerchief, wiped butter and a smattering of breadcrumbs off a small child's face. 'Good to see you, Letitia,' she said to a woman who was presumably the child's mother. 'Did you have a terrible rush to get in? Yes, so did we, in the end.' She turned back to Kitty. 'I'm sorry, dear. Well, that was very generous of your husband. Do you sail with him often?'

'Oh, yes, constantly.'

Mrs Geddes looked mildly shocked. 'Constantly? Just you and him and, er, the crew?'

'That's right.'

'How absolutely fascinating. Letitia, did you hear that?'

Kitty stifled a sigh — clearly all the women confined to Polack's Stockade would soon know about her unusual living arrangements. She wondered how long she should leave it before she attempted to slip away.

★ ★ ★

During the night a thick fog rolled off the sea and over Kororareka, and by four o'clock the next morning the town was blanketed in a thick haze: Hone Heke could not have been more pleased.

While he and his party made their way stealthily up through the scrub towards the flagstaff on Maiki Hill, Kawiti and one of his commanders, Pumuka, were leading two hundred men along the Matauwhi road towards the southern end of town. Approaching them through the fog from the opposite direction were forty or so sailors and marines from the *Hazard*, led by Commander Robertson. When Kawiti's advance party reached the gun at Matuawhi Pass and attempted to disable it, the weapon was fired and the escaping gunners ran back to warn Robertson that the rebels had attacked. When Robertson's men encountered Kawiti's main party, they saw that they were heavily outnumbered. The fighting was fierce: shouts, the clash of sword against patu, and the flat rattle of muskets rolled through the surrounding hills. Robertson was seriously wounded and Pumuka was killed.

At the same time, warriors from the Nga Puhi sub-tribe Te Kapotai had settled into the hills and were firing down at the town. When the sun began to rise shortly after, it became horribly clear to the armed settlers and troops that the flagstaff had been felled for a fourth time and that the upper blockhouse had been taken by the rebels.

All of this was very clearly audible from the

interior of Polack's Stockade, where only the youngest of the children had managed to sleep. As the battles progressed and the minutes passed, Kitty grew more and more frantic about Rian. Finally, unable to sit still any longer, she ran out of Polack's house and across to the stockade gate.

'*Stop!*' A soldier grabbed her arm and swung her around. 'Stay inside!' he yelled in her face. 'Get back inside!'

Kitty ducked away from him, stumbled, then righted herself as he made another lunge for her, shouting at her not to panic but to go back inside.

But she slipped through the gate; then, pausing for only a second to find her bearings, raced along the side of the stockade in the direction she knew would take her into the hills. Rian would be up there somewhere watching, she knew he would.

Holding up her skirts so she could run faster, she dodged through someone's vegetable garden and across a paddock in which a cow stood calmly chewing its cud despite the continual crack of muskets. Suddenly the roar of the *Hazard*'s guns joined the din, and Kitty involuntarily ducked. When she encountered a fence, she stopped, bundled up her skirts around her thighs, set her foot on the middle rail and climbed it. There was a sharp ripping sound as she jumped down the other side, but she didn't even stop to see what had torn.

She sped on, her hand clamped against her side now where a sharp stitch was forming. The grass was wet from early morning dew and she slipped and fell several times, but she refused to slow down. By the time she had reached the top of the first scrubby hill above Kororareka she was gasping for breath. She rested with her hands on her knees for several minutes, then straightened up and squinted down at the town.

There wasn't much to see: most of the troops and settlers seemed to be under cover, although she glimpsed the odd flash of red as soldiers ran from one shelter to another, and she knew that the Maoris would be even more skilfully concealed. Puffs of smoke came from the guns on the *Hazard*, followed a few seconds later by the actual sound of the guns firing. She saw that, once again, there was no flagstaff on Maiki Hill.

When Kitty had regained her breath, she turned and half-ran, half-slid down the other side of the hill and into a patch of bush, dim and still damp from the night. Once in among the trees and low scrub, she had to slow down to avoid getting caught up in vines and fallen branches. She wondered if she should look for a track, then changed her mind; her progress would be faster, but then again she might just meet someone she didn't want to meet. And the hill she was aiming for hadn't seemed too far away. It seemed the most likely spot Rian would have chosen — directly above the town but not too close, and crowned with a stand of totora for concealment.

She stopped: that was, of course, providing Rian and the crew had actually left the town.

What if they hadn't been able to? What if he had been shot and was lying down there somewhere, bleeding and in pain, wondering where she was? So far as he was aware she was still inside Polack's Stockade, and surely if he had been wounded he would have sent Hawk or Ropata or someone to fetch her?

She turned back, then hesitated again and, in frustration, swore aloud. It seemed very unlikely in all the confusion of the fighting, or even under the cover of the mist during the night, that Rian and the crew would not have been able to slip away. No, he would be up the hills somewhere, she was sure of it.

Halfway along the ridge of the next hill, she stepped suddenly out of the bush onto a rough track and recoiled in fright when she saw that she wasn't the only person on it. About twenty yards ahead stood a horse, and on its bare back sat a young Maori boy. He looked about eleven or twelve years old, was dressed only in a pair of ragged trousers, and was staring straight at her. There was a musket balanced across the horse's withers.

For what seemed an age, neither of them moved. Then the horse's ears twitched and the boy turned the horse away. He glanced briefly back at Kitty over his shoulder, then trotted around the corner of the track, his skinny frame bouncing loosely to the horse's gait.

Her heart still thudding wildly, Kitty moved off the track and back under cover of the bush. If she were to meet a group of soldiers she could say she had panicked at the sound of musket fire, run away and become lost, but if she walked into a party of Heke's or Kawiti's men she could well be taken prisoner. She doubted that she would be harmed, however, as a Pakeha woman would be seen as extremely useful should the need arise to negotiate.

She pushed on, climbing over fallen branches and moss-covered logs, slipping in damp mulch, snagging her wretched skirt every few yards it seemed, and swearing in a manner that would have made Sharkey proud. It wasn't until she paused at the base of the next hill to take a drink from a small stream that she realised she could no longer hear the sounds of battle. Listening intently, she turned in a full circle, but there was only the burble of the stream and the clear, ringing call of a tui in the trees above her.

Was she lost? She couldn't be, surely? The hairs on her arms rose and a flutter of cold panic filled her belly. Then she told herself not to be so silly; she hadn't even come that far yet. Or had she? She looked up to gauge the position of the sun, but couldn't see it through the canopy above her. Well, that was easily fixed — she would climb again until she could.

She looked back at the precipitously steep hill she had just negotiated, noting the deep gouges in the leaf litter where she had slipped and slid her way down, and mentally shook her head. She crossed the stream, shivering slightly as the cold water seeped inside her boots, and set off across the small clearing beyond it, heading for the slope leading up to the next hill.

But she had gone only five yards when suddenly there was nothing beneath her feet and she was falling.

8

She landed heavily on her side, and lay motionless with her eyes squeezed shut until she was sure she wasn't going to fall any further. Then she opened them to encounter an enormous weta only inches from her face, its eyes bulging from its revolting, shiny black head. Shrieking, she scrambled away.

But it wasn't the weta that made her heart almost leap out of her throat — it was the human skull upon which it was squatting. She crawled as far from it as possible, then sat back on her haunches and breathed deeply until her pulse started to steady again.

When she felt a little more composed, she checked herself for damage. Pulling up her skirts she saw that she had a large purple graze on her left thigh, scratches on her calf, and a cut on her right knee that was bleeding quite heavily. Her left hip hurt and so did her elbow, but she didn't think they were broken, and when she wiped her nose on the back of her hand there was blood. As soon as she saw it she realised she could taste it as well, in the back of her throat.

She gripped the hem of her petticoat and pulled, intending to tear off a strip to use as a bandage. But the stitching in the seam was a lot tougher than she expected, and after a lot of fruitless tugging and twisting she resorted to poking a piece of sharp stick through the fabric and ripping it, and even then it didn't tear off neatly. She took what she had and tied it around her knee, where it immediately turned bright red. Watching the stain spread like a lush red blossom, she noticed with a stab of dismay that her bangle had gone from her forearm.

Willing herself not to cry, she took a deep, wavering breath and made a thorough examination of her surroundings. She appeared to be at the bottom of a tomo, the word the Maoris gave to an underground cave. About twelve feet above her she could see a small patch of sky, partially obscured by the fallen branches and fronds of nikau that had concealed the opening. The hole she had fallen through wasn't very wide, and a lot smaller than the cave itself. The ground beneath her was damp and scattered with rocks, and rotting leaves and debris that had fallen in over time. She was surprised she hadn't hurt herself more when she'd landed. It was so quiet she could hear the blood pulsing in her ears, and from somewhere in the dark recesses of the cave she could hear the drip of water. The cave smelled wet, even there under the opening, and small ferns had taken hold between the rocks and in tiny fissures in the walls. The walls themselves sloped inward as they rose, and, with a sinking heart, Kitty could see that climbing them would be impossible. She was trapped like a crayfish in a pot.

Overwhelmed with sudden panic she screamed for someone to help her, and the echo of her voice bouncing off the cave walls almost deafened her so that she had to clap her hands over her ears. She closed her eyes for what felt like a very long time, but when she opened them again nothing had changed.

A second later she almost jumped out of her skin when she heard a sharp little scratching noise, but it was only the weta's claws as it climbed ponderously off its perch. The skull looked weathered, with long yellow teeth that appeared too large for the jaws, and there was moss growing across the back of it, like fuzzy green hair. The skeleton was tall and seemed to be intact, except for a break in one of the thighs, the bones arranged more or less as nature had intended. There were shreds of rotted fabric clinging to it, some little round things nearby that looked like metal buttons and the feet bones were still inside collapsed leather boots.

Then something inside the rib cage caught her eye and, moving slowly because her hip and elbow were beginning to throb now, she stepped gingerly across the slippery rocks and peered down.

The object was an ornate silver cross inlaid with ivory and it looked familiar, like the sort of thing a clergyman might wear. Where had she seen it before? Then, with a horrible jolt, she knew — it was the cross Uncle George had habitually worn. Tahi had been right: his father was under the ground. Her mouth opened in silent shock and she stared at the skeleton, realising that the mystery of her uncle's disappearance had finally been solved.

But only if she found a way out of the tomo herself. She glanced up at the opening, then at the skeleton, then back up again.

Then, finally, she started to cry. Not for her lost bangle or for miserable, dead Uncle George, but for herself.

* * *

At midday, acting commander Lieutenant Phillpotts made the decision to evacuate all women and children from Kororareka to HMS *Hazard* and to the other ships anchored just off shore; the fighting had died down for the time being and the Maoris had not yet invaded the town, but it seemed inevitable.

Observing from a hillside above Kororareka as women and children filed out of Polack's Stockade, Rian began to grow more and more uneasy as Kitty's familiar figure failed to appear.

'I can't see her,' he said to Hawk, and passed him the spyglass. 'You have a look.'

Hawk raised the glass to his eye, but half a minute later said, 'No, I cannot see her either.'

'Are they all out yet?' Mick asked, watching the scene below. 'Maybe there are more to come.'

They waited until it seemed that the last woman and child had emerged, but there was still no sign of Kitty.

Rian snapped shut the spyglass. 'Right, we're going down.'

They had been up in the hills since just after the fighting had begun at Matuawhi Pass earlier that morning. It had been a simple task to slip away from the town under cover of the sea mist, and they had been able to watch almost everything as it unfolded below them. It had been clear to them that Heke's men positioned on Maiki Hill had lost their enthusiasm once they had felled the flagstaff, as there had been only sporadic activity from them since. The sounds of battle from Matuawhi Pass had ended hours ago and the British troops involved had returned to the town. The Kapotai firing from the heights behind Kororareka also seemed to have quietened, so Rian wondered whether the fight was in fact over. But if it was, why had the order been given to evacuate the women and children?

At the gate to the stockade he grabbed the arm of a jittery-looking soldier.

'Have you seen a woman named Kitty Farrell?' he demanded. 'Tallish with black hair? Very pretty. Are the women all out?'

The young soldier, his eyes darting about as though expecting a horde of marauding Maoris to appear at any moment, jerked away from Rian and shook his head.

Exasperated, Rian snapped, 'No you haven't seen her, or no they're not all out yet?'

Sensing his impatience, the soldier replied quickly, 'The women and kids are all out, they're going out to the ships. Didn't you hear the order? You civilians are supposed to be going as well.' And then he darted off.

Hawk said to Rian, 'Why are the men also being evacuated?' But Rian was already walking away, through the stockade gate.

They checked every room in Joel Polack's

house, but Kitty was nowhere to be seen.

'What about the women?' Pierre suggested as they came out. 'Ask the women. They might know where she be.'

On the beach, among the throng of wounded soldiers, and women and children surrounded by piles of belongings, waiting to be collected by ships' boats, Rian finally found someone with news of Kitty.

'Yes,' said Martha Geddes, eyeing Gideon with poorly disguised alarm, 'I spent some time talking with her. She was in the house until just after dawn and then she ran out like a thing possessed. I tried to stop her but I couldn't, I'm afraid. Are you her husband?'

'Yes. And she didn't say where she was going?'

'No, all she said was something about 'I have to find him'. You don't have a son, do you? She seemed very upset. Mind you, we all were. The noise of the battle was terrific.'

They hurried back to Kororareka's main street, where Rian reluctantly admitted to Hawk, 'Oh, Christ, I think she might have gone out to look for me.'

Hawk nodded.

'Rian? I think that redcoat might be wantin' to talk to you,' Mick warned.

They all turned and stared at the soldier trotting towards them. He looked exhausted, the knees of his trousers were caked with dirt and there was a large tear in the sleeve of his jacket.

'I hear you're looking for someone, a woman?' the soldier said, panting.

'Yes, my wife,' Rian replied eagerly. 'Tall with

210

black hair. Have you seen her?'

'A lady of that description left the stockade at about six this morning. In a hell of a hurry, she was. I couldn't stop her. She was wearing . . .' He screwed up his face as he tried to remember.

' . . . a pale blue gown,' Rian finished for him.

'Yes, that was it!'

Pierre asked, 'Did you see which way she go?'

The soldier pointed towards the stockade gate. 'I tried to stop her there. It weren't safe, you see. But she ran off, up the side of the fence there and round the back. And then I got fired on and I couldn't go after her.'

Rian looked in the direction in which the soldier was pointing, but Daniel was already off and running.

★   ★   ★

Having rather tersely told Daniel to cool his heels and wait until he was given orders before he made a move of any sort, Rian led his crew through the handful of rough streets that made up Kororareka until they came to the last few cottages.

'Spread out,' he ordered. 'It looks like she might have been heading for the hills.' Where I said I would be, he thought angrily. This is my fault and if she's been hurt I will *never* forgive myself.

It was Pierre who found the small piece of pale blue fabric caught on the fence rail.

'Rian!' he called. 'She go this way!'

They drew together and stood scanning the

211

hills above them, hoping to see a flash of blue or even the wave of a hand, but there was nothing.

They climbed through the scrub, calling out every few yards.

'She would have been heading up and back slightly, wouldn't she?' Rian said, talking as much to himself as to Hawk. 'I think she would have been looking for somewhere with a good view but out of sight. She knew what I was intending to do so she wouldn't have gone too far into the bush. Would she?'

Hawk patted Rian's arm as reassuringly as he could. 'She is not a stupid woman, Rian. And she is not unfamiliar with this sort of terrain. She will have been careful.'

Rian wiped the sweat off his face with his sleeve then stood with his hands on his hips, his shoulders slumped and his head down. Hawk thought he had never seen a man look so dejected.

'Christ almighty, Hawk, I don't know what I'll do if — '

'We will find her,' Hawk interrupted, then set off again.

At the summit of the hill they heard a loud explosion and paused briefly to look back down at the town. Polack's Stockade seemed to have blown up; black smoke poured out of the house, partly obscuring the miniature figures scurrying madly around the conflagration.

'*Mon Dieu*, that is where the ammunition be,' Pierre muttered.

'Lucky they got the women and kids out, so it is,' Mick observed.

As they watched, the house next door caught alight, then the one next to that. Soon, all Kororareka would be aflame.

They spread out again and descended into the bush. Once they had entered the dense undergrowth Rian's heart began to grow cold. If she had become lost in bush like this, she might have wandered for miles. His voice was becoming hoarse from calling Kitty's name, and he knew the others were having the same problem because there was a lot of throat-clearing and spitting going on.

At the summit of the next hill they discovered that a track ran along the ridge and Hawk squatted to scrutinise the leaf litter and soil for footprints.

He straightened up. 'There are tracks here, small. They could be hers.'

'How fresh are they?' Rian asked.

Hawk shrugged. 'Four, five hours? These tracks of the horse are the same, but with some more recent.'

Rian frowned. 'She was on horseback?' He moved over to Hawk and stared at the ground. 'Was it shod?'

'No.'

'And it still isn't,' Mick said quietly.

They all looked up then and saw the boy on horseback a short distance down the track, a musket almost as tall as he was pointed directly at them. No one moved for a second. Then, slowly, they all drew their weapons. The boy remained motionless, the barrel of the musket unwavering.

Deliberately, Rian slid his pistol back into his belt. 'Have you seen a Pakeha woman?' he called in Maori, keeping his voice as neutral as possible.

The boy ignored the question and responded with one of his own. 'Are you the Queen's soldiers?'

'No,' Rian replied. Not trusting himself to get the words right, he said to Ropata, 'Tell him who we are and what we want.'

Ropata responded in Maori, 'No, we are not the Queen's soldiers and we are not armed settlers. We take no sides. We are searching for a Pakeha woman. She has black hair and a blue gown. She is alone.'

The boy lowered his musket an inch and nodded. 'I saw such a woman today. Up here.'

'This morning?' Rian asked, looking at Ropata for confirmation.

Ropata's eyes never left the boy's. 'Today? How many hours after sunrise?'

The horse impatiently stamped a hoof. Eventually the boy said, 'By the time the dew had dried.'

'Probably around nine o'clock,' Ropata relayed to Rian.

'Ask him which way she went.'

Ropata did, and the boy pointed with his musket.

Rian raised his hand in a gesture of thanks and turned away, eager to get going. The others filed after him, but Ropata waited, his eyes still on the rebel boy, for surely that was what he was, to make sure he didn't put a musket ball in their backs.

★　★　★

Half an hour later they crested the next ridge.

'She can't be far away,' Rian muttered yet again, his gaze following the slope of the hill down until it reached a small stream some distance below, barely visible between the trees.

'Which way?' Hawk asked, watching Rian carefully. He was becoming worried; the expression on his friend's face was growing increasingly anxious as they climbed further into the hills, and Hawk understood why. If Kitty had indeed come this far, she could be anywhere within a five-mile radius of rugged terrain covered with bush, hidden ravines and deep gullies. They might already have gone past her, or she could be miles away in the opposite direction.

'Will we go down for a drink? I'm gasping,' Mick announced, and set off down the steep hill.

He evidently soon lost his footing and they heard him cursing as he slid and slithered his way down. Then came a long moment of silence during which they wondered if he had perhaps knocked himself out, then his disembodied voice came echoing back up the gully.

'*Rian?*'

'*What?*' Rian shouted back.

'*There's something down here!*'

Rian hesitated only a moment before hurling himself down the slope, dodging around tree trunks and crashing through low branches and undergrowth. He was only part of the way down when he slid into Mick crouching over

215

something on the ground.

Mick grunted as he was knocked forward onto his hands and knees. 'It's hers, isn't it?' he asked as Rian snatched up the blue bangle half-buried in the leaf litter.

'*Kitty?*' Rian shouted. '*Kitty!!*'

They heard the undergrowth thrashing as the others scrambled down to join them.

'You've found her?' Daniel demanded, scraps of nikau leaf stuck in his hair and his eyes wide.

Rian held up the bangle. 'It's hers.'

Daniel knew it was Kitty's — he had noticed she was wearing it on the boat coming over from Paihia, just as he noticed every single thing about her every day.

'Quiet!' Hawk demanded.

Rian stared at him. 'What is it?'

'I hear something. Listen.'

They all strained to pick up whatever it was Hawk had heard, and it came again, a muffled, thin cry from somewhere below them.

Rian launched himself down the hill, shouting Kitty's name repeatedly and coming to an abrupt halt when he slid into the stream at the bottom of the gully. The others clambered down after him, then stood motionless like a small flock of wading birds, waiting for the cry to come again.

It did, but down here it was much more difficult to pick up the direction from which it was coming.

Rian splashed across the stream and stood at the edge of the clearing on the other side with his head cocked, waiting. The sound came again and he recognised her voice immediately.

Looking wildly around, he cried, 'Where the fuck is she?'

And then he saw it, a depression in the ground a few yards away. But he had taken only a few steps towards it when he found himself being forcefully tackled and knocked flat.

'What the hell are you doing!' he cried as he hit out at Ropata, whose arms were wrapped around his legs.

Ropata dodged the blow and sat up. 'I think it is the entrance to a tomo. If you go too close it may fall in. On top of her.'

Rian stared at him for a second, then rolled onto his belly and started inching his way towards the depression. As he neared he saw that it was indeed a hole.

He thrust his head over the rim and there she was, standing in a pool of sunlight surrounded by darkness, gazing up at him. She had been crying and her face was dirty and there was blood on her lip, and she was the most beautiful thing he had ever seen.

Fear and relief washing over him, he barked, 'What the *hell* are you doing down there?'

'Baking a cake,' she shot back. 'What do you think I'm doing?' Then her face crumpled. 'I've been stuck down here for hours, Rian. And I think I've found Uncle George.'

Part Two

The Found Child

9

Auckland, 13 March 1845

It's more settled than I thought it would be. You know, for a new town,' Kitty remarked to Simon, who was leaning on the ship's rail beside her.

Before them lay the short sweep of Commercial Bay, the principal water frontage to the town of Auckland. The bay itself was very picturesque, though the buildings that lined it had all the scruffy and untidy hallmarks of a rapidly established settlement, and the beach was crowded with ships' boats, waka, barrels, crates and stacks of timber. Behind the town rose a series of rolling, fern- and bush-covered hills, and in the middle distance, a range of low mountains that were curiously flat across their tops. Puia, Haunui had said they were called — volcanoes. Kitty sincerely hoped that they were all extinct.

Simon agreed. 'And it's growing by the day, it seems. I was here only last October, and I can see already that more buildings have gone up since then. Still, it is the capital, I suppose.'

'It's a pretty spot, isn't it?'

Simon pulled a doubtful face. 'From here it is, yes. It's not quite so pretty close up.'

They were aboard the government brig *Victoria*, along with approximately a hundred refugees from the sacked town of Kororareka.

Behind them at various points in the Waitemata Harbour were four more ships carrying the remainder of Kororareka's evacuated residents — almost five hundred in total — and the imperial troops who had fought there.

When the powder magazine had exploded in the basement of Polack's Stockade and it became clear that almost all the ammunition available for the town's defence had gone up with one very loud bang, Lieutenant Phillpotts had decided, to the anger of most of its inhabitants, to evacuate the whole settlement. In the end, though, they grudgingly consented to board the waiting ships; several buildings were already ablaze and everyone assumed that Heke and his followers would soon enter the town itself.

Indeed, Rian, Kitty and the crew only just made it back to the *Katipo*'s rowboat before the Maoris swept down from the hills. By the time they had rowed out to the middle of the harbour, Kororareka was completely ablaze, black smoke curling into the sky and drifting across the hills behind and to the south of the town. They sat and watched; then, when there was little left to see, they continued across to Paihia in the wake of the ships carrying the evacuees.

At Paihia the beach bustled with activity as the missionaries, together with their colleagues from Waimate, worked to sort the seriously injured from the merely frightened and exhausted, and administer spiritual succour and what medical care they could. The overriding sentiment was one of stunned disbelief: now that Heke's attack had actually happened, and with such utter destruction, the residents of Kororareka were overwhelmed. Many had lost their homes and their possessions, and all had lost any sense of security they might have once had. The only slightly cheerful person was Sarah, when Kitty presented her with the cross she had taken from the skeleton in the tomo.

'I'm truly sorry, Aunt Sarah,' Kitty said, 'but I really do think it was Uncle George.'

'Lying there all this time?' Sarah marvelled as she slipped the cross into the pocket of her apron and tried to arrange her features into an expression suggestive of someone who had just received terrible news. 'So close and we had no idea. He must have been running away.'

Kitty thought so, too, and for a moment imagined her uncle stumbling through the bush, gasping for breath, terrified that Tupehu would catch up with him, only to plunge into what would become his own grave. He must have lain there for days, perhaps crying out in fear and pain, perhaps waiting in silence for death to claim him.

'I wonder how he got across to Kororareka?' she said, but Sarah had already turned away and was tending to a woman with a toddler wailing monotonously with exhaustion.

That evening Kitty and Rian had the worst argument of their married lives when Rian ordered Kitty to go to Auckland for the duration of the war that he was convinced would follow the sacking of Kororareka. They had argued upstairs in their bedroom at Sarah's house, downstairs in the parlour (to the horrified fascination of Ngahuia and Rangimarie), and outside on the verandah — from where they could see across the bay the orange glow that was Kororareka still burning — until Kitty finally, and very reluctantly, agreed.

So at ten o'clock that night, Rian arranged for Kitty's passage to Auckland on one of the evacuee ships, and also for Simon's, whom he had coerced into accompanying her, insisting that it wasn't seemly for a woman to travel alone aboard a ship also carrying soldiers. Kitty thought that was a lot of rubbish, but she suspected Simon badly needed a break from the stress of the past few months, so she had agreed.

The next morning a few of Kororareka's residents returned to their smouldering homes to salvage whatever they could, while Henry Williams and Bishop Selwyn also went across to recover the dead and give them Christian burials. Kawiti's people were still in evidence, and even helped the settlers transport their salvaged possessions out to the ships. Then, inexplicably, Lieutenant Phillpotts ordered the *Hazard* to fire her guns into the town to deter looters, even though there were both settlers and rebel Maoris on the streets. As utu for this unchivalrous behaviour, Heke ordered most of the buildings still standing to be destroyed, although the Anglican and Catholic churches and Bishop Pompallier's house were to be left untouched. The evacuee ships sailed for Auckland later that day.

Now, Kitty shifted her weight from her left hip

224

to her right to ease the stiffness developing there. She was bruised from her left ankle all the way up to her waist and her elbow still throbbed, but Mrs Williams had examined her and declared that nothing appeared to be broken.

'Are there any decent stores here?' Kitty asked.

'Depends what you're looking for,' Simon replied.

'Nothing, really. I'm just wondering what on earth we're going to do. We could be here for weeks.'

Privately, Simon thought it more likely to be months. 'There's quite an active social scene, so I've heard. Not that I've ever been invited to be part of it, but Bishop Selwyn is apparently quite the social butterfly.'

The *Victoria*'s anchor chain gave a prolonged and deafening rattle as it paid out, and the ship turned slightly as her weight settled.

'We must be getting ready to disembark.' Kitty pointed towards the shore. 'What's that building with the flag?'

Simon followed the line of her arm. 'That's Government House, on Waterloo Quadrant.'

'And that two-storeyed building just below it?'

'I think that might be the Royal Hotel. I'm not sure. But that building down on the flat is the Commercial Hotel, and the one to the left of it is the Exchange, and the one further along is the Victoria. There are plenty of grog-shops here, too.'

'That's a lot of hotels,' Kitty remarked. She pointed again. 'Is that a stone building in the middle there? The big one? Aunt Sarah said all the buildings in Auckland were made of wood.'

Simon squinted. 'No, it's brick, but there are plenty of stone buildings. The brick one is Gibson & Mitchell's store.'

'That sounds promising,' Kitty said. 'What do they sell?'

'I don't know, I've never been in there. There are more shops on Shortland Street as well, the main street.'

Kitty frowned. 'But where are all the houses? Where do people live?'

'Everywhere, really. On Queen Street — that one going up the hill? And on Albert Street, and up near the barracks on Britomart Point. There are also quite a lot of homes at Official Bay. You can't see it from here, it's around the point.'

'Where do the well-to-do people live?'

'Official Bay, mostly. Or so I was told.'

Kitty grinned. 'Oh dear, that's a shame, I seem to have misplaced my 'at home' cards.' She indicated the shoreline around Commercial Bay. 'And are all those buildings warehouses and what have you?'

'No, most of them are shops, businesses and professional rooms. That one you can see just on the left of Gibson & Mitchell's is the theatre.'

'Really?' Kitty said, surprised. 'That's quite civilised, isn't it?'

'This *is* the capital,' Simon reminded her, '*and* the social hub of New Zealand. All the smart and cultured people live here.'

'Don't be sarcastic, Simon, it doesn't suit you.

What's that building up there? The really big one on the ridge?'

'St Paul's Church. Opened the year before last by Bishop Selwyn himself, no less.'

'It looks rather large for a town of this size,' Kitty remarked.

'Well, they say there are over three-and-a-half thousand living here now.'

'It's quite grand, isn't it?'

Simon looked disapproving. 'It's grandiose. But you know what Anglicans are like — everything has to be wildly ambitious.'

Kitty eyed her friend, noting that he needed a haircut, that the collar of his shirt was slightly grubby, and that his normally cheerful face was pale and weary-looking. Only half in jest, she said, 'That isn't a note of censure I hear in your voice, is it?'

Turning to face her, he blurted, 'Yes, it is, actually. I've had enough, Kitty.'

Surprised by his vehemence, Kitty waited for him to say something else, but in silence he turned once again towards the shore. Suspecting she knew what was at the root of his distress, she prompted gently, 'Of the Church Missionary Society, or of religion in general? Or of God Himself?'

Simon said nothing for a long moment, and when he did, Kitty was alarmed to hear tears in his voice. 'I don't think I've had enough of God. I've questioned my faith over and over and I think it's still as strong as it was. I *think* it is. But I'm fed up to my back teeth with the CMS. The missionaries always have to be right, don't they?

Right about what's best for people regardless of any other beliefs those people might have, always making moral judgements about what's right and what's wrong.' He turned to face her again, lowering his voice as several people had come to stand at the rail nearby. 'But it's the same no matter what religion you belong to, I'm sure of it. I've seen it. The Catholics are just as bad as the Protestants. They're all right and everyone else is wrong, and God help you if you don't or won't think the same way they do. Why is there such a *drive* to interfere with other people's lives, Kitty? Why can't they be happy just to live their own and leave other people be? I don't think it's right, and I don't think *they're* right. Not any more.'

'The Society, you mean?'

'Yes,' Simon answered bluntly. Then he sighed, partly in frustration and partly in defeat. 'I think it's time I left the CMS, Kitty. I don't think I can continue to do good works as a missionary. I'd rather just get on with living my life and keeping my faith the way I think I should.'

Kitty wondered how much of this had to do with Simon's very private preference for loving men rather than women. She wondered if he was lonely. But because she knew him well, and knew what an honest, honourable and decent man he was, she was sure he would never let his private needs get in the way of his faith.

'*Can* you leave the Society?' she asked. 'Officially?'

'Yes, or I can leave the same way you did,' Simon said. 'I can get on a ship and sail away.'

She looked at him admiringly. 'But would you? It would be a momentous thing to do, Simon. They'd never have you back. You'd definitely be burning your bridges.'

The corner of his mouth twitched. 'My britches?'

Kitty laughed. 'Your *bridges*, and you know very well that's what I said.'

There was another rattle of chains as the first of the *Victoria*'s boats was lowered into the slate-coloured waters of the harbour. There was no wharf, so everyone and everything would have to be rowed ashore, and the passengers had all been advised that the wounded would be disembarked first.

An hour or so later, Kitty and Simon stood on the beach alongside Kitty's small travelling trunk. They had been told to find private accommodation: as a woman with no children, Kitty was not eligible for one of the empty houses being made available to the evacuees.

'Any ideas about where you'd like to stay?' Simon asked.

'We're not refugees so we'll have to pay,' Kitty said, adding sourly, 'I'm only a wife whose husband doesn't think she can look after herself.'

Simon gave her a look. 'That's good, coming from a woman who recently spent six hours in an underground cave, calling for help and with nothing but a skeleton and a weta for company.'

Kitty ignored him. 'I think we should enquire about boarding houses. If there are any.'

'I'm sure there are,' Simon said, stooping to

hoist Kitty's trunk onto his shoulder and grunting with the effort. 'What have you got in here?'

'Clothes, bits and pieces,' Kitty replied as she hooked her arm through the strap of Simon's knapsack. 'My God, what have *you* got in *here?*'

'Books, my Bible, a spare shirt. My shaving things,' he said as an afterthought.

'Well, come on then, let's go and find somewhere before they all get taken,' Kitty grumbled, and headed off towards the unpaved road that was Auckland's main thoroughfare.

His boots kicking up sand as he went, Simon trudged behind her, dodging knots of people and their belongings on the crowded beach. They crossed the street and stopped at the first hotel they came to, the Commercial, and Simon went inside to ask about accommodation, leaving Kitty standing guard over their luggage.

He was back a few minutes later, clutching a grubby scrap of paper. 'They have rooms in there, but I thought it looked a bit rough. But the proprietor gave me the names of a couple of women who run boarding houses suitable, according to him, for the 'needs of a respectable lady'.'

'So ladies only?' Kitty asked.

'I imagine so.' Simon slipped the piece of paper into his pocket.

'But where will you stay?'

'I'll find somewhere. I stayed out at St John's College last time I was here, but I might try a hotel this time.'

The first boarding house Simon and Kitty

tried was already full, but the second, in Eden Crescent, had a room available. The landlady, Mrs Fleming, was a short, stringy woman with very thick spectacles.

'Only for ladies, mind,' she said. She gave Simon a hard look. '*Single* ladies.' Then she glanced at Kitty's left hand. 'Or are you married?'

'Well, actually, Mrs Fleming, I am,' Kitty explained, 'but my husband is up in the Bay of Islands at the moment. He's a trader, the captain of a schooner, and he's sent me down here for safety. The sacking of Kororareka, you know.'

Mrs Fleming's hands flew to her small, rather pinched mouth. 'Oh, my Lord, yes, that was a terrible business, wasn't it? We heard the day before yesterday. And now I hear that John Heke is on his way down here, with more rebels than you can count and every one of them armed with the latest in muskets and those dreadful poisonous spears they carry.'

'Is he?' Simon asked interestedly.

Mrs Fleming nodded vigorously, the lace flaps on her house cap wobbling in sympathy. 'So they're saying. But I for one refuse to leave Auckland. I will *not* be driven off by a band of bloodthirsty Maoris, even if they do number in the thousands.'

'Good for you,' Kitty said. 'Now, about this room?'

But something had occurred to Mrs Fleming. 'Excuse me, but if your husband is fighting in the Bay of Islands, who is this gentleman?'

Simon took off his hat. 'My name is Simon

231

Bullock, Mrs Fleming. I am a missionary at Waimate — '

'Waimate?' Mrs Fleming interrupted. 'That's the mission at Paihia, isn't it?'

'No, Paihia has a mission of its own. Waimate is a little further inland.'

'Have you all come down to Auckland, then, all the missionaries? I can't say I blame you,' Mrs Fleming said.

'No,' Simon answered patiently. 'I believe almost everyone has stayed at Paihia and Waimate. But Mrs Farrell's husband, a personal friend, asked me to accompany her to Auckland.'

'You would know Bishop Selwyn then?' Mrs Fleming said. 'A fine man.'

'I have met him,' Simon replied.

Losing patience with the gossip, Kitty interrupted. 'About the room, Mrs Fleming?'

'Oh, yes. It's an attic room and it has a lovely view.'

'How much is the tariff?'

'Three guineas per week and I'll require two weeks in advance.'

Kitty thought that was rather steep, but didn't argue. 'Fine, I'll take it, thank you.'

Mrs Fleming looked slightly taken aback. 'Do you not want to inspect it? Although I keep a very clean house, of course. No dirt, no cobwebs, no vermin. Certainly no cats, rats or mice. Filthy disgusting creatures, I can't abide them.'

Kitty supposed she had better cast her eye over the room. 'All right then, but I expect I'll still take it. I gather there will be a run on

232

accommodation because of the evacuees from Kororareka.'

'Very wise,' Mrs Fleming agreed.

Kitty followed her into the dimness of the hall while Simon waited outside.

The house itself was quite large; Kitty counted two bedrooms on the left of the central hallway, and a parlour and a large indoor kitchen on the right. The hall floor was lined with well-swept oilcloth and the wallboards were painted a fresh white. A steep, narrow staircase in a small foyer at the back of the house led up to two attic bedrooms.

'The view *is* very nice, isn't it?' Kitty said as she stood before a dormer window facing out over the Waitemata. From here she could see right across the harbour to the blue-green hills on the other side, and a collection of small and large ships at anchor.

The room wasn't very big, but it was pleasantly if rather plainly furnished with a chest of drawers, a wardrobe (goodness only knew how Mrs Fleming had got it up here), a ladder-backed chair and an iron bedstead. The unpainted walls were beginning to silver, and the floorboards were bare except for a bright rag rug. A flower-decorated bowl and ewer sat on the drawers, and the bed was covered with a pale yellow quilt. Most importantly, the room was indeed very clean.

Kitty opened her purse and counted out nine guineas into Mrs Fleming's hand. 'I'm not sure how long I'll be staying,' she said, very glad that Simon was downstairs. 'Not for any great length of time, but probably for at least three weeks.'

'And then will you be rejoining your husband?' Mrs Fleming asked, her face alight with both interest and curiosity. 'That's very brave of you.'

'Well, we'll see,' Kitty said.

Downstairs again, she asked Simon to carry her trunk up to her room, then waited in the parlour with Mrs Fleming until he came down again.

'How many other boarders do you have here?' she asked.

Mrs Fleming fussed about, moving a brass candlestick from one side of the mantelpiece to the other. Like the room upstairs, the parlour was simply but attractively furnished. 'I have two other ladies, so three now, counting your good self.'

'And where are these ladies this morning?' Kitty asked.

'Oh, they both have employment. One works for Mr Gorrie, the confectioner in High Street, and the other works for Mr Demmell, the watchmaker in Queen Street. Miss Whelan — she's the one who works for Mr Gorrie — occasionally brings home little bags of left-over butterscotch toffee, and very delicious it is too.'

'Does the other one bring home left-over watch springs?' Kitty asked.

Mrs Fleming looked at her blankly. 'Miss Langford? No.'

Oh dear, Kitty thought, no sense of humour.

'Miss Whelan arrived last year,' Mrs Fleming

mithered on, 'and she's affianced already, to a very nice young man named Mr Crow. He's a butcher at Flourday's Fine Meats on Chancery Street. Miss Langford, however, came out on the *Duchess of Argyle*, and she's been here for almost two-and-a-half years and *still* hasn't found herself a husband. I keep suggesting she try her luck at Port Nicholson, but no, she says she's very happy here.' She moved the candlestick back to its original position. 'How that can be when she remains a spinster I'm not sure, but still, each to her own, I suppose.'

Kitty quite liked the sound of Miss Langford. 'And when did you come to Auckland, Mrs Fleming?'

'Oh, I arrived on the *Anna Watson* in September of 1840. One of the first fleet, you know.'

'Really? And what does your husband do?'

Mrs Fleming sat down abruptly. 'Sadly, Mr Fleming passed away six months after we arrived.'

Kitty regretted asking now. 'Oh, I *am* sorry.'

'He *was* a printer. Fortunately he left me enough to purchase this house, and I've been taking in boarders ever since.'

At the parlour door, Simon cleared his throat.

Mrs Fleming bounced to her feet again. 'Oh dear, we're not keeping you from the business of saving souls, are we?'

'Not at all,' Simon replied. 'Mrs Farrell, may I have a private word, if you please?'

Kitty rose while Mrs Fleming extended her hand to Simon. 'Well, it's been lovely to meet

235

you, Mr Bullock. I hope that we may meet again.'

Simon clasped her hand and responded in kind. Outside, on the verandah that ran along the front of the house, he remarked, 'Well, it seems comfortable enough. Except for your landlady's incessant talking.'

Kitty shrugged. 'I expect she's just lonely. Apparently there are two other boarders — a Miss Whelan and a Miss Langford. Miss Whelan is engaged to be married but Miss Langford apparently is a spinster.'

Simon caught her eye. 'Well, don't look at me — I'm not in the market for a wife. Still.'

Kitty laid a hand on his arm and said with only a little bit of embarrassment, 'I do know that, Simon.'

Simon stared down at his boots for a long moment, then, with obvious difficulty, met her gaze again. A mottled flush spread up his neck. 'But do you know why?'

Her heart aching for him, Kitty said gently, 'Yes, I do. Rian told me.' And she gave him an affectionate kiss on his cheek, which made him go even more red. 'He guessed. I gather he was right?'

Simon nodded and stammered, 'You don't mind? It doesn't make you . . . ?'

Almost angrily, Kitty tugged on the lapel of his jacket. 'Of course I don't mind! Why should I? It's your business, Simon, no one else's, and it makes no difference to me. You are what you are and I'm *very* fond of you, so there.'

'I tried to tell you, that day on the beach at

236

Paihia, when you thought I was going to propose, I really did.'

Kitty almost blushed herself at the memory of it. 'Yes, well, we were rather at cross-purposes, weren't we?'

'Oh God,' Simon groaned. 'I suppose the entire crew of the *Katipo* know, do they?'

'I doubt it. At least, Rian wouldn't have said anything to them. He's very fond of you as well, you know. And he trusts you implicitly.'

'Well, he would, wouldn't he? I'm hardly likely to run off with you, am I?'

'No, not just with me, with everything. He thinks you have a very balanced view of the world — well, for a missionary — and that your decisions are always very sound.'

That cheered Simon up. 'Does he really?'

'Yes, he does. So, what are you going to do now?'

'I thought I'd go back to the Commercial and book a room. What will you do for supper?'

'I might stay in and meet my fellow boarders. Unless you wanted to dine?'

'No, I feel like an early night, actually. Shall we meet in the morning? We could go exploring.'

Kitty smiled. 'Yes, I think I'd like that, Simon. I'll see you then.'

★ ★ ★

When Kitty went back upstairs to her new room, she leaned on the windowsill and briefly closed her eyes. She missed Rian dreadfully already, and had no idea how she would manage even a week without seeing him, never mind three or four. And what if the trouble up north turned into a real war, one that went on for months and months?

She sighed and turned away, eyeing her trunk sitting neatly in the corner where Simon had left it. It really needed to be unpacked. She had brought two extra day dresses with her, underthings, her nightgowns and an extra bonnet, which would no doubt be well and truly squashed by now.

She knelt down and wrestled with the latches on the trunk; they were stiff and slightly rusty from the sea air, but eventually they opened with a short screech of protest. Setting her palms at the front corners of the lid she pushed it up and, with a small cry of disgust, lurched sharply back from the smell. It was *appalling*, and she recognised it immediately — cat shit.

The cat herself uncurled from her nest inside Kitty's bonnet.

'*Bodie!*' Kitty exclaimed, her hand over her nose.

Bodie blinked, stretched and creakily got to her feet.

Kitty lifted her out, noting with extreme distaste that the cat had emptied her bowels at least twice, and set her on the floor. 'You could have suffocated in there!'

Bodie gave the feline equivalent of a shrug, then sat down and began to clean her bottom.

Kitty gazed at her soiled belongings in despair, then gingerly began to unpack the trunk. Everything in it stank, but only one of her petticoats and her spare chemise had cat mess on them. At least Bodie had been tidy. Carefully, she lifted the offending items out and set them aside.

'How on earth did you get in my trunk?' she muttered. But she knew — it must have been when she'd left it open on her bed at Aunt Sarah's after she'd finished packing. 'I bet you're hungry,' she added, then started to laugh helplessly.

Still giggling, she poured water from the ewer into the bowl and set it on the floor; Bodie immediately rushed over to it and began to drink greedily.

'I don't have anything for you to eat, you know,' Kitty said.

Bodie's ears flicked back in response as she continued to lap up the water.

Kitty wondered if she could ask Mrs Fleming for something. But then she remembered her comment about not being able to abide cats, and her heart sank. 'Oh dear, what am I going to do with you?'

But she could quite legitimately say that *she* was hungry.

She found her landlady in the laundry off the back porch. 'I'm sorry, Mrs Fleming,' she said, 'but could I bother you for something to eat? There weren't enough rations on the *Victoria* to feed us all this morning.'

Mrs Fleming, her face red and sweaty from working over the copper, thought about it for a moment. 'Well, your board only covers breakfast. I'm more than happy to cook supper for you for an additional fee — I charge a shilling per meal

— but given that you've paid for the whole day today, I'll provide your dinner and we'll call it breakfast, shall we?'

'Yes. Yes, that would be lovely, thank you,' Kitty replied.

'It will just be some sort of cold collation. Will that suffice?'

'Wonderful, thank you.' Kitty eyed the boiling copper. 'And I would very much appreciate using your laundry facilities. I seem to have had a small spillage in my trunk.'

'Yes, of course,' Mrs Fleming said, wiping a trickle of sweat from her brow with the back of her wrist. 'I ask all my boarders to do their own laundry. I run a boarding house, after all, not a hotel. I'll call you when I've prepared your meal.'

Kitty went back upstairs and finished unpacking her trunk. Everything would have to be washed, except for her dresses — they were too delicate to go into the copper and anyway would take days to dry, so she would have to make do with airing them and perhaps liberally sprinkling them with rose water. Hanging out of the window, she vigorously flapped the petticoat and chemise to get rid of the hardened cat shit, then inspected her bonnet. It was squashed and lined with a layer of black fur, but salvageable.

'You really are a naughty cat, you know,' Kitty grumbled.

Bodie, stretched out on the yellow quilt, said, *Mrrrp*.

Kitty brought her meal back to her room. Bodie gobbled the cheese and a slice of ham and licked the butter off a piece of bread, then returned to the quilt where she sat contentedly washing herself. Kitty finished off what Bodie hadn't wanted — she had suspected that cats wouldn't like persimmon chutney on crackers — then collected up her things to take downstairs to the laundry, fervently hoping that Mrs Fleming wouldn't notice the smell.

★ ★ ★

Miss Langford and Miss Whelan arrived home within ten minutes of each other, just after six o'clock, surprising Kitty because they were both the complete opposite of what she had imagined they would be.

Hattie Whelan was chubby with a plain face, brown hair and eyes, and crooked teeth, which she showed frequently because she smiled and laughed a lot. Flora Langford, whom Kitty had expected to be the plain one as she hadn't managed to find herself a husband, had the potential to be very pretty, were she to make the effort. She had dark gold hair pulled back in a severe bun, blue eyes that tilted up at the outer corners hidden behind rather thick spectacles, and a prettily shaped mouth.

They both wanted to know all about Kitty, what her husband did, what it was like sailing around the world on a schooner, and what had happened at Kororareka.

'Were you frightened? I would have been,' Hattie said, helping herself to a third piece of bread. 'I would have been terrified.'

'It was frightening at times,' Kitty agreed,

recalling the long hours she'd spent in the cave wondering whether she would ever get out again, or if she was going to end up a pile of bones inside the rotting tatters of her clothes like Uncle George.

Mrs Fleming, who seemed to have an insatiable appetite for the details of what had happened at Kororareka, asked, 'And did you stay inside Polack's Stockade the whole time? It blew up, didn't it? I heard dozens of people perished in the explosion.'

'Actually, I believe only two people died. And no, I should have stayed inside the stockade but I . . . well, I panicked at the sound of the guns and ran outside.'

Hattie gasped. 'My Lord, not right into the middle of the fighting?'

'No, I ran around the back of the stockade and took shelter in a house there,' Kitty lied. 'I didn't come out until the order came to evacuate.'

Hattie shuddered. 'I would have been absolutely petrified hiding in a little house all by myself. Arthur, my intended — ' she said, interrupting herself and holding out her hand for Kitty to view the ring on her finger.

Kitty saw that it was a 'dearest' ring — the first letter of the name of each coloured gemstone spelled out the word — and looked rather expensive, especially for a butcher. 'Very nice,' she said.

'He sent to Sydney for it,' Hattie explained proudly. 'Anyway, Arthur said the fighting was all over in a matter of hours. Is that true?'

'I suppose it was,' Kitty agreed. 'Although it

242

seemed a lot longer.'

'And what did your dashing husband do, Mrs Farrell?' Mrs Fleming asked. 'I expect he was right at the forefront of the fighting?'

'No, he moved around a lot. I believe he was at the lower blockhouse for a while, then behind the town.'

'That was the way the Kapiti Maoris crept up, wasn't it? That's what I heard,' Mrs Fleming said, attacking a piece of particularly tough gristle with her knife.

'Te Kapotai, from Waikare,' Kitty corrected.

Flora Langford set her knife and fork neatly across her plate and dabbed at her mouth with a table napkin. 'And is it true that fifty imperial troops died and more than two hundred rebel Maoris?'

'I don't know about the Maoris,' Kitty replied, 'but the last I heard, on the morning after the battle, Bishop Selwyn buried nineteen British soldiers and marines. Some at Kororareka and some in the churchyard at Paihia.'

'It seems a bit silly to me,' Flora said. 'All that fuss over a flagpole.'

Mrs Fleming looked up, aghast. 'It's not just any flagpole, Miss Langford. A flagpole flying the *Union Jack*, the symbol of everything that is British and good!'

'Well, I suppose that could be considered vaguely insulting,' Flora conceded.

'Vaguely? *Vaguely!*' Mrs Fleming evidently couldn't believe her ears. 'Why, it . . . it was a blatant slap in the Queen's face, that's what it was!'

The conversation lapsed after that. As Mrs Fleming cleared the table, Kitty asked, 'Is there a good pharmacy here? I forgot to bring shampoo.'

Flora said, 'There's only Mr McKenzie, on Shortland Street. But he stocks most things, and he manufactures. You can borrow mine if you need some tonight. I'll bring it to your room.'

Flora was as good as her word, although Kitty had to hurriedly stuff Bodie into the wardrobe when she knocked on the door.

'Come in, please,' Kitty said as she opened it.

Flora handed her a jar of shampoo, walked in and sat down on the chair. 'This room is quite nice, isn't it? Mine's a bit dark in the mornings, but this one was taken when I moved in.' She wrinkled her nose. 'What's that smell?'

Kitty sniffed. 'I can't smell anything.' She couldn't, either; she had washed everything this afternoon and thoroughly scrubbed the inside of her trunk.

'Sort of an itchy smell,' Flora said, then sneezed incredibly loudly.

Kitty waited while Flora made the face that people do when they're not sure whether they're going to sneeze again, and then she did, four more times in quick succession.

'You've got a cat in here, haven't you?' she said, looking around suspiciously.

'No,' Kitty lied.

'Yes you have. Cats are the only thing that make me sneeze like that. Even just a few hairs will do it.'

Just then Bodie scratched violently on the inside of the wardrobe door. Kitty rolled her eyes in frustration and let her out. Bodie jumped onto the floor, walked up to Flora and hissed unpleasantly.

'I knew it,' Flora said, dabbing at her nose with her handkerchief. 'Mrs Fleming doesn't allow pets. Especially cats. She hates cats.'

'I know,' Kitty replied, and sat down on the bed. 'I didn't mean to bring her. She stowed away in my trunk.'

Flora laughed. 'What a clever cat you are,' she said to Bodie.

Bodie hissed again, then yawned.

'Did she shit in it, too?' Flora asked.

Kitty blinked at the crude word; she'd heard it thousands of times from the crew, but hadn't at all expected it to come out of Flora's pretty mouth. 'Er, yes, she did actually. Well, she was shut in it for two days.'

Flora made another face, this one expressing distaste. 'You'll have to smuggle her out to do her business, or your room will reek like a zoo. Lucky Mrs Fleming is as blind as a bat. Unfortunately, she has a nose as good as the one on your cat. What's her name?'

'My cat?'

'Yes.'

'Bodie, short for Boadicea.'

'How do you do, Boadicea,' Flora said, and sneezed again.

10

When Kitty told Simon the next day about
Bodie stowing away in her trunk, and what she
had managed to do in it during her two-day
incarceration, he roared with laughter and
suggested they go straight to the nearest butcher
to buy the cat a reward for her adventurous
exploits.

'It's all right for you to laugh,' Kitty grumbled.
'You didn't have to clean out my trunk or spend
three hours laundering my underthings.'

'Where is she now?' Simon asked, still
smirking. They were walking down to Mr
McKenzie's pharmacy on Shortland Street.

'Locked inside my room, and I hope that's
where she'll stay until I get back.'

Simon raised his eyebrows. 'What about
. . . you know?'

'I smuggled her out early this morning and
discovered a very convenient heap of soil behind
some bushes in Mrs Fleming's backyard.'

'She'll run away, you know.'

'Probably,' Kitty agreed gloomily. 'I really
don't know how long I'll be able to keep her out
of Mrs Fleming's sight. Apparently she hates
cats.'

'Couldn't you put her in a wicker basket and
send her back to Paihia?'

'Mrs Fleming?'

Simon gave Kitty a withering look. 'No: Bodie.

She survived in a trunk coming down to Auckland — surely she'll manage going back the other way.'

Kitty briefly considered the idea, then said, 'No, I couldn't do that to her. She might pine.'

'Over two days? I doubt it.'

'Simon, I'm not sure you know Bodie as well as you think you do.'

Simon took Kitty's arm and guided her across the dusty, uneven street, tipping his hat as they came abreast of two women walking towards them. 'What *are* you talking about, Kitty? Bodie's a cat — *nobody* knows her.'

'*I* know her,' Kitty insisted crossly.

'Well, what if she came and stayed with me at the Commercial? I'm sure the proprietor would turn a blind eye if I slipped him a couple of extra shillings a week.'

'No, she wouldn't like that either,' Kitty replied quickly.

Simon rolled his eyes. They walked on, then suddenly he said, 'I know what it is. You want her with you because she reminds you of Rian, doesn't she?'

Kitty saw that there was no point in lying, not to Simon. 'How did you know that?'

'Because I know *you*. You miss him very much, don't you?'

Kitty nodded, not trusting herself to speak.

Simon regarded her fondly, dismayed that she was so upset. 'Well, given that Rian has entrusted me to keep you away from the Bay of Islands until this war business is over, we'll just have to fill in our days in Auckland as interestingly and entertainingly as possible, won't we? And before you know, it will be time to go back. How's that?'

Kitty gave him a watery smile.

'And to start with,' he went on, 'we'll go into the very next draper's shop we come to, because if we're to spend some considerable time in civilised company, I desperately require some new clothes. And I need you to help me choose the fabric. You know I'm not very good at that sort of thing.'

This actually made Kitty feel a little better: she enjoyed shopping. Simon's wardrobe certainly needed attention, and she fully planned to buy for herself, too, as Rian had given her a purse full of money — to salve his guilty conscience, she righteously assumed, for sending her away.

They visited the pharmacy, which was quite well stocked as Flora had said, but ended up having to walk down to the bottom of Queen Street to find the shop where Auckland's largest draper had his premises. The condition of the streets was appalling — even worse than The Rocks, where there was at least paving in places. There were piles of fly-infested animal manure everywhere, deep ruts from wagon wheels just waiting to turn unsuspecting ankles, and no drains whatsoever. It clearly hadn't rained in Auckland for some time, because the ground was as dry as dust, but it was obvious that when it did the streets would be even more difficult and unpleasant to negotiate.

But the draper, Mr Graham, was a pleasant and, fortunately, very patient man. Simon dithered for so long over which of the fabrics to choose that Kitty wondered if he was doing it on purpose just to keep her occupied. He finally settled on a brown tweed and a dark grey herringbone for two suits, but then couldn't decide on the fabric for a fancy waistcoat.

'What about this?' he said, pointing at a pale lemon Indian doupion.

'No, too boring,' Kitty replied emphatically.

Simon gazed around. 'This?' he suggested doubtfully, lifting a bolt of rather fussy floral brocade.

'Er, it's a bit, well, feminine, don't you think?'

'Is it?' Simon muttered, and shoved the bolt back onto its shelf.

Mr Graham came to the rescue. 'Sir might appreciate this,' he suggested, sliding out, from the bottom of a pile, a bolt of dark blue fabric with a very faint paisley pattern in grey. 'See? It's China silk, but reasonably plain, and very pleasing to the touch.'

Simon hesitantly reached out and rubbed the silk between his fingers. 'Er, yes, very nice.'

'Is it to accompany the tweed or the herringbone?' Mr Graham asked.

Simon looked at Kitty, who answered, 'The herringbone. The grey will go nicely with that blue. And we'll take enough of the tweed to include a matching waistcoat, I think. Unless you wanted something different to contrast with the brown?' she said to Simon.

He shrugged, happy to leave it all to Kitty.

Knowing that Simon was unlikely to wear even one fancy waistcoat, never mind two, she said, 'Just the extra tweed, thank you,' as Mr Graham carried the various bolts of cloth over to his cutting table.

He deftly measured and cut the required lengths, folded and wrapped them in paper and tied the parcel with string, then calculated the cost.

Simon paid and signed the receipt.

'Thank you very much, Mr Bullock,' Mr Graham said. 'Did you have a tailor in mind?'

'No, we don't know Auckland well. We've only just arrived from the Bay of Islands.'

Mr Graham's face assumed an expression of concern. 'Yes, it's a dreadful state of affairs, isn't it? Very alarming. I do hope things are settled soon and then we can all get on with our lives. I would recommend Mr Donaven.'

Simon looked at him. 'Pardon?'

'Mr Donaven, a very accomplished gentlemen's tailor. On the corner of Chancery Street and Fields Lane. Fields Lane is off Shortland Street, if you don't know.'

'Oh, yes. Thank you.'

As Kitty and Simon left the shop, Simon with his parcel of fabric tucked under his arm, Mr Graham called after them, 'Good day, sir! Good day, Mrs Bullock!'

'It seems we're finally married after all,' Simon remarked as they wandered down the street. 'Now, where the hell is Fields Lane?'

'For a missionary, Simon, even a lay one, your language is deteriorating atrociously,' Kitty said.

'Yes, it is, isn't it?' he replied cheerfully.

They made their way down Queen Street, avoiding crumbling potholes and the more noisome piles of ordure, then turned into Shortland Street. About halfway along they came to the narrow alleyway that was Fields Lane. The premises of Mr Donaven the tailor were situated in a tiny shop at the far end. A bell over the door tinkled as they entered, and Mr Donaven soon had Simon measured for his new suits and waistcoats, promising that the garments would be ready in four days' time. Though he was rather busy, he said, because it seemed that more than a few of the evacuees from Kororareka were viewing their enforced exodus as an opportunity to have new clothes made.

'Perhaps we had better make that five days,' Mr Donaven amended after consideration.

'Well, whatever you can manage,' Simon said. 'I'm hardly likely to be invited to any glittering social events in the next week.'

'Oh, but you might be,' Mr Donaven said quickly. 'There's talk that the governor may be considering hosting an evening for the evacuees. Possibly an informal ball. To boost morale, so they say.'

'Really,' Simon murmured, who couldn't have cared less.

'Yes,' Mr Donaven said excitedly. 'So you have my word that I will have your suits finished as soon as I am able. I'll start on the herringbone first, as I assume you won't want to wear tweed to an evening event.'

Outside, Simon complained to Kitty, 'Why can't I wear tweed to an evening event? Not that I have any desire whatsoever to go galloping around a ballroom with a great gang of twittering would-be socialites.'

'No, but I might,' Kitty said. 'And if I do, I'll expect you to accompany me, Simon. Rian would want you to, after all.'

Simon glanced at her uneasily. 'But why would you want to go? I thought you didn't care for that sort of thing?'

'*Rian* doesn't, but actually sometimes I do.' Kitty pursed her lips in a thoughtful manner that unsettled Simon even further. 'And I've found that it pays to keep one's eyes and ears open. One never knows when one might come across a useful piece of information, does one?'

'Such as?'

'Oh, I don't know. When the next ship is scheduled to sail up to the Bay of Islands, perhaps?'

'*Kitty!*' Simon exclaimed in dismay. 'You promised Rian you would stay in Auckland!'

Kitty blinked her long black eyelashes. 'No, I didn't. *You* promised Rian you would look out for me. *I* don't recall making any promises at all. And anyway, I didn't say I want to go back, I just said I might be interested in when the next ship is sailing.'

'You've changed, Kitty,' Simon said. 'You used to be quite timid, even when you were being obstinate. You're a lot more sure of yourself now.'

Kitty met his gaze squarely. 'I know. Is it not to your liking?'

Simon thought about it. 'Yes, it is, funnily enough. But only if it isn't going to get me into trouble with Rian.'

★ ★ ★

April 1845

It rained almost solidly for the next two weeks, and the streets of Auckland were indeed reduced to stinking, muddy, almost impassable drains. Coming home one day from posting a letter to Rian, Kitty kicked off her filthy wet boots at Mrs Fleming's front door and, her hair dripping and her dress soaked, made her way soggily along the hall.

'Mrs Farrell?' Mrs Fleming called.

Kitty detoured into the parlour. 'Yes?'

'I'm afraid I had to use my master key to go into your room while you were out.'

Kitty's heart lurched. Was the cat out of the bag?

'I heard a dreadful ruckus up there,' Mrs Fleming went on, her spectacles glinting, 'and, thinking a bird may have flown in through the window, I went in to investigate. But nothing was amiss, which was very strange, although your window was open, so I closed it. I just thought I should tell you. I hope you don't mind.'

Hoping that her relief wasn't too evident, Kitty said, 'No, I don't mind at all. Thank you.'

Mrs Fleming nodded and went back to her sewing.

Kitty raced upstairs, her stockinged feet slipping on the floorboards, unlocked the door to her room and burst in.

She crossed the floor, gripped the bottom of the window sash and hauled it up. Bodie was crouched at the farthest edge of the outer sill, with her black fur plastered to her body, a very sour look on her face and a dead mouse clamped between her paws.

'I don't see why you can't hunt quietly,' Kitty said crossly as Bodie stood and shook each wet paw in turn. The mouse looked rather battered, as though it had been flung about repeatedly. So much for Mrs Fleming's vermin-free house.

Bodie took the dead creature in her mouth, edged along the sill and jumped agilely into the room where she sat on the rag rug, one paw proprietorially on the mouse, grooming her sopping fur.

Kitty warned, 'If you're not careful I *will* send you back to the Bay of Islands, you know.'

Bodie picked up the mouse and dropped it onto Kitty's foot.

'And currying favour won't work, either,' she added, throwing the poor dead thing out of the window.

Bodie stared at her for a long moment, then made an abrupt dash for the door, which Kitty belatedly realised she had left ajar. Across the landing the cat furiously scratched at Flora's bedroom door: the door creaked open and Bodie darted inside. Feeling intrusive and guilty, Kitty swore under her breath and followed her.

Flora's room was very similar to her own, though it was perhaps a little smaller and the window faced the hills behind Auckland instead of the harbour. The bed was very neatly made, but there were no personal items on the chest of drawers or the small bedside cabinet, as would be expected of someone who had lived in the same room for the past two years. There was also no sign of Bodie.

'Bodie,' Kitty whispered, crouching to peer beneath the bed. 'Bodie, here puss. Where are you?'

Kitty's heart sank as a scuffling sound came from Flora's wardrobe. She opened the door and there in one corner was Bodie, lying comfortably across a pair of beautiful red satin button boots with rather high heels and lace around the tops. Next to them sat another pair, but in black. Kitty frowned, thinking how inappropriate they would be for Auckland's rough and muddy streets.

'Get out of there,' she said to Bodie tersely, but Bodie didn't move, apparently happy where she was.

Kitty lifted her out, in the process knocking one of Flora's dresses off its hanger.

She swore again and carried Bodie back across the landing, shut her inside her bedroom, then returned to Flora's. She eyed the dress where it had fallen in a crumpled heap at the bottom of the wardrobe. It was of an ordinary style in a rather dull brown wool, and Kitty recognised it as one of the dresses Flora wore out to work. She gathered it up, slipped it back on the hanger and hung it in front of Flora's other dresses.

Flora's other dresses. Kitty frowned again. One was a good dress, a nice bottle green sateen and obviously one that Flora saved for best, but the two hanging behind it were very beautiful indeed — far too beautiful for a girl who worked for a watchmaker. They were in different colours

255

but of the same style and made of very good quality and expensive satin, heavily embellished with glittering beads. One was red and the other was black, presumably to match the boots lined up beneath them. By moving Flora's heavy winter cape only slightly, she saw that at the other end of the wardrobe were several very full petticoats, also of good quality and adorned with yards and yards of stunning lace.

Kitty reached in and withdrew the red dress, holding it against her body. The waist was tiny, though Flora might well have had a small waist under the ill-fitting clothes she wore during the day; the sleeves were almost non-existent and the bodice heavily boned in the manner of a corset. But it was the neckline that startled Kitty. It was so low that if she were to try it on without her chemise, she was sure the fabric would only just cover her nipples. Perhaps Flora wore it with a fichu? To wear such a daring gown in public without one would have been scandalous. The black dress had the same very low neckline, which was extremely unusual on a mourning gown. But surely no self-respecting grieving woman would wear such an outfit? Really, the only women Kitty had ever seen wearing clothes like this had been . . .

Slowly, Kitty returned the red dress to the wardrobe. Flora? Surely not? What a ridiculous notion. Flora was quite unprepossessing, even if she was somewhat candid in her manner, and anyway she was busy all day cleaning and assembling the insides of watches. Wasn't she?

That evening at dinner, Kitty asked Flora how

her day at work had been.

'Oh, you know, the same as it always is,' Flora replied, cutting into her rather tough pork chop.

'I've always wondered what it would be like to work for a watchmaker,' Kitty said, then winced inwardly as she realised how inane she sounded.

Hattie looked at her, her fork halfway to her mouth. 'Have you? How odd.'

'Yes, I suppose it is,' Kitty mumbled, staring at her plate and cursing herself for being so nosy.

'Well, if you're that interested, why don't you call in one day this week and I'll show you what I do,' Flora suggested. 'I work in Queen Street.'

Kitty felt deflated . . . until it occurred to her that Flora might only work for the watchmaker during the *day*.

'Are you going to your Bible studies class tonight, Miss Langford?' Mrs Fleming asked.

'Yes,' Flora replied after she had swallowed her mouthful. She took her glasses off and rubbed the bridge of her nose where they had rested. 'Would anyone like a glass of water?'

'Actually, the well is rather muddy at the moment,' Mrs Fleming said. 'I'd suggest a pot of strong tea. There's milk: I went to the dairy today.'

Flora pushed back her chair and crossed to the hearth to put the kettle over the fire. While her back was turned, Kitty tried on her spectacles. She looked down at her own hands then around the kitchen, noting that everything looked exactly the same as without the lenses.

She jumped when Flora remarked, 'They're not very powerful.'

Embarrassed, Kitty took the spectacles off, sure that they didn't have prescription glass in them at all. 'I've been wondering about getting a pair,' she said lamely.

'You wonder about a lot of things, don't you?' Flora observed.

'Tut tut, Miss Langford,' Mrs Fleming said. 'I'm sure Mrs Farrell is only curious.'

'I need spectacles, I'm sure I do,' Hattie said brightly. 'I gave a gentleman aniseed balls today instead of blackballs. Quite silly of me. Aniseed balls are brown, you see, and blackballs are, well, black.'

'What is this Bible studies class?' Kitty asked.

'It's a night class that's run by the Church Missionary Society,' Mrs Fleming replied. 'Miss Langford attends two nights a week as regular as clockwork, don't you? Tuesdays and Thursdays.'

Flora, who had sat down again, nodded.

'Where is it held?' Kitty asked.

'Oh, in town,' Flora replied vaguely.

'Why, are you interested in attending yourself?' Mrs Fleming asked Kitty hopefully. She approved wholeheartedly of religious instruction.

'Well, not really,' Kitty said. 'I'm not sure I'll be in Auckland long enough.'

Hattie asked, 'Was that you sneezing before, Flora? In your room? I could hear you from downstairs.'

'Yes, it was,' Flora said, giving Kitty a long, accusing look.

'I know you don't wish to be parted from your husband any longer than you have to be, Mrs Farrell,' Mrs Fleming said sympathetically, 'but

258

don't discount the possibility that you may be in Auckland for some time. I hear that more of Governor FitzRoy's reinforcements from Australia are due here in a fortnight. Apparently they are to join the troops already at the barracks, then sail north to the Bay of Islands. After that, well, it could be some time until the rebel Maoris are subdued, and if so, you should have ample opportunity for pursuing your spiritual advancement. On the other hand, of course, the rebels might scatter like a herd of panicked sheep, faced with the might of Her Majesty's troops.'

Kitty doubted it. 'I have no real need for spiritual advancement, Mrs Fleming. I was a missionary myself, at Paihia five or six years ago. I came out with my aunt and uncle. Uncle George was a minister at Paihia before he died.'

Mrs Fleming looked thoughtful. 'What was your maiden name, Mrs Farrell?'

'Carlisle.'

'No, I'm sure that wasn't it,' Mrs Fleming said, almost to herself. 'What was your uncle's name?'

'Kelleher.'

'Yes!' Mrs Fleming exclaimed. 'I remember now. Reverend George Kelleher. Wasn't there some sort of scandal?' Then she stopped. 'Oh, I do beg your pardon, dear.'

Kitty said nothing.

But Mrs Fleming apparently could not let it lie. 'There was . . . an incident, though, wasn't there? I'm sure I remember something.'

'My uncle did disappear, perhaps that's what

259

you were thinking of,' Kitty suggested.

'Yes, but wasn't there something to do with a housegirl? A Maori housegirl?' Mrs Fleming insisted.

Kitty blinked very slowly as she regarded her landlady. 'Not to my knowledge, Mrs Fleming. And I was there. My uncle simply, and tragically, disappeared on the eve of the signing of the treaty. It has since transpired that he became lost in the bush and died. I myself left very soon after that, for Australia.'

'To continue your work as a missionary?'

'To continue providing care and support to those in need, yes,' Kitty replied, recalling the long months she had spent looking after Wai and then baby Tahi. 'And then of course I married my husband.'

Mrs Fleming appeared confused, clearly unable, or unwilling, to equate Kitty's version of the story with the much more interesting one she had heard, but to her credit she said, 'Oh, well. I suppose these things often do get distorted in the telling.'

'Yes, I expect they do,' Kitty agreed.

Mrs Fleming patted her hand. 'But if you *are* to be staying at Auckland for any length of time, perhaps you could share some of your past experiences as a missionary with the Bible studies class. That's a wonderful idea, isn't it, Miss Langford?'

Kitty noticed that Flora looked rather cagey. 'Yes,' Flora said. 'Wonderful.'

Flora Langford was hiding something, and Kitty knew it.

'Surely what she gets up to after-hours is her business,' Simon said somewhat tetchily as he stirred sugar into his tea.

They were in the dining-room of Woods' Royal Hotel on Princes Street where, Kitty had been assured by Mrs Fleming, Auckland's 'fashionable circle' preferred to dine. Simon hadn't wanted to come, but Kitty, dispirited and missing Rian dreadfully, had insisted on having a treat. Also, her courses had started that morning, so that, as always, she was feeling flat and sharply disappointed.

'Yes, but a *prostitute*, Simon! Don't you find that fascinating?'

'No, I don't, and neither should you. I think you're being rather puerile about it, actually. And you don't even know if she is a prostitute. There might be some perfectly reasonable explanation for why she has risque dresses in her wardrobe and wears spectacles with ordinary glass in them.'

'Such as?' Kitty demanded.

'Well, I don't know.'

'And she goes out at night twice a week without fail, apparently.'

'Has she said where she goes?'

'Yes, to a Bible studies class! Ha!'

'Well, there you go, then,' Simon reasoned. 'She's just very devout.'

'With those gowns hanging in her wardrobe?' Kitty countered. 'And anyway, who goes to Bible studies classes twice a week?'

261

'I do,' Simon replied, reaching for a dainty ham and mustard sandwich. 'I teach them at Waimate, remember? And so did you when you were at Paihia.'

Kitty had forgotten that. 'Well, I don't believe her.'

Simon sighed. 'Do you not like this Flora Langford, Kitty? Is that what the problem is?'

'No, actually I do like her. Quite a lot.'

'Then why can't you just let her go about her business?' He made a pained face. 'God, this mustard's potent.'

'Because it's a *mystery*, Simon, and I want to get to the bottom of it.' Kitty's eyes lit up. 'I know! Let's follow her the next time she goes out!'

Simon laid his sandwich on his plate, carefully blotted his mouth with his napkin, leaned towards Kitty and said very firmly, 'No. Let's not.'

Kitty folded her arms and scowled, her afternoon tea untouched in front of her. After a minute she said, 'I still haven't received my invitation to the evacuees' ball.'

'Could that perhaps be because there isn't going to be one?' Simon suggested.

Kitty frowned. 'Isn't there? How do you know that?'

'I don't, but how do you know there *is*?'

'Because Mr Donaven said there was.'

'Mr Donaven said that there was talk, and only talk, of FitzRoy *considering* it,' Simon said patiently, 'not that he was on the verge of ordering invitations to be printed.'

He was wearing his new brown tweed suit, which Mr Donaven had tailored for him beautifully but which Simon, true to form, was managing to make look like an old potato sack.

'Why didn't you wear that shirt I gave you for Christmas with your nice new suit?' Kitty complained. 'It would look so much smarter than that scruffy old thing you've got on. And sit up straight, you'll spill food all down your front.'

Simon drew in a deep breath and let it out again very slowly. Then he said, 'You know, Kitty, not a day has gone by during this past week that I haven't thanked God that we never did actually marry.'

Kitty glared at him. 'Well, that's a lovely thing to say!' She opened her napkin, flapped it vigorously and laid it across her lap. 'Why are you being so difficult, Simon? We're supposed to be having a nice afternoon out.'

Simon nearly choked. 'Why am *I* being difficult? Kitty, you've done nothing but bicker and criticise since I came by to collect you! It's *you* who is being difficult!'

And then he felt a complete heel because her face fell and she fumbled in her reticule for her handkerchief, but not before a fat tear had escaped and trickled down her cheek. She was missing Rian terribly, and the crew, and probably the *Katipo* herself, and here he was chiding her for it when he should have been lending her a shoulder to cry on.

He reached across the table and took her hand. 'I'm sorry, Kitty, I really am. I know how much you miss Rian. Don't worry, you'll see him soon, I'm sure of it.'

But Kitty only cried harder, and people were starting to look.

'Look,' Simon said, desperate now and knowing he would no doubt deeply regret what he was about to say. 'Tell me what you want, and we'll do it, all right? Anything, so long as it cheers you up.'

⋆　⋆　⋆

'Here she comes,' Kitty said breathlessly, and ducked back into the shadows of the building two doors down from Mrs Fleming's house.

It was almost dark. Kitty had said she was going out for the evening to visit an acquaintance, but she and Simon had been waiting here for half an hour now for Flora to leave for her class. The temperature had cooled over the past few days, accompanied by a brisk wind that gathered up drying leaves and spun them around in miniature whirlpools, and Kitty was wishing she had packed her cape rather than just her shawl. Simon, leaning against the wall with his hands in his pockets and a resigned expression on his face, only grunted.

'Get back!' Kitty whispered, and they moved further into the shadows as Flora walked quickly past, carrying a portmanteau and with her yellow hair hidden beneath a bonnet.

They followed her at some distance all the way along Waterloo and Victoria Quadrants, then into Victoria Street itself. At the intersection of Victoria and Queen Streets, they had to stop and clutch at each other like lovers snatching an illicit cuddle in the shadows when Flora slowed and glanced over her shoulder, then walked briskly on.

Kitty and Simon held their embrace for a second or so longer, in case she looked back again, then moved apart. It was then that Kitty started giggling, and when she glanced at Simon she saw that he was having to make a supreme effort himself not to laugh. Kitty snorted loudly and was forced to wipe the back of her gloved hand under her nose. Simon looked quickly away, refusing to meet her eye, but she could hear him uttering a series of short, stifled whimpers as he struggled to contain himself.

'*Shssh*, she'll hear us!' Kitty hissed, then was overcome by another fit of giggles.

'Sorry,' Simon blurted, his eyes watering and his face red. And then he was away again.

Flora had by now crossed Queen Street and was striding off into the deepening evening gloom.

'Quick, we'll lose sight of her!' Kitty croaked, making a mighty effort to settle down.

Still giggling, they crossed the street, hurried past the wooden stocks outside the town gaol and negotiated the somewhat precarious bridging across the Ligar Canal, just in time to see Flora disappear around a corner into Albert Street. By the time they reached the corner themselves, she was entering a modest house tucked between the premises of a carpenter and a general merchant a hundred yards down the street.

'What's in there?' Kitty wondered.

Simon shrugged. 'I've no idea.'

Kitty edged closer to the house, whose front door opened almost directly onto the street. There was a carriageway running down one side, towards what looked like a stable at the rear. 'It looks like an ordinary house to me. Nothing like a school!'

'You can study the Bible in a house, you know,' Simon pointed out.

But Kitty wasn't to be dissuaded. 'Why don't you knock on the door and find out?'

Simon looked appalled. 'Me? What if it *is* a brothel?'

Kitty said crossly, 'Oh, you'll be all right. *You're* not likely to be tempted, are you?'

'But what if someone sees me?' Simon said worriedly. 'A missionary, banging on the door of a house of ill repute?'

'It's dark, no one will see,' Kitty assured him. 'Go on. Say you're looking for someone you thought lives around here.'

Much against his better judgement, Simon did as she asked. Looking nervously in all directions, he sidled up to the door of the house and knocked timidly. It was answered a few moments later by a mousy-looking girl in what appeared to be a servant's uniform.

'Good evening, sir,' she said. 'May I help you?'

Simon removed his hat. 'Er, good evening. I'm looking for a friend of mine, by the name of Mick Doyle. I was told that this is his residence.'

'No, sir, there's no one here by that name,' the girl replied flatly.

'Oh. But this *is* someone's residence, isn't it?'
A short pause. 'Yes, it is.'

'And do you hold Bible studies classes here?' Simon asked, feeling increasingly ill at ease as the exchange went on.

A very odd expression crossed the girl's face. 'No, sir, definitely not Bible studies.'

'Oh, well, obviously I'm mistaken,' Simon said, flustered. He didn't know what to say next so he thanked the girl, jammed his hat back on his head and marched smartly off.

'Is it a brothel?' Kitty demanded from her hiding place behind a fence several doors down.

'A servant said it *is* someone's house,' Simon replied, 'but no one said it was a brothel.'

'Well, they wouldn't, would they?'

'There are no classes held there, either. Can we go home now?'

'No, we can't. What time is it?'

Simon dug in a pocket for his watch. 'Half past eight. Why?'

'I think we should wait another thirty minutes, just in case.'

Not even bothering to ask in case of what, and knowing better than to argue, Simon crouched against the fence and settled down to wait.

The moon was almost full and the wind sharp, and they both suspected they could hear rats scurrying busily about somewhere nearby. A night bird hooted eerily in the scrubby trees across the street, and Simon complained that he was getting cramp in his legs.

But twenty minutes later, a sleek one-horse gig driven by a man in a long dark coat, wearing his hat low on his forehead, turned off Victoria Street, passed them and then turned into the carriage-way alongside the house Flora had entered.

'Who was that?' Kitty said, intrigued.

'How should I know?' Simon replied, massaging his aching calves.

Several minutes later the gig re-emerged and turned again in their direction. As it neared their hiding place, it slowed, then stopped.

Flora, whom Kitty barely recognised, was sitting on the seat next to the driver. Her spectacles were nowhere to be seen, her hair was pinned up in a gleaming cascade and she was wearing the black dress, which was indeed scandalously low at the neckline. A cape was draped over her shoulders and Kitty saw the glint of jewellery at her throat and ears. She looked devastatingly alluring and nothing like the woman who took her evening meals at Mrs Fleming's dining table.

Clearly amused, Flora leaned out of the gig in a cloud of expensive perfume and said, 'Kitty? Yes, you guessed correctly. I am in the business of, shall we say, entertaining gentlemen, but only a few, very wealthy, ones. And don't let that cat of yours play in my wardrobe again, if you don't mind. I sneezed for hours the other night.'

Then she gave Simon and Kitty a very gracious smile, arranged the hood of her cape over her head and signalled to the driver to continue on.

Speechless, Kitty could only stand in the street and stare after the gig as it disappeared around the corner.

* * *

Later that week Kitty, consumed with curiosity, summoned the courage to knock on Flora's door one night and ask her about her 'evening employment'.

Flora was sitting on her bed brushing her hair. 'Well, all right, but I'm only telling you this because you caught me out,' she said matter-of-factly, 'which I quite admire, because no one else has managed to do that yet.'

Flora had begun work as a prostitute six months after her arrival in New Zealand and exactly four months after she had realised she would never make her fortune helping Mr Demmell to repair and sell watches. She had looked around for more lucrative employment but, in a new town, there was very little for a single woman that paid well, and she had no wish to marry just to guarantee a roof over her head and food on her plate. Kitty, who had once faced the same dilemma, sympathised. So one night Flora had gone to the house on Albert Street, which was widely rumoured to be a brothel, and asked for a job, although she had refused the madam's offer of working from the Albert Street premises. Flora wanted only one or two clients, and only those who could pay the large fee she intended to charge. So the madam had arranged some suitable introductions and thereafter, for a mutually agreed percentage of Flora's earnings, had allowed Flora to 'prepare' there before she went out to her regular twice-weekly assignations.

Kitty, worldly-wise though she was these days, felt oddly disconcerted talking to a young woman with two vastly different lives, which she was clearly managing to juggle very successfully.

'But I would prefer you to keep this to yourself,' Flora added. 'I like living here, it suits me for the moment, and I rather suspect that would come to a very sudden end if Mrs Fleming were to become aware of my, er, after-hours activities. Is your friend Simon likely to say anything?'

'No, I'm sure he won't.'

'Good, because I don't want to move on until I'm ready.'

'I do have one question, Flora,' Kitty said, 'if you don't mind my asking.' Kitty actually had plenty of questions, but Flora, she was coming to realise, was a self-assured, intelligent and rather calculating woman who preferred to play her cards very close to her chest.

Flora parted her hair and began to plait it, ready for bed. 'What's that?'

'Why do you keep your clothes here, if you get ready at the house on Albert Street? Wouldn't it be easier, and safer, to keep everything there?'

'Yes, it would, but I don't trust the girls who work in the house an inch. They'd have their mucky hands on my lovely, and I might add very expensive, dresses the minute I was gone. They don't like me, you see. I make considerably more money than they do, for far less work.' Flora deftly tied a ribbon around the end of her plait and regarded Kitty candidly. 'Now, no more questions. I can see that you're bored and you miss your man, but as a woman with plenty of secrets of her own, Kitty, I'm sure you appreciate my need for privacy.'

They stared at each other for a long moment, during which Kitty realised that her companion wasn't just talking about Bodie, and suddenly appreciated how very perceptive Flora Langford was. But she felt somehow more at ease; as though their secrets were a sort of shared bond.

'I have a favour to ask of you,' she said.

When she had described what it was she wanted, Flora tapped her top lip thoughtfully and asked bluntly, 'Can you pay?'

'Yes, whatever is required.'

Flora nodded. 'I'll see what I can do.'

Then, in a gesture that was very unusual for a woman, she offered Kitty her hand. Kitty hesitated for a moment, then shook it firmly.

11

The press was full of the preparations for war. The twenty-eight-gun frigate HMS *North Star* had arrived in Auckland at the end of March, followed by the brig *Velocity* carrying two-hundred-and-eighty men of the 58th Regiment. A month later, the barque *Slains Castle* also beat into the harbour with a further two-hundred-and-fifteen men of the 58th. Immediately, an expeditionary force of almost five hundred men of the 58th, 96th, the Marines and Auckland Volunteers set off for the Bay of Islands.

It had also been widely reported that the great chief Tamati Waka Nene had become so enraged by Heke's actions at Kororareka that he now pledged to destroy him. This brought a modicum of relief to the people of Auckland, who surmised that imperial troops would have an even better chance of defeating Heke if they were aligned with pro-government natives. Despite a complete lack of evidence that Hone Heke was moving south, those living in Auckland continued their increasingly panic-stricken efforts to protect themselves. The Albert Barracks were hastily being built on the ridge above the town, and Point Britomart, with its grim scoria buildings, became Fort Britomart. Several blockhouses were erected, the windows of St

Paul's were bullet-proofed to create a haven for women and children, and the price of almost everything rose drastically as people rushed to stock up on provisions. Others had left Auckland for the south or sold their properties and fled the new colony altogether. There were also grave fears that the unrest among the northern Maoris would spread to those in other parts of the colony, such as the Waikato and the Arawa tribes, although level-headed observers pointed out that Auckland's Ngati Whatua were still trading perfectly peacefully and showed no signs of rebellion.

There were also loud grumbles from Aucklanders about the behaviour of some of the Bay of Island evacuees, who had gone from being 'unfortunate refugees' to 'that damned Kororareka rabble'. It seemed that a significant number of them had no interest in finding gainful employment for themselves, preferring instead to spend their days getting drunk in Auckland's grogshops. Women were no longer able to shop in Shortland or Queen Streets unchaperoned, and no self-respecting lady would even consider venturing along the waterfront, accompanied or not.

Kitty, however, who had slipped into such a state of agitated melancholia that Simon was becoming seriously alarmed, barely noticed what was happening around her. Rian had proved to be a less than enthusiastic letter-writer; Kitty had received only three from him since she had arrived in Auckland, and they had been only short notes, informing her he was well and she shouldn't worry. When she had opened and read the most recent letter, she had hurled it at Simon and shouted, 'Not worry? Not *worry!*' and burst into tears. He was so concerned for her, in fact, that he was considering taking her back to the Bay of Islands, regardless of Rian's wishes. But then something happened that both delighted and appalled him, in roughly the same measure.

Shopping on Shortland Street on the first day of May, Kitty had rounded on him. 'Why can't you leave me alone, Simon? You don't have to follow me *everywhere*, you know!'

'I do, actually. It isn't safe at the moment,' he replied.

'Well, I don't care,' Kitty snapped. 'You're making me feel like a prisoner in my own . . . clothes!' She had been going to say 'home', but Auckland wasn't her home, was it? The *Katipo* was, and she was missing the schooner and being at sea so much she ached. 'For God's sake, why can't I have just an hour to myself? I'm sure no one will accost me.'

Simon was fairly sure of that, too — the thunderous expression on Kitty's normally very pretty face would no doubt be enough to keep anyone away.

'If I do, will you promise not to go far?' he pleaded.

At his obvious concern and discomfort, Kitty's face softened. 'I promise. I just want some time alone with my thoughts, Simon. You understand what I mean, I know you do.'

Simon nodded, although he still had plenty of misgivings about leaving Kitty on her own. He looked at his watch. 'Shall I meet you back here at, say, midday? And then we could have some lunch, perhaps.'

'Yes, that would be nice,' Kitty said. 'I'll see you then.'

She watched him walk along the street until he was out of sight, then went into the nearest general store where she purchased a sturdy pair of trousers, a man's work shirt and a pea jacket.

'Shopping for your husband?' the man behind the counter asked brightly.

'Yes, I am,' Kitty said shortly, worried that Simon might come back and wishing the man would just get on with it.

'And a lucky man he is, too, if you don't mind me saying, missus.' The man frowned. 'Small, though. You sure you've got the right sizes?'

'Positive, thank you,' Kitty replied.

'Ah well, you know the man you're married to, I suppose.'

Kitty did — and that he'd be almost apoplectic if he knew what she was planning. She paid for her purchases and left the shop.

But as she stood in the doorway of a shoemaker's further down the street considering whether she wanted a new pair of boots, she felt a determined tugging at her skirts. Looking down, she encountered the face of perhaps the scruffiest little child she had ever seen.

She was Maori, although quite light-skinned, and aged anywhere between three and five, Kitty guessed. Her dirty, matted hair hung past her shoulders, and her sweet, heart-shaped face was filthy with what looked like many months of accumulated grime. She was wearing a sleeveless man's shirt tied at the waist with a piece of string, and her small feet were bare, the toes stubbed and scabbed.

'Hello,' Kitty said.

The child, the whites of her eyes bright in her grubby face, stared determinedly up at Kitty and yanked even more vigorously on her skirts.

'What do you want?' Kitty asked kindly.

The child opened her free hand to show what it held. Kitty bent to look, and saw that it was a nugget of gum, or copal, from a kauri tree. It had been highly polished to enhance its beautiful gold and honey hues, and there appeared to be some sort of insect trapped within it.

'That's very pretty,' she said. 'Is it yours?'

The little girl didn't appear to understand her, so Kitty changed to Maori and said it again. After a few seconds, the child nodded.

'Well,' Kitty said, 'you need to take very good care of it. You don't want to lose it.'

The child shook her head angrily and again thrust the piece of amber forward. Then she pointed meaningfully at Kitty's reticule. Did the little girl want her to buy the amber?

'No, it's yours,' she said, still in Maori. 'You keep it. It's quite valuable.'

Angrily, the child stamped her bare foot.

Kitty looked up and down the street. 'Where's your mother, sweetheart?'

But the child remained mute.

'Look, wait here a minute,' Kitty said. 'I'll be right back.'

She went into the shoemaker's and rapped on

276

the counter. A man wearing a heavy leather apron appeared from the back of the shop.

'Good morning, madam. How can I help you?'

'There's a little Maori girl outside,' Kitty explained. 'I'm trying to find out where her mother is.'

Realising he probably wasn't going to make a sale, the man's demeanour changed. 'A scruffy little kid, about three or four?' he asked. When Kitty nodded, he said, 'Don't know if she has a mother, that one. She's often hanging around in the street hawking bits and pieces. Stolen, I've no doubt. Just shoo her away — that usually gets rid of her eventually.'

Aghast, Kitty stared at him. 'But she's only a tiny child!'

The man shrugged, said, 'Not one of ours, though, is she?' and turned away.

Kitty glared at the back of his head and felt like swinging her reticule at it.

From the doorway into the back of his shop he said over his shoulder, 'And watch it, she's a known pickpocket.'

Kitty marched outside, expecting the little girl still to be there, but she was nowhere to be seen.

'Damn,' Kitty swore and set off down the street, looking down the narrow alleyways between shops and peering into doorways in case the child was hiding. She couldn't possibly just forget about her, not after looking into those enormous brown eyes and seeing with horror the way her arm and wrist bones had protruded so pathetically.

Where the hell had she gone? Kitty passed a grog-shop, then a grocer's, a general merchant's, a hotel, the offices of an auctioneer, a cabinetmaker's and a butcher, when something registered in her mind. Had that pile of rags in among those barrels just moved? She turned around and went back, then cautiously made her way between two buildings, holding up her skirts and carefully avoiding the worst of the fly-ridden butcher's offal and rubbish. She slowed, then peeked over the top of a barrel.

The little girl was squatting with her back to it, contemplating half a putrid-looking scotch egg. Her brown fingers extended and she delicately picked the maggots off it, then raised it to her mouth.

Kitty reached over the barrel and knocked the disgusting thing out of the child's hand. She squawked and leapt to her feet, her face a picture of childish rage. Then she had a tantrum, shrieking and stamping her bare feet, which was a great relief to Kitty — at least the girl was showing some signs of being a normal child. She scooped her up and carried her back out onto the street, then set her down. The girl immediately produced the nugget of amber again and offered it to Kitty.

'No,' Kitty said firmly in Maori, 'I'm not buying it, but you are coming with me.' She reached out to grasp the little girl's arm, but the child was off again, quickly disappearing into an alleyway on the opposite side of the street.

But Kitty had seen something in the girl's eyes for a fleeting second, something approaching an uneasy mix of fear and hope. So she set off herself, her heart thumping wildly with anticipation, walking slowly along Shortland Street and stopping every few yards to look into shops, up at the sky, along the street, anywhere so that the child had time to come out of hiding. By the time she reached the intersection with Bank Street, she knew the girl was following her. But she forced herself not to look, and when she paused to cross the street, she felt a small hand slip into hers.

As they crossed the street together, Kitty was shocked to feel tears streaming down her face.

★   ★   ★

'Oh, Kitty, no,' Simon said in dismay.

'I'm just going to take her back to Mrs Fleming's and give her a hot bath and something to eat,' Kitty explained quickly before he could say anything else. 'And then I'm going to find out who she belongs to, if in fact she actually has parents or a guardian. I wonder if she's an orphan?'

'That's kidnap, Kitty,' Simon warned. 'You can't just waltz off with her.'

'But we've been standing here for ages in full view, and no one's approached us,' Kitty reasoned.

'Have you asked her who her guardians are?'

'Of course I have, but she doesn't seem to be able to speak.'

Simon's belly squirmed with anxiety as he gazed down at the little girl. She stared boldly back at him, her hand firmly gripping Kitty's skirts. He closed his eyes and blew out a heartfelt sigh, knowing that this could only lead to trouble and wishing he had never agreed to leave Kitty to her own devices.

'Come on then,' he said with a very deep sense of foreboding. 'I'll carry your shopping. Did you buy something nice?'

'Just a few bits and pieces,' Kitty replied, feeling a twinge of guilt as she handed him her parcel.

Kitty had a key to Mrs Fleming's front door so they let themselves in. Kitty was hoping to smuggle the child up to her room, but unfortunately Mrs Fleming rushed out of the kitchen to meet them.

'Good morning, Mr Bullock. You'll never guess, Mrs Farrell, I was at the grocer's earlier — ' She stopped abruptly. 'What on earth have you got there?' she said, regarding the little girl with a look of extreme distaste.

'I found her on Shortland Street. I think she may be an orphan.'

'She's *filthy*,' Mrs Fleming correctly observed. 'She can't stay here.'

Kitty fixed her with a stern look. 'Mrs Fleming, where is your sense of Christian charity? The child is hungry and in need of help. Who am I, or indeed you, to turn her away from God's succour?'

Mrs Fleming tried unsuccessfully to arrange her expression into one of compassion, then bent down and peered into the child's hair. 'Oh my Lord, she's got head lice!' she exclaimed in horror, and scurried off down the hall. From the safety of the kitchen she called, 'You can put her in the bath on the back porch.'

Kitty left the little girl sitting on the back steps with Simon, and waited while Mrs Fleming put together a plate containing two thick slices of fresh bread, several of roast pork, some pickled cucumber and a square of cheese. She handed it to Kitty, saying gruffly, 'I'll agree, she does look very undernourished.'

The child pounced on the food, shoving the bread into her mouth and tearing at the meat.

'Hey, hey,' Simon said, 'slow down, you'll get heartburn.' He reached to take the meat off her, but she slapped at his hand and jammed the entire slice of pork into her mouth. It was too much and a moment later she choked. Simon patted her firmly on the back until the meat flew out and landed in the dirt at the foot of the stairs. Kitty watched in appalled fascination as the child lunged after it and pushed it back into her mouth.

'My God,' she said. 'When do you think she last had a square meal?'

'Not for some time, I'd say,' Simon muttered. He looked sadly up at Kitty. 'I think you're right. I think she must be an orphan.'

'But surely her people would have been looking after her? She must belong to one of the tribes around here,' Kitty said, her heart aching. 'And she can't be completely wild, she understands some Maori.'

'She looks like a half-caste to me,' Simon said. 'Perhaps she was abandoned because of it.'

'Oh, surely not? How could anyone be that cruel?' But Kitty knew that people could in fact be that unkind, Maoris and Europeans alike, and indeed plenty of other peoples she had encountered around the world.

The child poked the last bite of cheese into her mouth and sat there chewing it until she finally swallowed. She burped, looked up at Kitty with a very odd expression on her face, then opened her mouth wide and vomited everything back up. Kitty skipped out of the way, but the steps were splattered and so were the girl's feet.

Cursing, Simon jumped up and went inside for something to clean up the mess.

He returned with several pieces of rag and said, 'Perhaps we should have started her with something like bread soaked in milk. Her stomach's obviously not used to a lot of food at once. Mrs Fleming's got hot water on the fire for a bath.'

He knelt and began to clean the sick off the little girl's feet. Kitty watched him, thinking what a good, loving father he might have made. The child watched him, too, and a moment later started to make a strange sort of whimpering noise that Kitty realised was weeping. Huge tears rolled down her dirty cheeks and a dollop of watery snot slid out of her nose.

'Oh, the poor wee thing,' Kitty murmured, feeling fresh tears prick at her own eyes. Digging out her handkerchief, she bent down and wiped the girl's nose and upper lip.

'I don't suppose she has a name,' Simon said, sitting back on his heels.

'Yes, she does, actually,' Kitty replied with no hesitation at all. 'It's Amber.' Then she went inside to remonstrate with Mrs Fleming about the child having to have her bath on the porch.

'The breeze is rather brisk,' she insisted. 'I don't want to be responsible for her catching a cold. I think she would be better off in front of the fire in the parlour.'

Mrs Fleming looked alarmed. 'But she's infested with vermin. They can jump yards, those lice.' Then she shook her head in defeat and added reluctantly, 'I suppose I can put down a piece of oilcloth. But mind she doesn't wander around until she's been thoroughly cleaned. I've got my other boarders to think of, you know.'

Kitty said gratefully, 'Yes, Mrs Fleming, I know. Thank you. I'll start the fire now.'

When the fire in the parlour had been lit, Kitty carried in the tin bath and set it down near the hearth on the oilcloth Mrs Fleming had provided — a piece almost as wide as the parlour itself. Then she started to bring the water through from the kitchen and pour it into the bath.

Mrs Fleming appeared and held out a small bottle.

Kitty took it. 'What is it?'

'Lavender water. It might make her smell a little sweeter.'

'That's very thoughtful, Mrs Fleming.' Kitty beamed at her. 'Thank you.' Mrs Fleming was right — Amber did smell rather pungent.

The landlady blushed, firelight glinting off her spectacles. 'Don't use it all, mind.'

Kitty promised she wouldn't, and went outside

to fetch Amber, who was now wading her way through a bowl of bread and milk, topped off, if Kitty wasn't mistaken, with brown sugar.

'Did you make her that?' she asked Simon.

He shook his head. 'Mrs Fleming did.'

When Amber had finished, Kitty took her inside and was in the process of testing the temperature of the water when Amber suddenly lifted the hem of her filthy shirt, squatted and began to urinate on the oilcloth. It was too late for Kitty to stop her so she watched helplessly, and then, praying that Mrs Fleming wouldn't choose that moment to come in, hastily dropped a towel over the puddle. It hadn't occurred to her that the child probably wouldn't be, well, house-trained.

'We're going to have to do something about that, aren't we?' she said as she untied the string at Amber's waist, then opened the buttons on her shirt.

Kitty gasped as the shirt slid off the child's thin shoulders and fell to the floor: Amber's torso was covered with ugly, mottled bruises. Kitty turned her around and saw that the same bruising marked her back and skinny buttocks.

'Oh, my poor darling, what's happened to you?' she whispered.

But Amber said nothing, merely stood with her head down and her hair falling across her face.

Kitty went to the door and called out to Simon. When he appeared in the hallway she said angrily, 'Someone has kicked or beaten the hell out of her, Simon. We need to get a doctor to come and look at her.'

Simon looked as shocked as she felt. 'What? Is she hurt?'

'I don't know. The bruises don't look new, but there are a lot of them.'

Mrs Fleming emerged from the kitchen to stand in the hallway, her face grim.

Then Simon's hand crept up to cover his mouth as something truly horrible occurred to him. 'What about, well, is she . . . has she . . . ?'

With a jolt that almost sent her heart into her throat, Kitty realised what he was trying to say. She felt sick, and tasted bile rising up into the back of her mouth. 'I didn't look. I mean, how would you tell? Oh my God, Simon, please go and get a doctor. *Please.*'

Simon nodded and strode purposefully off down the hall, then stopped at the front door when he realised he didn't know where he was going. 'Mrs Fleming? Can you recommend a good physician?'

'Doctor Moffitt in Princes Street is very efficient. He attends me and Miss Whelan. He's expensive, however.'

Simon was out the door and away. Kitty returned to the parlour to find Amber sitting on the floor near the fire, her bony arms wrapped around her knees.

Kitty took her hand and encouraged her to step into the bath and sit down. At first Amber was hesitant, and Kitty wondered if she had ever had a hot bath in her life. Finally, though, she sat down, and Kitty began to soap her poor bruised back with some of her own special castile soap.

Amber splashed, then splashed some more so that water slopped over the edge of the bath onto the oilcloth, then gave a little tinkling giggle. She lifted a cupped handful of the lavender-scented water to her nose and sniffed noisily, like a small animal, then looked up at Kitty with a smile of such startled delight that Kitty had to bite her lip to stop herself from crying.

'That's lavender,' she said, her voice cracking. 'A pretty flower.'

Kneeling on the floor beside the bath, she leaned close to Amber and inspected her hair — again Mrs Fleming was right: it was infested with nit eggs.

'Mrs Fleming?' Kitty called. When the landlady put her head around the door, she asked, 'Do you have any tea-tree oil? I need to attend to Amber's hair.'

'I believe I have some somewhere,' Mrs Fleming said, and hurried off to look for it.

While she waited, Kitty tackled Amber's tangled and matted hair with a comb. She winced every time the comb caught and jerked Amber's head, but the little girl simply sat, apparently content, and played with the water.

After a few fruitless minutes, Kitty realised she was going to have to cut some of the hair off.

When Mrs Fleming reappeared with the oil, Kitty asked, 'And do you have a pair of good scissors? This is hopeless.'

Kitty cut a good six inches off Amber's hair, leaving it sitting just above her shoulders, then threw the ends onto the fire where they hissed and burned with a sharp, unpleasant smell. She applied the tea-tree oil to the child's scalp, using almost the whole bottle, and started the arduous process of combing it through and picking out the nit eggs. It took her an hour, during which she had to add more hot water to the bath so Amber wouldn't get cold. But at least the little girl was getting a thorough soak.

Finally, when she had removed all the eggs she could see, she began diligently to wash Amber with soap. Her hands and feet were ingrained with dirt and there was a ring of grime around her neck where the collar of her shirt had rubbed for God only knew how long. Then she massaged a liberal dollop of shampoo into what remained of Amber's hair, and rinsed it several times. To Kitty's distress, Amber struggled violently when she tipped her backwards into the water, as though she thought she was going to be drowned, so Kitty rinsed her hair by pouring water over it.

When Kitty judged Amber to be as clean as she was going to be, she lifted her out of the bath and wrapped her in a towel, then sat her on the floor in front of the fire while she combed out her hair.

'She's almost asleep,' Mrs Fleming said from the doorway.

'You can come in now,' Kitty said, trying not to smile. 'I think she's vermin-free.'

Mrs Fleming disappeared briefly, then came back with a bucket of water, a scrubbing brush and a jar of chloride of lime, which she sprinkled on the oilcloth around the bath and began to scour.

'I'm going to put her to bed until the doctor comes,' Kitty said.

Her head down over her scrubbing brush, Mrs Fleming casually suggested, 'Perhaps you could tuck her in with that cat of yours. They'd be good company for each other.'

Kitty felt her face growing hot. How long had Mrs Fleming known?

'I've a good mind to charge you an extra shilling a week for its keep, you know,' Mrs Fleming went on. 'But the mouse problem seems to be abating, so I suppose I won't.'

'Er, thank you,' Kitty said sheepishly.

She carried Amber, who was indeed almost asleep, up to her room and tucked her into bed. Bodie, who had been sitting on the windowsill, jumped onto the coverlet, sniffed at Amber's face and neck, then settled down beside her. Amber sighed, closed her little fist around Bodie's tail and shut her eyes.

'Well, that's a surprise,' Kitty said softly to herself. And was it also an omen? Oh, if only it was.

★   ★   ★

When the doctor arrived, Kitty had to wake Amber from a deep sleep. She immediately struck out at Kitty, stared around wildly, then burst into tears. But when she saw that Bodie was still nestled by her side, looking only vaguely affronted at having been woken herself, her wails subsided to sobs and she gradually settled.

'Poor little thing,' Kitty murmured, stroking

Amber's hair. 'Did you get a fright? Did you not know where you were?'

But if Kitty was hoping that something to eat, a good wash and a nap would be enough to restore Amber's voice, she was disappointed. Amber remained silent, although her fingers played restlessly over Bodie's sleek black fur.

Kitty called downstairs for Simon and the doctor to come up, then sat on the bed next to Amber.

'Sorry I took so long,' Simon apologised as he entered Kitty's bedroom. 'Doctor Moffitt was out on a house call.'

The doctor himself appeared, a short, round man with a kindly face and whiskers that were turning grey.

'What have we here then, eh?' he said cheerfully as he set his bag on the end of the bed.

'I found her on Shortland Street,' Kitty explained. 'And when I left to return here she followed me.'

'And she was by herself?' Doctor Moffitt asked.

Kitty nodded. 'She appeared to be. She was wearing an old rag of a man's shirt, and she was absolutely filthy and eating rubbish from behind the butcher's.'

Doctor Moffitt shook his head sadly. 'Yes, we're seeing more and more of this sort of thing. Often with the half-caste children. They're not wanted by anyone, you see.'

Kitty didn't believe that that could be an entirely accurate assessment — look at how precious Tahi was to his family — but perhaps the situation was different in the larger towns. Still, she found it difficult to accept that a child could be so completely abandoned, as Amber appeared to have been.

'We fed and bathed her,' she said, 'and I think we've managed to get the lice out of her hair, but she's covered in the most appalling bruises. And she doesn't seem to be able to speak. And we were worried about, well, whether she has been . . . otherwise hurt.' The doctor's expression was one of such pained distaste that Kitty knew he comprehended her meaning. 'So I was hoping you could examine her, please. And perhaps also give me an indication of her age, if possible.'

'Of course,' Doctor Moffitt said, and removed his coat.

Simon went downstairs as Kitty encouraged Amber to sit up. With her body cleansed of the worst of the dirt, the bruises on her tawny skin stood out in even sharper relief.

'Yes, I see what you mean,' the doctor said grimly. 'Could you remove the cat from the bed, please?'

Kitty lifted Bodie out of the way, which immediately sent Amber into a fit of screaming that gave Kitty an awful fright. She glanced at the doctor.

He shrugged. 'Perhaps we should leave it there, if it makes her feel better.'

Kitty returned Bodie to the bed and watched as the doctor gently palpated the bruises on Amber's chest and back, presumably checking for broken bones, felt up and down her arms and legs and around her neck, pressed his fingers into her belly and had a long look inside her mouth. Amber bore it all in silence, once again holding onto Bodie's tail. Then Doctor Moffitt made the examination Kitty had been dreading.

After a minute he patted Amber's hand and pulled the bedclothes up over her chest.

'Her teeth suggest that she is around four years old, perhaps a little younger,' he announced, 'although she is rather small, due to malnutrition I expect. And I'm fairly sure she hasn't been . . . got at, if you'll pardon my vulgarity.'

Blinking hard, Kitty breathed a deep sigh of relief.

'But I'm at a loss to explain why she can't, or won't, speak,' the doctor went on. 'You say she has uttered no words at all?'

'Not in my hearing,' Kitty replied. 'I've heard her giggle, and you heard her screaming, of course. I've spoken to her in both English and Maori, and I believe she was able to understand at least some of the Maori.'

'So she probably isn't deaf,' Doctor Moffitt said. 'And I can see no damage to her larynx and no deformity of the palate, although I'm not an expert in that particular branch of medicine. But she has received a fairly severe beating at some point in the not-too-distant past. Fortunately I can't feel any broken bones, but she will need bed rest for several days. The sores on her legs, buttocks and stomach are, I strongly suspect, ringworm. She also appears to have intestinal worms. For the ringworm I'd suggest a lotion of flax root. I believe Mr McKenzie the pharmacist keeps a stock. For the bruises, rub in arnica lotion, and for the intestinal worms administer an aperient followed by santonin on an empty stomach. What did you use to douse her hair?'

'Tea-tree oil,' Kitty said. 'And I cut quite a lot of it off.'

'Well, if the tea-tree oil doesn't work, and sometimes it doesn't, I'd recommend a paste. I can write out the ingredients for you. Two doses over the space of a week should suffice. However . . . ' Doctor Moffitt paused. 'I'm sorry, I don't believe your friend introduced us.'

Kitty hadn't even noticed. 'Oh, I beg your pardon, I'm Mrs Kitty Farrell.'

'Mrs Farrell, how long do you intend to, er, keep this child?'

'I hadn't really thought about it,' Kitty replied, untruthfully.

'Yes, well,' the doctor said, 'it's all very commendable doing good works, Mrs Farrell, but I'm not entirely sure it would be fair on the child if you fed and kept her for a few days, then sent her back to the streets when she becomes a burden. There's no orphanage in Auckland, you know.'

Kitty was thoroughly jolted. Good works? Send Amber back to the streets? Did the man think she was some sort of drawing-room socialite looking for a short-term hobby?

Frostily, she replied, 'I can assure you I will have her best interests at heart.'

Doctor Moffitt eyed her benignly. 'I see I have offended you, Mrs Farrell, and I apologise, but it

292

does happen, you know. Christian charity can tend to be a passing fad for some people.'

Kitty inclined her head in acknowledgement of his apology. 'I have every intention of searching for her guardians as soon as possible, Doctor. If she has any, I will find them. If it seems she does not, well, I will consider the situation again then.'

'Well, I wish you luck,' Doctor Moffitt said. 'And remember, if she is a truly feral child, she is quite likely to run off once her belly is full.'

'Well, we'll wait and see, shall we?' Kitty replied. 'Now, how much is your professional fee?'

Doctor Moffitt waved the question away. 'I do not view Christian charity as a passing fad, Mrs Farrell, so there will be no charge.'

'Oh,' Kitty said, slightly chastened. 'Thank you.'

Bodie squeaked half-heartedly as Amber picked her up and cuddled her. Doctor Moffitt and Kitty both looked down at her for a moment.

'I suggest you try and encourage her to eat eggs, meat, fresh vegetables and sugar, Mrs Farrell. That way, if she does run off, she will have something inside her to sustain her for at least a few days. You could also ask at the police station whether they've received any reports of a missing child, although I doubt they will have. Not regarding this child, anyway.'

'Yes, yes I will, Doctor. Thank you again.'

Kitty saw the doctor out, then turned to Simon, who was waiting in the hall.

'Well, it could have been worse news, I

293

suppose,' he said when she had repeated the doctor's diagnoses.

'I told him I would try to track down her guardians,' Kitty added unenthusiastically.

'And so you will, starting tomorrow morning,' Simon said quickly, alarmed by her reluctant tone. 'You can't keep her, you know. She's not a . . . a cat.'

But Kitty had already turned away.

★ ★ ★

Amber slept for the rest of the day, but was awake by the time Hattie and Flora came home from work. It was then that Kitty realised she didn't have anything Amber could wear, so she improvised by knotting the straps of her spare chemise, cutting off the hem and slipping it over Amber's head and tying a length of ribbon around the waist.

Hattie and Flora both thought she was the sweetest little thing they'd ever seen, although everyone soon agreed her manners were shocking. At the dinner table she stood on her chair and snatched food from everyone else's plates, and when she had her hands crammed full, scampered off to a corner of the kitchen to eat it. The meat dish was chicken, and when she had finished shovelling it into her mouth with her hands, she dropped the bones on the floor, where Bodie — allowed out of Kitty's room now that her presence had been acknowledged — happily pounced on them. Then Amber let out a remarkably loud burp, given her small stature, which made Flora laugh out loud, Hattie giggle and Mrs Fleming almost faint with disapproval.

'I'm sorry,' Kitty apologised, trying not to laugh herself. 'But we need to remember that she's probably never been taught table manners or anything like that.'

'Indeed,' Mrs Fleming said, still frowning. 'Well, I'm afraid I can't countenance such uncivilised behaviour at my table, I really can't. If she is still here tomorrow, Mrs Farrell, I'm afraid you'll have to do something to . . . to control her.'

'I'll certainly do my best, Mrs Fleming,' Kitty replied, not daring to meet her landlady's bespectacled eye.

After she had eaten, Amber lay down in the corner and fell asleep, so Kitty carried her upstairs and tucked her into bed again. When she retired herself, she slipped in beside Amber and cuddled behind her, gently stroking the little girl's hair over and over.

12

When Kitty awoke the next morning, Amber was no longer beside her. For a horrid moment Kitty thought she might have run away, but then she found her, on the floor beneath the bed curled around a very contented-looking Bodie, her piece of amber clutched tightly in her hand.

'Amber? Amber, sweetheart, it's time to wake up.'

Bodie and Amber both stirred, stretched and then blinked at her. As Amber began to crawl out from under the bed, Kitty stepped back, into a suspiciously damp patch on the rug.

'Oh, sweetheart, you're going to have to stop doing that,' she said, disheartened rather than annoyed. Then, with more than a little alarm, she realised that sometime in the near future the forces of nature would come into play and Amber would be compelled to produce more than just a puddle. Mrs Fleming most definitely would not be impressed with *that* in the parlour or in a corner of the kitchen.

As if able to read her mind, Amber emitted a small fart as she stood up, her belly rumbling ominously.

Kitty ducked beneath the bed for the chamber pot, set it on the floorboards, lifted Amber's chemise and sat her on it, gently holding her in place in case she decided to get off.

Amber looked up at Kitty, clearly not quite

knowing what was required.

Kitty encouraged her in Maori and, obviously having caught the general gist of Kitty's words, Amber frowned in concentration and bore down. There was a result a few seconds later.

'Good *girl*, Amber.' Kitty beamed.

Amber beamed back.

Then Kitty said, 'Oh, hell,' as she realised she had nothing with which to wipe Amber's bottom.

'Stay there,' she said. 'Nohoia.'

Amber didn't move, so Kitty rushed down the stairs for some newspaper, dreading what might confront her if the little girl decided to get off the pot before she returned.

But she was still there. 'You're such a good girl, aren't you, sweetheart?' Kitty said as she cleaned her up. Amber clearly knew when she needed to relieve herself, so it was going to be more a matter of teaching her *where* to do so.

She led Amber over to the bowl on the chest of drawers, poured in some water from the ewer and showed the little girl how to wash her hands. Amber sniffed the soap, her face breaking into a beatific smile at its perfume. Then Kitty combed out her hair and they went downstairs.

Breakfast passed without too much incident and, after some rather skilful persuasion, Kitty prevailed upon Mrs Fleming to look after Amber while she went into town to look for children's clothing, and to visit a printery to have some posters made up.

Hattie asked, 'Kitty, you speak Maori, don't you?'

297

'Yes.'

'Well, have you asked Amber who her mother is? In Maori, I mean? What *is* the Maori word for mother?'

Kitty's heart began to thump wildly. She'd deliberately only asked her in English, which she was fairly confident Amber couldn't understand. She had been dreading this moment. Then she sighed. She couldn't keep on pretending to herself that Amber didn't have any family; she might, and if she did, then she should go back to them. But beneath this reluctant acknowledgement of needing to do the right thing was still the hope that she was a genuine orphan, a little lost girl waiting for someone to love her and take care of her. Perhaps someone who couldn't have children of her own, but who would be so very grateful for the chance to be a mother.

Finally, she said, 'There are several words in Maori that mean mother.' As she spoke, she kept her gaze on Amber, hoping against hope that there would be no reaction to any of the words she was about to use. 'There's whaea, which is quite common.' Amber, thank God, continued to chew happily on her toast. 'And matua wahine.' Still no response. 'That means female parent, and isn't normally used as a form of address. And there's also ukaipo, which is more of a poetical description.' Again, Amber didn't stir. 'But no Maori child calls their mother that.' Trying not to wince, Kitty hesitated before saying the word to which Amber would most likely respond. 'And there is . . . mama.'

Not even looking up, Amber reached out and

stuck her fingers in the marmalade jar.

Heartened, and feeling somewhat braver, Kitty said in Maori, 'Amber? Do you know who your mother is? Do you know what her name is?'

For the briefest of seconds Amber was suddenly still, a dollop of marmalade in her small brown hand, and Kitty's heart plummeted. Then the child jammed the marmalade into her mouth and proceeded to lick her fingers, the sticky orange mess going all over her face and in her hair.

'I'd say that was a no, wouldn't you?' Hattie remarked.

Suddenly filled with a soaring sense of elation, Kitty said, 'No, she couldn't give me an answer, could she?'

Flora said shrewdly, 'You sound almost as though you're pleased she couldn't. You're not planning to keep her yourself, are you?'

'Well, no, of course I'm not,' Kitty replied quickly. 'Not if she already has parents or a guardian somewhere.' Hurriedly, she changed the subject. 'Actually, are there any printers in Auckland?' Though she knew perfectly well there were — she'd seen five or six shingles out during her walks around the town.

'There are several, I believe,' Mrs Fleming said. 'I use Mr Skean in Bank Street. He has very reasonable rates.'

'What will they say?' Flora asked as she spread honey on a piece of toast.

Feeling suddenly drained, Kitty drank the last of her tea. 'What will who say?'

'These posters you're going to have printed.

What will they have on them?'

'I'm not entirely sure,' Kitty said, sitting back in her chair. 'I haven't really thought about it. I'll have to ask Simon what he thinks.'

So she did, when he arrived to escort her into town.

He thought about it for a few minutes as they walked along Eden Crescent. 'What about, "Seeking the parents or guardian of a Maori girl, approximately four years old, found in Shortland Street on Thursday, 1 May. Possibly half-caste, dark hair, brown eyes and wearing a sleeveless man's shirt. Informants please apply to 10 Eden Crescent." Would that do?'

'I suppose so,' Kitty said, 'although it makes her sound a bit like a lost umbrella or a snuff box.'

'And you could offer a reward. It's probably the most effective way to get a result,' Simon added bluntly. 'You'll have to make sure any informants are genuine, though. Does she have any distinguishing features?'

Kitty frowned, casting her mind back to Amber in the bath. 'Yes, she has a birthmark on her back, just under her right shoulder-blade, sort of heart-shaped. I won't put that on the poster, though.'

'No, that would just be asking for trouble,' Simon agreed. 'But you could use it to test anyone who does come forward.'

'How much should I offer as a reward?'

'How much do you want to offer?'

Kitty didn't want to offer anything; the smaller the chance of any of Amber's family coming forward the better, as far as she was concerned. 'A pound?'

'That won't be enough,' Simon said. 'What about five pounds? Can you afford that much?'

Reluctantly, Kitty said she could.

They visited Mr Skean's printery and ordered fifty posters, to be collected the following morning. Then Kitty dragged Simon down to Queen Street to Mr Graham's drapery. The waterfront was very busy, as a ship laden with cargo had anchored early that morning and was being unloaded. Those shopkeepers whose premises weren't near the shore were standing by with carts and drays to collect the goods they'd ordered. There was a lot of running about and shouting going on, but, although it was an interesting spectacle, Kitty had better things to do.

'Come on,' she said to Simon, grasping him firmly by the elbow and leading him along the street to the drapery.

'What are we going in here for?' he asked.

'To choose fabric for clothes for Amber,' Kitty replied, in a tone suggesting that even a simpleton might be expected to know that.

Simon said uneasily, 'Can you not wait at least until the posters have been up for a week and we see if anyone comes forward?'

'Yes, but what is she supposed to go about in until then, Simon? My chemise? A tablecloth, perhaps? She needs drawers, she needs boots, she needs at least one dress, she needs a pinafore — ' Kitty replied, counting off each item on her fingers.

Simon shook his head despairingly. 'Kitty, stop. Look, I know you've . . . fallen in love with her, but I'm worried you're setting yourself up for a very bitter disappointment.' He paused, seeing again the longing that had burned in Kitty's eyes ever since she had found the child. 'And what will Rian say, eh? Will he want her? Have you thought about that?'

'Of course I've thought about it, Simon!' Kitty snapped. 'I've thought of little else since yesterday! But don't you think it's meant to be? Come on, you're a missionary, you're supposed to believe in miracles and divine intervention. Is that not what this is?'

His faith was something Simon had been trying not to think about of late, and he pushed it aside again now. 'I just don't want to see you hurt, that's all.'

'Well, why don't we just wait and see what happens?' Kitty said, talking quickly to dispel her own dread at the thought that her dream might not come true. 'But in the meantime, she must have something to wear. I mean, it really isn't appropriate that she go about in my underthings, is it?'

Simon sighed and followed her into the drapery.

⋆   ⋆   ⋆

Kitty selected three lengths of material for frocks; a rust, blue and green plaid wool (because the weather was turning), an unusually fine red and blue-sprigged linsey-woolsey, and an indigo-dyed calico. She also chose plain cream cotton and some pretty flannel for petticoats, and crisp white cotton for two chemises, several pairs of drawers and two pinafores.

'Do you stock fancy goods?' she asked Mr Graham.

'Some,' he replied, ushering her over to a set of shelves that held a selection of laces, reels of ribbon and trim, and a small assortment of embroidery thread. 'I don't carry a great range, though. You may prefer to shop around.'

'No, I think I'll find what I want here, thank you, Mr Graham,' Kitty said, gently rubbing a piece of lace between her fingers. 'Is this Irish?'

'Yes.'

'Good. I'll have enough of that to hem all of the underthings, and to go across the top and bottom of one of the pinafores.'

'It's rather expensive,' Mr Graham warned.

'Yes, I know. I suppose you don't stock children's bonnets?'

Simon, aware of the fun Kitty was having, nevertheless thought she was getting a little carried away, but found he didn't have the heart to try to stop her.

Instead, he said lamely, 'Do you really think she's the sort of child who will happily wear a bonnet?'

Kitty gave him a look. 'Simon, every little girl needs at least one bonnet.'

Mr Graham said, 'Unfortunately, no, I don't stock them, and this town at present does not have a milliner. But you could try at any good general merchant's. Do you know Gibson &

Mitchell's in Shortland Street? I recommend you try there first. And did you have anyone in mind for the dressmaking?'

'No, I've had no need of a dressmaker.'

'I'd recommend Mrs Hemmings, on the corner of Bank and Chancery. She's highly skilled, and very prompt.'

Kitty paid for her purchases and handed them to Simon to carry as they headed up to Shortland Street. He thought it rather amusing that a dressmaker would be named *Mrs Hemmings*, and said so.

At Gibson & Mitchell's, Kitty bought a blue bonnet, which she thought would match all Amber's new dresses. She also purchased seven pairs of children's lisle socks, a small pair of boy's trousers, a boy's shirt and a small jacket and cap. They were not particularly well tailored, but were made of a sturdy fabric and would be more than adequate.

Simon said, 'Are they for Amber?' When Kitty said yes, he asked, 'But why are you buying boy's clothes?'

'Because she has to wear something while her new clothes are being made.'

'Oh,' Simon said. And then it occurred to him: Kitty said she often wore men's clothes on board the *Katipo*, so this was obviously going to be Amber's shipboard outfit. Again, he winced inwardly at the thought of the bitter disappointment Kitty was probably courting.

Their next visit was to a shoemaker's, where Kitty announced she wanted two pairs of children's boots. 'One brown and one black, I think,' she told the shoemaker.

When he asked what size she required, Kitty withdrew a folded page of the *Auckland Times* from her reticule, and spread it out on the counter. 'This is her left foot and this is her right,' she explained. 'I drew around them this morning.'

The shoemaker regarded the template. 'How old is the child?'

'Four,' Kitty replied.

'These are very wide feet for a four-year-old. Is she a native child, or just not accustomed to wearing shoes?'

'Both,' Kitty said, fixing the shoemaker with a look that dared him to comment further.

He chose not to, and went to his shelves to select several pairs of boots.

Kitty chose styles that laced up rather than buttoned, assuming that the former would be easier for small fingers to manage than tiny buttons.

Their last port of call was Mrs Hemmings the dressmaker, who produced several patterns for Kitty to consider. While Simon sat twiddling his thumbs, the two women spent a pleasant half-hour discussing the merits of pin tucks on children's bodices and where exactly the waist should sit. After securing an assurance from Mrs Hemmings that the garments would be ready by the following Monday, Kitty and Simon walked back to Eden Crescent.

Amber and Mrs Fleming were in the kitchen making scones. Mrs Fleming's cheeks were flushed, while Amber was kneeling on a chair at the table, her hands, arms, face and the floor around her liberally dusted with flour. Bodie was sitting patiently beneath the table, clearly waiting for morsels to appear.

'Has she been good?' Kitty asked as she removed her bonnet and set it on a chair.

Mrs Fleming blew out her cheeks and tucked a strand of greying hair back under her house cap. 'Well, I'm not sure you can quite apply the word 'good' to a child like this one,' she said. 'But she has certainly been enthusiastic.'

'Have you been enthusiastic, have you?' Kitty asked Amber, who smiled at her and presented a handful of rather grey-looking scone dough.

'I don't know how many times I've told her not to eat uncooked dough,' Mrs Fleming remarked, 'but she has continued to shovel it in. And she had a good breakfast, too.'

Kitty regarded Amber's floury little face, and felt desperately sad that any child could have suffered such hunger.

Mrs Fleming deftly cut the scone dough into squares and slid the tray into the bread oven. 'Mr Bullock, would you care for a cup of tea? I have Souchong, Gunpowder and Black.'

'Souchong would be very nice, thank you,' Simon said as he sat down on a kitchen chair, then quickly stood again as he realised the seat was covered with flour. He turned around, revealing white imprints on his backside. Amber laughed merrily.

Kitty took a damp cloth, wiped the flour and dough from Amber's hands and face and lifted her down.

'No little accidents?' she asked.

'Almost,' Mrs Fleming said, 'but I managed to get her on the pot in time. Somebody really needs to take the time to train her.' She looked pointedly at Kitty. 'Although that certainly won't be me.'

'Of course not,' Kitty replied. 'You've been a great help already, Mrs Fleming, and I very much appreciate it.'

Mrs Fleming blushed with reluctant pleasure.

'But you do know about training a child?'

Mrs Fleming darted a look at Simon, who was still trying to dust the flour off the back of his trousers. 'I do,' she said, 'I've had children of my own, of course. But it isn't really a subject suitable for, well, the ears of a gentleman.'

'Oh. Yes, of course,' Kitty said.

'So perhaps we shall discuss the matter a bit later?' Mrs Fleming suggested.

'Yes, that would be very helpful,' Kitty agreed. 'Now,' she said, crouching to address Amber, who had crawled beneath the table to play with Bodie. 'I have some nice things for you, sweetheart. Would you like to see them?'

Amber took no notice, continuing to roll a ball of filthy dough past Bodie, who eyed it distastefully.

Kitty opened the box containing Amber's new bonnet, and handed it to her under the table. Amber took it, sniffed at the fabric, rubbed it across her face, then set it on Bodie's head and giggled delightedly.

'At least she knows what it's for,' Simon observed.

'Well, of course she does,' Kitty replied defensively. 'I very much doubt she's feeble-minded.'

Simon very much doubted it, too: the child's eyes exhibited far too much intelligence and cunning.

Kitty unwrapped the parcel that contained the boots. 'And look, Amber, look what else we've got for you.'

Amber came out from under the table.

'Lovely new boots!' Kitty said excitedly, handing her the brown pair.

Amber tugged them onto her bare feet and stood up. She took a few hesitant steps, then made a face, pulled them off again and went back to annoying Bodie.

Kitty sighed. 'Oh, well, I suppose she'll need to get used to them. But I'm sure she'll like her new dresses.'

'New dresses?' Mrs Fleming said, glancing at Simon, who shrugged.

'Yes, I'm having some dresses made. And underthings,' Kitty explained.

Mrs Fleming looked concerned. 'Oh dear, Mrs Farrell, you don't think that was a little unwise, do you? And such an expense, as well. I mean, she may not be here for very much longer.'

'Perhaps not,' Kitty said, pretending to be blithe about it. 'But she has to have something to wear.'

Still looking vaguely anxious, Mrs Fleming asked, 'You did arrange to have the posters printed?'

'Yes, they should be ready tomorrow morning.'

Mollified, Mrs Fleming said, 'Oh, well, that's good. And it will be interesting to see what comes out of the woodwork, won't it?'

★ ★ ★

Simon and Kitty, accompanied by Amber wearing her boy's shirt, jacket and trousers with the cuffs turned up and her hair tucked under the cap, went the following day to collect the posters and put them up in various places around the town. They left two at the post office in High Street, one on the notice board outside the Colonial Government Printing Office in Jermyn Street, one at the *Auckland Times* office in Shortland Street (with instructions to print it as an advertisement in the next issue), one at each of the town's churches, and the rest in various hotels, grogshops, grocers and general merchants along the main shopping streets.

When they had finished, Simon, carrying Amber's discarded boots under his arm, said, 'Well, if that doesn't get some sort of response, I don't know what will.'

Kitty looked around for Amber and suddenly couldn't see her. 'Oh God, Simon, where is she?'

Simon's mouth fell open, then he shut it and gazed up and down the street. 'She was here a second ago, I swear she was.'

Kitty had been holding tightly to Amber's hand almost all morning. But she had let go for just a few minutes, and now the child had gone. 'Oh, no, what if she's run away?' Kitty wailed, panic rising in her chest like a huge ocean wave.

'What if I can't find her again?'

Simon said calmly, 'Don't worry, she can't have gone far. She really was here a second ago. Perhaps if we — '

But his suggestion was interrupted by shouting from the interior of a grocer's shop several doors down the street. Then Amber came racing out, her legs pumping, her eyes wide and her arms wrapped around a watermelon almost as big as her head. The grocer, his apron flapping, emerged a second later and pounded down the street after her.

'Stop thief!' he bellowed. 'Stop him, the bugger's stolen my merchandise!'

Amber skidded to a halt in front of Kitty, then ducked around her, hiding behind her skirts.

The grocer lumbered up and, panting, reached behind Kitty and grabbed Amber by the ear.

'Sir!' Kitty cried. 'Unhand my child!'

'*Your* child?' the grocer said, looking from Kitty's face to Simon's equally European countenance, clearly assuming they were husband and wife. 'But the little beggar's a Maori!'

'What does that have to do with anything?' Kitty demanded.

'Well, how can . . . ' The grocer paused, let go of Amber and rubbed his florid face. 'Ah, never mind, but the little tyke just stole one of me watermelons. I'll want that paid for.'

'How much?' Kitty said tersely, opening her reticule.

A look of cunning slowly crossed the man's face. 'A shilling for the melon, and you might be interested in some of me other fine goods. If you are, I could be convinced not to go to the constabulary about this little matter,' he said, inclining his head at Amber.

Simon exclaimed, 'That's extortion!'

'It's me only offer, take it or leave it,' the grocer replied. 'I do hear that the gaol cells in this town can be a mite unpleasant for a little boy.' He frowned down at Amber, whose hair was falling out from beneath her cap. 'Actually, that's a lass, isn't it?'

Gripping Amber very firmly by the sleeve of her jacket, Kitty swept past him into his shop. 'Right,' she snapped when he'd caught up with her and squeezed himself behind his counter. 'Show me what you've got.'

Glancing at the doorway to make sure Simon wasn't yet within earshot, the grocer said leeringly, 'I could do *that* all right, missus.'

Kitty fixed him with a glare of such icy intensity that the man took an involuntary step back and bumped into the shelf behind him, knocking off several tins of tobacco.

Absolutely livid now, Kitty leaned across the counter. 'This is a commercial transaction, *sir*, not a social one, so get on with it.'

Wiping his sweaty hands on his apron, the grocer seemed to regain a little of his composure. 'Well, I've got some nice Patras currants, come in to port only yesterday, and some juicy muscatelles. Normandy pippins, Barcelona nuts, you name it. A bit pricey, but well worth it. Good sugar — Mauritius, Havannah or Manilla — citron, nutmeg, tapioca. Take your pick.'

Gritting her teeth, Kitty asked for a pound of

311

the muscatelles, two of the Manilla sugar and a pound of very expensive Java coffee.

When she opened her reticule again, the grocer reminded her, 'And a shilling for the melon.'

While the purchases were being wrapped, Kitty glanced angrily at Simon, who very gently shook his head, warning her to keep her temper in check. Fuming, Kitty turned back to the counter until the grocer slid the parcel across to her.

Picking it up, she said very clearly, 'You are the most unpleasant piece of ordure I have come across in a long time. May you rot in hell.'

As the grocer gaped, she turned to leave the shop. Unfortunately, Amber chose that moment to raise the watermelon she was still clutching high above her head and gleefully drop it, hooting as it exploded everywhere.

Kitty and Simon grabbed a hand each and whipped her out the door, her feet barely touching the ground. Outside, as they hurried down the street as quickly as was seemly, Simon said, 'Why did you have to say that? He'll go straight to the police now.'

'No he won't, not if he doesn't want to be brought up in front of the magistrate on charges of extortion.'

Between them, Amber was still chortling.

★ ★ ★

The first of the informants knocked on Mrs Fleming's door that evening. She was a young

312

Maori woman, bare-headed and bare-footed and wearing a plain brown dress.

'Good evening,' Kitty said in Maori.

'Good evening,' the woman replied. 'I have come about the found child. She is my daughter.'

'I see,' Kitty said. 'Can you describe her to me, please?'

The woman frowned slightly, and held out her hand at hip height, palm down. 'She is this big, with brown skin and black hair.'

She had just described every four-year-old Maori girl in New Zealand. Kitty said, 'Anything else?'

'Brown eyes.'

'No distinguishing marks? No . . . ' Kitty struggled to recall the Maori word for birthmark, then finally remembered it.

The woman stared at her for a long moment, as though trying to work out what Kitty was thinking. Eventually, she said, 'No.'

'That is a shame. This child has a birthmark.'

'Where?' the woman asked.

'On her face,' Kitty replied, pointing to her left cheek.

'Yes, that is her, that is my daughter!' the woman cried passionately. 'I have just remembered. It has been such a long time since I have seen her.'

Kitty shut the door in her face.

Simon, standing in the hallway, said, 'You're a cunning article, Kitty Farrell.'

'Clearly I'm going to have to be,' Kitty muttered. She was very relieved that the woman had been an impostor, but deeply disappointed that anyone would lie like that just for five pounds. What might have happened if she had believed the woman and handed Amber over? Would Amber have been dumped at the corner of the next street?

The next person to present themselves was an elderly Maori man whose missing grandchild, it was progressively revealed, had birthmarks on her feet, both legs, her belly, one arm and in the middle of her forehead.

'Was he referring to a child or a piebald pony?' Simon wondered after Kitty had sent the old man on his way.

At ten o'clock that evening some more 'informants' arrived, a pair of Pakeha men so drunk they could barely stand. This time Simon did the honours and shut the door in their faces.

The following morning, two little Maori boys knocked on the door. One, about eight years old, was wearing trousers, a vest with the buttons missing, and a gentleman's black silk top hat. His companion, probably about six, Kitty guessed, sported either long shorts or short longs, and a snotty upper lip.

'The found girl,' the elder of the two boys announced in English, 'she is our sister.'

Kitty assumed that, because he spoke quite good English, he was a pupil at one of the town's small, church-operated native schools.

'And what does she look like, this sister of yours?' she said, not unkindly.

The boys exchanged a quick glance before the elder one replied, 'Like us, but a girl.'

'Can you be a bit more precise?' Kitty asked.

314

The boys didn't appear to know what the word precise meant, so Kitty switched to Maori. They managed to come up with a very vague and obviously fabricated description of their 'sister', then trailed off into silence.

The longer they stood staring at her, the sorrier Kitty felt for them, even though they were clearly trying to hoodwink her. Mentally she gave them full marks for initiative, and for being able to read the poster in the first place, and told them to wait on the verandah. She closed the door and went into the kitchen to find the biscuit tin.

They were still standing there when she opened the front door again. 'No five pounds, but you can have a biscuit,' she said, handing them each one of Mrs Fleming's enormous ginger snaps. They seemed happy enough with those, and wandered off down the street with their mouths full.

Nobody else knocked that day, or Monday either, after the advertisement had run in the *Auckland Times*. Kitty was finding the tension almost intolerable as she waited to see whether someone with genuine information would eventually come knocking. Amber herself seemed to be settling well, although she still hadn't spoken. Kitty suspected that she actually could talk, or had once been able to, because she appeared to understand quite a lot of Maori and responded to it non-verbally when she felt like it. Kitty had begun to teach her the English words for various things, such as 'cat' and 'boot' and 'milk', and was convinced Amber was

315

absorbing them, even if Flora had pointed out that Amber seemed to pay attention only if the subject was related to either food or Bodie. Kitty thought she was being a little cynical, and said so; Flora thought Kitty was being somewhat gullible and overly optimistic, and said so. Mrs Fleming said they were both being rather irritating, and at least as undisciplined as Amber.

On Monday afternoon Kitty went along to Bank Street to collect Amber's new clothes. Mrs Hemmings had made a marvellous job of them and Amber seemed to be delighted, parading through the house and twirling around so that the lacy hem on her drawers peeked out from beneath her skirt. An unforeseen but happy outcome of the new underthings was that she seemed very reluctant to soil them, and got the pot out herself the next time she needed to empty her bladder.

'See, I told you she was a clever little girl!' Kitty said delightedly.

'Well, I can't argue with that,' Mrs Fleming replied, very pleased that she would no longer have to scrub her rugs.

But late that night someone came to the door with news that almost froze Kitty's heart. She was a Maori woman with a demeanour thoroughly unlike any of the others who had responded to the poster.

'I have information about the child,' she said without preamble when Kitty answered the door. She was a tall, handsome woman, with the chin moko that denoted considerable rank. She also spoke excellent English. 'I believe she is the daughter of my niece.'

Warily, Kitty asked, 'Can you tell me, has she any — '

'Yes,' the woman interrupted briskly, 'she does. She has a namu, a birthmark, on her back. In the shape of a heart.'

A bolt of pain lanced Kitty's chest and her eyes filled with hot, stinging tears. She swallowed and clutched at the doorframe for support, struggling to accept that the worst had happened, that she was about to lose Amber.

She swallowed again, the lump in her throat burning like a hot coal. 'Well, what was she doing wandering around on her own like that? What was she doing *all by herself?!*' she suddenly blurted, wanting to lash out at this woman who had brought such awful news. Then, with an almighty effort, she composed herself. 'I beg your pardon,' she said stiffly. 'One moment, please. I will fetch her for you.'

But the woman reached out and grasped her sleeve. 'No. You do not understand. I do not want her back. I want you to keep her, and to take her away from here if you can.'

Kitty could not understand what she was saying. 'But . . . you said she has a mother.'

'No, I said she is the daughter of my niece. My niece is not fit to be a mother.' The woman's face remained expressionless. 'The child's father was a Pakeha. He . . . defiled my niece. She became insane because of it. No one in my hapu would look after the child because they feared they would also become tainted by the madness. I include myself in this. We gave her food, but she slept in a hut by herself. Then, a year ago, she ran away.' The woman sighed and dropped her gaze. 'She cannot come back to my village, but my heart is heavy because of what we have done to her. I have recently been baptised and I have asked the Lord Jesus Christ for guidance, and He has advised me what to do. So please, take her and give her a better life than the one we inflicted upon her. I believe it is God's will.'

Kitty suddenly felt so light-headed she knew she had to sit down, and subsided in a heap of skirts on the hallway floor.

Unperturbed, the woman looked down at her. 'So, will you take her?'

'Yes. I will,' Kitty answered hoarsely. 'Do you want the five pounds?'

'No. Thank you.'

And she turned to go, but stopped when Kitty said, 'Wait. What is her name? What did you call her?'

Over her shoulder, the woman said quietly, 'We never gave her a name.'

Kitty stayed where she was and watched as the Maori woman walked away into the darkness. Then she started to cry.

13

Kitty tore open Rian's letter while she was still in the post office and read it immediately before folding it again, thoughtfully, and slipping it into her reticule.

'Any news?' Simon asked, when she reappeared. He and Amber had been sitting on the verandah, waiting.

'Yes, although it's much the same as we've already read in the newspaper. The British returned to Kororareka with the usual pomp and ceremony and now Hulme's marching overland after Heke. He's landed his force at Onewhero Bay.'

'Does Heke have a new pa at Puketutu?'

'Yes, it seems so,' Kitty replied.

'Puketutu's a fair march inland,' Simon remarked. 'And a difficult one, for soldiers not accustomed to the bush.' Kitty hadn't mentioned the last part of Rian's letter:

We knew of the landing place because the wife of one of Waka's men has a cousin married to someone at Pukera, and naturally it came to Haunui's ears. So we travelled overnight by waka to Onewhero, went ashore, found a comfortable vantage point and watched as Her Majesty's finest trudged off inland, laden with ammunition and provisions and hampered from the outset by the weight of several 3 lb rockets from the Hazard. Mick has bet they will manage ten miles by nightfall, although I have wagered only seven as the Weather looks certain to deteriorate. The quicker, though perhaps more challenging, route would have been to head inland from Hararu, but of course it is not my place to offer such advice.

I will write again when I can. I miss you very much, mo ghrá, but I still believe that you are, for the meantime, safer in Auckland.

Your Loving Husband,
Rian

Kitty was silent for some time. Then she said, 'Simon, I think it's time we went back.'

Simon had been dreading this moment for almost ten weeks, but now the prospect of returning to the Bay of Islands somehow didn't feel quite as daunting as he had imagined. Nevertheless, he said gloomily, 'Rian won't be pleased.'

'Well, I'm not pleased about being stuck in Auckland.'

'What will you do?' Simon asked, digging in his pocket for a bag of lemon drops and offering them to Amber. 'When you get back, I mean?'

'Leave the two younger members of our party with Aunt Sarah, and try to find Rian.'

'You don't have to talk in code, you know. I doubt she can understand you,' Simon said, inclining his head at Amber, who was busy trying to accommodate five lemon drops in her mouth at once.

Kitty held a gloved hand beneath the girl's chin to catch the inevitable spillage. 'Don't be too sure about that. Sometimes I think she understands more than we realise. Or more than *you* realise.'

Simon frowned. 'Will she be happy staying with your aunt, do you think? She's already had a lot of changes.'

'I know. It *is* bothering me. I really don't want to leave her at Paihia. But she's only a child, I can't go dragging her from battleground to battleground.'

Simon looked alarmed. 'But you won't be going near any battlegrounds, will you?'

'If Rian is, then I am,' Kitty said simply. 'But Haunui and Tahi will be at Paihia and I'm sure they'll help. And you'll keep an eye on her, won't you? She knows you. Perhaps you can come in from Waimate now and then?'

She glanced at Amber, who, sucking noisily, was now busy filling the pockets of her pinafore with gravel. Would she think she had been abandoned again? The words of the Maori woman echoed in Kitty's head: 'My heart is heavy because of what we have done to her.' If only there were some way to know how Amber was feeling. Physically, she had changed noticeably: her hair was clean and shiny, the ringworm that had marked her body was clearing up, and she had put on some much-needed weight. And she seemed happy enough, playing with Bodie and with Kitty and Simon and the other women in the house. But sometimes there were tears and tantrums, and she still awoke on the floor under Kitty's bed each morning. And, from time to time, Kitty had seen something in the child's eyes, a look of mistrust and suspicion.

Simon followed Kitty's gaze, and gave a regretful sigh. 'Actually, no, Kitty, I can't keep an eye on her.'

Kitty blinked. 'Why not?'

Simon stood up and brushed off the seat of his trousers. 'Because I'm coming with you. Rian asked me to look after you, and that's what I'm going to do.'

'But what about Waimate? What about your duties there?'

'They're managing now, I've no doubt, so they can manage for another month or two without me.'

Not caring who was looking, Kitty kissed Simon's cheek and hugged him tightly. 'Oh Simon, my lovely friend,' she said. 'Thank you.'

★ ★ ★

Kitty was absurdly pleased. She had been steeling herself to strike out from Paihia on her own to find Rian, because she knew she couldn't bear to be separated from him any longer, and the thought of him gallivanting all over the north getting into God only knew what sort of trouble terrified her. She felt as she had during the short battle at Kororareka, only now her fear had multiplied tenfold. This time there were many more soldiers involved and what had started off as a local skirmish was becoming a fully-fledged war. But with Simon at her side, she knew she would find the strength to do what she had to do to reunite her small family.

However, there were preparations to be made before they left Auckland. Four days after she'd come to her decision, Kitty and Simon walked with Flora late one afternoon to an area of sloping, fenced paddocks bordering Hobson Street. In one paddock stood two horses, a grey and a bay.

'Will they suffice?' Flora asked. 'They're properly schooled.'

Kitty gathered her skirts and rather laboriously climbed the fence, then approached the horses. The grey was a very fine mare, around sixteen hands high, and her slightly concave nose suggested she had Arab blood in her veins. The bay, a gelding, stood a little taller, and was also a beautifully built animal. Kitty ran her hands expertly along their flanks and up and down their elegant legs, and smiled. It had been a long time since she'd had much to do with horses, and their comforting smell brought back memories of riding out along Norfolk lanes on her mare, a pastime that had both soothed and invigorated her. It would be wonderful to be back in the saddle again.

Flora came up behind her, followed rather more cautiously by Simon. 'I had arranged the mare a month ago,' she said. 'But then when you said you wanted two animals, I had to ask my friend to find another one.'

Kitty nodded. This was the favour she had asked of Flora: that she use her 'contacts' to procure a horse suitable for cross-country riding, a horse that was strong, fit and reliable enough to trail British regiments and Maori war parties across the rugged terrain of the upper North Island. 'Were they expensive?' she asked, stroking the bay's velvety nose.

'Very,' Flora replied. 'Apparently prime horse-flesh is hard to find in this town. But that's not a problem, is it?'

'No. And were you able to get the tack I wanted?'

'It will be delivered to the boarding house tonight. And I'm glad you didn't ask for a side-saddle. My friend said they're more scarce than hen's teeth at the moment.'

Kitty noticed that Simon was contemplating the horses with a very odd look on his face. 'What's the matter?'

'Is one of those for me?' he asked nervously.

'Yes. You can have the bay, I think, as you're taller.'

Simon swallowed. 'Well, thank you,' he said, 'but actually, I don't know how to ride a horse.'

Flora burst out laughing.

Kitty didn't. 'Oh Simon, you must, surely? Everyone can ride a horse!'

'Everyone with money enough to afford one,' Simon amended ruefully. 'I've never had that, and I've always walked everywhere.'

'Well, it's time to remedy that then, isn't it?' Kitty declared firmly. 'And as time is short, I think we'll start tomorrow morning, don't you?'

Simon's expression remained one of extreme misgiving.

'It's easy, really,' Kitty insisted. 'It's just a matter of confidence and a touch of balance. You'll see.'

★ ★ ★

Simon's first riding lesson was a disaster, albeit a very entertaining one. He, Kitty and Amber set out for Hobson Street the next morning, Kitty happily anticipating being on horseback again, Amber catching the mood and bouncing about excitedly, and Simon dreading what lay ahead.

Kitty had prevailed upon Mrs Fleming's neighbour, a man named Joshua Leach, to transport the saddles, bridles and other paraphernalia in his horse and cart. Unfortunately for Simon, his three children, who did not attend school, came along for the ride, sensing that something interesting was about to take place.

'You don't mind, do you?' Mr Leach said as he hoisted his youngest child up onto the cart. 'It's just that the wife has had a gutsful of them under her feet, and it's washing day and she thought they might like a look at the nice horses.'

Although aware of Simon's discomfort, Kitty felt she couldn't really say no, as Joshua Leach was providing the transport and his services free.

When they arrived at the paddock, the three Leach children tumbled off the cart and ran to climb the fence, perching themselves along the top rail like sparrows on a clothesline. Amber, however, slipped through the fence and walked straight up to the horses.

Kitty's heart missed a beat as the little girl wove between them, her hand trailing along their gleaming sides, and walked only inches from their hind legs, a kick from which could easily kill her.

'Amber!' she called. 'Amber, come away from there!'

But as usual Amber ignored her, and ducked under the grey's belly, emerging on the other side with a wide grin on her face.

'Oh God,' Kitty muttered, and prepared to climb the fence to fetch her back.

'No, leave her,' Simon said. 'I think she's all right. I think she's enjoying herself.'

Reluctantly, Kitty had to agree as she watched Amber run her small hands down the bay's nose and rub her cheek against his soft, rubbery lips.

'Your little girl's naughty, isn't she, missus?' the youngest Leach child, a girl of about five, said delightedly. 'Are you going to smack her bottom?'

Her light-brown hair was tangled and the bib of her pinafore was stained with whatever it was she'd had for breakfast. Clearly Mrs Leach had been in a hurry to get them out of the house.

'No, she hasn't done anything wrong,' Kitty said.

'But you told her to come away,' the child insisted. 'You said to her, 'Come away from there', and she didn't.'

'Never mind,' Kitty said brightly, leaning into the cart for one of the saddles.

But the questions continued. 'Is she deaf, your little girl? And why is she brown and you're — '

The eldest Leach child, a boy, said, 'Shut up, Annabel.'

'I only *said* — ' Annabel began.

'Annabel,' her father said sharply, 'if you can't be quiet, you can go and sit on that log over there. By yourself.'

Annabel clamped her mouth shut.

Kitty handed Simon a bridle. 'The first thing you need to do is catch the horse.'

Simon looked first at the bridle, then rather more doubtfully at the animals in the paddock, then said, 'Why don't you do it? Otherwise we could be here all day.'

Kitty withdrew two carrots from the pocket of her dress. She was wearing her oldest one today, over her recently purchased men's trousers, to preserve her modesty when she climbed into the saddle. When they were back up north she would do away with the dress altogether, but here in Auckland she thought it prudent not to make too much of a spectacle of herself.

Holding out a carrot, Kitty walked up to the grey, patted her nose while she munched, and then slipped on the bridle. When she led the horse back to the fence, the bay placidly followed.

Kitty showed Simon how to correctly fit a bridle and a saddle. 'You need to make sure that the bit is properly between the horse's teeth. If it isn't, you won't have any control when you pull on the reins because the horse won't feel it. And some horses will hold their breath while you're fastening the girth. Then, when you mount, the saddle will slip off. A well-placed knee in the belly will fix that.'

'Isn't that a bit cruel?'

'Well, I suppose you could just ask the horse to breathe out, but I've never had much luck with that method,' Kitty said, which made Mr Leach snort with amusement.

When they were ready, Kitty explained to Simon how to mount.

'Reins gathered in the left hand, holding onto the pommel, left foot in the stirrup iron. You can set your other hand on the pommel, too, but try not to pull on it too hard. Then swing yourself up and take your right leg over the saddle, then put your foot into the stirrup iron on the other side. See?' she said, showing him how easy it was but noting with some alarm that she wasn't quite as supple as she had once been.

Simon tried to copy her, but the second he put any weight at all on the stirrup, the bay walked off, forcing Simon to hop along beside him.

The children on the fence tittered, and Mr Leach busied himself putting a nosebag on his own horse.

'No,' Kitty said, 'gather your reins in tighter. He thinks you're giving him his head.'

Simon did as he was told and, with a grunt, heaved himself up into the saddle and fumbled around trying to get his right foot into the stirrup. The bay walked off again.

Panicked, Simon cried, 'How do I stop it?'

Kitty came alongside him and said calmly, 'Let go of the pommel, and take hold of the reins again. See, they're just dangling loose on his neck. Now, pull on them gently.'

Simon did, and the bay came to a halt. Simon grinned and said incredulously, 'It worked!' Then his smile slipped as he glanced down. 'They're quite a distance off the ground, aren't they?'

'Not really,' Kitty said. 'You'll get used to it.'

They walked side by side around the paddock several times, stopping and starting until Simon had gained a little confidence, then Kitty announced that they were going to try trotting.

'Do you know what posting to the trot is?' she asked.

Simon looked at her blankly.

'Posting to the trot is when you deliberately rise and fall to the rhythm of the horse's trot. Otherwise it can be very uncomfortable. Try trotting and see.' Kitty urged her horse to trot, and the bay followed, Simon hanging on for grim death as he bounced all over the place in the saddle.

Kitty posted beside him with effortless elegance. 'No, like this, see? Grip with your knees and push yourself up and down until it feels smooth. You'll know when you get it right.'

And suddenly, Simon did get it right. A wide smile spread across his face as he found the rhythm, and the pressure on his testicles eased.

The bay, no doubt also relieved to no longer have a large sack of potatoes crashing around on his back, sped up, his head high and his mane flying. Unfortunately, his tail was also up and, just as Simon and Kitty approached the audience on the fence, the bay emitted a series of farts like musket shots, then proceeded to defecate, leaving a trail of dung in a neat line behind him.

The children could hardly contain themselves, and Kitty noticed that Joshua Leach, too, was having a thoroughly good laugh. Worse, however, was to come. Halfway around the paddock the bay slowed, then stopped and straddled his legs. A moment later his long penis emerged and he started to release a powerful stream of urine.

Oh dear, Kitty thought, biting her lip. 'Simon?'

'What?' Simon looked around. 'What the hell's he doing?'

'He's relieving himself. Can you lean forward to take the weight off his kidneys?'

Simon looked at her suspiciously, as though suspecting her of trying to make him look even sillier than he felt.

'It's true,' Kitty said. 'It's not good for them.'

Self-consciously, Simon rose in the stirrups and leaned forward over the horse's neck, embarrassingly aware that his backside was now in the air. Hearing shrieks of hysterical laughter from the other side of the paddock, he knew he must look a complete fool. Beneath him he could hear and smell the horse's pungent urine as it splattered onto the grass.

'He'll take ages,' Kitty warned.

But eventually the bay finished and decided to walk on, leaving an enormous puddle soaking into the ground behind him and Simon wondering what else was in his repertoire.

Wryly, he said, 'He's not shy, is he?'

Kitty grinned. They trotted again until Simon

was beginning to feel he was mastering the gait, then Kitty suggested they try a canter.

'I don't think I'm ready for that,' Simon said quickly.

'Yes, you are. Urge him forward, go on.'

With some misgiving Simon squeezed with his knees, and the bay broke into a smooth canter.

Simon looked happily surprised. 'This is a lot easier than trotting, isn't it?'

Thrilled to be allowed to go faster than a trot, the bay gave a tiny buck, which didn't unseat Simon but did put him slightly off balance. Gradually, he began to slide sideways out of the saddle. Clinging desperately to the horse's mane he looked across to Kitty, cantering beside him as though, he thought sourly, she had been born on a horse.

'Are you going to fall?' she called calmly.

He nodded vigorously.

'Then take your feet out of the stirrups, and roll when you hit the ground.'

Slowly, and with rather majestic inevitability, Simon slid further and further to one side and finally let go, rolling as instructed and keeping his head and hands tucked in so they wouldn't be struck by the bay's hooves. Kitty slowed and wheeled back to where Simon sat dejectedly in the grass, elbows on his knees.

'Are you hurt?'

'Only my pride.'

'Well, that's not so bad then, is it? Come on, get back on.'

But Simon had decided he'd had enough for one day. Hat in his hands, he trudged back to the fence in search of some sympathy from Joshua Leach.

Kitty rode for a little longer, then let each of the children sit on the saddle in front of her as she cantered slowly around the paddock. Amber squealed with excitement, which caused the grey to toss her head and flick her ears back and forth in alarm, but the child had a natural rhythm, and soon wasn't even bothering to hang on, relaxing into the horse's gait and allowing it to hold her in the saddle.

'Did you see that?' Kitty said proudly when she came to a halt and she and Amber had dismounted. 'I think she's going to be a natural equestrienne.'

'Which is more than I can say for myself,' Simon muttered, rubbing his aching thighs.

★   ★   ★

Kitty booked a passage on a barque named the *Irish Bride* which was due to sail up to the Bay of Islands in six days' time. They could have departed Auckland sooner, but the *Bride* was the only ship currently at anchor in the Waitemata fitted to transport large livestock, and even then Kitty had to bribe the captain because he was convinced the horses would be more trouble than their fare was worth.

But there was plenty to do while they waited. Simon had riding lessons every day, even though he insisted that they were crippling him and prematurely turning him into an old man. By the time they were ready to go, however, he was reasonably confident in the saddle and had fallen off only twice more.

There were also supplies to buy, the sorts of things Kitty knew would be difficult to obtain at Paihia and Pukera because of the fighting. It was now getting on for the middle of May, and the *Auckland Times* had reported at length on Lieutenant-Colonel Hulme's major victory against Heke's force of two hundred at Puketutu on 8 May. Hulme had attacked the incompletely built pa with a storming party of more than two hundred soldiers and a party of pro-government Maoris, known as kupapa, including Tamati Waka Nene's people, only to find his troops being attacked from the rear by a number of Kawiti's men who had coincidentally arrived on the scene. The struggle had been bitter and there had been losses on both sides, but eventually Heke had retreated from his pa and Hulme had chosen to withdraw, leaving at least two hundred dead and wounded Maoris in his wake.

Having lived among Maoris for some time, both Kitty and Simon had their doubts about the veracity of the *Times*'s reports. Simon insisted that Heke, being the cunning strategist that he was, would most certainly have co-ordinated with Kawiti, whose arrival at Puketutu during the battle would not have been a matter of chance. And Kitty, who had already seen how estimates of numbers killed and wounded had been exaggerated in the press after Kororareka, simply did not believe that Heke had lost two hundred men. They were not the only observers to doubt that the Maoris had been so roundly and comprehensively beaten; while some in Auckland celebrated the end of the rebellion, there were louder mutters about the war having only just begun. Kitty's resolve to return to the Bay of Islands was only strengthened, and the lack of any further letters from Rian worried her enormously.

While waiting for the *Irish Bride* to sail, she also paid a visit to Doctor Moffitt to inform him that she had decided to adopt Amber. The doctor had congratulated Kitty on her extremely charitable decision, although he did warn her that raising a wild, abandoned child could well be a very daunting task.

'And how does your husband view the matter?' he asked Kitty across his gleaming mahogany desk.

'Well, my husband is up north at the moment, so unfortunately I haven't been able to tell him that we now have a daughter.'

The doctor raised his bushy, greying eyebrows. 'So this is a decision you've made independently?'

'Er, yes.'

'I see. Well, how do you *think* Mr Farrell will view the matter?'

'Captain Farrell,' Kitty corrected.

'Military?'

'No, a sea trader.'

Doctor Moffitt regarded Kitty over the top of his spectacles. 'May I respectfully suggest that some men may not be altogether delighted to discover that their wives have adopted a waif off the streets? And a little half-caste waif at that.'

'Yes, I know.' Kitty looked down at her hands folded in her lap. 'Although I very much doubt that the colour of her skin will bother him. But I will be honest with you, Doctor, I'm not entirely sure how he will feel about it.'

And somehow she ended up telling this man she barely knew the story of how Rian had lost his first wife and child at sea, and about her fears that the awful tragedy had put him off ever wanting to be a father again.

'Mmm, it is a very difficult situation, isn't it?' the doctor murmured. 'And is that why you don't have any children of your own? Assuming that you don't, of course.'

'No, we don't. But, actually, that isn't the reason. We've been married now for five years and our private life is . . . well, let's just say that we love each other very much. And I've taken no measures to prevent a pregnancy, but nothing at all has happened.' She paused. 'I've remained barren.'

'Barren is a very harsh and rather unkind word, Mrs Farrell. May I ask, have you had any medical investigations regarding this state of affairs?'

Kitty considered the doctor's question, and after a minute answered as honestly as she was able.

'No, I haven't — perhaps, I suspect, because I don't wish to be given bad news.'

'If you choose, I could perform an examination now,' Doctor Moffitt suggested gently. 'I'm not a specialist in matters of the female reproductive system, I confess, but I can probably tell you whether there's anything obviously amiss.'

Kitty regarded him for a long and thoughtful moment, then started to smile. 'Thank you, but no, I don't believe that will be necessary. I have a child now.'

Doctor Moffitt returned her smile. 'I was hoping you might say something like that. You see, it's my belief that when some women are unable to bear children, it's often because God has something else in mind for them. And in your case, Mrs Farrell, He has seen fit to send you this little Maori child. Had you already been a mother, you might not have been in the right frame of mind to consider adopting her. Do you see what I mean?'

Kitty's smile widened into a grin. 'Yes. Yes, I do. I hadn't considered it in that light before.'

Doctor Moffitt moved his pen from one side of his blotter to the other. 'May I offer you some advice regarding your husband?'

'You may.'

'I think it would be best for you to simply introduce the child to Captain Farrell,' the doctor said, 'then leave them to get on with it. Men are far more capable of forming bonds with children than many people believe. She is an endearing and, I suspect, rather bright little girl, and if, as you say, your marriage is a strong one, then matters should take care of themselves.'

Kitty inclined her head. 'Thank you, Doctor Moffitt. That's very sensible advice and I shall remember it.'

The *Irish Bride* was scheduled to sail at one o'clock and Mrs Fleming and Joshua Leach went down to Commercial Bay to see Kitty, Amber, Simon and Bodie off. Hattie and Flora were already there, having ducked out during their lunch breaks. Bodie, now at least a pound heavier from eating Mrs Fleming's mice and too much scone dough, made the trip to the waterfront tucked into Simon's knapsack, her black head poking out of the top. The two horses had been brought down earlier, and were now in a temporary pen on the beach, waiting to be barged out to the ship.

To Kitty's surprise, as they stood on the sand waiting for the ship's boats to collect them and the handful of other passengers, Mrs Fleming intermittently touched her handkerchief to her eyes.

'I'm sorry, Mrs Farrell,' she said through the fine embroidered linen, 'I'm not usually like this. It's just that, well, I've become quite fond of you and Amber. And yes, even that little cat of yours, although I never thought I'd hear myself say that.'

Kitty patted her arm. 'Well, perhaps one day we'll come back and visit,' she said comfortingly.

'You take care of that child now,' Mrs Fleming said. 'And you take care of your new mama,' she added, bending down to address Amber.

Amber blinked at her but said nothing.

'And Mr Bullock, it has been *lovely* to know you,' Mrs Fleming went on. 'You keep up with

God's good works now, won't you?'

Simon nodded noncommittally and clasped Mrs Fleming's hand.

Hattie gave them all a hug, except for Simon, of course, because she was an affianced woman, and then it was Flora's turn.

'Take care of yourselves and, who knows, we may cross paths again on our various travels,' she said, as she gave Kitty a quick embrace.

Kitty hugged her back. 'Thank you, and good luck with your, er, career,' she said.

Flora laughed.

'Is Miss Langford looking for new employment?' Mrs Fleming said in an aside to Hattie. 'I didn't know that.'

Then Joshua Leach finished unloading the cart, shook Simon's hand and thanked him for the entertainment over the past few days. 'Never laughed so hard in my life,' he said, his face crinkling into a smile. 'And neither has the wife, when I told her.'

'Glad I could be of service,' Simon said, grinning.

When the ship's boat arrived, the luggage was loaded before the passengers climbed in, the women holding the hems of their dresses above the tiny waves. Apart from Kitty, Simon and Amber, there were only two small families wanting to return to their homes at Kororareka, and hoping that their homes were still standing.

As the rowboat headed out towards the *Irish Bride*, Kitty waved back at the shore, then simply watched as the people on it grew smaller and smaller. She noticed Simon eyeing her, and gave him a little smile.

The barge that would ferry the horses out to the *Bride* was towed from the Point Britomart side of the bay, then swung around and eased into the shallows. Shading her eyes, Kitty could make out Joshua Leach leading the animals one at a time onto the barge's wooden deck, then closing the gate of the high wooden pen. He had volunteered to accompany the horses out to the ship, and Kitty had been grateful, as she knew they would be frightened and disoriented. She had blinkered them, but still the roll of the barge beneath their hooves and the brisk sea breeze would surely unnerve them.

The rowboat came alongside the *Bride* and Kitty made sure all their luggage was securely closed, before tightening her shawl around her shoulders. She would usually climb the ship's ladder to board, but today she asked for a chair to be lowered so she could take Amber up on her lap. Although she was an agile little girl, Kitty was worried about her slipping and falling if she became frightened. But as the chair swung gently on its slow ascent up to the gunwale, Amber merely grinned and gave the occasional hoot of excitement as though it were all a great adventure.

By this time the barge had arrived and, above the rhythmic splashing of the sea against the hull of the *Bride*, Kitty could hear the hollow ring of the horses' hooves as they stamped nervously. When the winch was lowered this time it had a wide canvas sling attached, which Mr Leach unclipped, passed beneath the belly of the grey, then fastened again. Kitty winced and closed her eyes as the grey squealed and kicked as she was lifted, smashing the top rail of the pen, but opened them again in time to see her being lowered gently onto the deck, where she staggered once, then righted herself. The bay followed, a little less noisily but equally inelegantly.

Kitty took their lead ropes and led them into a covered pen on the deck, where they were going to have to spend the afternoon and night until the *Irish Bride* dropped anchor at the Bay of Islands and they were once again taken ashore. She gave them a carrot each and, with Amber, stayed with them until they had settled somewhat. By that time the *Bride* had unfurled her sails and was turning with the tide to head out into the Rangitoto Channel.

14

Bay of Islands, May 1845

When the *Irish Bride* arrived in the Bay of Islands the next morning, Kitty noted that, along with the *Katipo*, there were several government vessels moored in the harbour, flying the Union Jack. But there were fewer military ships at anchor than the *Auckland Times* had implied, and she wondered whether they were further up the coast on some manner of sortie.

'Does the mission station here have a barge?' the *Bride*'s surly captain asked as he joined Kitty at the ship's rail.

'No, I don't think so,' she said. 'Actually, I don't know.'

'In that case, there will most certainly be a problem getting your animals off this ship,' the captain said shortly.

Kitty looked at him. 'Then I shall have to go ashore and see what I can arrange.'

The captain, who was very keen to move on out of the harbour's rebel-infested waters, replied, 'Yes, you will. And I'd thank you to do it sharpish. I've the rest of the passengers to disembark across the bay.'

Not waiting for a chair this time, Kitty went down the ship's ladder with Amber clinging to her back like a little monkey and Simon waiting in the boat below with Bodie. Their luggage was sent down and the crewmen set out for the Paihia shore.

As they neared, Kitty could see the mission's animals grazing contentedly in their enclosures, and a cluster of chickens pecking at the grass beyond the sand; the little settlement certainly didn't look like a town in the middle of a war. A few minutes later the rowboat grounded on the beach and a crewman jumped out to hold it steady. Unlike their previous arrival when almost all of Pukera had turned out to meet them, this time only a few curious Maori children loitered on the beach. But as she waded through the shallow waves lapping onto the sand, Kitty spotted Albert, Rebecca Purcell's boy, among them.

He approached as Kitty stood wringing the sea water from her hem.

'Hello, Mrs Farrell,' he said with a smile. 'We didn't know you were coming back today.' Then he noticed Simon. 'Morning, Mr Bullock.'

'Good morning, Albert,' Simon replied, decanting Bodie from his knapsack. 'Is your father about?'

'No, he's over at Waitangi this morning.'

'Reverend Williams?'

'He's at Waitangi as well.'

Bodie looked about, sniffed the air, then bolted across the sand and disappeared into the long grass.

'You don't know where my husband is, do you?' Kitty asked hopefully.

Albert shook his head. 'He's been away for a couple of weeks now. Him and his crew. Except for that French fellow, I think he went back out

342

to Captain Farrell's schooner.'

Kitty's heart sank with a disappointment so sharp she felt momentarily sick. 'Well, who *is* here then? We have a small problem and we need some help.'

Frowning, Albert said, 'No one, really.' Then his face lit up. 'No, I think Mr Haunui and Mr Jenkins are in the carpentry shop. Shall I fetch them?'

'Yes, please,' Kitty said, removing her bonnet and tucking stray locks of hair behind her ears.

Albert's eyes settled on Amber, who was still standing in the shallows, watching something near her feet. Then she crouched and snatched an object out of the water — a starfish, which she held aloft, grinning.

'Who's that little girl?' he asked curiously.

Kitty said, 'She's mine, actually. Her name is Amber.'

Too polite to ask anything else, although he clearly wanted to, Albert only nodded and trotted off up the beach.

Kitty and Simon set to piling up the luggage as it was unloaded from the rowboat until Albert returned a few minutes later with Haunui, Tahi, Caleb Jenkins and Rebecca Purcell.

'Kitty, you're back! How lovely!' Rebecca exclaimed happily and pecked Kitty on the cheek. 'And who do we have here?' she asked brightly, nodding at Amber.

Kitty extricated herself from Haunui's bear-hug and nodded warmly at Caleb Jenkins.

'Rebecca, this is Amber,' Kitty announced. 'My daughter.'

Rebecca's eyes widened comically and Kitty laughed. 'I've adopted her,' she explained, then added, 'After a fashion. But I'll tell you about all that later. Right now, we need some help.'

Haunui, who was squatting in front of Amber and speaking to her in Maori, glanced up, alarmed. 'What is it? What is wrong?'

The sharp look of consternation on his face told Kitty that, although Paihia appeared quiet, the situation had obviously been very tense of late. 'It's nothing serious,' she said quickly. 'Does the mission have a barge?'

Caleb Jenkins answered. 'No, only a pair of rowboats.'

'Damn,' Kitty said, for a moment forgetting she was now back in Church Missionary Society territory. 'I have two horses on the *Irish Bride*.' She pointed out into the harbour. 'And I need to get them ashore but I'm not quite sure how.'

One of the crewmen from the ship's boat called, 'Hurry up, if you please, missus.'

Haunui stood, grunting slightly. 'We will swim them in.'

'That sounds rather dangerous,' Simon said.

'No, it is easy, if they do not whakaoho,' Haunui replied.

Simon looked doubtful. 'Yes, well, they both panicked when they were taken on board at Auckland.'

'No, only the grey,' Kitty reminded him. 'How would you do it, Haunui?'

'Put them in the water, tie a rope around their heads and swim with them. We have brought cattle and bullocks ashore that way.'

Kitty could see no other option, and she trusted Haunui to know what he was doing, so she climbed into the boat with him, leaving Amber on the shore with Simon.

As the crew pushed off, Haunui said, 'It is good to have you back, Kitty.'

Kitty met his eye. 'I stayed away as long as I could, but I had to come back, Haunui. I just had to.'

'I know,' he said, patting her hand.

'Albert said Rian has been away for some weeks. Do you know where he is?'

'There was a battle at Puketutu five or six days ago. I know he was there,' Haunui admitted.

'Yes, we read about that in the paper. But where is he now?'

'Not too far away, I hope,' Haunui replied, although he didn't sound very convinced.

They were silent for several minutes, then Haunui remarked, 'The little girl does not say much.'

'She doesn't say anything. I think she's mute.' And Kitty gave him a quick explanation of how she had found Amber, and what her kinswoman had said about her.

Haunui shook his head in sad resignation. 'What will Rian think about her?'

'I don't know,' Kitty replied uneasily. 'People keep asking me that.'

Soon they had come alongside the *Irish Bride*, and Haunui suggested that the less excitable horse should be lowered into the water first. Kitty relayed the instruction up to the captain, who was leaning impatiently over the rail, and several minutes later they heard the winch start to turn as the bay was hoisted above the gunwale above them. Hastily, the crew manoeuvred the rowboat out of the way.

The winch descended slowly, the bay hanging limply and bumping gently against the hull. He struggled slightly as he met the water, but Haunui slipped out of the rowboat and paddled over to take hold of his head halter and attach a rope to it. Kitty talked constantly to the horse and when he had calmed, Haunui unfastened the sling around the horse's belly and signalled for the winch to be wound up again. The grey followed and when Haunui had fastened a rope to her halter as well, then removed the sling, he set out for the shore in a sort of sideways stroke, both ropes looped around his arm.

The crewmen in the rowboat followed at a distance that wouldn't frighten the horses, who were soon almost towing Haunui in their desperation to reach solid land. Ashore once again, Kitty thanked the crewmen and they struck out for the *Irish Bride*, already turning to cross the harbour.

The horses stood on the sand shaking themselves like enormous dogs and looking happier than they had since the previous afternoon. Kitty found another carrot in her pocket and gave them half each.

'They are fine horses,' Haunui said, water dripping from his wiry hair and his clothes. He raised his eyebrows. 'I think just right for tracking people across-country?'

'Something like that,' Kitty said, wiping horse

slobber off her hand.

By this time Sarah and her housegirls, Ngahuia and Rangimarie, were also on the beach, along with Eliza Henry, Charlotte Dow and several of Rebecca's children.

Sarah embraced Kitty. 'It's lovely to have you back, dear,' she said. 'And Simon has said you have become the guardian of this delightful little child?'

'Yes. Her name is Amber.'

'And what will Rian have to say about that, I wonder?'

Kitty rolled her eyes and opened her mouth to speak, but was interrupted by a childish bellow of anger; Tahi was lying on his back in the sand, where Amber had evidently just shoved him. He kicked out at her with his bare foot, but she jumped nimbly out of the way.

'What are you doing down there, boy?' Haunui asked his grandson.

'She pushed me down!' Tahi complained loudly, his face contorting with outrage.

'Why?' Haunui asked.

'I only said she was rude for not talking to me, Koro. And then she pushed me down!'

'Oh, Tahi,' Kitty said gently, 'she can't talk. She's mute.'

Tahi climbed to his feet and glanced from Kitty to Amber, then back at Kitty again. 'What is mute?'

'It's what I just said,' Kitty replied. 'It means she's unable to talk.'

'So you say to her you are sorry, boy,' Haunui ordered.

Amber was now standing well out of range behind Kitty, but Tahi walked slowly over to her and said stiffly, 'I am sorry for being rude.'

Kitty touched him on his shoulder. 'She doesn't understand English, sweetheart.'

He looked up at her. 'Does she understand Maori?'

'I'm not sure,' Kitty said. 'Perhaps a little bit.'

'Did her mama and papa not teach her?' Tahi asked.

'She's never had a mama or a papa,' Kitty explained.

So Tahi apologised again, this time in Maori. Amber stared at him for a moment, her head on one side and her dark shining hair falling over her face. Then she smiled, reached out to touch the end of Tahi's nose and giggled.

'Does she like me?' Tahi asked, surprised.

Exchanging an amused glance with Kitty, Haunui said, 'Perhaps she does, boy, perhaps she does.'

★   ★   ★

Kitty made sure that Amber was sitting safely in the centre of the small waka and holding onto Bodie firmly, then pushed off from the shallows. As soon as the waka was free of the sand she stepped in, sat down and took up the paddle.

'All right?' she said to Amber sitting behind her.

Amber only blinked at her, but Bodie, in a headlock under Amber's arm, let out a muffled squawk.

'You can probably let her go now, sweetheart,' Kitty suggested, but Bodie was already wriggling free. She stepped daintily past Kitty and sat down in the prow of the waka, the stiff sea breeze ruffling her whiskers and turning one of her ears inside out.

Kitty soon found her rhythm with the paddle and struck out for the *Katipo*, anchored in the middle of the bay. She knew that if anyone had an idea of Rian's whereabouts it would be Pierre, providing he was indeed aboard.

The wind grew stronger as she paddled beyond the shelter of the small island of Motumaire and out into the more open waters of the bay. The skies had darkened during the morning and were threatening rain, but Kitty couldn't smell it yet, which meant they might be lucky and stay dry. Her arms were aching already; clearly, ten weeks languishing in Auckland had made her soft. Behind her, Amber chuckled as a sea bird ponderously launched itself from a wave and flapped heavily along until it caught the wind and began to rise.

'I once lost a very good bonnet on this harbour, you know,' Kitty said conversationally. 'Not quite here, though. I think it was a little closer to Kororareka.'

She wondered sadly if Amber would ever speak, and how they would communicate if she never did. When she had been a child herself, there had been a family in Dereham with a girl of Kitty's age who was profoundly deaf and, as a result, as good as mute. She could make noises, and did so frequently, but they were awful sounds — grunts and strange loud groans that had always frightened Kitty. At least Amber didn't do that. And often, she did appear to be listening when people spoke to and around her, and occasionally even seemed to respond. On board the *Irish Bride*, Kitty had shouted at her for hanging over the ship's rail and she had stepped quickly away from it. She supposed they could get by with a system of pointing at things and some sort of sign language if they had to, but she was sure that behind Amber's silent mouth there was a very quick mind. So why couldn't, or wouldn't, she speak?

Perhaps a specialist physician in London might know, Kitty thought as she gritted her teeth against the cramps that were now beginning to grip her shoulder muscles. Yes, that's what they would do — they would take her to London and have her seen by an expert. Doctor Moffitt had been kind and very efficient, but by his own admission unfamiliar with the field of medicine that concerned speech, so perhaps he had missed something that someone with more knowledge and experience might pick up. The thought gave Kitty hope, and spurred her to paddle the last aching furlong until she reached the *Katipo*.

The schooner's rowboat was tied alongside but the ship itself looked deserted, and for a defeated moment Kitty wondered if in fact anyone was on board. Then, suddenly, a ratty, moustachioed face peered cautiously over the gunwale.

'Pierre!' Kitty cried. 'It's me, Kitty!'

Pierre's face broke into a delighted grin, and a second later the ladder came tumbling over the side.

Kitty secured the waka to the base of the ladder and indicated to Amber that she should climb onto her back. But Amber had other ideas: she wriggled past Kitty, grasped the sides of the rope ladder and scampered up it.

'Amber, be careful!' Kitty shouted, her heart in her mouth. Then she breathed a sigh of relief as Pierre's sinewy arm appeared and hauled the child over the rail.

Kitty grabbed Bodie, unceremoniously stuffed her into Simon's knapsack, borrowed expressly for that purpose, and followed Amber up the ladder. At the top, Pierre helped her onto the deck and gave her an enthusiastic embrace.

'Kitty, Kitty, it is very good to see you!' he declared, kissing both her cheeks flamboyantly. 'We have been missing you!'

Kitty set the knapsack on the deck; Bodie struggled out of it, looking very affronted, then stalked off a few feet before she sat down and began to groom herself.

'I've missed you, too, Pierre,' Kitty said, feeling ridiculously weepy. 'I had to come back. I couldn't bear it in Auckland.'

'Then I am glad,' Pierre replied, his gaze shifting to Amber. 'And *la petite fille*, she is who?'

'This is Amber. I've, er, adopted her,' Kitty said nervously. 'I found her wandering the streets in Auckland. I made extensive inquiries, but she had no one to look after her and, well, I brought her with me. Permanently,' she ended lamely.

Pierre bent down and extended his hand to Amber. She took it hesitantly, shooting a look of uncertainty at Kitty.

'It's all right,' Kitty assured her. 'Pierre is a nice man.'

Amber looked doubtful a moment longer, then reached out and vigorously tweaked the end of Pierre's long moustache. He gave a yelp of surprise and she giggled irreverently.

'She is a cheeky one,' he remarked, his eyes watering. 'And how many years have you, Mademoiselle Amber?'

'She can't speak, Pierre,' Kitty said. 'Or, at least, she hasn't yet. But she isn't slow.'

'I see that,' Pierre muttered. 'And how has Madame Boadicea been? We thought she must have stole away with you.'

'She did, and she's been her usual self,' Kitty said. 'Pierre, where is Rian? I was hoping you would know. I'm desperate to see him.'

Pierre gave her a sympathetic look. 'Not far. We were at the fight at Puketutu six days ago. *Mon Dieu*, what a *débâcle*. Then we pass through here on the way to following the Queen's men to the Waikare River. Hulme has gone to Auckland and Major Bridge commands now. He is in pursuit of the Kapotai warriors to steal back the loot from Kororareka. Gideon was watch on the *Katipo*, then I draw the straw and she is the shortest, so now I am here.'

Kitty nodded. 'When did they leave for Waikare, Rian and the others?'

'Not yesterday, the day before.'

'On foot or by sea?'

'On foot. Less easy to be seen that way,' Pierre said.

For a second Kitty was again overwhelmed with annoyance at Rian's absurd need to sneak around after the British soldiers and generally put himself at risk for no good purpose. But she thrust her anger to the side — she needed a clear head.

'Simon and I are going to find them,' she said abruptly. 'We brought horses up with us.'

A shadow crossed Pierre's weathered face, but then he simply shrugged. 'Then you need to leave today.' He squinted up at the sky. 'The weather, she is setting in.'

'I know. Shall I leave Bodie here with you?'

'*Oui*. It is boring and she will be company,' Pierre said. 'And the little girl?'

Kitty made a regretful face. 'I was going to ask Aunt Sarah if she will look after her. I hope she won't mind. I don't expect it will be for long, do you?'

She looked at Pierre but, disconcertingly, his countenance remained impassive.

★   ★   ★

When Kitty told Sarah that she and Simon planned to go after Rian, Sarah was very much against the idea.

'It's far too dangerous, Kitty,' she insisted. 'Heke and Kawiti's men are everywhere. You may even be shot at by the British if you're wandering around in the bush.'

'I don't care,' Kitty said stubbornly. 'I've mouldered away in Auckland for months and I've had enough. I have to see him, Aunt Sarah.'

For a long moment, Sarah regarded her with some compassion: if it had been Caleb, she would almost be tempted to go out and look for him, too. But what she said was, 'I wouldn't call adopting a little orphan girl 'mouldering', dear. I would call that doing God's work in the best way you know how.'

'I wouldn't,' Kitty snapped. 'I'd call it doing what any decent person would do.'

'It's the same thing, isn't it?' Sarah countered. Then she sighed, aware that her niece was behaving in such a short-tempered manner only because she was worried and desperately missing her husband. 'He *will* come back, Kitty, you know he will. Hasn't he always been a very competent and capable sort of man?'

'Yes, but — '

'Then can you not wait here until Major Bridge's men come back from Waikare?' Sarah frowned. 'Rian *is* fighting with the Volunteers, isn't he?' Then, seeing Kitty's hesitation, she raised her hand. 'No, never mind, I don't want to know. And either way, I still believe a man the cut of Rian Farrell is perfectly capable of looking after himself.'

'Perhaps, but I'm still going to find him,' Kitty said flatly.

Sarah had an inspiration. 'You can't. You can't leave that little girl here by herself. She'll think she's been abandoned all over again.'

This struck at the very centre of Kitty's heart.

'I *know* that, Aunt Sarah!' she almost shouted. 'Don't you think I don't? But I can't help it, I *have* to find him!'

Sarah's cat's-bum mouth from the old days appeared for a moment, then disappeared just as quickly: she knew Kitty wouldn't be taking the decision to leave the little girl at Paihia lightly.

'Very well,' she said reluctantly. 'I can see I can't talk you out of it. I'll look after Amber, on one condition — and that is that you must come back here after a week. That poor child won't know whether she's Arthur or Martha if you're away any longer than that.'

Kitty thought furiously — she wasn't going to cover much distance in a week, given the way the weather was setting in. On the other hand, Waikare wasn't all that far away, and that meant Rian wasn't, either.

And then she stopped, realising with an unpleasant jolt how just selfish she was being. She was desperate to know Rian was safe, but at what cost to Amber? Feeling tears approaching, she bit her lip and said, 'Yes, I know, you're right. It will have to be no more than a week. I'll try to be back before that.'

'Yes, you do that, Kitty,' Aunt Sarah said, slightly reprovingly. 'I've not been a mother myself, as you well know, but I've been around children long enough now to know that they need the constant presence of someone they love. And that little girl is very attached to you, Kitty, it's as plain as the nose on my face. So you must be back as soon as you can, for her sake if no one else's.'

The next morning dawned cool and overcast, and it began to drizzle as Kitty and Simon saddled the horses. Kitty had named the grey Tio, which in Maori meant oyster, because that was her colour. Simon, however, had settled on something rather more pragmatic for the bay — Horo, the word for fast.

Despite Sarah's disapproving looks, Kitty was wearing her moleskin trousers, a man's blue serge shirt and heavy jacket, a broad-brimmed hat and a rainproof oilcloth cape. On either side of her saddle hung bags containing a change of clothes, a tinder box and some basic food items, including bread and cheese, and tea and sugar in twists of paper. There was also a pistol Haunui had somehow acquired and passed on to her, and which Kitty had no idea how to fire.

Simon was attired in a similar fashion to Kitty, although he looked as miserable as the day and his old felt hat had collapsed around his ears like a sodden cabbage.

'We'd better set off, I suppose,' he said, looking at his watch.

Kitty nodded and walked across Sarah's lawn to say goodbye. She hugged her aunt, Rebecca and Haunui, and bent down to say farewell to Tahi, who gazed back at her with big, serious eyes. Then she sat down on the edge of the verandah and put Amber on her knee.

'I have to go away for a few days, Amber,' she said in Maori. 'But I promise I'll be back. All right? I promise, sweetheart, I promise with all my heart.'

Amber looked at her for a long moment. Then, with a curiously blank face, she slid off Kitty's knee and went and stood at the other end of the verandah, staring out into the rain.

Kitty's heart almost broke. She glanced over at Simon, who shook his head sadly, then at Sarah, who said, 'I told you that would happen, didn't I?'

'Thank you, Aunt Sarah, that's a helpful thing to say,' Kitty said angrily as she stood up and made herself walk back to the horses before her guilt got the better of her.

She and Simon mounted and squelched across the grass towards the beach. Blending into the low sky, the sea was the colour of gunmetal, the waves small but choppy. Kitty itched to look back for one last glimpse of Amber, but was frightened that, if she did, she wouldn't leave at all.

But at the last moment she did turn her head, and there was Amber standing at the edge of Sarah's garden, her hands parked on her hips and a furious expression on her face.

'Mama,' she cried in a rusty, cracking voice. She stamped her foot and, bent almost double with the effort, shrieked it again. 'Mama!'

Kitty reined in Tio and closed her eyes. Then she pulled the horse around.

⋆   ⋆   ⋆

Simon dismounted, groaned theatrically and knocked the rain off his hat. They had been following various tracks south from Paihia and around the Haumi rivermouth for almost four hours now, and he had demanded a stop so he could ease his legs, which, he moaned to Kitty, were surely on the verge of snapping off. They were heading for the eastern reaches of the harbour, where Major Bridge's troops had allegedly been going. It would have been very much quicker to take the horses across the bay to Kororareka and go south-east from there, or even by water straight down the harbour to the mouth of the Waikare River. But there had been no suitable transport for the horses, so their only choice was to ride all the way around the harbour, which was probably going to take them several days.

'Oh, bear up,' Kitty said benignly as she passed Amber down to him then slid off Tio. 'Although I have to admit, I'm a bit sore myself. It does take a little while to get used to being in the saddle for long stretches.'

Amber had been riding in front of her, leaning back against Kitty. At one point, Kitty suspected, she had even gone to sleep. She was wearing the little trousers and jacket Kitty had bought for her in Auckland, and Kitty thought she looked rather sweet with her hair fluffing out from beneath her cap. She had stopped shouting the minute Kitty had turned back on the beach at Paihia and had shrieked with delight when it became clear to her that Kitty was packing her things so she could go with them. Since then she had said 'Mama' no less than eleven times, and Kitty had been absolutely thrilled. She had also said something that sounded like 'potie', which Kitty assumed was Amber's version of 'Bodie'. The letters 'B' and 'D' were not part of the Maori tongue, so naturally they would be difficult for her to pronounce, at least to start with, as Kitty had said to Simon at least three times.

Amber ran happily around, helping Simon collect sticks and dry leaves for the fire while Kitty unpacked the saddlebag containing the food. Simon soon had a small fire going in the shelter of an enormous kauri log, and crouched in front of it, warming hands that were chafed red from gripping wet leather reins. Amber watched him for a moment, then did the same thing, squatting down and reaching out little brown hands towards the small flames.

Kitty smiled. Even though it was wet and cold and they were going to be tired and sore for the foreseeable future, she hadn't felt this happy in months. She had Amber now, and they were on their way to find Rian, and as far as she was concerned everything was right with the world. She cut several slices of bread from one of the loaves they had packed, and skewered them with green sticks.

'I thought your aunt was going to have a hysterical fit when you said Amber was coming with us,' Simon remarked as he poked at the fire. Then he added, in a very good approximation of Sarah's outraged voice, 'If even just a single hair on that child's head is harmed, Kitty Farrell, you'll not be able to live with yourself!'

'I know, she *was* rather upset, wasn't she?'

Kitty made a rueful face as she sliced cheese to put on the bread after it had been toasted. 'But she did tell me I shouldn't leave Amber behind. So, in the end I was only following her advice, wasn't I?' She poured water from a bottle into a billy and set it on the fire for tea. 'I couldn't leave her behind, Simon, not after her crying out like that. I wonder if she could always do it — speak, I mean — but just didn't want to.'

'Who knows?' Simon said. 'But obviously she was upset enough to try, which I suppose is a good sign. She's clearly regarding you as her mother now.'

'Yes, but how did she know to say 'Mama'? Do you think someone taught her?'

Simon shrugged, then swore softly as his piece of bread fell off the stick and into the fire. He wriggled the stick under it and flipped it out, wiping the ash off onto the leg of his trousers. 'That's toasted enough, I think. Pass me some cheese, please?' Kitty obliged. 'Actually,' Simon continued, 'I think she's been listening to us when we've been talking, and picked it up that way.'

A strong gust of cold wind blew into the shelter created by the kauri log and fat drops of rain sizzled in the fire.

'I think it's really setting in,' Simon observed dolefully, nodding out at the grey wall of rain. 'Do you want to press on or find somewhere better to shelter?'

'What time is it?' Kitty asked, putting a slice of cheese on Amber's toast.

Simon looked at his watch, then slipped it

back into his pocket. 'Half past one. A bit early to stop, I suppose.'

'Yes, I'd rather press on,' Kitty said, anxious to get as near as possible to the area where they suspected Rian was before night fell.

Simon withdrew the map Haunui had drawn for him, and carefully opened it and spread it out on dry ground, away from the rain. 'If we carry on across-country towards Kawakawa, but turn back towards the coast before we get there, we should be able to ford the Kawakawa River somewhere near Taumarere. Here, see? We *should* be able to,' he emphasised, 'providing it isn't too swollen by all this rain.'

Kitty said, 'Can you move out of the light, please?'

'What? Oh, sorry.'

Amber came over, too, and huddled beside the map, her little features taking on the same expression of studied concern Kitty had no doubt was on her own and Simon's faces.

'Which part of the river?'

'Here,' Simon said, pointing with an ash-smudged finger. 'Then if we go across-country again, from here to here, in theory we should arrive at Waikare where the Kapotai stronghold is and where Major Bridge was heading.'

Kitty rescued Amber's cheese on toast, which she had left too near the fire and was now smoking, and carefully picked off the charred crusts. 'Well, we'll have a cup of tea, shall we, then keep on. I wonder if we'll get as far as the river tonight?'

'Perhaps,' Simon said, 'although I don't think

we should try and cross it tonight. Not in the dark.'

'No,' Kitty agreed. Then she frowned. 'Did you hear that?'

'What?'

'Over there.' Kitty pointed to a stand of bush beyond the kauri log. 'I thought I heard something moving.'

Simon looked, then listened intently. 'I can't hear anything. A branch breaking, do you think?'

Kitty stared into the trees a moment longer, then shrugged and turned back to her food.

They finished their meal, such as it was, and pushed on again through the rain. Amber became tired and grizzly, but, as the rain began to lift later in the afternoon, so did her mood. Every time they passed something interesting — a bird, a tree, some sort of geographical formation of note — Kitty told Amber the name for it in both English and Maori, and soon the little girl was repeating the words after her quite recognisably. She was much better at Maori than English, though, which reinforced Kitty's suspicion that she had learned at least some of her native tongue before she'd run away from her family's village. *Family!* Kitty thought in disgust, still not quite able to comprehend the callousness that could have deliberately ignored a helpless child.

They saw very few people as they travelled, only a handful of Maoris also apparently on the move, and a small family of English settlers inland and south of Opua, who warned them that 'John Heke was still on the warpath' and that they had better keep their eyes open if they knew what was good for them.

Kitty knew what would be good for her — a hot bath, a good dinner and a nice, soft mattress — and she expected that Amber and Simon felt the same way. She had two sore spots on her backside from sitting in a wet saddle all day, the insides of her calves were rubbed raw from the stirrup leathers, and she was getting a headache. Soon they would need to find shelter for the night and make themselves something hot and filling to eat.

'Where are we?' she said to Simon as she urged Tio abreast of him. The poor horses looked as fatigued as Kitty felt. Tio's lovely, elegant head was drooping, and Horo's hindquarters were caked with mud from sliding down the bank of a stream they had crossed an hour earlier.

'I don't know,' he said after a moment.

They were in a patch of bush but the track was gradually rising, so Kitty expected that they would soon encounter a vantage point that would allow them to establish their bearings. But the sun was beginning to go down and in another hour it would be too dark to see.

So they plodded along until they came to a clearing at the top of a hill. It was lighter up there, out of the trees, and Kitty realised that she had underestimated the amount of daylight left; they probably had closer to an hour and a half. Behind and below them they could see where they had been — a long and dense stretch of forest that had already fallen into evening's shadow.

Kitty suddenly shivered. 'It's going to be chilly tonight.'

But she was unsettled by more than just the prospect of a cold night outdoors: she had the unnerving impression that they were being followed. Two or three times that afternoon the hairs on the back of her neck had risen and she had been sure they were being secretly observed, but had seen no one — neither behind them nor in the bush as they passed through it. She had thought to tell Simon, but in the end had kept it to herself in case he insisted they return to Paihia.

'See that down there?' he said, pointing. 'I think that's the river.'

'The Kawakawa?'

'Yes. But if it isn't, we're hopelessly lost.'

Kitty looked at him in alarm. 'Do you think we are?'

'No, I'm pretty sure that's the Kawakawa. I've been in this area before with Reverend Burrows, on one of his flock-finding journeys.'

And that reminded Kitty of something she had been meaning to ask. 'Why didn't you go out to Waimate when we were at Paihia? You would have had the time.'

Simon removed his hat and flicked off a weta that had suddenly appeared over the edge of the brim. Conversationally, he remarked, 'That was a tusk weta.'

Amber's keen eyes followed the insect as it sailed into the scrub at the side of the track.

Kitty shuddered. 'It was appallingly ugly, that's what it was.'

'Yes, it was,' Simon agreed. 'Did you know that 'weta' is a shortened form of the word 'wetapunga', the name the Maoris give to the giant weta? It means, more or less, 'God of ugly things'.'

'Thank you for the entomology lesson, Simon. Why didn't you go out to Waimate?'

'Because I didn't want to,' Simon said, putting his hat back on.

'Why not?'

'Because I'm thinking.'

'What about?' Kitty demanded, prying relentlessly.

Simon twisted in his saddle to give her a hard look. 'About whether or not I *ever* want to go back. And I don't particularly want to discuss it at the moment, if you don't mind.' And he tapped Horo's flanks with his heels and headed off down the hill.

'Oh, very well then,' Kitty muttered, and followed him.

They rode for another hour until it really was becoming too dark to see. But just as they thought they would have to bed down in the cold, damp darkness of the bush, they emerged from the undergrowth and saw before them the glittering expanse of the Kawakawa River.

'It's wide, isn't it?' Kitty said doubtfully.

'Yes,' Simon agreed. 'And clearly, at the moment, rather deep.'

'Damn,' Kitty said.

15

They slept that night in a shelter they made from nikau branches on the edge of the marshland bordering the river. Kitty lay awake half the night worrying that wetas would creep out from the foliage and inside her blanket. And it was cold, but unfortunately not cold enough to keep the mosquitoes away; the next morning all three of them were covered in large red welts.

'That was possibly one of the worst night's sleeps I've ever had,' Kitty complained as she came back from relieving herself in the bushes and washing her face in the cold waters of the Kawakawa. Her neck was stiff from using a saddlebag as a pillow, her body sweaty and grimy under the clothes she'd slept in, and her eyes felt gritty. 'Do I look as bad as I feel?'

'Yes,' Simon said.

You don't look much better, Kitty thought. He had a large mosquito bite on his cheek and his hair was sticking up all over the place.

He sniffed under his armpit, made a face and said, 'A bath wouldn't go amiss.'

Amber was the only one who seemed in high spirits. She was dancing about collecting sticks and leaves for the breakfast fire, humming something tuneless and pointing at various things and saying their names. Now that she had rediscovered her voice, she appeared intent on using it as often as possible.

Kitty dug out the horses' nosebags and filled them with a mixture of chaff and oats. Tio and Horo had been allowed to graze intermittently during the journey yesterday, but she knew they would be consuming a lot of energy so had made sure to provide them with something extra. She hooked the nosebags over the horses' ears and knelt next to the newly smoking fire with the remainder of the day before's loaf of bread and a billyful of oats.

'Porridge and toast?' she suggested to Simon.

Amber said, 'Podge.'

Simon held out his hand for the billy. 'I'll refill the water bottles while I'm at it.' He limped stiffly off towards the river.

Poor Simon, Kitty thought. A fortnight ago he had never even ridden a horse, and now here he was perched on the back of one for ten hours a day. No wonder he was moving slowly. She cut up the last of the loaf and stuck the slices onto sticks.

Today, if the going wasn't too difficult, they would perhaps make Waikare by late afternoon, depending of course on where they crossed the river; if they had to follow it all the way inland until it turned into a stream, it could be days before they reached their destination. Kitty sighed inwardly. She knew that this was the point at which she was supposed to say to herself that she had waited so long now to see Rian that a few days more wouldn't matter — but they would. They would matter a lot. She didn't think she could bear it if they were to be held up just because it had rained and the river had risen.

She glanced up to check on Amber. Oh God, what was Rian going to say when she told him? What was *she* going to say? Hello, Rian, this is your new daughter? The thought of it made her stomach churn with nerves. Once he came to know Amber he would love her, of course. Kitty was sure of that, because what decent person wouldn't love a child as sweet and as clever as Amber? But then her mind started to echo with Rian's comments about a schooner being no place to raise a child, and wasn't Kitty happy with the way things were? Angrily, she swatted at a mosquito buzzing noisily around her ear and reflected that yes, she had been happy — she'd been happier than she ever could have imagined. But now there was Amber, and some essential part of her had changed forever. How could she explain to Rian how her spirit soared whenever the little girl smiled at her, and how she had thought her heart might break with grief and happiness when Amber had first called her 'Mama'?

Kitty closed her eyes and whispered, 'Oh, please don't make me choose.'

'Kitty? What's the matter?'

She opened her eyes. Simon was standing on the other side of the fire, the billy in his hand.

'Nothing.' She set the billy over the flames and added a good pinch of salt to the oats and water.

'It didn't look like nothing,' Simon remarked as he positioned the bread around the edge of the fire. 'You're worried about what Rian is going to say, aren't you?'

'Is it that obvious?'

'To me it is, yes.'

Kitty sat back on her heels. 'Oh, Simon, I want to see him so much it hurts, it actually physically *hurts*. But I'm terrified. What if he doesn't, well, what if he won't . . . ' She trailed off, unwilling to actually say it aloud.

Simon jabbed a stick into the billy and gave the oats a vigorous stir. 'Why don't you try praying about it?' He set the stick aside and gave Kitty a long, fond and slightly frustrated look. 'Go on, try it. You've nothing to lose. And this is me talking now, not Simon Bullock the CMS missionary.'

'Pray to God?' Kitty said disbelievingly.

'You can pray to whomever or whatever you like,' Simon replied. 'Just as long as you do pray. You might find that it stops things going around and around in your mind. You *might* find that it gives you a bit of, well, balance.'

Balance, Kitty thought wistfully. Yes, that would be nice.

⋆ ⋆ ⋆

They crossed the Kawakawa three miles upstream, at a sweeping curve where the channel widened and the river spread out and became less deep. But the horses still had to swim part of the way, and Kitty found the moment when Tio's hooves left the riverbed and she became waterborne extremely unnerving. Tio clearly did, too: her ears flattened against her skull and the powerful muscles of her shoulders pumped as she struck out for the far bank. Kitty slid out of the saddle and swam jerkily alongside, trying to hold Amber securely in place on Tio's back.

'All right?' Kitty called out to Simon who, like her, had dismounted and was hanging grimly onto Horo's mane. He nodded quickly, too busy trying to remain upright to speak.

The water was swift in the middle of the channel, and surprisingly cold. Glancing back, Kitty saw with a surge of fear that the current had already swept them some distance downstream. She looked ahead again and, gritting her teeth, concentrated on keeping Amber in the saddle and her own legs out of the way of Tio's.

But a minute later Tio stumbled as her hooves struck the riverbed and she righted herself, then lunged up the incline to the bank. On dry land she shook herself, dislodging Amber, who slid to the ground.

Kitty picked her up and hugged her, and together they watched as Horo launched himself out of the river and staggered up the bank, dragging Simon along beside him. Kitty's hands and feet were numb with cold and she could hear her own teeth chattering.

They sat on the bank in silence, all three of them, river water running out of their clothes, panting as they regained their breath. A few feet away the horses quickly settled, then bent their heads to graze.

'I didn't realise it would be so cold,' Simon gasped.

'No,' Kitty replied, 'but at least it isn't raining any more.'

Simon looked at her and suddenly they were

laughing like loons, tears running down their faces as the fear and tension drained away. Amber laughed too, but as she was pointing at them they could only assume she was laughing *at* them, not with them. Which only made them laugh harder.

Eventually they managed to compose themselves.

Simon suggested, 'Shall we walk for a while, to warm up and try to dry off a bit?'

Kitty nodded; her backside was still sore and she didn't relish sitting on it in soaking wet trousers.

As they picked their way across the boggy ground that bordered the river, leading the horses behind them, a dark figure appeared unseen on the far bank. It crouched, watching for several minutes until the small party ahead had disappeared from sight, then slipped soundlessly into the swollen, fast-flowing waters.

By midday Kitty and Simon were feeling better, and certainly a lot warmer, so decided to push on for another hour or so before they stopped to eat. Ahead of them lay an expanse of hills and valleys clad in thick bush, and they were both beginning to doubt now that they would make Waikare by nightfall.

'We could follow the coastline,' Simon said as they repacked the saddlebags after they finally did stop. 'Although I doubt that would be any quicker. I've been into some of those bays by sea and they're fairly rugged. A lot of them don't even have beaches, just cliffs.'

'No,' Kitty said as she tightened Tio's

surcingle. 'I think it's better that we stick to the tracks and keep going overland. At least we know the tracks actually go somewhere.'

They had been following the narrow but distinct paths that local Maoris had worn across the landscape for so long that the ancestors who had originally walked them were remembered only in whakapapa and legend. Haunui had done his best to include in his map all the tracks he knew of, but had admitted that he hadn't walked them all himself and didn't know where some of them led. He had, however, included as many landmarks as he could recall, and they were using these as a guide.

Late in the afternoon, just as the sun began its descent behind the forested hills at their backs, they came across a small group of Maoris walking along the track towards them — an elderly man and woman, two younger women carrying several large ketes, and three children. The old man had a bundle of blankets rolled up and tied to his back. Kitty and Simon pulled off the track to let them pass, but the old man signalled to his companions to stop.

'Good day,' he said in Maori.

Kitty saw that he had only one eye, and a hollow of knotted scar tissue where the other one should have been. He reminded her strongly of Wai's assumed father, Tupehu, and for a moment she felt disconcerted.

'Good day, Koro,' Simon replied, also in Maori.

'What is your destination?' the old man asked.

Simon said, 'We are heading for Waikare.'

The women glanced at each other and almost imperceptibly shook their heads.

The old man hesitated for a moment, then said, 'Waikare is not a good place today.'

'In what way, Koro?' Simon asked uneasily.

Grunting, the old man adjusted the bundle on his back. 'There has been a battle there. Of sorts. The Queen's men came and burned the Kapotai pa to the ground.'

Simon shot a worried look at Kitty, then said to the old man, 'When was that? When was this battle?'

'At dawn.'

'Today?'

'Yesterday.'

Simon leaned forward in his saddle. 'And are you Te Kapotai yourselves? Were you in the battle?'

One of the younger women spoke up. 'No. We were only visiting. But we saw it.'

The old man frowned at her for interrupting. 'The pa has gone and so have the Kapotai people. But they are not far away and they are angry. You Pakeha should watch out for yourselves.' Then his wrinkled face relaxed. 'But no matter. They will build another pa. Little was lost.' He laughed and tapped his head. 'Those Queen's men in their little boats!'

And with that he walked on, chuckling to himself.

The others followed, one of the children giving a little wave to Amber, who waggled her fingers in reply.

When they were out of earshot, Simon said, 'I

wonder what he meant by that? The comment about the boats?'

Kitty shrugged. 'Obviously Major Bridge has launched his attack. And that means Rian won't be far away.'

'*Probably* won't be far away,' Simon amended, not wanting Kitty to get her hopes up.

Kitty urged Tio back onto the track. 'I wonder how much further it is? We should have asked the old man.'

'We should be able to see for ourselves soon. We've been travelling uphill for a while now, so with luck we'll come across a vantage point. Or even a lookout.'

But the bush at the summit of the hill they had been climbing was as dense as it had been in the valley below. They rode for another hour and finally came to a clearing on the eastern aspect of a hill that afforded them a view of the terrain ahead, but by then it was too dark to make out much more than a dimly gleaming stretch of water. In the darkness, they could only assume that they were looking down on the Waikare River, where the Kapotai pa now lay in ashes.

★   ★   ★

'Mimi,' Amber announced. It was early next morning and Simon had gone in search of water. But when Kitty bent to help Amber with the buttons on her trousers, she pushed her away and said, 'No!'

'Do you want to do it by yourself?'

'Ae. *Myself!*'

Kitty rolled her eyes; it was wonderful that Amber was learning to manage her own toileting, but rather time-consuming and slightly pointless since she hadn't yet got the hang of doing up her own buttons. She watched as Amber ducked behind a ponga to do her business in private.

She waited for several minutes, then called, 'Amber, are you all right?'

There was no answer.

'Sweetheart? Do you need any help?'

Still nothing. Kitty turned and pushed her way around to the other side of the ponga.

Amber had gone.

Kitty gave a moan that was half-panic and half-fear, and crouched to peer beneath the ponga's drooping, browning branches in case Amber had crawled under there. She straightened, then turned in a full circle, but could see no sign of the little girl. A scream rose up in her throat but she stifled it, forcing herself to stand very still and listen.

At first all she could hear were the sounds of the forest — the wet wind in the taller branches, the whisper and rustle of leaves heavy with the rain from the day before, and the gurgle of some invisible stream not far away. And then she heard it, a faint crackling of twigs and branches as something large moved through the bush, heading away from her. She lunged after it.

But common sense somehow prevailed over her terror and she stopped and slid Haunui's pistol from her saddlebag. With hands that were shaking with shock, she fumbled in powder and a ball, then jammed the pistol into her belt, hoping she wouldn't blow a hole in her own thigh.

She set off again, this time moving stealthily and straining to listen for the tell-tale noises ahead of her, the sounds she knew in her heart were being made by a war-crazed and blood-thirsty rebel warrior dragging her precious daughter to certain death.

At one point she thought she saw a flash of something in the bush beyond, and realised that the trees had thinned slightly and that she was approaching another track. A moment later she had stepped onto it and saw, up ahead, a figure carrying a smaller one clamped under its arm like a rolled-up mat. A noose of terror tightened around Kitty's heart.

'*Stop!*' she cried.

But the figure merely broke into a jog, although not before Kitty had realised that Amber's abductor was a woman, and that there was something vaguely familiar about her heavy but powerful gait. She set off after them, her boots slipping and sliding on the muddy track.

She had been running for almost five minutes when she came to a fork and knelt to inspect the mud for footprints: they were there, a clear set made by wide bare feet, but where the track branched they stopped, as though whoever had made them had vanished into thin air. Kitty stifled a groan and remained very still, straining to hear any sound that might indicate the direction the abductor had taken. But there were only the normal rustling sounds of the bush.

After a long minute Kitty stood and walked a couple of paces along the left-hand track, looking for bent branches, broken twigs, fresh fallen leaves — any sign that might suggest something had recently passed by. But there was nothing. She did the same along the other track, but again there was nothing. She bit her lip and blinked back tears, wishing she had Hawk with her — Hawk, who could track anything anywhere.

The sharp crack of a twig made her whirl around, aiming her pistol at the undergrowth. Holding her breath, she steadied her pistol hand with the other, but when nothing more happened, she stepped forward cautiously and peered into the bushes.

A kiwi stared back up at her, its small black eyes blinking resentfully in the sunlight before it turned and shuffled further into the gloom, presumably to return to sleep.

Kitty let her breath out, turned to the fork in the track again and withdrew from her jacket a pocket compass she'd purchased in Auckland. She flipped up the smooth brass lid and watched as the needle wavered, then settled. Then she turned the compass so that the needle sat over the reading for north, which told her that the left-hand track headed south-west, while the other went north-west. Neither direction could be guaranteed, of course, because the tracks could change direction at any stage, but Kitty felt a surge of hope as she contemplated the track on the right. Hadn't Haunui mentioned a rumour about Heke and Kawiti building a new pa at Ohaeawai? And Ohaeawai, she knew, was inland and slightly south-west of Paihia, which meant that it lay directly north-west of where she was now. If whoever had Amber was in cahoots with the rebel Maoris — and who else was likely to steal a child belonging to Pakehas? — then it stood to reason that they were probably heading for Ohaeawai. Kitty pocketed the compass and ran off along the right-hand track, praying that the abductor was in fact ahead of her.

After more than forty minutes, her lungs felt as though they might tear themselves out of her chest and the stitch in her side had become unbearable. Cursing her diminished physical fitness, she slowed and then stopped, bent at the waist and hoicking inelegantly to clear her throat. Then all of a sudden she remembered Simon. He would surely have returned to their camp by now and be wondering where on earth she and Amber had got to. Would he come looking for them? She knew he'd be desperately worried, and cursed herself for not thinking to leave even a scribbled note.

She straightened and stretched painfully, the muscles made stiff from riding complaining mightily at being exerted even further, and then took a moment to review her surroundings. Her resting place was on the crest of a steep hill, and in the gully below ran a small stream bordered by rocks and scrub and, a short distance upstream, a wide fan of what appeared to be freshly fallen debris. A movement caught her eye and she squinted, her heart leaping as Amber's kidnapper stepped out of the scrub and knelt to drink from the stream. The little girl had a rope tied around her neck and, when she made a move to break away, the kidnapper viciously jerked the rope and Amber sprawled onto her side.

Kitty stifled her cry of outrage and, bent double to avoid attracting attention, moved along the exposed ridge to the point where the track began its descent into the gully. But she was dismayed to discover that the track itself had gone, washed away by the recent heavy rains, leaving only a vast, eroded, scree-covered slope extending to the bottom of the hill. The bush on either side was thick and tangled, and Kitty knew it would take too long to pick her way down through it.

She quickly emptied her outside pockets, shoving everything inside her jacket, removed the ball from the pistol and jammed it back into her belt, buttoned the jacket itself, and prepared to launch herself onto the scree. In the second before she jumped, however, she glanced down into the gully. The kidnapper had seen her.

But it was too late — Kitty was already on her way. She soon discovered that remaining upright was going to be very difficult. She went over once and managed to scramble wildly back up again, but halfway down the slope, a hissing avalanche of small rocks preceding her, her feet went out from under her a second time and she crashed heavily onto her back, her head connecting sharply with a lump of rock.

* * *

For a moment after regaining consciousness, Kitty had no idea where she was. Then she remembered and let out an involuntary cry of fear and despair. Her head was pounding atrociously, and when she gingerly probed at the base of her skull her hand came away sticky with congealing blood. Oh God, how long had she been knocked out? Glancing up at the sun, hazy behind low, grey cloud, she was relieved to note that it had barely moved across the sky.

Feeling too dizzy and nauseous to stand, she slithered the rest of the way down the hill on her backside, her fingernails clogging with dirt as she used her hands to steady herself. At the bottom she sat for a moment, then crawled to the stream and ducked her head completely beneath the water. It was extremely cold and bit viciously at the wound at the back of her skull, but the shock of it helped to clear away the fogginess that was threatening to overwhelm her. She took a long and welcome drink.

In a few minutes she began to feel better, although her head hurt like hell and she'd torn several fingernails to the quick on her left hand. She'd lost the tie binding her hair, so she used her right hand to comb the wet strands back from her forehead, then checked the inside pockets of her jacket to make sure that nothing had been lost or damaged. The small powder horn and bag of lead balls were still there, as was the compass, although the glass over the dial had cracked. Her short, bone-handled knife was still in her boot, but had left a small purple gouge on her ankle, and her pistol was secure beneath her belt. But the latest letter from Rian, which she'd folded into the breast pocket of her shirt, had gone. She turned and squinted up the slope; was that a piece of note paper snagged in a bush near the summit, or simply the pale underside of a leaf? She briefly debated fetching the precious missive, then shook her head. She might be able to climb back up, but she doubted she could get down again in one piece, and, she thought desperately — *Amber needs me*. Repeating those three words over and over, she reloaded and primed the pistol.

When she was sure her legs would support her, and the stabbing pain in her head had subsided to a dull throb, she waded across the stream and began the long climb up the hill, water squelching from her boots and her torn fingers smarting. At the top, after stopping several times to catch her breath and wait for waves of dizziness to wash over her, she stood and surveyed the terrain that unfolded to the north-west. Below, and slightly to her right, snaked the Kawakawa River. Had it only been the day before that she, Amber and Simon had crossed it with such giddy bravado? To the left of the river lay mile after mile of dense rolling bush, and somewhere, hidden beneath its lofty canopy, was Amber.

The river — yes! She would follow the river inland: paddle up it, in fact, if she could find a waka or a rowboat. That would take her some miles past Kawakawa, and then she could continue on to Ohaeawai on foot.

But an unpleasant little voice in Kitty's head

suddenly said: But what if Amber's being taken somewhere completely different, and you won't see her again and you'll *never* know what happened to her?

'But it must be Ohaeawai they're heading for,' Kitty countered aloud, saying it with enough force to drown out the other voice. She had been putting together snippets of information she'd heard in recent months, and now had a strong suspicion she knew who Amber's abductor was. Her mouth set in a line of fierce resolve: if she was right, then she would have no compunction at all in doing whatever it took to get Amber back.

Heartened by her own sense of determination, she set off in the direction of the river.

★   ★   ★

It took Kitty longer than she had expected. By the time she reached the southern bank of the Kawakawa, at a spot several miles further inland than where they had crossed the previous day, the sun was beginning its late afternoon slide towards the western hills. Now all she needed was a boat of some sort. She knew that small 'communal' waka were often left on the riverbanks for people who wanted to cross without getting themselves or their possessions wet, and she'd been praying for the last few hours that there would be one somewhere near the point at which she emerged from the bush.

However, there was nothing on either side of the river as far as she could see in either

382

direction, so she set off again, heading inland, at times wading through the shallows when the bush crowded her off the narrow track bordering the water.

But as she rounded a bend almost an hour later, she spied something that made her spirit leap with triumph — a small waka, beached on the bank, with a single oar propped against the prow. She hurried towards it, her boots slipping in the mulch of wet, fallen leaves littering the track, and was only yards away when she heard a human voice — an *angry* human voice, as though someone was indulging in a good telling-off. Her heart racing, she ducked for cover.

A moment later, two people appeared on the bank near the beached waka — one, her back to Kitty, was the kidnapper, and the other was Amber, once again tucked under an arm. The little girl was struggling, and for her efforts was receiving a rain of blows about the head, which served only to make her struggle and kick out even more energetically.

In Maori, the kidnapper demanded fiercely, 'Stop that! Now, get in the waka before I drown you.'

Kitty's rage rose like a boiling red tide. Launching herself from the shelter of the trees, she bellowed, *'Put her down!'*

The kidnapper slowly turned and Kitty recognised her immediately. She was a little older, of course, and had grown heavier, but it was definitely her.

Amber cried out, *'Mama!'* and the woman

clamped a hand over her mouth.

'Amiria,' Kitty croaked, her voice thick with anger and fear.

Hoisting Amber more securely under her arm, Amy moved a few steps closer. 'Ae, you remember me,' she said.

'Of course I remember you,' Kitty spat. 'How could I ever forget?'

Amy shrugged, raising her heavy, slanted brows. The rims of her eyes were red, as though she hadn't slept for some time. 'Wai was a long time ago. She is dead. What do you care now?'

'I care because she was my *friend*, Amy. And what you did contributed to her death.'

'No,' Amy said petulantly, and then she laughed, a horrible, high, cackling sound. 'The baby of the Pakeha minita did that, not me. He should not have lain with someone as silly and as weak as Wai, he should have lain with *me! I* was the one worthy of him, not *her!*"

It was then that Kitty realised that there was something terribly wrong with Amy's mind. Very slowly, she took a step towards her.

'Do not move!' Amy warned. She stood Amber on the ground, holding her still by her hair. A trickle of blood ran across Amy's palm from what appeared to be a bite wound.

'Mama!' Amber wailed again.

Kitty hesitated. 'What do you want with the child?'

'She is yours, is she not,' Amy said. It was a statement, not a question. 'I have been watching you for days, you and the Pakeha man. I have been *watching*.'

Amber suddenly tried to twist away. Amy slapped her across the side of the head and she went limp, crouching on the muddy ground, the ends of her hair still tangled in Amy's fist.

'Amy, please, let her go,' Kitty pleaded, suddenly desperate. 'What can you want with her?'

'To trade,' Amy said simply.

Kitty stared at her. 'What?'

'When the next battle comes, at Ohaeawai, there will be prisoners. We will trade this one for one of ours.'

Kitty felt cold fingers dance down her spine. 'Amy, who is *we*?'

'Who is we?' Amy parroted. '*Who is we?!* We are the greatest army ever to face the Queen's men! We are the saviours of the Maori race, and we will not rest until every Pakeha skin has been banished from this land!' And she launched into a vicious haka, hissing and springing from one foot to the other and throwing out her arms, jerking Amber about by her hair like a life-sized doll.

'Stop!' Kitty cried. She thought furiously. 'Amy, what value can a child have?'

'One of yours for one of ours!'

'But I'm not part of the fighting! I'm looking for my husband!'

A tiny flicker of doubt appeared in Amy's eyes. 'No. You are fighting for the Queen. I have a prisoner already. Kawiti will be pleased.'

Kitty took a tentative step closer.

Amy yanked Amber in front of her and a second later a blade glinted in her hand. 'Come closer and I will slit her throat!'

Kitty froze. Oh God, what should she do? But then Amy did something that made up her mind for her — she passed the sharp blade of the knife across Amber's throat, leaving behind the shallowest of cuts. A single bead of blood began to trickle into the little girl's collar.

With her own blood roaring in her ears, Kitty snatched the pistol from her belt, cocked it and aimed it at Amy's face. 'Let her go or I will shoot, I swear it.'

'You do not have the strength to do that,' Amy sneered. 'You never did.'

Nothing moved for several seconds, not even the wind in the trees, then Kitty squeezed the trigger and a ragged red hole appeared in the centre of Amy's forehead. For a moment she looked comically surprised, then crashed onto her back, her legs spread and the knife spinning off into the undergrowth. She twitched once, then lay still.

Kitty sank to her knees, sure she was going to be sick, the pistol on the ground before her.

Amber ran over and snatched it up, aimed it at Amy's dead body and shouted, '*Ka mate!*'

Then Kitty gathered her in her arms, smelling the sharp tang of fear in the child's sweat, and hugged her tightly, rocking her gently back and forth. Slowly, as the minutes passed, their heartbeats gradually returned to normal.

Kitty was immensely grateful for the comfort of the little warm body pressed against her chest. She knew she would never be the same again. She had deliberately taken a life, and that knowledge would stay with her forever. But in truth she felt very little regret, which startled and frightened her. Amy had threatened Amber's life, therefore she had to be stopped: it had seemed so clear and simple when she pulled the trigger, and it seemed no more complicated now. Is this what love for a child means? A willingness to go to any lengths to protect and deliver from harm? If so, then she could accept this unexpected and violent turn of events. And in that moment, she also knew she would kill again if she had to.

Amber's lips tickled Kitty's cheek as she whispered, 'Mama?'

'What is it, sweetheart?' Kitty replied, smoothing Amber's hair away from her grubby face and turning to see what had caught her daughter's eye.

There stood a heavily tattooed man, the muzzle of his musket pointed directly at them.

16

The warrior reached down and deftly removed the pistol from Amber's grasp, then gestured at her and Kitty to stand. As Kitty got shakily to her feet, fresh fear surging through her, but she retained enough wit to slip the compass unseen from her own pocket into Amber's, and breathe 'Kahore korero' into her ear, praying that she understood the words and kept silent. Better, in fact, if they both feigned ignorance of the Maori language.

The man gave a whistle that sounded exactly like the call of a kokako, and two more warriors stepped soundlessly from the bush. They were kitted out for war in maros, garments like short aprons, and not much else, and it was clear to Kitty that they belonged to either Hone Heke or Kawiti. She sincerely hoped they weren't Kawiti's men: the chief had lost a son in the battle at Puketutu and would surely be in no mood for carting a Pakeha woman and a scruffy half-caste child about the countryside, regardless of Amy's comments about the usefulness of prisoners.

One of the warriors approached Amy's body, spread-eagled on the narrow shore with one arm trailing in the water, and prodded hesitantly at her flank with the barrel of his musket.

'Ka mate,' he said in an unnerving echo of Amber's earlier proclamation.

The others grunted, apparently not in the least perturbed by Amy's death.

The first man eyed Kitty, then gruffly ordered in Maori, 'Shoes off.'

Kitty pretended she didn't understand him.

'Shoes!' the man repeated, and pointed agitatedly at her boots, then at his own bare feet. 'Off!'

Then Kitty was suddenly sitting on the ground again while one of the warriors wrestled with her bootlaces.

'*I* will do it!' she snapped in English, and very reluctantly removed her boots. The knife she had been concealing fell out onto the sand.

No one said anything, but the first man reached roughly into her pockets, emptied them and tucked the contents into the waistband of his maro, then barked, 'Ngaru, Hapi — prepare the waka.'

The two clearly subordinate warriors shoved their way into a thicket of bushes near the river's edge and set to dragging out armfuls of nikau branches that were concealing a second waka, somewhat larger than the one Kitty had been intending to steal. Grunting, they hauled it out and shunted it towards the river so that the stern sat in the water.

'Get in,' the first man said to Kitty, and gestured at the waka.

'Wiripo, what about the body?' Ngaru asked the leader.

Wiripo glanced at Amy's prostrate form and frowned.

'Leave her, she was mad,' Hapi said, waving

his hand about his head and making a strange face.

'Ae,' Wiripo agreed, 'but she was still fighting for us. Put her in the waka. We will bury her later.'

With obvious reluctance, Ngaru and Hapi struggled to hoist Amy's heavy body off the sand and manoeuvre it into the waka's stern, breaking into a sweat even though the day wasn't at all warm.

Kitty glanced at Amber, and nearly smiled at the sight of the little girl's lips clamped deliberately together — clearly she had understood the warning. She took Amber's hand and squeezed it comfortingly, although she herself felt far from confident.

She bit her lip: how on earth were they going to get out of this? What would Rian do? Would he fight his way out? Kitty eyed the trio of burly and very fit captors and mentally shook her head. They'd rendered her pretty much defenceless by taking her pistol and her knife. The only thing still in her favour was the fact that they thought she couldn't understand what they were saying: surely something would be mentioned sooner or later that she could use to her and Amber's advantage?

Ngaru grasped her arm and propelled her, not roughly but certainly insistently, towards the waka. Hapi bent to take Amber's hand, but she reciprocated by delivering a well-aimed kick to the base of his shin.

'Ah!' he exclaimed, hopping around on one foot and grimacing.

Wiripo and Ngaru both laughed, but, before Amber could inflict any more damage, Ngaru picked her up and deposited her in the middle of the waka. Kitty knelt and put her arm around her daughter, feeling the child's thin shoulders shuddering with either fear or rage. To hide her own shaking hands, she put her boots back on and busied herself tying the laces.

Wiripo stepped into the waka and sat in silence as Ngaru and Hapi launched the vessel off the sand and into deeper water, then climbed in themselves and each took up a paddle.

As the waka turned against the current, Wiripo pointed to a blanket bundled in the bottom of the hull and said to Kitty, 'Lie down under the blanket.'

She made an uncomprehending face.

Wiripo frowned again, his patience obviously wearing thin. Making what appeared to be a supreme effort, he said in English, 'Blanket. Sleep. Hide.'

Kitty obstinately shook her head.

'I am glad she is not my wife,' Ngaru muttered. 'Too stubborn.'

'I would have the woman,' Hapi said, rubbing his bruised shin resentfully, 'but not if I also had to take the child.'

Wiripo told them to shut up, then leaned in close and shouted in Kitty's face, '*Blanket!*'

When she still refused to obey, he produced a piece of thin rope and tied her wrists together, then pushed her to the bottom of the waka and pulled the blanket completely over her. Kitty stifled her panic, trying to keep a clear head. The waka began to rock alarmingly, there was a curse in Maori, and a moment later Amber was also shoved under the blanket.

Then there was silence, broken only by the quiet splash of oars dipping into the water. Kitty assumed that they were heading upriver, but to what destination she had no idea. She wriggled her shoulders, trying to make herself more comfortable — the bottom of the waka was very unforgiving, and the timber was transferring the cold of the river directly into her bones. She extended her legs, then retracted them quickly as her foot met some part of Amy's body.

Above her, the one called Ngaru asked, 'Who are they?'

Another voice — Wiripo, Kitty thought — replied, 'I have not seen them before.'

'She is wearing men's clothes.'

Someone chuckled. 'Ae.'

'The child has very poor manners,' Hapi grumbled. 'If she were mine, I would beat her.'

Kitty drew up her knees, protectively nudging Amber closer to her belly.

'But instead she beat you!'

More laughter.

'They could be useful,' Wiripo said. 'As prisoners of war. We will ask Kawiti.'

Under the blanket, her face pressed against the cold hull, Kitty flinched.

The warriors paddled for some time, then a faint hail of greeting came and Hapi returned the call. Kitty struggled to sit up, but was pressed firmly down again by a large foot. She strained to feel any change in the rhythm of the paddles, a sign that the waka might be slowing, but the men continued smoothly on, their voices fading into a drone and then, eventually, silence.

★ ★ ★

Something floated past and scraped against the side of the waka, waking Kitty and making her cry out. She shuffled the blanket off her head and saw that it was now almost dark, and that it was raining again. How long had she slept? How on earth had she even managed to?

Amber wriggled, then stretched. 'Mama?'

Kitty grimaced, praying that the men hadn't heard her. 'Ssshh,' she warned gently.

The waka was slowing: above her, Kitty watched the dark branches of trees and ferns glide past in the gloom as they neared the bank. Where were they? She knew the river was still too substantial to be near its source, so how far inland had they travelled? How close were they now to Ohaeawai, where Kawiti himself was rumoured to be camped?

The waka jolted as it grounded in the shallows: Ngaru leapt out, took hold of the low prow and began to pull. When the vessel was secure on dry land, Wiripo hoisted out Kitty and deposited Amber on the sand beside her, then inclined his head towards Amy's body and ordered Hapi to bury her somewhere fitting. They started to walk then, leaving Hapi behind with his unpleasant task, and soon were so deep into the dense bush that Kitty realised, with a rush of panic, that she could no longer hear their lifeline, the river. Or perhaps its sound had only been drowned out by the increasingly heavy rain, the patter and drumming on the broad leaves of the forest canopy creating a muted but steady tattoo.

Ngaru led the way at a cracking pace, rainwater sluicing down his broad back as he slogged through the mud and shoved aside drooping, water-laden branches. The soles of her boots collecting more mud with every step, Kitty slipped and slid on the track, her tied hands no help at all when she repeatedly fell to her knees. Each time, she felt Wiripo's rough grip on her shoulders as he dragged her up again and urged her on. At one point she turned to him and snapped, 'Get your bloody big hands off me!', but whether he understood or not, he merely shrugged and gave her another little push.

Amber trotted along in front of Kitty, her small hands grasping at leaves and branches to keep her footing. Somewhere her cap had been lost and her dark hair hung in streaming rivulets down her back, and with every few steps she looked over her shoulder to make sure Kitty was still behind her.

'Keep going, sweetheart, we'll be there soon,' Kitty urged.

The rain suddenly stopped, but the day had disappeared altogether now, leaving the forest in complete darkness except when the heavy, scudding clouds parted and briefly allowed the pale yellow of the moon to light the way. After an indeterminate amount of time, they turned off the track into a natural clearing several hundred yards square, the flattened grass indicating that the occupants had been there for at least a day or two. From what Kitty could see there were six other men in the camp, sitting around a fire that had been built under a thatch of green ponga branches to keep the rain off. The smell of cooking meat permeated the air, and, as they staggered into the clearing, every face turned towards them.

Kitty stopped in her tracks; Wiripo shoved her forward again.

'What do you have there?' one of the men near the fire asked with interest.

'Something Kawiti might find useful,' Wiripo replied shortly, and herded Kitty and Amber past the fire to the opposite side of the clearing. There, he produced another length of the thin, strong rope, tied it firmly to the binding already around Kitty's wrists, then secured the free end to a narrow tree trunk and knotted it repeatedly. He did the same with Amber, except that the rope was fastened around her waist instead of her wrists, and by the time he'd finished they were both firmly attached to the slender tree, unable to move more than three or four feet in any direction. The more Kitty pulled on the water-sodden ropes around her wrists, the tighter they became. In her anger and frustration, she kicked violently out at Wiripo with her muddy boot: he sidestepped neatly, his face impassive, and walked away.

She sat, gesturing at Amber to do the same, then nervously stood again almost immediately as Ngaru approached carrying a rolled-up mat and an evil-smelling blanket, which he offered to Kitty. She took them, hesitated, then forced herself to thank him.

He was wearing a kind of cape now, against the cold that was creeping back into the bush after the rain, and had wrapped an extra length of some sort of cloth around his waist. The mokos patterning his cheeks, nose and stubbled chin were complex, indicating that he was a man of some mana, but he didn't look any older than Rian and was possibly younger. When he crouched in front of Amber, Kitty quickly pulled her back beyond his reach.

Ngaru's expression became rather wistful. 'I have a daughter just like you,' he said in Maori. 'I miss her very much.' But when Amber remained silent, after a moment he smiled sadly, then returned to the fire.

Kitty unrolled the mat and she and Amber sat on it, grateful to be off the cold, wet ground. From their position on the edge of the clearing, they could hear some of what the men were saying, but not all of it, although Kitty certainly tried to pick up as much information as she could. There was talk about what had happened at Waikare several days earlier — evidently the sortie had not been a success for Major Bridge, even though the Kapotai pa had been destroyed — speculation about the upcoming battle at Ohaeawai, and desultory comments about the atrocious weather.

When one of the men silently presented Kitty and Amber with some roasted pork half an hour later, they ate it ravenously. After they'd picked off every last edible shred, Kitty tossed the bones away, then watched with wary interest as Hapi trudged into the camp. He did not look at all happy.

'Did you bury her well?' one of the men asked, his voice betraying a note of unease.

Hapi nodded, warming his hands near the fire, then reached for a piece of meat.

'We should have returned her to her people,' Ngaru said.

Wiripo shook his head. 'She said she had no people.'

'She might walk, that one,' someone else commented. 'I hope you put plenty of rocks on her grave.'

Kitty shivered and drew Amber closer.

Some time in the night it began to rain again, not as torrentially as earlier, but very steadily. Kitty decided she would do better to stay awake, but only minutes later found herself barely able to keep her eyes open. At regular intervals someone came to check that the ropes around the tree remained secure, dashing Kitty's hopes of escaping and stealing away under cover of darkness.

★ ★ ★

Dawn broke damp and grey, the wretched rain still falling. Kitty had slept after all, and lay blinking in confusion as Ngaru looked down at her and Amber huddled together on the mat. In silence he checked the ropes, then deliberately twisted the knots around to the far side of the tree trunk. Bastard, Kitty thought angrily as he returned to the fire and began to talk animatedly to the others.

Amber sat up, stretched, scratched her armpit and whispered, 'Mimi.'

Kitty's heart sank. She sat up herself, wincing at the stiffness in her bones and the headache that still lingered after yesterday's fall, and watched as Amber clambered to her feet and moved a short distance away to relieve herself.

It wasn't until Amber had unbuttoned her trousers and squatted that Kitty, with a start that almost made her cry out, realised that the end of Amber's rope was trailing along the ground behind her. Hardly daring to hope, she pulled surreptitiously on her own rope and stared in amazement as the loose end appeared around the base of the tree.

Sweating now, Kitty prayed that Amber would remember that they were supposed to be tied up, and not wander around and attract attention. But as usual, Amber had trouble with her buttons and came back to Kitty for help.

As she struggled one-handed to fasten Amber's trousers, Kitty whispered hoarsely in Maori, 'Go into the forest when I say to.'

Amber regarded her for a long moment, then nodded.

Kitty glanced across the clearing: the men were eating and talking around the fire, except for one who was relieving himself against a tree. Ngaru turned and gave Kitty a meaningful look, then resumed energetically relating to the others what Kitty assumed was a complicated and entertaining story. Now no one was looking in their direction at all.

Kitty whispered into Amber's ear, 'Go!', and the little girl obediently melted into the bush. Kitty gathered up the rope attached to her wrists so she wouldn't fall over it, and crept after her. In the gloom of the undergrowth, she hastily wound Amber's rope around her waist, then urged, 'Run!'

Amber set off, jumping over small obstacles and dodging around larger ones, her feet slipping in the soggy leaf litter but never losing her balance, and Kitty realised with wonder that, even in the grip of terror, she still had the capacity to feel immensely proud of her daughter.

They circled the camp until they came to the track leading to the river. The mud sucked hungrily at their boots and forced them to slow down, but finally they reached the place where, the day before, the waka had been beached. The river was hugely swollen from the rains and the waka was almost afloat already, and Kitty was profoundly grateful to see that the paddles had been left neatly inside it.

She dug about in Amber's pockets until she found the compass, then set it on a rock, opened the lid and stamped on it as hard as she could. Pieces of compass flew everywhere, but all Kitty wanted was the glass. She retrieved the largest shard and placed it carefully between her teeth, then lifted Amber into the waka, pushed off and jumped in herself. The waka was immediately caught by the current and began to move downstream. Behind them, from the depths of the bush, came a series of angry shouts.

Kitty took the piece of glass in one hand and started to saw at the ropes around her wrists, but knew almost immediately that the angle was wrong and it would never work.

'Mama?'

Amber extended her hand and Kitty, trying not to think about what might happen if Amber cut herself, reluctantly gave her the piece of glass. With the shard held delicately between thumb and forefinger and her tongue poking out in concentration, Amber carefully sliced each strand until the ropes fell away and Kitty's hands were free. Kitty gave her a delighted squeeze, then quickly cut the rope at Amber's waist and snatched up a paddle: the waka was being swept along side-on to the current now, and was in real danger of capsizing. She plunged the paddle deep into the water and brought the waka around so that the prow was facing downstream again, then settled into a rhythm, changing sides with each stroke. Only then did she allow herself a small sigh of relief.

The cries had faded behind them, but they were still a long way from safety. Kitty noticed with alarm that the Kawakawa had breached its banks as far as the eye could see, the thick brown water eddying into the very bush itself. Logs, small trees and, at one point, a dead pig swirled about in the shallows, and the surface of the river was littered with branches and clods of earth. There was no hope of dodging anything, so Kitty resolutely paddled straight through the debris, her head up and her eyes fixed on what lay ahead.

They went on that way for almost an hour, paddling past great gouges where angry waters had taken huge bites out of the banks and flooded the new, raw contours. The sky was a curious yellow colour, bordered by yet more rain clouds gathering in great phalanxes of grey and white, and they saw absolutely no one, Maori or Pakeha, friend or foe.

Then Amber's head lifted. She sat very still, then turned to Kitty and frowned.

'What is it, sweetheart?'

'Turituri nui!' Amber exclaimed, and flung her arms wide.

Kitty listened, and now she could hear it, too — a deep, dull, roaring sound that seemed to be coming from the river itself.

When they rounded the next bend they discovered the cause. Here, the river narrowed and entered a gorge. Between the elevated banks of volcanic rock there was nowhere for the floodwaters to go, so the river simply picked up speed, carrying the debris along at a breakneck pace and sending spray high into the air.

Kitty's shrieked warning to Amber to hold on was torn from her mouth as they were plunged into the torrent. The paddle was instantly ripped from Kitty's hands, and the waka spun sideways, then straightened, turned again and finally flipped over, spilling both of them into the murky, tumultuous waters. Amber went under immediately, disappearing from sight before Kitty was sucked down herself, her legs tangling in a mass of submerged branches.

The light beneath the churning water was very dim, and the rush of air bubbles past Kitty's head seemed extraordinarily loud. Struggling violently, and feeling a painful band begin to tighten around her lungs, she kicked free of the branches and struck out for the surface. She broke through, treading water and coughing, and staring wildly around for Amber. Grabbing hold of a log hurtling past her head, she shrieked her daughter's name over and over, unable to see her anywhere as the madly bobbing detritus shot through the gorge, then gradually began to slow as the river widened once more.

At last she caught a glimpse of something that could be a small, pale face. She pushed off from the log and swam with the current, gritting her teeth as she was jostled and scraped by the rubbish sweeping past. But when she blinked, she lost sight of the little scrap that might have been her daughter, and let out such a shriek of frustration and dismay that she felt the back of her throat tear and tasted blood.

Then she saw it again, bobbing a few yards ahead, half-submerged and caught in the fork of a large branch. Still coughing, Kitty fought her way towards it, not daring to let the branch out of her sight, chanting to herself over and over, '*Hold* on, love, *hold* on, love, *hold* on, love', until finally her hand closed on Amber's hair and she hauled her head up and out of the water.

Somehow, Kitty managed to struggle to the bank and drag Amber onto dry land, where she sat, cradling the child and keening with despair.

Around her a small group of people had begun to gather, but Kitty ignored them because she thought they were ghosts, and she didn't have time for ghosts — not now, not while her precious little girl needed her and had to be kept warm in case she had decided to stay after all.

A hand settled on Kitty's trembling shoulder and a familiar voice said, 'Kitty, *mo ghrá*, it's me.'

Kitty raised her eyes, and there he was. 'Oh God, Rian, help her!' she cried, holding Amber up to him. '*Please help her!*'

But Rian, staring in mute horror now at the small, limp form cradled in his wife's arms, was paralysed and unable to move.

It was Hawk, moving quickly, who plucked Amber from Kitty's grasp, laid her on the ground and felt in her neck for a pulse. Grimly he noted the way her limbs flopped lifelessly, and how her eyes had rolled up into her head, and feared that they were too late.

★ ★ ★

Simon had been distraught when he'd discovered that Kitty and Amber had apparently vanished into thin air. He'd searched the area around their campsite and shouted himself hoarse for over an hour before he'd finally succumbed to despair and collapsed in a heap with his head in his hands. That was how Rian had found him — babbling repeatedly that it was all his fault for not looking after them.

Rian and the crew were heading overland back

to Paihia, dirty, tired and deeply disillusioned by the shambles they'd witnessed at the Kapotai pa. Major Cyprian Bridge had proved himself completely incompetent, Tamati Waka Nene's two most trusted lieutenants had performed almost as poorly, and, worst of all, the Kapotai themselves had behaved no better than children. Rian's mood, therefore, was already fairly dire, and the discovery that Kitty had taken it upon herself to return to the Bay of Islands and had now gone missing made him white with fear and anger.

As soon as Simon had managed to relate what had happened, giving only a very garbled explanation of why Kitty had a child with her, Rian ordered Daniel to return to Paihia with the horses, and Hawk to begin tracking. Hawk had picked up Kitty's trail fairly quickly, despite the wet conditions, and had tracked her back to the Kawakawa, where he'd found a small amount of blood near the river's edge. Keeping the unpleasant discovery to himself, he advised Rian that it looked as though several people had gone onto the river at that point, although he couldn't say whether they'd travelled upstream or downstream. Rian, convinced that Kitty had been taken captive by either Heke's or Kawiti's people, guessed that they had gone inland, heading for the new pa at Ohaeawai.

It had taken them all that night to walk upriver, never daring to leave the riverbank in case Kitty and her captors had come ashore again somewhere and they missed the signs. The sun had been up for several hours and they were almost asleep on their feet and beginning to fear that Kitty had been lost, when she had crawled out of the swollen river only yards in front of them. Later, Rian told everyone it had been extreme good luck, but Hawk thought it far more likely to be the work of some benevolent god.

Now they were crossing the wide mouth of the Kawakawa and heading back to Paihia in a waka 'borrowed' from a landing place near the ruins of Pomare's pa at the southern end of the harbour. Rian had said very little to either Kitty or Amber, although Kitty noticed him glancing at Amber frequently, as though he couldn't quite believe what he was seeing. Amber was pale and clearly exhausted, but she was all right: Hawk had held her upside-down and whacked her across the back until she'd given an enormous start and vomited up what had seemed like several pints of river water. Then she'd cried for a few minutes, sat up, pointed at Gideon's bald head and smiled.

Kitty had no idea what Rian was thinking because he'd been so reticent, and it was hardly the sort of thing she could discuss with him here, jammed between the crew in a waka in the middle of the harbour. He was very angry, though, she could see that — especially with her.

Haunui greeted them as they landed at Paihia, eager to know whether the stories of the shambles at Waikare were true.

'Yes,' Rian said shortly, then stomped off across the sand.

Unfortunately, he had to stomp back a minute

later to ask Kitty whether she was staying with Sarah and was it still acceptable if he stayed there too.

'Of course it is,' she replied tersely, unable to decide whether she was feeling anger, frustration or disappointment. She stayed on the beach, talking to Haunui about what had happened, and of her deep shock at the ease with which she had despatched Amy when she'd believed Amber's life to be at stake, hoping to give Rian enough time to settle down. Then, when Amber started to yawn hugely, she realised she couldn't delay the confrontation any longer.

Sarah greeted Kitty and Amber warmly as they trudged in through the front door, clearly relieved that they had returned more or less unscathed, then warned them in a loud whisper that Rian was sitting on the bench in the back garden with a bottle of her best port and a face like thunder.

'Have you had a tiff?' she asked bluntly.

'It seems so,' Kitty replied.

'About . . . ?' Sarah nodded her head at Amber, who was yawning *and* rubbing her eyes.

'Yes,' Kitty admitted, and related the events of the past few days to her appalled aunt, adding, 'So, yes, I think it *has* come as a bit of a shock.'

'Well, I'd be very surprised if it hadn't,' Sarah said. 'It's not just any man who'd be willing to take on another's child, you know.' She dampened the corner of her apron with spit and wiped a dirty mark off Amber's face. 'Still, you're not married to just any man, are you?' She laid a hand on Kitty's cheek. 'Don't fret, dear. God has a way of making sure these things work out.'

'I hope you're right,' Kitty said.

★ ★ ★

She gave Amber a thorough wash with soap and hot water and made her something to eat. As the little girl's eyes started to droop, she tucked her into bed and sat with her for the few minutes it took her to fall into a deep sleep. Then she went downstairs.

Rian was still slumped on the bench in the garden, his eyes closed and the half-empty bottle of port at his elbow. Ngahuia and Rangimarie were picking vegetables for supper, but after a glance from Kitty, which they returned with a sympathetic look of their own, they went inside.

Kitty moved the port and sat down on the bench.

'Are you awake?' she whispered.

'Yes,' Rian mumbled, although he didn't open his eyes.

'I'd like to talk to you. About Amber.'

Rian said nothing.

So Kitty told him exactly what had happened from the first moment she had encountered Amber in Shortland Street, and how she had been thinking and feeling, and how her love for the child had grown to the extent that she'd had no option but to take Amy's life. It took her half an hour, during which Rian drank another quarter of the port.

When she had finished, he sat forward with his

elbows on his knees and turned his head to Kitty. 'Do you think it's right to take a child away from everything she knows and push her into a life completely foreign to her?'

'I think it's right if all that child knows is hunger and loneliness and deprivation. She was wearing rags, Rian, and she was starving and someone had been beating her.'

Rian made a face, although whether it was at the thought of a small, defenceless child being battered or because he was finding this conversation so difficult, Kitty couldn't tell.

'How the hell are you going to look after her, though?' he demanded. 'Have you thought about that? Have you thought about the practicalities of it?'

'I'll look after her — *we'll* look after her — the way any child would be looked after in a good home.'

'But the *Katipo* isn't a good home,' Rian countered. 'The *Katipo*'s a schooner and people can fall off schooners. People can fall off any sort of ship. Especially children.'

He sat back and contemplated the bottle on the grass at his feet, but didn't reach for it. Instead, he rubbed his hands over his face and said something so unexpected and so profoundly moving that Kitty could barely swallow around the lump in her throat.

'My son was so young when he died that we hadn't even had time to name him. That was the worst thing of all, Kitty. I loved him so much, and he died without a name.'

Kitty slid her hand across the bench, took hold

of Rian's, and waited.

After a moment, he spoke again. 'What if we took her in, Kitty, and somehow we lost — ' He stopped. 'Christ, I can't even say it.'

'Rian,' Kitty said quietly, without looking at him, 'I've already taken her in. I can't undo that. I've made my choice.'

She let the implication hang in the air between them, shocked by what she had just said, and even more shaken by the fact that she meant it.

Rian closed his eyes. 'Then I don't *have* a choice, do I?'

Kitty squeezed his hand. 'This is . . . just how I feel about it, Rian. This isn't blackmail.'

'No, I know it isn't,' he said eventually. Then he sighed. 'But you're more important to me than anything else on this earth, Kitty, and I'm not willing to live my life without you.' He opened one eye and asked, 'Do you think she has the makings of a good sailor?'

Epilogue

Halfway between New Zealand and Panama, just east of the Marquesas Islands, the *Katipo* skimmed swiftly and elegantly across the Pacific Ocean as the wind snapped in her sails. Soon she would be drawn by the Peru current up and across the equator and into the south-east trades, and it would be all hands on deck. But for now they were all below in the mess-room, having a party.

Kitty stuck her head into the galley and said to Pierre, 'Are you ready? We are.'

Pierre nodded and, unable to keep the enormous grin off his face, lifted a platter and carried it through, the crew launching into a rowdy rendition of 'For She's a Jolly Good Fellow' as he set it on the table in front of Amber. On it was a large, round cake that Pierre had spent almost the entire day decorating with marzipan, and Amber's eyes almost popped out of her head.

'Me?' she said incredulously, looking up at Kitty.

Kitty laughed with delight at the look on her daughter's face. 'Yes, sweetheart, it's for you. It's a birthday cake.'

Still uncertain, Amber repeated, 'Birfday?'

Rian nodded solemnly. 'Yes. Everyone has

410

one, and we're making yours today. And that'll be every year, of course.'

Amber didn't understand what he'd said, but she clapped her hands and let out an 'oooh' of amazement as Pierre lit the four miniature candles set in the marzipan.

'Blow!' Kitty urged.

Puzzled, Amber looked at her.

'You blow them out, like this, see?' Kitty said, bending over the cake and pretending to blow out the candles. 'And then you close your eyes and make a wish.'

Amber did as she was told — for a change — and grinned delightedly as everyone clapped and cheered.

They were all there: Pierre, Gideon, Mick, Hawk and Ropata. And of course Bodie, sitting contentedly on the end of the table. Daniel was there, too, having proved so useful over the past few months that Rian had asked him to sign on as Sharkey's replacement, despite Hawk's muttered misgivings. And so was Simon, who had finally decided to leave the CMS and sail the high seas as ship's boy while he contemplated his faith and what he was going to do next.

Amber beamed up at her big, noisy, unconventional family, her little face radiant.

She looked, Kitty thought with an immense rush of love, like a child who had finally come home.

We do hope that you have enjoyed reading this large print book.

Did you know that all of our titles are available for purchase?

We publish a wide range of high quality large print books including:
Romances, Mysteries, Classics
General Fiction
Non Fiction and Westerns

Special interest titles available in large print are:
The Little Oxford Dictionary
Music Book
Song Book
Hymn Book
Service Book

Also available from us courtesy of Oxford University Press:
Young Readers' Dictionary
(large print edition)
Young Readers' Thesaurus
(large print edition)

For further information or a free brochure, please contact us at:
Ulverscroft Large Print Books Ltd.,
The Green, Bradgate Road, Anstey,
Leicester, LE7 7FU, England.
Tel: (00 44) 0116 236 4325
Fax: (00 44) 0116 234 0205

Other titles published by Ulverscroft:

THE LAST OF THE BONEGILLA GIRLS

Victoria Purman

1954: Hoping to escape life as a refugee in post-war Germany, sixteen-year-old Hungarian Elizabeta arrives in Australia with her family. Her first stop is the Bonegilla Migrant Camp in rural Victoria, a temporary home for thousands of new arrivals. There, Elizabeta becomes firm friends with the feisty Greek Vasiliki; quiet Italian Iliana; and the adventurous Frances, daughter of the camp's director. In this vibrant and growing country, the Bonegilla girls rush together towards a life that seems full of promise, even as they cope with ever-present adversity. So when a ghost from the past reaches out for Elizabeta, there is nothing that her friends wouldn't do to keep her safe. But secrets have a way of making themselves known. Can the Bonegilla girls defeat their past? Or has it finally come to claim them?

PHOTOS OF YOU

Tammy Robinson

When Ava Green turns twenty-eight, she discovers this will be her last birthday. The cancer she thought she'd beaten three years ago is back, only this time it's terminal — and she's not going to waste any of the time she has left. She's been dreaming of her wedding since she was a little girl, but there's only one problem: there's no groom. Her friends and family decide they will help her throw the wedding of her dreams, without the vows; and as word spreads, the whole country seizes the story of a woman whose dying dream is simple, uniting to give her a wedding to remember. But when photographer James Gable volunteers to help document the whole event, it becomes painfully clear that it's never too late to discover the love of your life . . .

NICOLA'S VIRTUE

AnneMarie Brear

1867: With no family, but a good education, Nicola Douglas boards a ship to Australia with high hopes of a fresh start in a new country as a governess. Sydney is full of young women with similar ambitions and equally poor prospects — but when a wealthy benefactor appears, she finds a foothold. What she never anticipated was the attention of two suitors: Nathaniel, a privileged and attractive English gentleman; and Hilton, a beguiling American. Nicola reaches a crisis — the prospects of finding love, and being married, show how empty her life has been since her parents' deaths. However, her position at the Governess Home is vital to her. Can she have both? Or would her career alone ever be enough to sustain her?

THE ROSIE RESULT

Graeme Simsion

I was standing on one leg shucking oysters when the problems began . . . Don and Rosie are back in Melbourne after a decade in New York, about to face their most important project. Their son, Hudson, is having trouble at school: his teachers say he isn't fitting in with the other kids. Meanwhile, Rosie is battling Judas at work, and Don is in hot water after the Genetics Lecture Outrage. The life-contentment graph, recently at its highest point, is curving downwards. For Don, geneticist and World's Best Problem-Solver, learning to be a good parent as well as a good partner will require the help of friends old and new. It will mean letting Hudson make his way in the world, and grappling with awkward truths about his own identity. And opening a cocktail bar.